W9-AYW-366

"TWO MEMBERS OF OUR FAMILY HAVE BEEN SHOT."

Rose had to stop and swallow her grief before she could continue. "We need your help, Ms. Nelson, to find the killer."

Murder. That was definitely more serious than Vicki had been expecting. "Have the local police not turned up any leads?"

"They don't exactly know."

"What do you mean by 'don't exactly know'?" Vicki could think of several things it might mean and none of them appealed to her.

"Why don't you show her, Rose," Henry said quietly.

Rose slipped out of her sandals and rose to her feet. In one quick movement she stripped off the sundress she was wearing, stood naked for a heartbeat, and then, where there had been a pale-haired young woman there was a large white dog.

"Werewolves," Vicki heard herself say aloud, amazed at her composure. *Odds are good it's Henry's influence. This is what comes of hanging around with vampires. . . . I'll get the bastard for this!*

BLOOD TRAIL

Tanya Huff

DAW BOOKS, INC.

DONALD A. WOLLHEIM, FOUNDER

375 Hudson Street, New York, NY 10014

ELIZABETH R. WOLLHEIM
SHEILA E. GILBERT
PUBLISHERS

www.dawbooks.com

Copyright © 1992 by Tanya Huff.

All Rights Reserved.

Cover art Copyright © 2007 Lifetime Entertainment Services.

DAW Book Collectors No. 873.

DAW Books are distributed by Penguin Group (USA) Inc.

All characters in this book are fictitious.
Any resemblance to persons living or dead is coincidental.

The scanning, uploading and distribution of this book via the
Internet or any other means without the permission of the
publisher is illegal, and punishable by law. Please purchase
only authorized electronic editions, and do not participate in
or encourage the electronic piracy of copyrighted materials.
Your support of the author's rights is appreciated.

Nearly all the designs and trade names in this book are
registered trademarks. All that are still in commercial use are
protected by United States and international trademark law.

First Printing, February 1992
19 18 17 16 15 14 13

DAW TRADEMARK REGISTERED
U.S. PAT. AND TM. OFF. AND FOREIGN COUNTRIES
—MARCA REGISTRADA
HECHO EN U.S.A.

PRINTED IN THE U.S.A.

For DeVerne Jones,
who patiently answered hundreds of questions
including a few it never occurred to me to ask.

With special thanks to Ken Sagara,
whose generosity was responsible for me
finishing this manuscript on time,
vision intact.

PRIVATE INVESTIGATOR VICKI NELSON
HAS A DETECTIVE TO KEEP HER COOL,
AND A VAMPIRE TO KEEP HER WARM.

SOME WOMEN HAVE IT ALL...

DON'T MISS

BLOOD TIES

THE HIT TELEVISION SERIES
BASED ON TANYA HUFF'S BLOOD BOOKS,
AIRING ON LIFETIME.

GO TO LIFETIMETV.COM FOR SHOW TIMES.

Lifetime.

One

The three-quarter moon, hanging low in the night sky, turned even tamed and placid farmland into a mysterious landscape of silver light and shadows. Each blade of grass, toasted golden brown by two months of summer heat, had a thin black replica stretching out behind it. The bushes along the fence bottom, highways for those too timid to brave the open fields, rustled once and then were silent as some nocturnal creature went about its business.

Their summer-shorn fleece turned milky white by the moonlight, a large flock of sheep had settled for the night in one corner of the meadow. Except for the rhythmic motion of a number of jaws and the occasional flick of an ear or twitch of a lamb unable to be still for long, even in sleep, they appeared to be an outcropping of pale stone. An outcropping come suddenly to life as several heads rose at once, aristocratic noses pointed into the breeze.

They were obviously familiar with the creature that bounded over the fence and into the meadow, for although the ewes remained alert they watched it approach with mild curiosity rather than alarm.

The huge black beast paused to mark a fence post, then trotted a few steps into the field and sat down, gazing back at the sheep with a proprietary air. Something in its general outline, in the shape of its head, said wolf just as its coloring, its size, its breadth of chest, and the reaction of the flock said dog.

Convinced that all was as it should be, it began to

lope along the edge of the fence bottom, plumed tail streaming behind it like a banner, moon-silvered highlights rippling through its thick fur with every movement. Picking up speed, it leapt a thistle—more for the sheer joy of leaping than because the thistle was in its way—and cut diagonally across the lower end of the pasture.

With no more warning than a distant cough, the gleaming black head exploded in a shower of blood and bone. The body, lifted off its feet by the impact, spasmed for a frenzied moment and then lay still.

Bleating in terror at the sudden blood scent, the sheep panicked, racing to the far end of the field and pressing in a huddled noisy mass against the fence. Fortunately, the direction they'd taken had moved them upwind, not down. When nothing further happened, they began to calm and a few of the older ewes moved themselves and their lambs out of the crowding and began to settle once again.

It was doubtful that the three animals who leapt the fence a short time later even noticed the sheep. Huge paws seeming to barely touch ground, they raced to the body. One of them, russet hackles high, started back along the slain animal's trail but a growl from the bigger of the two remaining called it back.

Three pointed muzzles lifted and the howl that lifted with them panicked the sheep yet again. As the sound rose and fell, its primal cadences wiped out any remaining resemblance the three howling might have had to dogs.

Vicki hated August. It was the month in which Toronto proved what a world class city it had become; when the heat and humidity hung on to the car exhaust and the air in the concrete and glass canyon at Yonge and Bloor took on a yellowish-brown hue that left a bitter taste in the back of the throat; when every loose screw in the city decided to take a walk on the wild side and tempers were baked short. The police, in their navy blue pants and hats and heavy boots, hated August for both personal and professional reasons. Vicki had moved quickly out of uniform, and out of the force entirely a year ago, but she still hated August. In fact, as August was now forever linked with her leaving a job she'd loved, this least congenial of months had been blackened beyond redemption.

As she unlocked the door to her apartment, she tried not to smell herself. She'd spent the day, the last three days, working as an order picker in a small coffee processing factory up on Railside Drive. In the last month the company had been plagued with a number of equipment failures that the owners had finally come to realize were sabotage. Desperate—a small specialty company couldn't afford the downtime if they hoped to complete with the multinationals—the owners had hired Vicki to find out what was going on.

"And Vicki Nelson, private investigator, comes through again." She closed the door behind her and thankfully peeled off her damp T-shirt. She'd been able to pinpoint who was jamming the processing machines on her first day but even knowing that, it took her two further days to discover how and to gather enough evidence to bring charges. Tomorrow she'd go in, lay the report on Mr. Glassman's desk and never go near the place again.

Tonight, she wanted a shower, something to cat that didn't smell like coffee, and a long vapid evening spent sucking at the boob tube.

She kicked the filthy T-shirt into a corner as she peeled off her jeans. The only up side about the entire experience was that smelling as she did, she'd gotten a seat on the subway coming home and no one had tried to crowd her.

The hot water had just begun to pound the stink and stiffness away when the phone rang. And rang. She tried to ignore it, to let the shower drown it out, but had little success. She'd always been a compulsive phone answerer. Muttering under her breath, she turned the water off, quickly wrapped herself in towels, and raced for the receiver.

"Oh there you are, dear. What took you so long?"

"It's a very small apartment, Mom." Vicki sighed. She should've known. "Didn't it occur to you at about the seventh ring that maybe I wasn't going to answer the phone?"

"Of course not. I knew you were home or you'd have had your machine plugged in."

She never left her machine on when she was home. She considered it the ultimate in rudeness. Maybe it was time to reconsider. The towel began to unwind and she made a grab for it—a second floor apartment was not high enough up for walking around in skin. "I was in the shower, Mom."

"Good, then I didn't get you away from anything important. I wanted to call you before I left work . . ."

"So that the Life Sciences Department would pay for the call," Vicki added silently. Her mother had been working as a secretary at Queen's University in Kingston for longer than most of the tenured professors and she stretched job perks as far and as often as she could.

". . . and find out when you had vacation this year so maybe we could spend some time together."

Right. Vicki loved her mother but more than three days in her company usually had her ready to commit matricide. "I don't get vacations anymore, Mom. I'm self-employed now and I have to take what jobs come my way. And besides, you were here in April."

"You were in the hospital, Vicki, it wasn't exactly a social visit."

The two vertical scars on her left wrist had faded to fine red lines against the pale skin. It looked like a suicide attempt and it had taken some extremely fancy footwork to avoid telling her mother how she'd actually gotten them. Being set up as a sacrifice for a demon by a sociopathic hacker was not something her mother would deal with well. "As soon as I get a free weekend, I'll come by. I promise. I have to go now, I'm dripping on the carpet.''

''Bring that Henry Fitzroy with you. I'd like to meet him.''

Vicki grinned. Henry Fitzroy and her mother. That might be worth a weekend in Kingston. ''I don't think so, Mom.''

''Why not? What's wrong with him? Why was he avoiding me at the hospital?''

''He wasn't avoiding you and there's nothing wrong with him.'' *Okay, so he died in 1536. It hadn't slowed him down.* ''He's a writer. He's a little . . . *unusual*.''

''More unusual than Michael Celluci?''

''Mother!''

She could almost hear her mother's brows rise. ''Honey, you may not remember this, but you've dated a number of *unusual* boys in your time.''

''I'm not dating boys anymore, Mom. I'm almost thirty-two years old.''

''You know what I mean. Remember that young man in high school? I don't recall his name but he kept a harem. . . .''

''I'll call you, Mom.''

''Soon.''

''Soon,'' Vicki agreed, rescued the towel again and hung up. ''Dated unusual boys in my time. . . .'' She snorted and headed back toward the bathroom. All right, a couple of them may have been a bit strange but she was over one hundred percent certain that none of them were vampires.

She turned the water back on and grinned, imagining the scene. *Mom, I'd like you to meet Henry Fitzroy. He drinks blood.* The grin widened as she stepped under the water. Her mother, infinitely practical, would probably ask what type. It took a lot to disrupt her mother's view of the world.

She'd just dumped a pan of scrambled eggs onto a plate when the phone rang again.

''It figures,'' she muttered, grabbing a fork and

crossing into the living room. "Damn thing never rings when I'm not doing anything." Sunset wouldn't be for a couple of hours yet—it wasn't Henry.

"Vicki? Celluci." With so many Michaels on the Metropolitan Toronto Police Force, most of them had gotten into the habit of perpetually referring to themselves by their last names, on duty and off. "You remember the name of Quest's alleged accomplice? The guy who never got charged."

"Good evening, Mike. Nice to hear from you. I'm fine thanks." She shoveled a forkful of egg into her mouth and waited for the explosion.

"Cut the crap, Vicki. He had some woman's name . . . Marion, Maralyn. . . ."

"Margot. Alan Margot. Why?"

Even over the sounds of traffic, she could hear the self-satisfied smile in his voice. "It's classified."

"Listen you son of a bitch, when you pick my brains 'cause you're too lazy to look it up, you don't come back with 'it's classified.' Not if you want to live to collect your pension."

He sighed. "Use the brain you're accusing me of picking."

"You pulled another body out of the lake?"

"Mere moments ago."

So he was still at the site. That explained the background noise. "Same pattern of bruises?"

"Near as I can tell. Coroner just took the body away."

"Nail the bastard."

"That," he told her, "is the plan."

She hung up and slid into her leather recliner, eggs balanced precariously on the arm. Two years ago, the case had been hers. Hers the responsibility of finding the scum who'd beaten a fifteen-year-old girl senseless and then dropped the unconscious body in Lake Ontario. Six weeks of work and they'd picked up a man named Quest, picked him up, charged him, and made it stick. There'd been a another man involved, Vicki had been sure of it, but Quest wouldn't talk and they hadn't been able to lay charges.

This time. . . .

She yanked her glasses off her nose. This time, Celluci would get him, and Vicki Nelson, ex-fair-haired girl of the metro police would be sitting on her duff. The room in front of her blurred into an indistinguishable mass of fuzz-edged colors and she shoved the glasses back on.

"Shit!"

Breathing deeply, she forced herself to calm. After all, what mattered was catching Margot—not who made the collar. She scooped up the remote and flicked on the television. The Jays were in Milwaukee.

"The boys of summer," she sighed, and dug into her cooled eggs, giving herself over to the hypnotic accents of the announcers doing the pregame show. Like most Canadians over a certain age, Vicki was a hockey fan first but it was almost impossible to live in Toronto and not have baseball make inroads into your affections.

It was the bottom of the seventh, the score three to five, the Jays behind two runs, two out and a man on second with Mookie Wilson at bat. Wilson was hitting over three hundred against right-handers and Vicki could see that the Brewers' pitcher was sweating. At which point, the phone rang.

"It figures." She stretched a long arm down and dragged the phone up onto her lap. Sunset had been at eight forty-one. It was now nine oh five. It had to be Henry.

Ball one.

"Yeah, what?"

"Vicki? It's Henry. Are you all right?"

Strike one.

"Yeah, I'm fine. You just called at a bad time."

"I'm sorry, but I have some friends here who need your help."

"My help?"

"Well, they need the help of a private investigator and you're the only one I know."

Strike two.

"They need help right now?" There were only two innings left in the game. How desperate could it be?

"Vicki, it's important." And she could tell by his voice that it was.

She sighed as Wilson popped out to left field, ending the inning, and thumbed the television off. "Well, if it's that important . . ."

"It is."

". . . then I'll be right over." With the receiver halfway back to the cradle, a sudden thought occurred to her and she snapped it back up to her mouth. "Henry?"

He was still there. "Yes?"

"These friends, they aren't vampires are they?"

"No." Through his concern, he sounded a little amused. "They aren't vampires."

Greg gave the young woman a neutral nod as he buzzed her through the security check and into the lobby. Vicki Nelson her name was and she'd dropped by a number of times over the summer while he was on the desk. Although she looked like the kind of person he'd have liked under other circumstances he simply couldn't get over the impressions he'd formed during their initial meeting last spring. It didn't help when observation confirmed that she was not the sort who would normally answer the door half dressed, proving, to his mind, his feeling that she'd been hiding something that night.

But what?

Over the last couple of months his belief that Henry Fitzroy was a vampire had begun to fade. He liked Mr. Fitzroy, respected him, realized that all his idiosyncrasies could stem from being a writer rather than a creature of the night but one last lingering doubt remained.

What had the young woman been hiding that night? And why?

Occasionally, just for his peace of mind, Greg considered asking her outright, but a certain set to her jaw had always stopped him. So he wondered. And he kept an eye on things. Just in case.

Vicki felt a distinct sense of relief as the elevator doors closed behind her. Scrutiny by that particular security guard always made her feel, well, dirty. *Still, it's my own fault. I'm the one who answered the door practically naked.* It had been the only solution she could think of at the time and as it had worked, distracting the old man from his intention of pounding a croquet stake through Henry's heart, she supposed she shouldn't complain about the aftereffects.

She pushed the button for the fourteenth floor and tucked her white golf shirt more securely into her red walking shorts. The little ''adventure'' last spring had melted off a few pounds and so far she'd managed to keep them from finding their way back. She carried too much muscle to ever be considered slim—a secret desire she'd admitted to no one—but it was nice to have a little more definition at the waist. Squinting in the glare of the fluorescent lights, she studied her reflection in the stainless steel walls of the elevator.

Not bad for an old broad, she decided, shoving the hated glasses up her nose. She wondered briefly if maybe she should have dressed more formally then decided that any friends of Henry Fitzroy, bastard son of Henry the VIII, ex-Duke of Richmond, et cetera, et cetera, were not likely to care if the private investigator showed up in shorts.

When the elevator reached Henry's floor, Vicki settled her purse on her shoulder and put on her professional face. It lasted right up until the condo door swung open and the only creature in the entrance hall was a huge russet colored dog.

It—no, he—has to be a dog. Vicki extended her hand

for him to sniff. *Wolves don't come in that color. Or that size. Do they?* She could have added that wolves don't generally hang out in condominiums in downtown Toronto, but given that it was *Henry's* condo all bets were off.

The animal's eyes were outlined in black, adding to a remarkably expressive face. He enthusiastically sniffed the offered hand, then pushed his head demandingly under Vicki's fingers.

Vicki grinned, pulled the door closed, then obediently began to scratch in the thick ruff behind the pointed ears. "Henry?" she called as a tail heavy enough to knock a grown man to the ground slammed rhythmically into the wall. "You home?"

"In the living room."

Something in the tone of his voice drew her brows down but a saucerlike paw on her instep almost instantly distracted her. "Get off, you great brute." The dog obediently shifted his weight. She grabbed his muzzle lightly in one hand and shook his massive head from side to side. "Come on, fella, they're waiting for us."

He smiled—there really was no other word for it— whirled around and bounded into the living room, Vicki following at a slightly more sedate pace.

Henry stood in his usual place by the huge wall of windows that looked down on the city. The lights he used on the infrequent occasions he had company picked up the red highlights in his fair hair and turned his hazel eyes almost gold. Actually, Vicki was guessing about the effect on his eyes as she couldn't see details over that great a distance. She never tired of looking at him though, he had a presence that lifted his appearance from merely pleasing to extraordinary and she could certainly understand how poor Lucy and Mina hadn't stood a chance against his well-known fictional counterpart.

He wasn't alone. The young woman fiddling with the CD player turned as Vicki came into the living room and Vicki hid a smile as she found herself being thoroughly and obviously looked over. She took a good long look in return.

A dancer? Vicki wondered. Although small, the girl was sleekly muscled and held herself in a way that could almost be interpreted as challenging. *Don't try it, kid. If I'm not quite twice your age*—the girl could be no older than seventeen or eighteen—*I'm definitely meaner.* The short mane of silver blond hair, Vicki realized with a start, was natural; the brows could have been lightened but not the lashes. While not exactly pretty, the pale hair made for an exotic contrast with the deep tan. *And that sundress certainly leaves little tan to the imagination.*

Their eyes met and Vicki's brows rose. Just for an instant she almost had a grasp of what was really going on, then the instant passed and the girl was looking up through her lashes and smiling shyly.

The large red dog had gone to sit by Henry's side, his head level with Henry's waist, and now the two of them walked forward. Henry wore a carefully neutral expression. The dog looked amused.

"Vicki, I'd like you to meet Rose Heerkens. Her family is having some trouble I think you can help them with."

"Pleased to meet you." Vicki held out her hand and after a quick glance at Henry—*What did he tell her about me?*—the younger woman put hers in it. Very few women are any good at shaking hands, not having been raised to do it, but Vicki was surprised by both a grip that matched her own and a callus-ridged palm.

As Rose released her hold, she extended the motion to indicate the dog now leaning against her legs. "This is Storm."

Storm held up a paw.

Bending over to take it, Vicki grinned. "Pleased to meet you too, Storm."

The big dog gave a short bark and leaned forward,

dragging his tongue across Vicki's face with enough force to almost dislodge her glasses.

"Storm, stop it!" With both hands buried in the russet ruff, Rose yanked the dog back. "Maybe she doesn't want to be covered in slobber."

"Oh, I don't mind." She wiped her face off with her palm and resettled her glasses on her nose. "What kind of a dog is he? He's beautiful." Then she laughed, for Storm obviously recognized the compliment and was looking smug.

"Please don't encourage him, Ms. Nelson, he's vain enough already." Rose dug her knee in behind the big dog's shoulder and shoved, knocking him over. "And as for what kind he is—he's a nuisance."

Storm didn't look at all put out by being so unceremoniously dumped. Tongue lolling, he rolled over on his back, all four feet in the air, and looked expectantly up at Vicki.

"Do you want your stomach rubbed, then?"

"Storm." Henry's command brought the animal off the floor, to stand looking remarkably chastened.

Vicki glanced at Henry in astonishment. What was with him?

"Perhaps," he met Vicki's eyes then swept his gaze over the girl and the dog, "we should get on with things."

Vicki found herself moving toward the couch without having made a conscious decision to move. She hated it when he did that. She hated the way she responded to it. And she really hated not being sure if it was the vampire or the prince she was responding to—somehow knuckling under to a supernatural ability seemed less reprehensible than giving in to a medieval petty dictator. *His undead highness and I are going to have to have a little talk about this. . . .*

Tossing her bag down, she settled back against the red velvet upholstery, watching Rose curl up in the armchair and Storm throw himself to the floor at her feet. He looked splendid against the cream colored

carpet but the russet fur clashed a little desperately
with the crimson of the chair. Henry dropped one
denim-clad leg on the arm of the couch and perched
beside her, so close that, for a moment, Vicki was
aware of him alone.

"It's too soon, Vicki, you lost a lot of blood."

*She felt her face flush. It had never occurred to her
that he wouldn't want to. . . . It was what they were
leading up to, wasn't it? "They put most of it back at
the hospital, Henry. I'm fine. Really."*

*"I believe you." He smiled and she suddenly found
the air available in the hallway inadequate.*

*He's had over four hundred and fifty years to prac-
tice that smile, she reminded herself. Breathe.*

*"We have to be very careful," he continued, plac-
ing his hands lightly on her shoulders. "I don't want
to hurt you."*

*It sounded so much like dialogue out of a bad soap
opera that Vicki grinned. "Just so long as you remember I haven't got a couple of hundred years to spare,"
she told him, digging for her apartment keys, "I'll try
not to rush you."*

That had been almost four months ago, the first time
they'd gone out after she'd been released from the hospital. And they still hadn't. Vicki had tried to be patient but there were times, and with him sitting so
close this was one of them, when she wanted to kick
his feet out from under him and beat him to the floor.
With an effort, she brought her attention back to the
business at hand.

As everyone appeared to be waiting for her to speak,
she arranged her face into her best "the police officer
is your friend" expression and turned to Rose. "What
is it you need me to help you with?"

Again, Rose glanced at Henry. Although Vicki
couldn't see the vampire's response it seemed to re-
assure the younger woman for she took a deep breath,
brushed her hair back off her face with trembling fingers, and said, "In the last month two members of our

family have been shot.'' She had to stop and swallow grief before she could continue. ''We need your help, Ms. Nelson, to find the killer.''

Murder. Well, that was definitely a little more serious than Vicki had been expecting. And a double murder at that. She pushed her glasses up her nose and let sympathy soften her voice as she asked, ''Have the local police not turned up any leads?''

''They don't exactly know.''

''What do you mean by 'don't exactly know'?'' Vicki could think of several things it might mean and none of them appealed to her.

''Why don't you show her, Rose,'' Henry said quietly.

Vicki swiveled around to look up at him, her peripheral vision too poor to allow her the luxury of glancing from the corner of her eye. His expression matched his tone. Whatever Rose had to show her was very important. More than slightly apprehensive, she turned around again.

Rose, who had been waiting for her attention, slipped out of her sandals and rose to her feet. Storm, after giving the sandals a quick sniff, padded over to her side. In one quick movement she stripped off the sundress she was wearing, stood naked for a heartbeat, and then, where there had been a pale-haired young woman and a large russet dog there was a red-haired young man and a large white dog.

The young man bore a strong resemblance to the young woman; they shared the same high cheekbones, the same large eyes, the same pointed chins. *And the same lithe dancer's body*, Vicki noted after one quick glance at the obvious difference.

''Werewolves,'' she heard herself say aloud, amazed at her composure. *Odds are good it's Henry's influence. This is what comes of hanging around with vampires. . . . I'll get the bastard for this.*

The young man, completely undismayed by both her scrutiny and his nakedness, winked.

Vicki, considerably nonplussed, especially when she remembered how she'd been treating the dog—*No, wolf. No, wer. Oh hell.*—earlier, felt herself flushing and glanced away for an instant. When she looked back, she found she'd missed the actual moment of transformation and Rose was tugging her dress back over her head. The young man—Storm?—was resignedly pulling on a pair of bright blue shorts that offered minimal coverage.

Feeling her gaze on him, he looked up, smiled, and advanced with his hand held out. "Hi. I guess further introduction are in order. My name's Peter."

"Uh, hi." Apparently the names changed with the form. A little stunned, Vicki took the offered hand. It had the same pattern of heavy callus that Rose's had. Made sense actually if they ran on four feet part of the time. "You're, uh, Rose's brother?"

"We're twins." He grinned and it reminded Vicki so much of the expression the russet dog had worn that she found herself grinning in return. "She's older; I'm better looking."

"You're noisier," Rose corrected, curling back up in the armchair. "Come and sit down." With a martyred air, Peter did as he was told, throwing himself gracefully down into the same spot he'd occupied as Storm, his back pressed against his sister's knees. "We're sorry about the theatricality of all this, Ms. Nelson," she continued, "but Henry suggested it was the best way to present it, that you . . ."

She hesitated and Henry smoothly finished the sentence. ". . . that you weren't a person who denied the evidence of your own eyes."

Vicki supposed he meant it as a compliment so she contented herself with a quiet snort and an only moderately sarcastic, "Well, you should know."

"You will help us, won't you?" Peter leaned forward, and placed one hand lightly on Vicki's knee. There was nothing sexual in the touch, and the expression accompanying it held only a combination of worry and hope.

Werewolves. Vicki sighed. *First vampires and demons, now werewolves. What next?* She crossed her legs, dislodging Peter's hand, and settled back into a more comfortable position; odds were good that this was going to be a long story. "Perhaps you'd better start at the beginning."

Two

"At the beginning," Rose repeated, her tone turning the statement into a question. She sighed and pushed a shock of pale hair back off her face. "I guess it started when Silver got shot."

"Silver?" Vicki asked. She had a feeling that if she didn't stay on top of this explanation it was going to get away from her pretty quickly.

"Our aunt," Rose began but Peter cut in when he saw the look on Vicki's face.

"We have two names," he explained. "One for each form." He laid a short-fingered hand against the tanned muscles of his chest. "This is Peter, but it was Storm who met you at the door. And, in her fur-form, Rose is called Cloud. It's easier than explaining to outsiders why all the farm dogs have the same names as members of the family."

"I can imagine it must be," Vicki agreed, pleased that her earlier assumption about the names had been verified. "But doesn't it get a little confusing?"

Peter shrugged. "Why should it? You have more than one name. You're Ms. Nelson to some people, Vicki to others, and you don't find it confusing."

"Not usually, no." Vicki conceded the point. "So your aunt was shot in her . . . uh, wolf form." Well, they were called werewolves so she supposed wolf was the preferred term. It certainly seemed more socially acceptable than dog. *And just think, before Henry came into my life, I never used to worry about things like that.* . . . She'd have to remember to thank him.

"That's right." Peter nodded. "Our family owns a large sheep farm just north of London, Ontario . . ."

The pause dared her to comment but Vicki kept her expression politely interested and her mouth shut.

". . . and Silver was shot in the head when she was out checking the flock."

"At night?"

"Yes."

"We thought about telling the police that someone had shot one of our dogs," Rose continued, "and at the time that's all we thought it was, some dickhead with a gun who had no way of knowing she was anything more. These things happen, people lose dogs all the time." Her voice broke on the last word and Peter butted his head against her knees. She threaded her fingers through his hair and went on. Touch appeared to be important to them Vicki noted. "But the last thing we need is police roaming around and asking questions, you know, seeing things, so the family decided to deal with it."

Peter's lips drew back off his teeth; long and white, they were his least human feature.

If "the family" had caught up to Silver's killer, Vicki realized, justice would have little to do with the law and the courts. A year ago she would have been appalled at the idea, but a year ago she'd had a badge and things had been a lot simpler. "So what did you tell people who asked where your Aunt Sylvia had gone."

"We told them she'd finally decided to join Uncle Robert up in the Yukon. She always talked about doing it so no one was very surprised. Aunt Nadine—she was Aunt Sylvia's twin. . . ." Rose swallowed again, hard, and Peter pressed closer. "Well, she stayed out of sight for a while. Twin bonds are pretty strong with our people and she kept having to howl. Anyway, Monday night, Ebon—Uncle Jason—was shot in the head while he was out checking on the ewes with fall lambs. No one heard anything and we couldn't find a scent anywhere near the body."

"High velocity rifle, probably with a silencer and a scope," Vicki guessed. She frowned. "Sounds like quite a marksman; to hit a moving target at night. . . ."

"Monday was a full moon," Henry broke in. "There was plenty of light."

"Wouldn't matter with a scope. And there wasn't a full moon the night Silver was killed." She shook her head. "A shot like that, two shots. . . ."

"That isn't all," Rose interrupted, tossing something across the room. "Father found this near the body."

Vicki flailed at the air and the small lump of metal landed in her lap. Silently cursing her lack of depth perception, she dug around in the folds of her shorts and when she fished it out, stared down in puzzlement at what could only be—in spite of its squashed appearance—a silver bullet. She closed her teeth firmly on her instinctive response. *Your uncle was killed by the Lone Ranger?*

Henry reached over her shoulder and plucked the dully gleaming object from her palm, holding it up to the light between finger and thumb. "A silver bullet," he explained, "is one of the traditional ways to kill a werewolf. The silver is a myth. The bullet alone is usually enough to do the job."

"I can imagine." A .30 caliber round—and Vicki knew the slug had to have been at least that large to have maintained any kind of shape at all after traveling through flesh and bone and then impacting into the dirt—fired from a high velocity rifle would have left very little of Ebon's head in the wake of its passing. She turned again to Rose and Peter who had been watching her expressionlessly. "I take it that a similar bullet was not found by your aunt's body or you'd have mentioned it?"

Rose frowned down at her brother then they both shook their heads.

"Doesn't really matter. Even without the bullet, the pattern points to a single marksman." Vicki sighed and leaned forward on the couch, resting her forearms on her thighs. "And here's something else to think about; whoever shot Ebon was shooting specifically at werewolves. If one person knows you're wer, others will too; that's a given. These deaths could be the result of a community. . . ."

"Witch hunt," Henry put in quietly as she paused.

She nodded, not lifting her gaze from the twins, and continued. "You're different and different frightens most people. They could be taking their fear out on you."

Peter exchanged a long look with his sister. "It doesn't have to be that complicated," he said. "Our older brother is a member of the London police force and Barry, his partner, knows he's a wer."

"And his partner is a marksman?" All things considered, it wasn't that wild a guess. Nor would it be unlikely that said partner would own a .30 caliber rifle when any six people in any small town would likely own half a dozen between them.

The twins nodded.

Vicki let her breath out in a long, low whistle. "Messy. Has your brother confronted his partner about this?"

"No, Uncle Stuart won't allow it. He says the pack keeps its trouble within the pack. Aunt Nadine convinced him to call Henry, and Henry convinced them both that we should talk to you. That you might be our only chance. Will you help, Ms. Nelson? Uncle Stuart said we were to agree to whatever you charge."

Peter's hand was back on her knee and he was staring up at her with such single-minded entreaty that she said without thinking, "You want me to find out that Barry didn't do it."

"We want you to find out who did do it," Rose

corrected. "Who *is* doing it. Whoever they are."
Then, just for an instant, the fear showed through.
"Someone is killing us, Ms. Nelson. I don't want to
die."

*Thus lifting this whole discussion out of the realm
of fairy tales.* "I don't want you to die either," Vicki
told her gently. "But I might not be the best person
for the job." She pushed her glasses up her nose and
took a deep breath. Both deaths had occurred at night
and her eyes simply didn't allow her to function after
dark. It was bad enough in the city, but in the country
with no streetlights to anchor her, she'd be blind.

On the other hand, what choice did they have? Surely
she'd be better than nothing. And her lack of vision
didn't affect her mind, or her training, or her years of
experience. And this was a job that would count for
something, it was important, life or death. *The kind
of job Celluci still does.* God damn it! She could work
around the disability.

"I can't leave right away." Dawning expressions of
relief mixed with hope told her she'd made the right
decision. "Unfortunately, I have appointments I can't
break. How about Friday?"

"Friday evening," Henry interrupted smoothly.
"After sunset. Meanwhile, no one is to go anywhere
by themselves. No one. Both Ebon and Silver were
shot while they were alone, and that's the only part of
the pattern you can change. Make sure the rest of the
family understands that. And as much as possible, stay
in sight of the house. In fact, as much as you can, stay
in sight of non-wer. Whoever is doing this is counting
on you not being able to tell anyone, and as long as
there are witnesses around you should be safe. Did I
miss anything, Vicki?"

"No, I don't think so." He'd missed asking for her
opinion before he started his little lecture, but they'd
discuss that later. As for his assumption that he'd be
going along, well, it solved her transportation problem
and created all sorts of new ones that would have to

be dealt with—again, later. She wasn't looking forward to "later."

"Over the next two days," she told the twins, "I want you to write me up a list—two lists actually; the people who know what you are on one and the people who might suspect on the other. Get the input of everyone in the family."

"We can do that, no problem." Peter heaved a sigh of relief and bounded to his feet.

Apparently the fact that she and Henry operated as a team had come as no surprise to him. Vicki wondered what Henry had told them before she arrived. "First thing tomorrow," she buried the slug in tissues and sealed it into one of the small freezer bags she always carried in her purse, "I'll drop this off at ballistics and see if they can tell me anything about the rifle it came from."

"But Colin said . . ." Rose began.

Vicki cut her off. "Colin said it would lead to awkward questions. Well, it would in London and, considering your family's situation, it's not the sort of thing you want talked about. Good cops remember the damnedest bits of information and Colin handing around silver bullets could lead to your exposure later on. However," she pitched her voice for maximum reassurance, "this is Toronto. We have a much broader crime base, God forbid, and the fact that *I* was handing around a silver bullet won't mean squat even if someone does remember it."

She paused for breath and tucked the small plastic bag containing the tissues and the slug down into a secure corner of her purse. "Don't expect anything though, this thing is a mess."

"We won't. And we'll tell Aunt Nadine to expect you on Friday night." Peter smiled at her with such complete and utter gratitude that Vicki felt like a heel for even considering refusing to help. "Thanks, Ms. Nelson."

"Yes, thank you." Rose stood as well and added

her quieter smile to the brilliance of her brother's. "We really appreciate this. Henry was right."

What Henry was right about *this time* got a little lost in Peter shucking off his shorts. Vicki supposed she'd have to get used to it but at the moment all that naked young man left her a little distracted. The reappearance of Storm came as a distinct relief.

He shook himself briskly and bounded toward the door.

"Why . . ." Vicki began.

Rose understood and grinned. "Because he likes to ride with his head out the car window." She sighed as she stuffed the discarded shorts back into her bag. "He's such lousy company in a car."

"Well, he certainly seems anxious to get going."

"We don't like the city much," Rose explained, her nose wrinkling. "It stinks. Thanks again, Ms. Nelson. We'll see you Friday."

"You're welcome." She watched Henry walk Rose to the door, warn them to be careful, and return to the living room. The look on his face rerouted the accusation of high-handedness she was about to make. "What's wrong?"

Both red-gold brows rose. "My friends are being killed," he reminded her quietly.

Vicki felt herself flush. "I'm sorry," she said. "It's hard to hang onto that amidst all the," she waved a hand as she groped for the word, "strangeness."

"It is, however, the important thing to be hung onto."

"I know. I know." She forced herself not to sound sullen. She shouldn't have had to be reminded of that. "You never thought for a moment that I might say no, did you?"

"I've come to know you over these last few months." His expression softened. "You need to be needed and they need you, Vicki. There aren't too many private investigators they can trust with this."

That was easy to believe. As to her needing to be

needed, it was a facetious observation that could easily be ignored. "Are all the wer so," she searched for the right word and settled on, "self-contained? If my family were going through what theirs is, I'd be an emotional wreck."

Somehow he doubted that, but it was still a question that deserved answering. "From the time they're very young, the wer are taught to hide what they are, and not only physically; for the good of the pack you never show vulnerability to strangers. You should consider yourself honored that you got as much as you did. Also, the wer tend to live much more in the present than humans do. They mourn their dead, then they get on with life. They don't carry the burden of yesterday, they don't anticipate tomorrow."

Vicki snorted. "Very poetic. But it makes it nearly impossible for them to deal with this sort of situation, doesn't it?"

"That's why they've come to you."

"And if I wasn't around?"

"Then they'd die."

She frowned. "And why couldn't you save them?"

He moved to his usual place by the window, leaning back against the glass. "Because they won't let me."

"Because you're a vampire?"

"Because Stuart won't allow that kind of challenge to his authority. If he can't save the pack, neither can I. You're female, you're Nadine's problem, and Nadine, at the moment, is devastated by the loss of her twin. If you were wer, you could probably take her position away from her right now, but as you aren't, the two of you should be able to work something out." He shook his head at her expression. "You can't judge them by human standards, Vicki, no matter how human they seem most of the time. And it's too late to back out. You told Rose and Peter you'd help."

Her chin went up. "Did I give you any indication that I might back out?"

"No."

"Damned straight, I didn't. She took a deep breath. She'd worked with the Toronto City Council, she could work with werewolves. At least with the latter all the growling and snapping would mean something. In fact, the wer were likely to be the least of her problems. "There might be difficulties. I mean, with *me* taking this case."

"Like the fact you don't drive." She could hear the smile in his voice.

"No. Real problems."

He turned and spread his arms, the movement causing the hair to glint gold in the lamplight. "So tell me."

It's called retinitis pigmentosa. I'm going blind. I can't see at night. I have almost no peripheral vision. She couldn't tell him. She couldn't handle the pity. Not from him. Not after what she'd gone through with Celluci. *Fuck it.* She shoved her glasses up her nose and shook her head.

Henry dropped his arms. After a moment, when the silence had stretched to uncomfortable dimensions, he said, "I hope you don't mind that I've invited myself along. I thought we made a pretty good team the last time. And, I thought you might need a little help dealing with the . . . strangeness."

She managed an almost realistic laugh. "I do the day work, you cover the night?"

"Just like last time, yes." He leaned back against the glass and watched her turning that over in her mind, worrying it into pieces. She was one of the most stubborn, argumentative, independent women he'd met in four and a half centuries, and he wished she'd confide in him. Whatever the problem was, they could work it out together because whatever the problem was, it couldn't be big enough to keep her from giving everything she had to this case. He wouldn't allow it to be. Friends of his were dying.

"I don't want to die, Ms. Nelson."

I don't want you to die either, Rose. Vicki worried

her lower lip between her teeth. If they worked together, he'd find out, eventually. She had to decide if that mattered more than the continuing loss of innocent lives. *And put like that, it's not much of a choice, is it?* If she wasn't their best chance on her own, together she and Henry were. *Screw it. We'll work it out.*

Henry watched her expressions change and smiled. Over his long existence he'd grown very good at reading people, at picking up the delicate nuances that mirrored their inner thoughts. Most of the time, Vicki went right past nuance; her thoughts as easy to read as a billboard.

"So, Friday night after sunset. You can pick me up."

He bowed, the accompanying smile taking the mocking edge off the gesture. "As my lady commands."

Vicki returned the smile, then yawned and stretched, back arched and arms spread out against the red velvet.

Henry watched the pulse beating at the base of her throat. He hadn't fed for three nights and the need was rising in him. Vicki wanted him. He could scent her desire most times they were together, but he'd held back because of the blood loss that she'd taken in the spring. And, he had to admit, held back because he wanted the timing to be right. The one time he'd fed from her had been such a frenzied necessity that she'd missed all the extra pleasures it could bring to both parties involved.

The scent of her life filled the apartment and he walked forward, his pace measured to the beat of her heart. When he reached the couch, he held out his hand.

Vicki took it and hauled herself to her feet. "Thanks." She yawned again, releasing him to shove a fist in front of her mouth. "Boy, am I bagged. You wouldn't believe the time I had to get up this morning and then I spent the whole day working essentially two jobs in a factory that had to be eighty degrees C.'' Dragging her bag up over her shoulder, she headed for the door. ''No need to see me out. I'll be waiting for you after sunset Friday.'' She waved cheerfully and was gone.

Henry opened his mouth to protest, closed it, opened it again, then sighed.

By the time the elevator reached the lobby, Vicki had managed to stop laughing. The poleaxed look on Henry's face had been priceless and she'd have given a year of her life to have had a camera. *If his royal undead highness thinks he's got* this *situation under control, he can think again.* It had taken almost more willpower than she had to walk out of that apartment, but it had been worth it.

''Begin as you mean to go on,'' she declared under her breath, wiping sweaty palms against her shorts. ''Maybe Mom's old sayings have more value than I thought.''

She was still smiling when she got into the cab, still flushed with victory, then she leaned back and looked up at the fuzzy rectangles of light that were Henry's building. She couldn't see him. Couldn't have even said for certain which fuzzy rectangle was his. But he was up there. Looking down at her. Wanting her. Like she wanted him—and she felt like a teenager whose hormones had just kicked into overdrive.

Why the hell wasn't she up there with him, then?

She let her head drop down against the sweaty leather of the seat and sighed. ''I am *such* an idiot.''

''Maybe,'' the cabbie agreed, turning around with a gold-toothed grin. ''You wanna be a moving idiot? Meter's running.''

Vicki glared at him. ''Huron Street,'' she growled. ''South of College. You just drive.''

He snorted and faced forward. ''Just 'cause you unlucky in love, lady, ain't no reason to take it out on me.''

The cabbie's muttering blended with the sounds of the traffic, and all the way down Bloor Street, Vicki could feel Henry's gaze hot on the back of her neck. It was going to be a long night.

The tape ended and Rose fumbled between the seats for a new one with no success. The long drive back from Toronto had left her stiff, tired, and too tense to take her eyes off the road—even if it was only an empty stretch of gravel barely a kilometer from home.

"Hey!" She poked her brother in the back. "Why don't you do something useful and dig out. . . . Storm, hold on!'' Her foot slammed down on the brake. With the back end of the small car fishtailing in the gravel and the steering wheel twisting like a live thing in her hands, she fought to regain control, dimly aware of Peter, not Storm, hanging on beside her.

We aren't going to make it! The shadow she'd seen stretched across the road, loomed darker, closer.

Darker. Closer.

Then, just as she thought they might stop in time and relief allowed her heart to start beating again, the front bumper and the shadow met.

Good. They were unhurt. It was no part of his plan to have them injured in a car accident. A pity the change in wind kept him from his regular hunting ground, but it need not stop the hunt entirely. He rested his cheek against the rifle, watching the scene unfold in the scope. They were close to home. One of them would go for help, leaving the other for him.

"I guess Dad was right all along about this old tree being punky. Rotted right off the stump.'' Peter perched on the trunk, looking like a red-haired Puck in the headlights. "Think we can move it?''

Rose shook her head. "Not just the two of us. You'd better run home and get help. I'll wait by the car."

"Why don't we both go?"

"Because I don't like leaving the car just sitting here." She flicked her hair back off her face. "It's a five minute run, Peter. I'll be fine. Jeez, you are getting so overprotective lately."

"I am not! It's just. . . ."

They heard the approaching truck at the same time and a heartbeat later Rose and Storm came around the car to face it.

Only the Heerkens farm fronted on this road. Only the Heerkens drove this road at night. His grip tightened on the sweaty metal.

"They spray the oil back of the crossroads today. Stink like anything." Frederick Kleinbein hitched his pants up over the curve of his belly and beamed genially at Rose. "I take long way home to avoid stink. Good thing, eh? We get chain from truck, hitch to tree, and drag tree to side of road." He reached over and lightly grabbed Storm's muzzle, shaking his head from side to side. "Maybe we hitch you to tree, eh? Make you do some work for your living."

"There are none so blind as those who will not see. . . ." There would be no chance of a shot now.

"Thanks, Mr. Kleinbein."

"Ach, why thank me? You do half of work. Truck did other half." He leaned out of the window, mopping his brow with a snowy white handkerchief. "You and that overgrown puppy of yours get home now, eh? Tell your father some of the wood near top is still good to burn. If he doesn't want, I do. And tell him that I return his sump pump before end of month."

Rose stepped back as he put the truck into gear, then

forward again as he added something over the sound of the engine that she didn't catch. "What?"

But he only waved a beefy arm and was gone.

"He said," Peter told her, once the red banner of taillights had disappeared and it was safe to change, "Give my regards to your brother. And then he laughed."

"Do you think he saw you as he drove up?"

"Rose, it's a perfectly normal thing for him to say. He might have meant me, he might have meant Colin. After all, Colin used to help him bring in hay. You worry too much."

"Maybe," she acknowledged but silently added as Storm's head went out the window again, *Maybe not.*

He remained where he was, watching, until they drove away, then he slipped the silver bullet from the rifle and into his pocket. He would just have to use it another time.

"Are you sure of this?" The elder Mr. Glassman tapped a manicured nail against the report. "It will hold up in court?"

"No doubt about it. Everything you need is right there." Behind her back the fingers of Vicki's right hand beat a tattoo against her left palm. Every time she faced the elder Mr. Glassman, she found herself standing at parade rest for no reason she could discern. He wasn't a physically imposing man, nor in any way military in bearing so she supposed it must be force of personality. Although he'd been hardly more than a child at the time, he'd managed to not only survive the death camps of the Holocaust but bring his younger brother Joseph safely through the horror as well.

He closed the report and sighed deeply. "Harris." The name put an end to months of petty sabotage, although as he said it, he sounded more weary than angry. "Our thanks for your quick work, Ms. Nelson." He stood and held out his hand.

Vicki took it, noting the strength beneath the soft surface.

"I see your bill is included with the report," he continued. "We'll issue a check at the end of the week. I assume you'll be available for court appearances if necessary?"

"It's part of the service," she assured him. "If you need me, I'll be there."

"Yo, baby-doll!" Harris, spending the last of his lunch break outside in the sun with a couple of cronies, heaved himself to his feet as Vicki left the building. "Packin' it in, eh? Couldn't cut it."

Vicki had every intention of ignoring him.

"Pity that your tight little ass is gonna be wiggling its way somewhere else."

And then again. . . .

He laughed as he saw her reaction and continued to laugh as she crossed the parking lot to stand in front of him. A jock in his younger days, he had the heavy, bulgy build of a man who'd once been muscular, his Blue Jays T-shirt stretched tight over the beer belly he carried around instead of a waist. He was the kind of laughing bigot that everyone tends to excuse.

Don't mind him, it's just his way.

Vicki considered those the most dangerous kind but this time he'd gone beyond excuses. He could complain about people not being able to take a joke all the way to court.

"What's the matter baby-doll, couldn't leave without a good-bye kiss." He turned to be sure the two men still sitting by the building appreciated the joke and so missed the expression on Vicki's face.

She'd had a bad night. She was in a bad mood. And she was more than willing to take it out on this racist, sexist son-of-a-bitch. He had a good four inches on her and probably a hundred pounds but she figured she'd have little trouble dusting his ass. *Tempting, but no.* Although her eyes narrowed and her jaw clenched,

years of observing due process held her temper in
check. *He's not worth the trouble.*

As she turned to leave, Harris swung around and, grinning broadly, reached out and smacked her on the ass.

Vicki smiled. *Oh what the hell. . . .*

Pivoting, she kicked him less hard than she was able
on the outside edge of his left knee. He toppled, bel-
lowing with pain, as if both feet had been cut out from
under him. A blow just below his ribs drove the air
out of his lungs in an anguished gasp and given that
she resisted stomping where it would hurt the most,
she treated herself to slamming a well-placed foot into
his butt as he drew his knees up to his chest. Then she
grinned at his buddies and started home again.

He could press charges. But she didn't think he
would. He wasn't hurt and she was willing to bet that
by the time he got his breath back he'd already be
warping the facts to fit his world view—a world view
that would not include the possibility of his being taken
down by a woman.

She also realized that this wouldn't have been the
case if she still carried a badge, police brutality being
a rallying cry of his kind.

You know, she shoved her glasses up her nose and
ran for the bus she could now see cresting the Egling-
ton Avenue overpass, *I think I could grow to like being
a civilian.*

The euphoria faded along with the adrenaline and
the crisis of conscience set in barely two blocks from
the bus stop. It wasn't so much the violence itself that
upset her as her reaction to it; try as she would, she
simply couldn't convince herself that Harris hadn't got
a small fraction of exactly what he had coming. By the
time she was fighting her way to the back of the Dundas streetcar in an attempt to actually make it off at
her stop, she was heartily sick of the whole argument.

*Violence is never the answer but sometimes, like with
cockroaches, it's the only possible response.* By physically moving two semi-comatose teenagers out of her

way, she made it out the door at the last possible second. *Harris is a cockroach. End of discussion*. It was too damned hot to deal with personal ethics. She promised herself she'd take another crack at it when the weather cooled down.

She could feel the heat of the asphalt through the soles of her sneakers and, walking as quickly as the seething crowds allowed, she turned up Huron Street toward home. Dundas and Huron crossed in the center of Chinatown, surrounded by restaurants and tiny markets selling exotic vegetables and live fish. In hot weather, the metal bins of food garbage heated up and the stench that permeated the area was anything but appetizing. Breathing shallowly through her mouth, Vicki could completely understand why the wer had hurried out of the city.

As she passed, she checked *the puddle*. Tucked up against the curb in a spot where the asphalt had peeled off and a number of the original paving bricks were missing, the puddle collected local runoff as well as assorted organic flotsam. As the temperature rose, foul smelling bubbles occasionally broke through the scummy surface, adding their own bit of joy to the bouquet. Vicki had no idea how deep the puddle was. In five years, she'd never seen it dry. She had a theory that someday, something was going to crawl out of this little leftover bowl of primordial soup and terrorize the neighborhood, so she kept an eye on it. She wanted to be there when it happened.

By the time she reached her apartment, she was covered in a fine sheen of sweat and all she wanted was a cold shower and a colder drink. She suspected it'd be some time before she got either when she could smell the coffee brewing inside as she put her key in the lock.

"It's a hundred and twelve degrees in the shade," she muttered, swinging open the door, "how the hell can you drink hot coffee?"

It was a good thing she didn't expect an answer, because she didn't get one. Snapping the lock back

on, she threw her bag down in the hall and went into
the tiny living room.

"Nice of you to drop by, Celluci." She frowned.
"You look like shit."

"Thank you, Mother Theresa." He raised his mug
and drank deeply, barely lifting his head off the back
of the recliner. When he finished swallowing, he met
her eyes. "We got the son of a bitch."

"Margot?"

Celluci nodded. "Got him cold. We picked the little
bastard up at noon."

*At noon. While I was proving I was more macho
than Billy Harris.* For an instant Vicki was so blindly
jealous she couldn't speak. That was what she should
be doing with her life, making a difference, not making a fool of herself in the parking lot of a coffee factory. Lower lip caught between her teeth, she managed
to wrestle the monster back into its pit although she
couldn't quite manage the smile.

"Good work." When she'd allowed Mike Celluci
back into her life, she'd allowed police work back in.
She'd just have to learn to deal with it.

He nodded, his expression showing exhaustion and
not much more. Vicki felt some of the tension go out
of her shoulders. Either he understood or he was too
tired to make a scene. Either way, she could cope. She
reached over and took the empty mug from his hand.

"When was the last time you slept?"

"Tuesday."

"Ate?"

"Uh. . . ." He frowned and rubbed his free hand
across his eyes.

"Real food," Vicki prodded. "Not something out
of a box, covered in powdered sugar."

"I don't remember."

She shook her head and moved into the kitchen.
"Sandwich first, then sleep. You'd better not mind cold
roast beef, 'cause that's all I've got." As she piled the
meat onto bread, she grinned. It was almost like old

times. They'd made a pact, she and Celluci, years ago when they'd first gotten involved; if they couldn't take care of themselves, they'd let the other one do it for them.

"This job has enough ways of eating at your soul," she'd told him as he worked the knots out of her back. *"It makes sense to build up a support structure."*

"You sure you just don't want someone to brag to when the job is done?" he snorted.

Her elbow caught him in the solar plexus. She smiled sweetly as he gasped for breath. "That, too."

And as important as someone who'd understood when it went right, was someone who understood when it went wrong. Who didn't ask a lot of stupid questions there were no answers to or give sympathy that poured salt on the wound failure had left.

Someone who'd just make a sandwich and turn down the bed and then go away while the last set of clean sheets got wrinkled and sweaty.

Six hours later, Celluci stumbled out into the living room and stared blearily at the television. "What inning?"

"Top of the fourth."

He collapsed into the only other chair in the room, Vicki being firmly entrenched in the recliner. "Goals scored?" he asked, scratching at the hair on his chest.

"It's runs, asshole, as you very well know, and it's a no-run game so far."

His stomach rumbled audibly over the sounds of the crowd cheering an easy out at first. "Pizza?"

Vicki tossed him the phone. "It's my place, you're buying."

One lone slice lay congealing in the box and the Jays had actually managed to acquire and hang on to a two-run lead when she told him she was heading for London.

"England?"

"No, Ontario."

"New case?"

"Right first time."

"What's it about?"

I'm looking for the person, or people, involved in shooting a family of sheep-farming werewolves with silver bullets. At least it was real work. Important work. "Uh, I can't tell you right now. Maybe later." *Maybe in a million years.* . . .

Celluci frowned. She was hiding something. He could always tell. "How are you getting there? Train? Bus?" Stretching out his leg, he poked her in the side with a bare foot. "Jogging?"

Vicki snorted. "I'm not the one carrying the love-handles."

In spite of himself, he sucked in his gut.

Vicki grinned as he tried to pretend he hadn't done it, visibly forcing himself to relax. *Pity,* Vicki mused, *because he's just going to get tense again.* "Henry's giving me a lift down tomorrow night."

"Henry?" Celluci kept his voice carefully neutral. She had, of course, every right to spend time with whoever she wished but there was something about Henry Fitzroy that Celluci most definitely didn't like. Casual inquiries had turned up nothing to make him change his mind—given that they'd turned up nothing at all. "He's involved in this case, is he?" The last of Vicki's cases Henry Fitzroy had been involved with had ended with her half dead at the feet of a grade B movie monster. Celluci had been unimpressed.

Vicki pushed her glasses up her nose. How much to tell him. . . . "He's friends with the people I'm working for."

"Will he be staying after he drops you off?" Correctly interpreting her lowering brows, he added, "Calm down. You know and I know how much trouble a civilian can be around a case. I just want to be sure that you're not complicating things for yourself." He could see that she wasn't convinced of his purity of motive. Tough.

"First of all, Celluci, try to remember that *I* am

now a civilian.'' He snorted and she scowled. ''Secondly, he's just giving me a lift and filling me in on some of the background details. He won't be interfering.'' *He'll be helping. We'll be working together.* She had no intention of letting Mike Celluci know that, not when she didn't know how she felt about it herself. Besides, it would involve an explanation it wasn't her place to give. And if she wanted to work with Henry Fitzroy, it was none of Celluci's damned business.

Celluci read the last thought off her expression and almost got it right. ''I was thinking about your career, not your sex life,'' he growled, tossing back the last inch of tepid beer remaining in the bottle. ''Get your mind out of the gutter, Vicki.''

''My mind?'' It was her turn to snort. She peeled herself out of the recliner, sweaty skin coming away from the vinyl with a painful tearing sound. ''I didn't bring it up. But seeing as you have. . . .''

He recognized her next move as a distraction, an attempt to pull his attention away from Henry Fitzroy. As distractions went, it wasn't bad and he decided to cooperate. Time enough later to do a little investigating into the elusive Mr. Fitzroy's background.

Halfway to the bedroom, he asked with mock seriousness—or as close as he could get given his current shortness of breath—''What about the game?''

''They're two runs ahead with an inning an a half to play,'' Vicki muttered. ''Surely they can win this one without us.''

As Henry's teeth opened the vein in Tony's wrist he looked up to find the eyes of the younger man locked on him. The pupils dilated and orgasm weighted the lids, but through it all, Tony watched avidly as the vampire drank.

When it was over, and he was sure the coagulant in his saliva had stopped the bleeding, Henry raised himself up on one elbow. ''Do you always watch?'' he asked.

Tony nodded drowsily. "S'part of the turn on. Seeing you do it."

Henry laughed and pushed a long lock of damp brown hair back off Tony's forehead. He'd been feeding from Tony as often as had been safe for the last five months, ever since Vicki had convinced the young man to help save his life. "And do you watch while I do other things?"

Tony grinned. "I don't remember. You mind?"

"No. It's pleasant not to have to hide what I am."

Letting his gaze drift down the length of Henry's body, Tony yawned. "Not hiding much now," he murmured. "You gonna be around on the weekend?"

"No," Henry told him. "Vicki and I are going to London. Some friends of mine are in trouble."

"More vampires?"

"Werewolves."

"Awesome." The word blurred, his voice barely audible. Then his eyes slid closed as he surrendered to sleep.

It was *very* pleasant not having to hide what he was, Henry reflected, watching the pulse slow in Tony's throat. It had been a long time since he'd had the luxury of removing all masks, and now he had not one but two mortals who knew him for what he was.

He smiled and stroked the soft skin on the inside of Tony's wrist with his thumb. As he couldn't feed from the wer, this trip would finally see him and Vicki . . . better acquainted.

Three

'JAYS LOSE IN NINTH'

'JAYS LOSE IN NINTH'

"Damn!" Vicki squinted at the headline and decided it wasn't worth thirty cents to discover how the Jays had blown it this time. With no streetcar in sight, she leaned against the newspaper box, immediately regretting it as the box had spent the day basking under an August sun and its metal surface was hot enough to grill steak.

"Well, *that* was *just* what I needed," she growled, rubbing her reddened forearm. Her eyes itched and ached from a combination of the drops and the contortions her ophthalmologist had just put them through, and now she'd fried six square inches of skin. And the streetcar *still* wasn't coming.

"Fuck it. Might as well walk while I can still see the sidewalk." She kicked the newspaper box as she went by and stepped out onto the street, challenging a Camaro crossing Broadview on the yellow light. The driver hit the horn as she dodged the front fender, but the expression she turned toward him closed his teeth on the profane comment he'd been about to add. Obviously not *all* young men driving Camaros had a death wish.

She crossed the Gerrard Street Bridge in a fog, fighting to keep her emotions under control.

Until this morning she'd thought she'd come to grips with the eye disease that had forced her off the Metro Police. She hadn't accepted it graciously, not by any means, but anger and self-pity had stopped being the

motivating factors in her life. Many, many people with
retinitis pigmentosa were in worse shape than she was
but it was hard to keep sight of that when another two
degrees of her peripheral vision had degenerated in the
last month and what little night sight she had remaining had all but disappeared.

The world was rapidly taking on the enclosed dimensions of a slide show. Snap on the scene in front
of her. Turn her head. Snap on the scene in front of
her. Turn her head. Snap on the scene in front of her.
And could someone please get the lights.

*What bloody good am I going to be to a pack of
werewolves anyway? How am I supposed to stop a
killer I can't see?* The more rational part of her mind
tried to interject that the wer were hiring her for her
detective abilities and her experience, not her eyes, but
she was having none of it. *Maybe I'll get lucky and
one of them's been trained as a guide dog.*

"Yo! Victory!"

Frowning, she looked around. Her anger had carried her almost to Parliament and Gerrard, farther than
she'd expected. "What are you doing in this part of
town?"

Tony grinned as he sauntered up. "What happened
to, 'Hi, how are ya?' "

Vicki sighed and attempted not to take the day out
on Tony. When she'd gone to him for help and together
they'd saved Henry, their relationship had changed,
moved up a level from cop and kid—not that he'd actually been a kid for some time. Four years ago, when
she first busted him, he'd been a scrawny troublemaker
of fifteen. Over the years, he'd become her best set of
eyes and ears on the street. Now, they seemed to be
moving toward something a little more equal, but old
habits die hard and she still felt responsible for him.

"All right." She flicked a drop of sweat off her chin.
"Hi. How are you?"

"How come," he asked conversationally, falling
into step beside her, "when you ask, 'How are you?'

it comes out sounding like, 'How much shit are you in?' ''

"How much?"

"None."

Vicki turned her head to look at him but he only smiled beatifically, the picture of wronged innocence. He was looking pretty good, she had to admit, his eyes were clear, his hair was clean, and he'd actually begun to gain a little weight. "Good for you. Now back to my first question, what are you doing in this part of town?"

"I got a place here." He dropped that bombshell with all the studied nonchalance a young man of almost twenty could muster.

"You what!" The exclamation was for Tony's benefit, as he so obviously wanted her to make it. Her mood began to lighten under the influence of his pleasure.

"It's just a room in a basement." He shrugged—no big deal. "But I got my own bathroom. I never had one before."

"Tony, how are you paying for this?" He'd always turned the occasional trick, and she hoped like hell he hadn't gone into the business full time—not only because it was illegal but because the specter of AIDS now haunted every encounter.

"I could say it's none of your business. . . ." As her brows drew down, he raised his hands appeasingly. "But I won't. I got a job. Start on Monday. Henry knows this guy who's a contractor and he needed a wiffle."

"A what?"

"Guy who does the joe jobs."

"Henry found you this?"

"Yup. Found me the place too."

All the years she'd known Tony, the most he'd ever been willing to take from her had been the occasional meal and a little cash in return for information. Henry Fitzroy had known him less than five months and had taken over his life. Vicki had to unclench her teeth before she could speak. "Have you been spending a lot of time with Henry?" The question held an edge.

Tony glanced over at her appraisingly, squinting a little in the bright afternoon sun. "Not much. Hear you're gonna be doing some howling with him this weekend though." At her frown, he leaned closer and in an excellent imitation of a monster movie matinee, intoned, "Verevolves."

"And did he discuss the case with you too?"

"Hey, he just mentioned it."

"I'm surprised he didn't invite you along."

"Jeez, Victory," Tony shook his head. "There's just no talking to you in this mood. Get laid or something and lighten up, eh." He waved jauntily and raced to catch the streetcar at the lights.

Vicki's reply got lost in traffic sounds and it was probably just as well.

"Is it something I said?"

Vicki didn't bother to lift her head off the cool glass of the car window. The highway lights were less than useless as illumination so why bother turning to face a man she couldn't see. "What are you talking about?"

Her tone was so aggressively neutral that Henry smiled. He concentrated for a moment on slipping the BMW into the just barely adequate space between two transports then out the other side to a clear section of road where he actually managed to achieve the speed limit for seven or eight car lengths before he caught up to another section of congested traffic. "You haven't said two civil words to me since I picked you up. I was wondering if I'd done something to annoy you."

"No." She shifted position, drummed her fingers on her knee, and took a deep breath. "Yes." Personal differences must not be allowed to influence the case; things were going to be difficult enough already. If they didn't deal with this now, odds were good it'd turn up sometime a lot more dangerous. "I spoke with Tony today."

"Ah." Jealousy, he understood. "You know I must feed from a number of mortals, Vicki, and you yourself chose the other night to. . . ."

She turned to glare at the indistinct outline his body made against the opposite window. "What the hell does that have to do with anything?" Her left fist slammed down on the dash. "For four years I couldn't get Tony to take anything from me but a couple of hamburgers and some spare change. Now all of a sudden you've found him a job and a place to live."

Henry frowned. "I don't understand the problem." He knew her anger was genuine, both her breathing and her heartbeat had accelerated, but if it wasn't the sexual aspect that bothered her. . . . "You don't want Tony to be off the streets?"

"Of course I do, but . . ." . . . *but I wanted to be the one to save him.* She couldn't say that, it sounded so petty. It was also completely accurate. Abruptly anger changed to embarrassment. ". . . but I don't know how you did it," she finished lamely.

The pause and the emotional change were as clear an indication of her thoughts as if she'd spoken them aloud. Four hundred and fifty years having taught discretion if nothing else, Henry wisely responded only to Vicki's actual words. "I was raised to take care of my people."

Vicki snorted, grateful for a chance to change the subject. "Henry, your father was one of the greatest tyrants in history, burning Protestants and Catholics impartially. Disagreement of any kind, personal or political, usually ended in death."

"Granted," Henry agreed grimly. "You needn't convince me. I was there. Fortunately, I wasn't raised by my father." Henry VIII had been an icon for his bastard son to gaze at in awe and, more than that, he'd been king in a time when the king was all. "The Duke of Norfolk saw to it that I was taught the responsibil-

ities of a prince.'' And only fate had prevented the
Duke of Norfolk from being the last death of King
Henry's reign.

''And Tony is one of 'your people'?''

He ignored the sarcasm. ''Yes.''

It was as simple as that for him, Vicki realized, and
she couldn't deny that Tony had responded to it in a
way he'd never responded to her. She was tempted to
ask, *''What am I?''* but didn't. The wrong answer
would likely throw her into a rage and she had no idea
of what the right answer would be. She fiddled with
the air-conditioning vents for a moment. ''So tell me
about werewolves.''

Definitely a safer topic.

''Where should I start?''

Vicki rolled her eyes. ''How about with the basics?
They didn't cover lycanthropy at the police academy.''

''All right.'' Henry drummed his fingers on the
steering wheel and thought for a moment. ''For starters, you can forget everything you've ever seen at the
movies. If you're bitten by a werewolf, all you're going to do is bleed. Humans cannot become wer.''

''Which implies that werewolves aren't humans.''

''They aren't.''

''What are they then, small furry creatures from Alpha Centauri?''

''No, according to the oldest of their legends, they're
the direct descendants of a she-wolf and the ancient
god of the hunt.'' He pursed his lips. ''That one's
pretty much consistent throughout all the packs, although the name of the god changes from place to
place. When the ancient Greek and Roman religions
began to spread, the wer began calling themselves
Diana's chosen, the hunting pack of the goddess.
Christianity added the story of Lilith, Adam's first
wife, who, when she left the garden, lay with the wolf
God created on the fifth day and bore him children.''

''What do you believe?''

''That there are more things in heaven and earth than are dreamed up in your philosophy.''

Vicki snorted. ''What a cop-out,'' she muttered. ''And misquoted.''

''How do you know? Remember, I heard the original. Had the hardest time convincing Shakespeare not to call the poor guy Yoluff.'' He sounded perfectly serious but he had to be pulling her leg. ''Yoluff, Prince of Denmark. Can you imagine?''

''No. And I don't really care about mythic wer. I want to know what I can expect tonight.''

''What do you know about wolves?''

''Only what I've learned from National Geographic specials on PBS. I suppose we can discount the character assassination indulged in by the Brothers Grimm?''

''Please. Brothers Grimm aside, wer function much the same way wolves do. Each pack is made up of a family group of varying ages, with a dominant male and a dominant female in charge.''

''Dominant? How?''

''They run the pack. The family. The farm. They do the breeding.''

''The Stuart and Nadine you mentioned the other night?''

''That's right.''

Vicki pulled thoughtfully on her lower lip. ''For something this important, you'd think that *they'd* have come and spoken to me.''

''The dominant pair almost never leave their territory. They're tied to the land in ways we just can't understand.''

''You mean, in ways *I* can't understand,'' she said testily, his tone having made that quite clear.

''Yes.'' He sighed. ''That's what I mean. But before you accuse me of, well, whatever it was you were about to accuse me of, you might consider that four hundred and fifty odd years of experience counts for something.''

He had a point. And an unfair advantage. "Sorry. Go on."

"Donald, Rose and Peter's father, used to be the alpha male, so I imagine the hold is still strong on him. Sylvia and Jason are dead and Colin works nights, which makes it difficult to use me as an intermediary. Rose and Peter, while not adults by wer standards, were the only remaining choice."

"And they were, after all, only the icing on a cake you were perfectly capable of baking on your own."

Henry frowned, then smiled as he worked his way through the metaphor. "I didn't think you'd be able to turn them down," he said softly. "Not after you'd seen them."

And what makes you think I'd be able to turn you down, she wondered, but all she said aloud was, "You were telling me about the structure of the pack."

"Yes, well, about thirteen years ago, when Rose and Peter's mother died, their Uncle Stuart and Aunt Nadine took over. Stuart was originally from a pack in Vermont but had been beta male in this pack for some time."

"He'd just wandered in?"

"The young males often leave home. It gives them a better chance to breed and mixes the bloodlines. Anyway, Donald gave up without a fight. Marjory's death hit him pretty hard."

"Fight?" Vicki asked, remembering the white gleam of Peter's teeth. "You mean that metaphorically, I hope?"

"Not usually. Very few dominant males will just roll over and show their throat and Stuart had already made a number of previous attempts."

Vicki made a bit of a strangled sound in her own throat and Henry reached over and patted her on the shoulder. "Don't worry about it," he advised. "Basically, the wer are just nice, normal people."

"Who turn into wolves." This was not the way Vicki had been raised to think of normal. Still, she was sitting in a BMW with a vampire—things couldn't get much stranger than that. "Do, uh, all you supernatural creatures hang out together or what?"

"What?" Henry repeated, confused.

Vicki pushed her glasses up her nose. It didn't help in the dark but it was a reassuring gesture nevertheless. "Just tell me your doctor's name isn't Frankenstein."

Henry laughed. "It isn't. And I met Perkin Heerkens, Rose and Peter's grandfather, in a perfectly normal way."

Slowly, as the day released its hold on the world, he became aware. First his heartbeat, gaining strength from the darkness, the slow and steady rhythm reassuring him that he'd survived. Then breathing, shallow still for little oxygen reached this far below ground. Finally, he extended his senses up and out, past the small creeping things in the earth to the surface. Only when he was sure that no human lives were near enough to see him emerge, did he begin to dig his way out.

His hiding place was more a collapsed foxhole than anything else, although, if discovered, Henry hoped that the Nazis would believe it a shallow grave. Which, he supposed as he pushed through the loose dirt, was exactly what it would be if the Nazis discovered it. Being unearthed in daylight would kill him more surely than enemy fire.

"I really, really hate this," he muttered as his head broke free and he unhooked the small perforated shield that kept the earth out of his nose and mouth. He dug in only as a last resort, when dawn caught him away from any other shelter. Once or twice he'd almost left it too long and had had to claw the dirt aside with the heat of the sun dancing fire along his back. Burial reminded him too much of the terror of his first awakening, trapped in his common coffin, immortal and alone, hunger clawing at him.

He had all but one leg clear when he caught sight of the animal lying motionless in the pool of darker night under a fir.

Wolves? In the Netherlands? he wondered as he froze. No, not a wolf, for the russet coloring was wrong, but it definitely had wolf in its bloodline and not so very far back. It crouched carefully downwind, ears back flat against its skull, plumed tail tucked in tight against its flanks. It was reacting to the scent of another hunter, preparing to attack to defend its territory.

White teeth gleamed in the darkness and a low growl rumbled deep in the massive throat.

Henry's own lips drew back and he answered the growl.

The animal looked surprised.

And even more surprised a second later when it found its spine pressed against the forest floor and both Henry's hands clamped deep in its ruff. It struggled and snapped, digging at its captor with all four feet. Although the growls continued, it made no louder noises. When it found it couldn't get free, it squirmed around until it managed to lick Henry's wrist with the tip of its tongue.

Cautiously, Henry let it up.

It shook itself vigorously, had a good scratch, and sat, head to one side, studying this strange creature, nose wrinkled and brows drawn down in an expression so like a puzzled frown that Henry had to hide a smile—showing his teeth at this moment would only start the whole thing off again.

With dominance determined, Henry brushed the worst of the dirt from his heavy workman's clothes and slipped a hand beneath the shirt to check the canvas pouch taped around his waist. He knew the documents were safe, but the faint crackle of the papers reassured him anyway.

He'd need most of the night to reach the village where he'd meet his contact in the Dutch Resistance

and as he needed to feed before he arrived—it made
working with mortals bearable—he'd better be on his
way. Checking his course with the small compass SOE
had provided, he started off toward the northeast. The
dog rose and followed. He heard it moving through
the brush behind him for a time, its movements barely
distinguishable from the myriad sounds of a forest at
night. As he began to pick up speed, even that trace
faded away. He wasn't surprized. A full blood wolf
would have trouble keeping up. A dog, regardless of
its heritage would have no chance at all.

The German patrol crossed his path about three
hours before dawn, not far from the village. As they
passed him, standing motionless beside the trail with
barely inches to spare, Henry smiled grimly at the
skull and crossbones that fronted each cap. Totenkopf.
An SS unit used for internal security in occupied territory, especially where the Resistance was active.

The straggler was a barrel-chested young man who
somehow managed to strut in spite of the hour and the
ground condition, and whose *more-master-race-than-
thou* attitude radiated off of him. It seemed safe to
assume that his comrades had deliberately let him fall
a little behind; there were limits, apparently, even in
the SS.

Henry had a certain amount of sympathy for the
common soldier in the German army but none what-
soever for the Nazis among them. He took the young
man from behind with a savage efficiency that had him
off the trail and silenced between one breath and the
next. As long as the heart continued to beat, damage
to the body was irrelevant. Quickly, for he was vulnerable while he fed, Henry tore open the left wrist
and bent his head to drink. When he finished, he
reached up, wrapped one long-fingered hand about the
soldier's skull, twisted, and effortlessly broke his neck.
Then he froze, suddenly aware of being watched.

The forest froze with him. Even the breeze stilled
until the only sound became the soft phut, phut of

blood dripping slowly onto leaf mold. Still crouched over the body, muscles tensed and ready, Henry turned to face downwind.

The big dog regarded him steadily for another few seconds, then faded back until not even the vampire's eyes could separate it from the shifting shadows.

The dog shouldn't have been able to track him. Foreboding ran cold fingers along Henry's spine. Swiftly he stood and moved toward the place where the huge animal had disappeared. A heartbeat later he stopped. He could feel the lives of the patrol returning, no doubt searching for the missing soldier.

He would have to deal with the dog another time. Grabbing a handful of tunic and another of trouser, he lifted the corpse up into the crotch of a tree and wedged it there, well above eye level. With one last apprehensive look into the shadows, he continued his journey to the village.

It wasn't difficult to find.

Harsh white light from a half dozen truck-mounted searchlights illuminated the village square. A small group of villagers stood huddled on one side, guarded by a squad of SS. A man who appeared to be the local commander strode up and down between the two, slapping a swagger stick against his leg in the best Nazi approved manner. Except for the slap of the stick against the leather boot top, the scene was surreally silent.

Henry moved closer. He let the sentry live. Until he knew what was going on, another unexplained death could potentially do more harm than good. At the edge of the square he slid into a recessed doorway, waiting in its cover for what would happen next.

The tiny village held probably no more than two hundred people at the very best of times, which these certainly weren't. Its position, near both the border and the rail lines the invaders needed to continue their push north, made it a focal point for the Dutch Resistance. The Resistance had brought Henry, but unfortunately it had also brought the SS.

There were seventy-one villagers in the square, mostly the old, the young, and the infirm. Pulled from their beds, they wore a wide variety of nightclothes and almost identical wary expressions. As Henry watched, two heavily armed men brought in five more.

"These are the last?" the officer asked. On receiving an affirmative, he marched forward.

"We know where the missing members of your families are," he said curtly, his Dutch accented but perfectly understandable. "The train they were to have stopped is not coming. It was a trap to draw them out." He paused for a reaction but received only the same wary stares. Although those of an age to understand were very afraid, they hid it well; Henry's sensitive nose picked up the scent, but the commander had no way of knowing his news had had any effect. The apparent lack of response added an edge to his next words.

"By now they are dead. All of them." A young boy smothered a cry and the commander almost smiled. "But it is not enough," he continued in softer tones, "to merely wipe out resistance. We must wipe out any further thought of resistance. You will all be executed and every building in this place will be burned to the ground as both an example of what happens to those civilians who dare support the Resistance and to those inferiors who dare oppose the Master Race."

"Germans," snorted an old woman, clutching at her faded bathrobe with arthritic fingers. "Talk you to death before they shoot you."

Henry was inclined to agree—the commander definitely sounded like he'd been watching too many propaganda films. This did not lessen the danger. Regardless of what else Hitler had done in his "economic reforms," he'd at least managed to find jobs for every sadistic son-of-a-bitch in the country.

''You.'' The swagger stick indicated the old woman. ''Come here.''

Shaking off the restraining hands of friends and relatives and muttering under her breath, she stomped out of the crowd. The top of her head, with its sparse gray hair twisted tightly into an unforgiving bun, came barely up to the commander's collarbone.

''You,'' he told her, ''have volunteered to be first.''

With rheumy eyes squinted almost shut in the glare of the searchlights, she raised her head and said something so rude, not to mention biologically impossible, that it drew a shocked, ''Mother!'' from an elderly man in the clutter of villagers. Just to be sure the commander got the idea, she repeated herself in German.

The swagger stick rose to strike. Henry moved, recognizing as he did so that it was a stupid, impulsive thing to do but unable to stop himself.

He caught the commander's wrist at the apex of the swing, continued the movement and, exerting his full strength, ripped the arm from the socket. Dropping the body, he turned to charge the rest of the squad, swinging his grisly, bleeding trophy like a club, lips drawn back from his teeth so that the elongated canines gleamed.

The entire attack had taken just under seven seconds.

The Nazis were not the first to use terror as a weapon; Henry's kind had learned its value centuries before. It gave him time to reach the first of the guards before any of them remembered they held weapons.

By the time they gathered their wits enough to shoot, he had another body to use as a shield. He heard shouting in Dutch, slippered feet running on packed earth, and then suddenly, thankfully, the searchlights went off.

For the first time since he entered the square, Henry could see perfectly. The Germans could see nothing at all. Completely unnerved, they broke and tried to run, only to find their way blocked by the snarling attack of the largest dog any of them had ever seen.

It was a slaughter after that.

Moments later, standing over his final kill, blood-scent singing along every nerve, Henry watched as the dog that had followed him all night approached stiff-legged, the damp stain on its muzzle more black than red in the darkness. It looked completely feral, like a wolf from the Brothers Grimm.

They were still some feet apart when the sound of boots on cobbles drew both their heads around. Henry moved, but the dog was faster. It dove forward, rolled, and came up clutching a submachine gun in two very human hands. As the storm troopers came into sight, he opened fire. No one survived.

Slinging the gun over one bare shoulder, he turned back to face Henry, scrubbing at the blood around his mouth with the back of one grimy hand. His hair, the exact russet brown of the wolf's pelt, fell in a matted tangle over his forehead and the eyes it partially hid were the eyes that had watched Henry emerge from the earth and later feed.

"I am Perkin Heerkens," he said, his English heavily accented. "If you are Henry Fitzroy, I am your contact."

After four hundred years, Henry had thought that nothing could ever surprise him again. He found himself having to rethink that conclusion.

"They didn't tell me you were a werewolf," he said in Dutch.

Perkin grinned, looking much younger but no less dangerous. "They didn't tell me you were a vampire," he pointed out. "I think that makes us even."

"That is *not* a perfectly normal way to meet someone," Vicki muttered, wishing just for an instant that she was back at home having a nice, *normal*, argument with Mike Celluci. "I mean, you're talking about a vampire in the Secret Service meeting a werewolf in the Dutch Resistance.''

''What's so unusual about that?'' Henry passed an RV with American license plates and a small orange cat sleeping in the rear window. ''Werewolves are very territorial.''

''If they were living as part of normal. . . .'' She thought for a second and began again. ''If they were living as part of human communities, how did they avoid the draft?''

''Conscription was a British-North American phenomenon,'' Henry reminded her. ''Europe was scrambling for survival and it happened so quickly that a few men and women in a few isolated areas were easy to miss. If necessary, they abandoned 'civilization' for the duration of the war and lived off the land.''

''All right, what about British and North American werewolves then?''

''There are no British werewolves. . . .''

''Why not?'' Vicki interrupted.

''It's an island. Given the human propensity for killing what it doesn't understand, there's not enough space for both humans and wer.'' He paused for a moment then added, ''There may have been wer in Britain once. . . .''

Vicki slumped lower in the seat and fiddled with the vents. *I don't want to die, Ms. Nelson.* ''So the wer aren't worldwide?''

''No. Europe as far south as northern Italy, most of Russia, and the more northwestern parts of China and Tibet. As far as I know there are no native North American wer, but I could be wrong. There's been a fair bit of immigration, however.''

''All post World War II?''

''Not all.''

''So my original question stands. How did they avoid the draft?''

Vicki heard him shrug, shoulders whispering against the thick tweed seatback. ''I have no idea but, as most

of the wer are completely color-blind, I'd guess they
flunked the physical. I do know that the allies used
color-blind observers in aerial reconnaissance; because they had to perceive everything by shape they
were able to see right through most camouflage.
Maybe some of that lot were wer.''

''Well, what about you, then? How does a vampire
convince the government he should be allowed to do
his bit for liberty?'' Then she remembered just how
convincing Henry could be. ''Uh, never mind.''

''Actually, I didn't even approach the Canadian government. I stowed away on a troop ship and returned
to England where an old friend of mine had risen to a
very powerful position. He arranged everything.''

''Oh.'' She didn't ask who the old friend was. She
didn't want to know—her imagination was already
flashing her scenes of Henry and certain prominent
figures in compromising positions. ''What happened
to the villagers?''

''What?''

''The villagers. Where you met Perkin. Did they all
die?''

''No, of course not!''

Vicki couldn't see any *of course not* about it. After
all, they'd wiped out an entire squad of SS and the
Nazis had disapproved of things like that.

''Perkin and I set it up so that it looked as though
they'd been killed in an allied air strike taking out the
railway line.''

''You called in an air strike?''

She could hear the grin in his voice as he answered.

''Didn't I mention this old friend had risen to a very
powerful position?''

''So.'' One thing still bothered her. ''The villagers
knew there was a pack of werewolves living amongst
them?''

''Not until the war started, no.''

''And after the war started?''

''During the war, any enemy of the Nazis was a

welcome ally. The British and the Americans even managed to get along.''

She supposed that made a certain amount of sense. ''And what about after the war?''

''Perkin emigrated. I don't know.''

They drove in silence for a while, one of only a few vehicles on the highway now that Toronto had been left behind. Vicki closed her eyes and thought of Henry's story. In some ways the war, for all its complications, had been a simple problem. At least the enemies had been well defined.

''Henry,'' she asked suddenly, ''do you honestly think that a pack of werewolves can live as a part of human society without their neighbors knowing?''

''You're thinking city, Vicki; the Heerkens' nearest neighbors live three miles away. They see people outside the pack when *they* choose to. Besides, if you didn't know me, and you hadn't met that demon last spring, would you believe in werewolves? Would anyone in North America in this century?''

''Someone obviously does,'' she reminded him dryly. ''Although I'd have expected blackmail over murder.''

''It would make more sense,'' Henry agreed.

She sighed and opened her eyes. Here she was, trying to solve the case armed only with a magnifying glass and a vampire, cut off from the resources of the Metro Police. Not that those resources had been any help so far. Ballistics had called just before she left to tell her that the slug had most likely been a standard 7.62mm NATO round; which narrowed her possible suspects down to the entire North Atlantic Treaty Organization as well as almost everyone who owned a hunting rifle. She wasn't looking forward to arriving at the Heerkens farm.

This was the first time she'd ever really gone it alone. What if she wasn't as good as she thought?

''There's a map in the glove compartment.'' Henry

maneuvered the BMW off Highway 2. "Could you get it out for me?"

She found both glove compartment and map by touch and shoved the latter toward her companion.

He returned it. "Multitalented though I may be, I'd rather not try to read a map while driving on strange roads. You'll have to do it."

Fingers tight around the folded paper, Vicki pushed it back at him. "I don't know where we're going."

"We're on Airport Road about to turn onto Oxford Street. Tell me how long we stay on Oxford before we hit Clarke Side Road."

The streetlights provided barely enough illumination to define the windshield. If she strained, Vicki could see the outline of the map. She certainly couldn't find two little lines on it.

"There's a map light under the sun visor," Henry offered.

The map light would be next to useless.

"I can't find it."

"You haven't even looked. . . ."

"I didn't say I wouldn't, I said I couldn't." She'd realized from the moment she'd agreed to leave the safe, known parameters of Toronto that she'd have to tell him the truth about her eyes and couldn't understand how she'd gotten herself backed into that kind of a corner. Tension brought her shoulders up and tied her stomach in knots. Medical explanation or not, it always sounded like an excuse to her, like she was asking for help or understanding. And he'd think of her differently once the "disabled" label had been applied, everyone did. "I have no night sight, little peripheral vision, and am becoming more myopic every time I talk to the damn doctor." Her tone dared him to make something of it.

Henry merely asked, "What's wrong?"

"It's a degenerative eye disease, retinitis pigmentosa. . . ."

"RP," he interrupted. So that was her secret. "I know of it." He kept his feelings from his voice, kept it matter-of-fact. "It doesn't seem to have progressed very far."

Great, just what I need, another expert. Celluci wasn't enough? "You weren't listening," she snarled, twisting the map into an unreadable mess. "I have *no* night sight. It drove me off the force. I am piss useless after dark. You might as well just turn the car around right now if I have to solve this case at night." Although she hid it behind the anger, she was half afraid he'd do just that. And half afraid he'd pat her on the head and say everything was going to be all right—because it wasn't, and never would be again—and she'd try to rip his face off in a moving car and kill them both.

Henry shrugged. He had no intention of playing into what he perceived as self-pity. "I turn into a smoldering pile of carbon compounds in direct sunlight; sounds like you've got a better deal."

"You don't understand."

"I haven't seen the sun in four hundred and fifty years. I think I do."

Vicki shoved her glasses up her nose and turned to glare out the window at a view she couldn't see, unsure of how to react with no outlet for her anger. After a moment she said, "All right, so you understand. So I have a comparatively mild case. So I can still function. I haven't gone blind. I haven't gone deaf. I haven't gone insane. It *still* sucks."

"Granted." He read disappointment at his response and wondered if she realized that she expected a certain amount of effusive sympathy from the people she told. Rejecting that sympathy made her feel strong, compensating for what she perceived as her weakness. He suspected that the disease was the first time she hadn't been able to make everything come out all right through the sheer determination that it would be.

"Have you ever thought about taking on a partner? Someone to do the night work?"

Vicki snorted, anger giving way to amusement. "You mean you helping me out as a regular sort of a job? You write romance novels, Henry; you have no experience in this type of thing."

He drew himself up behind the wheel. He was Vampire. King of the Night. The romance novels were just the way he paid the rent. "I wouldn't say. . . ."

"And besides," she interrupted, "I'm barely making enough to keep myself going. They don't call the place Toronto the Good for nothing you know."

"You'd get more jobs if you could work nights."

She couldn't argue with that. It was true.

His voice deepened and Vicki felt the hair on the back of her neck rise. "Just think about it."

Don't use your vampiric wiles on me, you son-of-a-bitch. But her mouth agreed before the thought had finished forming.

They drove the rest of the way to the farm in silence.

When they pulled off the dirt road they'd been following for the last few miles, Vicki could see only a vague fan of light in front of the car. When Henry switched off the headlights, she could see nothing at all. In the sudden silence, the scrabble of claws against the glass beside her head sounded very loud. She didn't quite manage to hold back the startled yell.

"It's Storm," Henry explained—she could hear the smile in his voice. "Stay put until I come around to guide you."

"Fuck you," she told him sweetly, found the release, and opened the car door.

"Yeah I'm glad to see you, too," she muttered, trying to push the huge head away. His breath was marginally better that of most dogs—*thanks, no doubt, to his other form being able to use a toothbrush*—but only marginally. Finally realizing that without better leverage the odds of moving Storm were slim to none, she sat back and endured the enthusiastic welcome. Her fingers itched to dig through the deep ruff, but the memory of Peter's naked young body held them in check.

"Storm, that's enough."

With one last vigorous sniff, the wer backed out of the way and Vicki felt Henry's hand touch her arm. She shook it off and swung out of the car. Although she could see the waning moon, a hanging, three-quarter circle of silver-white in the darkness, it shed a light too diffuse to do her any good. The blurry rectangles of yellow off to the right were probably the lights of the house and she considered striding off toward them just to prove she wasn't as helpless as Henry might think.

Henry watched the thought cross Vicki's face and shook his head. While he admired her independence, he hoped it wouldn't overwhelm her common sense. He realized that at the moment she felt she had something to prove and could think of no way to let her know she didn't. At least not as far as he was concerned.

He put her bag into her hand, keeping his own hold on it until he saw her fingers close around the grip, then drew her free arm gently through his. "The path curves," he murmured, close to her ear. "You don't want to end up in Nadine's flowers. Nadine bites."

Vicki ignored the way his breath against her cheek caused the hair on the back of her neck to rise and concentrated on walking as though she was not being led. She had no doubt that the wer, in wolf form at least, could see just as well as Henry and she had no intention of undermining her position here by appearing weak to however many of them might be watching.

Head high, she focused on the rectangles of light, attempting to memorize both the way the path felt beneath her sandals and the way it curved from the drive to the house. The familiar concrete and exhaust scents of the city were gone, replaced by what she could only assume was the not entirely pleasant odor of sheep shit. The cricket song she could identify, but the rest of the night sounds were beyond her.

Back in Toronto, every smell, every sound would have meant something. Here, they told her nothing. Vicki didn't like that, not at all; it added another handicap to her failing eyes.

Two sudden sharp pains on her calf and another on her forearm, jolted her out of her funk, reminding her of an aspect of the case she hadn't taken into account.

"Damned bugs!" She pulled her arm free and slapped down at her legs. "Henry, I just remembered something; I hate the country!"

They'd moved into the spill of light from the house and she could just barely make out the smile on his face.

"Too late," he told her, and opened the door.

Vicki's first impression as she stood blinking on the threshold was of a comfortably shabby farmhouse kitchen seething with people and dogs. Her second impression corrected the first: *Seething with wer. The people are dogs. Wolves. Oh, hell.*

It was late, nearly eleven. Celluci leaned back in his chair and stared at the one remaining piece of paper on his desk. The Alan Margot case had been wrapped up in record time and he could leave it now to begin its ponderous progress through the courts. Which left him free to attend to a small bit of unfinished business.

Henry Fitzroy.

Something about the man just didn't ring right and Celluci had every intention of finding out what that was. He scooped up the piece of paper, blank except for the name printed in heavy block letters across the top, folded it twice, and placed it neatly in his wallet. Tomorrow he'd run the standard searches on Mr. Fitzroy and if they turned up nothing. . . . His smile was predatory as he stood. If they turned up nothing, there were ways to delve deeper.

Some might call what he planned a misuse of authority. Detective-Sergeant Michael Celluci called it looking out for a friend.

Four

"I'm Nadine Heerkens-Wells. You must be Vicki Nelson."

The woman approaching, hand held out, shared a number of features with Peter and Rose; the same wide-spaced eyes and pointy face, the same thick mane of hair—in this case a dusty black marked with gray—the same short-fingered, heavily callused grip.

Her eyes, however, were shadowed, and lurking behind that shadow was a loss so deep, so intense, that it couldn't be completely hidden and might never be completely erased. Vicki swallowed hard, surprised by the strength of her reaction to the other woman's pain.

On the surface, Vicki had absolutely no doubt she faced the person in charge, and Nadine's expression proved that the welcoming smile had originally developed out of a warning snarl. *Still, I suppose she has no reason to trust me right off, regardless of what Henry's told her.* Keeping her own expression politely unchallenging, Vicki carefully applied as much force to the handshake as she received, despite the sudden inexplicable urge to test her strength. "I hope I'll be able to help," she said in her public service voice, meeting the other woman's gaze squarely.

Force of personality weighted with grief struck her almost a physical blow and her own eyes narrowed in response.

The surrounding wer waited quietly for the dominant female's decision. Henry stood to one side and watched, brows drawn down in a worried frown. For

Vicki to work effectively, the two women had to accept one another as equals, whether they liked it or not.

Nadine's eyes were brown, with a golden sunburst around the pupil. Deep lines bracketed the corners and her lids looked bruised.

I can take her, Vicki realized. *I'm younger, stronger. I'm . . . out of my mind.* She forced the muscles of her face to relax, denying the awareness of power. "I hadn't realized London was so far from Toronto," she remarked conversationally, as though the room were not awash with undercurrents of tension.

"You must be tired from your long drive," Nadine returned, and only Vicki saw the acknowledgment of what had just passed between them. "Come in and sit down."

Then they both looked away.

At that signal, Vicki and Henry found themselves surrounded by hearty handshakes and wet noses and hustled into seats at the huge kitchen table. Henry wondered if Vicki realized that she'd just been accepted as a kind of auxiliary member of the pack, much as he was himself. He'd spent long hours on the phone the last two nights arguing for that acceptance, convincing Nadine that from outside the pack Vicki would have little chance of finding the killer, that Vicki would no more betray the pack than she'd betray him, knowing as he did that Nadine's agreement would be conditional on the actual meeting.

"Shadow, be quiet."

The black pup—about the size of a small German shepherd—who had been dancing around Vicki's knees and barking shrilly, suddenly became a small naked boy of about six or seven who turned to look reproachfully up at Nadine. "But, Mom," he protested, "you said to always bark at strangers."

"This isn't a stranger," his mother told him, leaning forward to brush dusty black hair up off his face, "it's Ms. Nelson."

He rolled his eyes. "I know *that*, but I don't know *her*. That makes her a stranger."

"Don't be a dork, Daniel. Mom says she's okay," pointed out one of two identical teenage girls sitting on the couch by the window in a tone reserved solely for younger brothers.

"And she came with Henry," added the other in the exact same tone.

"And if she was a stranger," concluded the first, "you wouldn't have changed in front of her. So she *isn't* a stranger. So shut up."

He tossed his head. "Still don't know her."

"Then get to know her quickly," his mother suggested, turning him back to face Vicki, "so that we can have some peace."

Even though she was watching for it, Vicki missed the exact moment of change when Daniel became Shadow again. One heartbeat a small boy, a heartbeat later, a small dog. . . . *Not that small either, and I can't call them dogs. And yet, they aren't quite wolves.* A cold nose shoved into the back of her knee and she started. *And does that make this, him, a puppy or a cub? Ye gods, but this is going to get complicated.* Trying not to let any of this inner debate show on her face, she reached down and held out her hand.

Shadow sniffed it thoroughly then pushed his head under her fingers. His fur was still downy soft.

"If you start scratching him, Ms. Nelson, you'll be at it all night," one of his sisters told her with a sigh.

Shadow's nose went up and he pointedly turned his back on her, leaning up against Vicki's legs much the way Storm had leaned against Rose that night in Henry's condo. Which reminded Vicki. . . .

"Where's Peter and Rose? Peter. . . ." She paused and shook her head. "I mean, Storm, met the car and I was sure I saw Rose—I mean, Cloud—when I first came in."

"They've gone to get their Uncle Stuart," said the graying man next to Henry. Although he'd taken part in the welcome, those were the first words he'd actually spoken. He extended his hand across the table. An old scar puckered the skin of his forearm. Vicki wasn't positive, but it looked like a bite. "I'm Donald Heerkens, their father."

"I'm Jennifer." The closer of the two girls on the couch broke in before Donald could say any more.

"And I'm Marie."

And how the hell does anyone tell you apart? Vicki wondered. Sitting down, at least, they appeared to be the exact same size and even their expressions looked identical. *Mind you, I'm hardly one to judge. All kids look alike to me at that age. . . .*

The two of them giggled at their uncle's mock scowl.

"So now you've met everyone who's here," Marie continued.

"Everyone except Daddy," Jennifer added, " 'cause like you already met Rose and Peter." The two of them smiled at her in unison. Even their dimples matched.

Daddy must be Stuart, Vicki realized; Nadine's husband, Daniel's father, Donald's brother-in-law, Peter's and Rose's uncle. The dominant male. Meeting *him* should prove to be interesting.

"Nice thing to be ignored in my own home," growled a voice from the door.

Shadow flung himself out from under Vicki's fingers, charged across the kitchen barking like a furry little maniac, and leapt up at the man who'd just come into the house—who caught him, swung him up over his head, and turned Daniel upside down.

Vicki didn't need an introduction. The same force of personality that marked Nadine marked Stuart and he was *definitely* very male. He was also very naked and that added considerable weight to the latter observation. Vicki had to admit she was favorably impressed although at five ten she could probably give him at least four inches. Judging by human standards, which was all she had to work with, Henry's warning aside, he appeared to be younger than his wife by about five years. His hair—all his hair, and there was rather a lot of it all over his body—remained unmarked by gray.

"Stuart. . . ." Nadine pulled a pair of blue sweatpants off the back of her chair and threw them at her husband.

He caught them one-handed, Daniel tucked under the other arm, and stared at them with distaste. Then he turned and looked straight at Vicki. "I don't much like clothing, Ms. Nelson," he told her, obviously as aware of her identity as she was of his. "It stops the change and in this heat it's damned uncomfortable. If you're going to be here for a while, you're going to have to get used to the little we wear."

"It's your house," Vicki told him levelly. "It's not my place to say what you should wear."

He studied her face, then smiled suddenly and she got the impression she'd passed a test of some kind. "Humans usually worry about clothing."

"I save my worry for more important things."

Henry hid a smile. Since they'd met, he'd been trying to figure out if Vicki was infinitely adaptable to circumstances or just so single-minded that anything not leading to her current goal was ignored. In eight months of observation he'd come no closer to an answer.

Tossing the sweatpants in the corner, Stuart held out his hand. "Pleased to meet you, Ms. Nelson."

She returned both smile and handshake, careful not to come on too strong. *Come on too strong to a naked werewolf. Yeah, right.* "And you. Please, call me Vicki."

"Vicki." Then he turned to Henry and by the tiniest of changes, the smile became something else. He held out his hand again. "Henry."

"Stuart." The smile was a warning, not a challenge. Henry recognized it and acknowledged it. It could change to challenge very quickly and neither man wanted that. As long as Henry kept to his place, the situation between them would remain tense but stable.

Uninterested in all this grown-up posturing, Daniel twisted against his father's side, found the grip loose enough to allow change, did, and began to bark. His father put him down just as the screen door opened and Cloud and Storm came in.

For the next few moments, the two older wer allowed themselves to be attacked by their younger cousin, the fight accompanied by much growling and snapping and feigned—at least Vicki assumed they were feigned—yelps of pain. As none of the other adults seemed worried about the battle, Vicki took the time to actually look at her surroundings.

The kitchen furniture was heavy and old and a little shabby from years of use. The wooden table could seat eight easily and twelve without much crowding. Although the chairs had chew marks up each leg they—to judge by the one under Vicki—had been made to endure and still had all four feet planted firmly on the worn linoleum. The lounge that the twins were perched on, tucked under the window by the back door, had probably been bought in the fifties and hadn't been moved from that corner since. The refrigerator looked new, as did the electric stove. In fact, the electric stove looked so new, Vicki suspected it was seldom used. The old woodstove in the far corner would likely be not only a source of winter heat but their main cooking facility. If they cooked. She hadn't thought to ask Henry what the wer ate or if she'd be expected to join in. A sudden vision of a bleeding hunk of meat with a side of steaming entrails as tomorrow's breakfast made her stomach lurch. The north wall was lined with cupboards and the south with doors, leading, Vicki assumed, to the rest of the house.

To her city bred nose, the kitchen quite frankly *smelled*. It smelled of old woodsmoke, of sheep shit—and quite probably sheep, too, if she had any idea of what sheep smelled like—and very strongly of well, wer. It wasn't an unpleasant combination, but it was certainly pungent.

Housework didn't seem to be high on the list of wer priorities. That was fine with Vicki, it wasn't one of her top ten ways to spend time either. Her mother, however, would no doubt have fits at the tufts of hair piled up in every available nook and cranny.

Of course, my mother would no doubt have fits at this entire situation . . .

Peter stood up and dangled a squirming Shadow at shoulder level—front paws in his left hand, rear paws in his right—deftly keeping the pup's teeth away from the more sensitive, protruding, areas of his anatomy.

. . . so it's probably a good thing she isn't here.

Just as she was beginning to wonder if she shouldn't bring up the reason for her visit, Stuart cleared his throat. Peter released Shadow, smiled a welcome at Vicki and Henry, changed, and curled up on the floor beside his twin. Shadow gave one last excited bark and went over to collapse, panting, on his mother's feet. Everyone else, the two visitors included, turned to face Stuart expectantly.

And all he did was clear his throat. Vicki was impressed again. *If he could bottle that he could make a fortune.*

"Henry assures us that you can be trusted, Ms. Nelson, Vicki." His eyes were a pale Husky blue, startlingly light under heavy black brows. "I'm sure you realize that things would get very unpleasant for us if the world knew we existed?"

"I realize." And she did, which was why she decided not to be insulted at the question. "Although *someone* obviously knows."

"Yes." How a word that was mostly sibilants could be growled Vicki had no idea. But it was. "There are three humans in this territory who know of the pack. An elderly doctor in London, the local game warden, and Colin's partner."

"Colin the police officer." It wasn't really a question. A werewolf on the London Police Force was a phenomenon Vicki was unlikely to forget. She pulled a notebook and a pen from the depths of her purse. "The twins—Rose and Peter, that is—mentioned him."

Donald's expression seemed more confused than proud. "My oldest son. He's the first of us to hold what you could call a job."

"The first to finish high school," Nadine said. At Vicki's expression, she added, "Generally we find school very . . . stressful. Most of us leave as soon as we can." Her lips twisted up into what Vicki could only assume was a smile. "Trouble is, they're making it harder to leave at the same time they're making it harder to stay."

"The world is becoming smaller," Henry said quietly. "The wer are being forced to integrate. Sooner or later, they'll be discovered." He had no doubt as to how his mortal brethren would treat the wer; they'd be considered animals if they were allowed to live at all. When so small a thing as skin color made so large a difference, what chance did the wer have?

Vicki was thinking much the same thing. "Well," her tone brooked no argument, "let's just hope it's later. I personally am amazed you've managed to keep the list down to three."

Stuart shrugged, muscles rippling under the thick mat of black hair that covered his chest. "We keep to ourselves and humans are very good at believing what they wish to believe."

"And seeing what they wish to see," Donald added, the skin around his eyes crinkled with amusement.

"Or not seeing," Marie put in with a giggle.

The assembled wer nodded in agreement—regardless of shape—all save Shadow, who had fallen asleep, chin pillowed on his mother's bare instep.

"What about those who might suspect what you are?" Vicki asked. Murderers were almost always known to the victim. The times they weren't were usually the cases that never got solved.

"There aren't any."

"I beg your pardon?"

"There aren't any," Stuart repeated.

He obviously believed what he said, but Vicki thought he was living in a dream world. A noise from the right pulled her gaze down to the two wer on the floor. Cloud looked as though she wanted to disagree. *Or maybe she wants to go walkies. How the hell can I tell?*

"You do have contact with humans. The younger ones, at least, on a regular basis." Vicki's gesture covered both sets of twins. "What about other kids at school? Teachers?"

"We don't change at *school,*" Marie protested.

Jennifer's head bobbed in support, red hair flying. "We *can't* change when we're dressed."

"And as you're dressed at school, you *can't* change at school?" They seemed pleased she was so quick on the uptake. "It must be frustrating. . . ."

Marie shrugged. "It's not so bad."

"Don't you ever want to tell people what you can do? Show them your other shape?"

Stuart's growl sounded very loud and very menacing in the shocked silence that followed. The girls looked as though she'd suggested something obscene. "Okay. I guess not." *Don't judge them by human standards. Try to remember that.* "What about special friends?"

Storm and Cloud were unreadable. Marie and Jennifer looked puzzled. "Boyfriends?"

Both girls wrinkled their noses in identical expressions of disgust.

"Humans don't smell right," Stuart explained, shortly. "That sort of thing never happens."

"They don't smell right?"

"No."

Vicki decided to leave it at that. She really wasn't up for a discussion of werewolf breeding criteria, not at this hour of the night. There were, however, two things that had to be covered. The first still made Vicki uncomfortable and, in almost a year of working for herself, she hadn't come up with a less than blunt way of bringing it up. "About my fee. . . ."

"We can pay it," Stuart told her and only nodded when she mentioned the amount.

"All right, then," she laced her fingers together and stared into the pattern thus formed for a moment, "one more thing. When I find whoever is doing this, what then? We can't take him to court. He can't be held accountable for murder under the law without giving away the existence of your people."

Stuart smiled and, in spite of the heat, Vicki felt a chill run up and down her back. "He will be accountable to our law. To pack law."

"Revenge, then?"

"Why not? He's killed two of us for no reason, no cause. Who has better right to be judge and jury?"

Who indeed?

"There's no other way to stop him from killing again," Henry said quietly. He thought he understood Vicki's hesitation, if only in the abstract. Ethics formed in the sixteenth century had an easier time with justice over law than ethics formed in the twentieth.

What it came down to, Vicki realized, was a question of whose life had more value; the people here in this room or the maniac, singular or collective, who was picking them off one by one? Put like that, it didn't seem to be such a difficult question.

"The three people you have, then, I'd like to check them out."

"We already checked," Donald began but Stuart cut him off.

"It's too late to do anything tonight. We'll get you the information tomorrow."

As Vicki had already been told, they'd attempted to deal with this themselves after Nadine's twin had been shot. She wasn't surprised that they'd done some checking. She wished they hadn't; in her experience, amateurs only muddied the waters. "Did you find anything?"

Stuart sighed and ran both his hands back through his hair. "Only what we already knew; Dr. Dixon is a very old man who hasn't betrayed us in over forty years and isn't likely to start now. Arthur Fortrin went north at the end of July and won't be back until Labor Day weekend. And Colin's partner, Barry, had both the skill and the opportunity."

Vicki tapped her pen against the paper. "That doesn't look good for Barry."

"No," Stuart agreed. "It doesn't."

"Hey, Colin! Wait a minute. . . ."

Colin sighed and leaned against the open door of the truck. There really wasn't anything else he could do; leaping inside and roaring off in a cloud of exhaust fumes would certainly not make things any better. He watched his partner cross the dark parking lot, weaving his way around the scattered cars belonging to the midnight shift, brows drawn down into a deep vee, looking very much like a man who wanted some answers. Exactly the situation Colin had been trying to avoid.

"What is with you, Heerkens?" Barry Wu rocked to a halt and glared. A line of water dribbled down his face from his wet hair and he swiped at it angrily. "First you act like a grade A asshole all shift, then you slink out while I'm in the shower without so much as a 'See you tomorrow,' or a 'Go fuck yourself.' "

"You're my partner, Barry, you're not my mate." As an attempt to lighten the mood, it was a dismal failure; Colin could still smell the anger. He did his best not to react to it, catching the growl in his throat before it rose to an audible level.

"That's right, your partner—let's set aside the fact I thought I was your friend—and as your partner I have a right to know what it is that's got you tied in knots."

"It's pack business. . . ."

"Bullshit! When it affects your job—our job—like it did tonight, it's my business! Three to eleven shift has enough problems without you and your attitude adding to them."

All right. If you really want to know, we think you've murdered two of my family. Except Colin didn't think it, couldn't think it, had to think it. He'd searched Barry's locker, the trunk of his car, even quickly searched his apartment one evening when they went back there for a few beers after work. Nothing beyond the rifles the pack already knew he had. No indication that he'd been casting silver bullets. Nor had his scent been anywhere in the woods. If Barry was responsible for the two deaths, he wasn't leaving evidence lying around. If he wasn't responsible, Colin had found nothing that could clear him.

Colin wanted to confront him. The pack leader had refused to allow it. Torn between pack law and this newer loyalty, Colin had almost reached the point where he couldn't stand it any longer.

He swung up into the truck and slammed the door. "Look" he snarled, "I want to tell you but I can't. Just leave it!" Slamming the truck into gear, he screeched out of the parking lot, knowing full well Barry wouldn't leave it. He'd worry at it and tear at it like Shadow with a slipper until he had it in pieces and could see what it was made of. Colin wasn't looking forward to going to work tomorrow night.

Still, tomorrow night was a long time away and maybe this hotshot Toronto PI Henry Fitzroy had convinced the pack to hire could turn something up.

"When I get out of the city," he told his reflection in the rearview mirror, "I'm going to have a good long howl. I deserve it."

He watched Colin return home, bad mood obvious even through the scope. Finger resting lightly on the trigger, he tracked him from the truck to the house but, although he had a clear line of sight, he couldn't apply the necessary pressure. He told himself it was too dangerous—there were too many others too close—but in his heart he knew it was the uniform. Colin would have to die in his other form.

Shadows moved against the windows, then the kitchen light went off and the farmhouse stood in darkness. Fire would take care of the lot of them, but he doubted he could get close enough to set it.

Staying carefully downwind, he worked his way back to the road and his car, old skills put to new uses. Although tonight's reconnaissance had brought him little new information and no chance of making a kill, his penetration so close to their home had convinced him it would only be a matter of time before he won.

There were, however, the visitors to consider.

Until he found out who, and what, they were, he would not act against them. He would not have the murder of innocents on his conscience.

Henry stood by the bed and watched Vicki sleep. She had one arm thrown up over her head, the other across her stomach. The sheet, like the darkness, did little to hide her from his sight. He watched her breathe, listened to the rhythm of her heart, followed the path of her blood as it pulsed at wrist and throat. Even asleep, her life was like a beacon in the room.

He could feel his hunger growing.

Should he wake her?

She slept with the corners of her mouth curved slightly upward, as though she knew a pleasant secret.

No. There had been enough strangeness for her to deal with for one night. He could wait.

Lightly, very lightly, he drew his finger along the soft skin of her inner arm and whispered, "Tomorrow."

For the first moment after waking, Vicki had no idea where she was. Sunlight painted molten gold across the inside of her lids and, as pretty as it looked, it shouldn't be there. Her bedroom window faced a narrow alley and across that another bedroom window so, even if she'd left the curtains open, which she never did, it couldn't possibly be this light.

Then she remembered and opened her eyes. The ceiling was a blue blur with a yellow blur across it. Reaching out to the right, her fingers scuttled across the bedside table until they found her glasses. She settled them on her nose and the blurring vanished although the ceiling didn't change significantly. It was still blue. The yellow was a slanting bar of sunlight streaming through the space between the thin cotton curtains. Her room, Sylvia's old room, was obviously on the east side of the house. That settled, Vicki sat up.

The black shape stretched across the lower left corner of the bed gave her a second's panic until she recognized Shadow. Sliding carefully out from under the sheet so as not to wake him, she was just about to stand when she noticed that the bedroom door was wide open and, given the angle of the bed, she'd be fully visible to anyone who walked by.

Fully visible.

Vicki hated wearing pajamas and although she'd brought a T-shirt to sleep in, it had been so hot she hadn't bothered. She supposed she could handle Shadow—mostly because so far she'd avoided thinking of Daniel—but Shadow's cousins or uncle or father—especially Shadow's father—were another kettle of fish entirely and what's more, she could smell coffee so she knew *someone* was up.

Well, I can't stay in bed all day. . . . Girding her loins, metaphorically speaking, she dashed across the small section of open linoleum and eased the door closed. Shadow scrubbed at his muzzle with one oversized paw but didn't wake. Feeling considerably more secure, Vicki got into a pair of clean underwear and began to hook on her bra. She'd have to have a word with Sha . . . Daniel when he woke up as she knew she'd closed the door last night.

The door opened.

Jennifer, or maybe Marie, came into the room.

It didn't really help that of the two, Vicki was wearing more clothing.

"Hi. Mom sent me up to see if you were awake. Like it's really early still but Aunt Sylvia always said the sun in this room was like an alarm clock. You coming right down?"

"Uh, yes."

"Good." She shook her head at the bra. "Boy am I glad I'll never need one of those things." Glancing around, she sighed volubly. "So that's where the runt got to. If he bugs you just throw him out."

"I'll, uh, do that."

Vicki pushed the door closed again as soon as the bushy tail of the long legged, half-grown wer had cleared the threshold.

Something Henry had said last night as they walked up the stairs together now made sense.

"Inside the pack, the wer have no sense of personal privacy."

She got dressed in record time and decided to skip having a shower. After her father left when she was ten, it had been just her and her mother. With the exception of a year in university residence when she didn't have a choice, she'd lived alone all her adult life. Something told her that all this family togetherness she found herself in the midst of was going to wear thin pretty quickly. . . .

Elbows on the kitchen table, sipping at cup of very good coffee, Vicki tried to look as though a half-naked woman joined her for breakfast every morning.

"The vinyl seats stick," Nadine had explained as she sat, smoothing her cotton skirt. It had been wrapped so that a single tug would release it.

Apparently Stuart's decision the night before to leave

off the despised sweatpants had given the rest of the family the opportunity to dress as they chose. Or not. Given that the heat had already left a damp vee down the back of Vicki's T-shirt, she supposed the "or not" wasn't such a bad idea. She couldn't help but notice the various items of clothing scattered all over the house, ready to be pulled on if an outsider arrived. *"Although if it's someone we don't want to see,"* Nadine had confirmed, *"we just stay in fur-form and ignore them."* Considering the size of the fur-forms, Vicki was willing to bet the wer had no trouble with trespassers.

From where she sat, Vicki could see out the largest of the three kitchen windows. The view included a scruffy expanse of lawn, a weathered building with a slight list to the west that appeared to be a garage, and beyond that, the barnyard. Cloud and Storm were stretched out under the huge willow tree in the center of the lawn. As Vicki watched, Storm lifted his head and yawned. He got slowly to his feet, stretched, and had a vigorous shake, dark russet fur rippling with highlights in the early morning sun. He sniffed at Cloud who ignored him. Dropping into a half crouch, he pushed his muzzle under her jaw and lifted. Her head rose about six inches off the ground and then dropped. She continued to ignore him. He did it again. The third time, Cloud twisted, changed, and Rose grabbed his muzzle with both hands.

"We're at the end of a very long lane." Nadine anticipated Vicki's question. "You can't actually see the house from the road and, with the exception of mail delivery, almost no one uses the road but us."

Out on the lawn, Cloud chased her brother twice around the tree and out of sight.

The sound of claws on linoleum shifted Vicki's attention back into the house but it was only Shadow coming down the stairs and into the kitchen. He sat in front of the refrigerator, had a quick scratch, then changed so he could open the door.

"Ma, there's nothing to eat."

"Don't stand with the fridge door open, Daniel."

He sighed but obediently closed it and Vicki marveled at how universal some things could be . . .

"If you're hungry why don't you go out to the barn and hunt rats?"

. . . and how universal some things were not.

Daniel sighed again and dragged himself over to lean against his mother's shoulder. "Don't know as I'm hungry for rats."

Nadine smiled, brushing the hair back off his forehead. "If you catch one and you don't want to eat it, you can bring it to me."

This apparently solved all problems because it was Shadow who put both front paws up on Nadine's lap and swiped at her face with his tongue before bounding outside. The screen door, Vicki saw, had been hung so that it swung freely in both directions with no latch to prevent a nose or a paw from pushing it open.

"They grow up so fast," Nadine said reflectively, snatching a fly out of the air.

For one horrified moment, with the rats still causing her a little trouble, Vicki was afraid Nadine was going to eat it but the older woman only crushed it and threw it to the floor. All things considered, lousy housekeeping was much easier to deal with. Vicki brushed a fly off the edge of her own mug and tried very hard to be open-minded. *Rats. Right. If I don't eat until sundown maybe Henry'll take me to MacDonalds.*

"Cloud comes into her first heat this fall," Nadine continued in the same tone, wiping her hand against the fabric of her skirt, "so pretty soon now, Peter'll be leaving."

"Leaving?" Back on the lawn, Shadow was stalking the waving plume of Storm's tail.

"It's too risky to have him stay. We'll probably send him away in early September."

"But . . ."

"When Cloud goes into heat, Storm'll go crazy trying to get to her. Better for all concerned if the males are far away when their littermates—their twins—mature." Her voice shook a little as she added, "The bonds between twins are very strong with our kind."

"Rose said something similar." Vicki traced the pattern on her mug with the tip of one finger, unsure if she should say anything about Sylvia's death. The pain shadowing Nadine's eyes was so intensely personal, sympathy might be seen as an intrusion.

Nadine's nails tapped against the tabletop. "The wer see death as a natural result of life," she said, reading Vicki's hesitation. "Our mourning is specific and soon over. Jason was my brother and I miss him, but with the loss of my twin, I feel as though I've lost a part of myself."

"I understand."

"No, you don't. You can't." Then Nadine's voice twisted into a snarl and her lips lifted off her teeth. "When you have found this animal with a coward's weapon, he will pay for the pain he has caused."

It was so easy, Vicki realized, to forget why she was here; to get caught up in the strangeness and lose sight of the fact that two people had been murdered. So some aspects of the case were a little unusual. So what. She put down her mug, unaware her expression almost exactly mirrored Nadine's. "I'd better get started."

Five

"Why can't I come?" Daniel scowled fiercely up at Peter. "You always took me with you when you went places before."

"It's too dangerous." Peter shimmied the track shorts up over his hips. Vicki tried not to watch and wasn't significantly successful at it. "What if the human who shot Silver and Ebon is out there?"

Lips pulled back off small, pointed teeth. "I'd bite him!"

"He'd shoot you. You're not coming."

"But Peter. . . ."

"No."

"Cloud?"

She growled, her meaning plain.

"Okay, fine." Daniel threw himself down onto the grass. "But if you get in trouble out there, don't go howling for me." He thrust his chin into his cupped hands and only glowered when Cloud gave him a couple of quick licks as she went by.

Vicki fell into step beside Peter and the three of them headed for the nearly overgrown lane behind the barn.

"Hey, Peter!"

Peter turned.

"Ei kee ayaki awro!" The words rose and fell in a singsong cadence, practically dripping with six-year-old indignation.

Peter laughed.

"What did he say?"

"He said I mate with sheep."

It hadn't actually occurred to Vicki that the wer would have a language of their own although now she thought about it, it became obvious. It sounded a bit like Inuit—at least Inuit according to PBS specials on the Arctic; Vicki'd never been farther North than Thunder Bay. When she mentioned this to Peter, he kicked at a clump of yellowed grass.

"I've never heard Inuit but we sure got the same problems. The more we integrate with humans the more we speak their language and lose ours. Grandfather and Grandmother spoke Dutch and English and wer. Father still speaks a little Dutch but only Aunt Sylvia bothered to learn any wer." He sighed. "She taught me and I'm trying to teach Daniel but there's still so much I don't know. The dirt bag that killed her killed my best chance at keeping our language alive."

"You seem to be doing a good job." Vicki waved a hand back toward the willow. "Daniel's certainly using it. . . ." It might not be much comfort but it was all she had to offer so far.

Peter brightened. "True. He's like a little sponge, just soaks it right up. Cloud now," he made a grab for his twin's tail but she whisked it out of his way, "she learned to say Akaywo and gave up."

"Akaywo," Vicki repeated. The word didn't resonate the way it did when Peter said it but it was recognizable. Sort of. "What does it mean?"

"Uh, good hunting mostly. But *that* means hello, good-bye, how's tricks, long time no see."

"Like Aloha."

"Aloha. Alo-ha." Peter lengthened the second syllable until it trembled on the edge of a howl. "Good word. But not one of ours. . . ."

Suddenly, Cloud's ears went up and she bounded off into the underbrush. A second later, Peter shoved his shorts into Vicki's hands and took off after her.

Vicki watched their tails disappear behind a barrier of bushes and weeds and slapped at one of the billions of mosquitoes their passage through the grass had stirred up. "Now what?" she wondered. From all the crashing about, they were still after it, whatever it was. "Hey," she called, "I'll just keep walking to the end of the lane. You can catch up with me there." There was no response but to be honest she didn't expect one.

It was almost comfortable in the lane; a long way from cool but not nearly as hot as it would no doubt get later in the day. Vicki checked her watch. 8:40. *"You can make those calls this morning if you like,"* Nadine had said, *"but you might be better off heading out to the fields and having a look at where it happened before it gets too hot. When it warms up in a couple of hours, no one around here'll be awake to show you the place. Beside, Peter or Rose can tell you all about the three humans while you go."* A good theory if only Peter and Rose, or Peter and Cloud, or even Storm and Cloud—whatever—had stuck around.

She brushed aside a swarm of gnats, crushed another mosquito against her knee, and wondered if Henry was all right. The wer had apparently light-proofed a room for him, but at this point Vicki wasn't entirely certain she'd trust their good intentions. Still, Henry had been here other times and obviously survived.

Pushing her glasses up her nose, sweat having well lubricated the slope, she reached the end of the lane and paused, a little overwhelmed by the vast expanse of land now before her. Up above, the sky stretched on forever, hard-edged and blue. Down below, there was a fence and a field and another fence and a bigger field. There were sheep in both fields. In fact, there were three sheep not twenty feet away on the other side of the first fence.

Two of them were eating, the third stared down the arch of its Roman profile at Vicki.

Vicki had never heard that sheep were dangerous,

but then, what did she know, she'd never been this close to a sheep before.

"So," leaning carefully against the fence, she picked a tuft of fleece off a rusty bit of wire and rolled it between her fingers, "I don't suppose you saw anything the night that Jason Heerkens, aka Ebon, was murdered?"

At the sound of her voice, the staring sheep rolled its eyes and danced backward while the other two, still chewing, peeled off to either side and trotted a few feet away.

"So much for interviewing witnesses," she muttered, turning back to look down the lane. "Where the hell are Cloud and Pe . . . Storm?"

As if in answer to her summons, the two wer burst out of the bushes and bounded toward her, tongues lolling, tails waving. Cloud reached the fence first and without pausing sailed over it and came to a dead stop, flattened against the grass on the other side. Storm, only a heartbeat behind, changed in midair, and Peter landed beside his sister in a very human crouch. The sheep, obviously used to this sort of thing, barely bothered to glance up from their grazing.

Vicki, less accustomed, tried to maintain an unruffled expression. Silently, she offered Peter his shorts.

"Thanks." He slid them on with practiced speed. "We almost had him that time."

"Had who?"

"Old groundhog, lives under a pile of cedar rails alongside the lane. He's fast and he's smart, but this time he made it to his den with only about a hair between him and Cloud's teeth."

"Couldn't you just change and move the rails."

Peter shook his head, bits of bracken flying out of his hair. "That'd be cheating."

"It's not like we're hunting for food," Rose put in, stretching out on the grass. "There'd be no fun in it if we used our hands."

Vicki decided not to point out that there probably

wasn't much fun in it for the groundhog either way. She slung her bag over the fence and followed a little more slowly. Rails she might have flag-jumped but wire offered no surface solid enough to push off from. *Besides, if I try to keep up with a couple of teenage werewolves, I'll probably strain something. Besides credibility.*

She pushed her glasses up her nose. "Where to now?"

"Toward the far side of the big pasture." Peter pointed. "Near the woods."

The woods offered sufficient cover for a whole army of assassins.

Vicki picked up her bag. Time to start earning her money. "Who owns the woods?"

"The government, it's crown land." Peter led the way along the fence, Cloud staying close by his side. "We won't cut straight across 'cause these ewes are carrying late fall lambs and we don't want to bother them any more than we have to. Our property ends at the trees," he continued, "but we're butted up against the Fanshawe Conservation Area." He grinned. "We help maintain one of the best deer herds in the county."

"I'm sure. Let me guess, that's how you met the game warden?"

"Uh huh. He came on one of the pack's kills, knew it hadn't been dogs, thought he recognized the spoor as wolf but couldn't figure out what the occasional bare human footprint was doing in there, and tracked us. He was really good. . . ."

"And you, that is, the pack, wasn't being as careful as it could have been." In Vicki's experience, complacency had exposed the majority of the world's secrets.

"Yeah. But Arthur turned out to be an okay guy."

"He could have turned out to be disaster," Vicki pointed out.

Peter shrugged. What was done was done as far as

the pack was concerned. They'd taken steps to see it
would never happen again and thought no more about
it.

"What about the doctor?" She watched Cloud snap
at a grasshopper and wondered if the separate forms
had separate taste buds.

"Dr. Dixon's ancient history." Peter told her,
snatched a high-leaping insect out of the air and
popped it in his mouth.

Vicki swallowed a rising wave of nausea. The
crunch, crunch, swallow, gave the snack an immedi-
acy the earlier episode with the rats hadn't had. And
while it was one thing to see Cloud do it. . . . *Well, I
guess that answers my question.* Then she saw the look
on Peter's face. *The little shit ate that on purpose to
gross me out.* She gave her glasses a push and two
steps later plucked a grasshopper off the front of her
shorts—fortunately, it was a small one.

A long time ago, on a survival course, an instructor
had told Vicki that many insects were edible. She
hoped he hadn't been pulling her leg.

Biting down wasn't easy.

Actually, it tastes a bit like a squishy peanut.

The expression on Peter's face made the whole thing
worthwhile. The last time she'd impressed a young man
to that extent, she'd been considerably younger herself
and her mother had gone away for the weekend.

Mike Celluci would maintain that she was insanely
competitive. That wasn't true. She merely liked to
preserve the status quo and her position at the top of
the heap. And no teenage anything was getting the
better of her. . . .

"Now, then," she tongued something out of her
tooth and swallowed it quickly—there were limits—
"you were telling me about Dr. Dixon?"

"Uh, yeah, well. . . ." He shot her a glance out of
the corner of one eye but made an obvious decision
not to comment. "When our grandparents emigrated
from Holland after the war, Grandmother was preg-

nant with Aunt Sylvia and Aunt Nadine. They got as far as London when she went into labor. We don't normally use doctors, the pack helps if it's needed. I went out to the barn when Daniel was born but Rose watched."

Cloud looked up at the sound of her name. She'd run ahead and was urinating against a fence post.

"Anyway," Peter continued, nostrils flared as they passed the post, "there was this young doctor in the crowd and before Grandfather could carry Grandmother away, he'd hustled the both of them and Father, who was about five, into his office." He snickered. "Boy, did he get a shock. As soon as they were alone, Grandfather changed and almost ripped his throat out. Lucky for the doctor, Aunt Sylvia was wrong—somehow, I don't know—anyway, Dr. Dixon acted like a doctor and Grandfather let him live. He's been taking care of all our doctor stuff ever since."

"Handy man to know." The amount of "doctor stuff" necessary in Canada for government documents alone could be positively staggering. The wer were lucky they'd stumbled onto Dr. Dixon when they had. "So that leaves only Barry Wu."

"Yeah." Peter sighed deeply and scratched at the patch of red hair in the center of his chest. "But you better talk to Colin about him."

"I intend to. But I'd also like to hear your opinion."

Peter shrugged. "I like him. I hope he didn't do it. It'll kill Colin if he did."

"Have they been partners long?"

"Since the beginning. They went to police school together." They'd reached the second fence. Cloud sailed over it, just as she had the first. Peter slipped his thumbs behind the waistband of his shorts, changed his mind, and started climbing. "Barry's an okay guy. He reacted to us the same way you did . . ." Twisting his head at an impossible angle, he grinned back over his shoulder at her. ". . . kind of shell-shocked but accepting."

Cloud had run on ahead, nose to the ground. About three quarters of the way across the field, she stopped, sat back on her haunches, pointed her nose at the sky, and howled. The sound lifted every hair on Vicki's body and brought a lump into her throat almost too big to swallow. From not very far away came an answer; two voices wrapping about each other in a fey harmony. Then Peter, still in human form, wove in his own song.

The sheep had begun to look distinctly nervous by the time the howl trailed off.

"Father and Uncle Stuart." Peter broke the silence to explain the two additional voices. "They're checking fences." He turned a little red under his tan. "Well, it's almost impossible not to join in. . . ."

As Vicki had felt a faint desire—firmly squelched—to add in her own two cents worth, she nodded understandingly. "Is that where it happened?"

"Yeah. Right here."

At first glance, "right here" looked no different than anywhere else in the field. "Are you sure?"

"Of course, I'm sure. It hasn't rained and the scent's still strong. Besides," one bare foot brushed lightly over the cropped timothy grass, "I was the first one to the body." Cloud pushed up against his legs. He reached down and pulled gently on her ears. "Not something I'm likely to forget."

"No, probably not." Maybe she should have told him that he'd forget in time but Vicki didn't believe in lying if she could avoid it, even for comfort's sake. The violent death of someone close *should* make a lasting impression. Given that, she gentled her voice to ask, "Are you going to be up to this?"

"Hey, no problem." His hand remained buried in the thick fur behind Cloud's head.

The wer touched a great deal, she realized, and it wasn't just the youngsters. Last night around the kitchen table, the three adults had seldom been out of contact with each other. She couldn't remember the last time she'd spontaneously touched her mother. *And why am I thinking about that now?* She dug out her pad and a pencil. "Let's get started, then."

Ebon had been traveling northeast across the field. The bullet had spun his body around so that the ruin of his head had pointed almost due north. Even without Peter's description, there were enough rust brown stains remaining on the grass to show where what was left of Ebon's head had come to rest. The shot had to have come from the south.

Vicki sat back on her heels and stared south into the wood. *Brilliant deduction, Sherlock.* She stood, rubbing at the imprints of dried grass on her knees. "Where was your aunt shot?"

Peter remained sitting, Cloud's head in his lap. "In the small south field, just off that way." He pointed. The small south field wrapped around a corner of the woods. "Ebon was coming from there."

"Similar shot?"

"Yeah."

Head shots, at night, on moving targets. Whoever he was, he was good. "Which way was the body facing?"

"Like this." Peter shoved Cloud's body around until it was aligned to the northwest. She endured the mauling but didn't look thrilled.

Silver's tracks had been coming from the south and the shot had spun her in an arc identical to Ebon's.

The Conservation Area woods ran east of the small south field.

"I think we can safely assume it's the same guy and he shot from the cover of the trees," Vicki muttered, wishing for a city street and a clear line of sight. Trees shifted and moved about the way buildings never did and, from where Vicki stood, the woods looked like a solid wall of green and brown, with no way of knowing what they hid. A dribble of moisture rolled out of her hair and down the back of her neck. Someone could be watching now, raising the rifle, taking aim. . . . *You're getting ridiculous. The killings have happened at night.* But she couldn't stop a little voice from adding. *So far.*

Her back to the trees and an itching she couldn't control between her shoulder blades, she stood. "Come on."

"Where?" Peter rose effortlessly. Vicki tried not to be annoyed.

"We're going to have a look for the bullet that killed your aunt."

"Why?" He fell into step beside her as Cloud bounded on ahead.

"We're eliminating the possibility of two killers. So far, the pattern of both deaths are identical with only one exception."

"The silver bullet?"

"That's right. If the deaths match on all points, the odds are good there's a single person responsible."

"So if that's the case, how do you find them?"

"You follow the pattern back."

Peter frowned. "I don't think I understand what you mean."

"Common sense, Peter. That's all." She scrambled over another fence. "Everything connects to everything else. I just figure out how."

"After Aunt Sylvia died, the pack went hunting for her killer but we couldn't find any scents in the wood that didn't belong."

"What do you mean, didn't belong?"

"Well, there's a lot of scents in there. We were looking for a strange one." He squirmed a little under Vicki's frown and continued in a less condescending tone. "Anyway, after Uncle Jason was shot, Uncle Stuart wouldn't let anyone go into the woods except Colin."

Good way to lose Colin, Vicki thought, amazed as she often was at the stupid things otherwise intelligent people could do, but all she said aloud was, "And what did Colin discover?"

"Well, not Barry's scent, and I think that was mostly what he was looking for."

Cloud was making tight circles, nose to the ground, in roughly the center of the field.

"Is that where it happened?"

"Uh huh."

Teeth clenched, Vicki waited for the howl. It didn't come. When she asked Peter why, he shrugged and said, "It happened weeks ago."

"Don't you miss her?"

"Of course we do, but . . ." He shrugged again, unable to explain. Everyone but Aunt Nadine had finished howling for Silver.

Cloud had found the bullet by the time they reached her and had dug it clear with more enthusiasm than efficiency. Her muzzle and paws had acquired a brown patina and the rest of her pelt was peppered with dirt.

"Good nose!" Vicki exclaimed, bending to pick up the slug. *And a good thing there wasn't anything else to learn from the scene,* she added silently, surveying the excavation. A quick wipe on her shorts and she held the prize up in the sunlight. It certainly wasn't lead.

Peter squinted at the metal. "So it's just one guy?"

Vicki nodded, dropping the bullet into her bag. "Odds are good." One marksman. Who killed at night with a single shot to the head. One executioner.

"And you can find him now?"

"I can start looking."

"We should've found the dirtbag," Peter growled, savagely ripped up a handful of grass. "I mean, we're hunters!"

"Hunting for people is a specialized sort of a skill," Vicki pointed out levelly. The last thing she wanted to do was inspire heroics. "You have to train for it, just like everything else. Now, then," she squinted at the woods then looked back at the two young wer, "I want the both of you to return to the house. I'm going to go in there and have a look around.''

''Uh, Ms. Nelson, you don't have much experience in woods, do you?'' Rose asked tentatively.

''No. Not especially,'' Vicki admitted, ''but . . . Rose, what the hell do you think you're doing?''

''It's just that, you're from the city and. . . .''

''That's not what I meant!'' She positioned herself between the woods and the girl. ''You *know* someone is watching your family from those trees. Why are you changing? Why take such a stupid risk?''

Rose rubbed at the dirt on her face. ''But there's no one there now.''

''You can't know that!'' Why the whole damned county wasn't in on the family secret, Vicki had no idea.

''Yes, I can.''

''How?''

''It's upwind.''

''Upwind? The woods are upwind? You can smell that there's no one there?''

''That's right.''

Vicki reminded herself once again not to judge by human standards and decided to drop it. ''I think you two should get home.''

''Maybe we should stay with you.''

''No.'' Vicki shook her head. ''If you're with me, you'll influence what I see.'' She raised a hand to cut off Peter's protest and added, ''Even if you don't intend to. Besides, it's too dangerous.''

Peter shrugged. ''It's been safe enough since Ebon died.''

It took her a moment to understand. ''You mean that two members of your family were shot out here and you're still coming in range of the woods? At night?''

''We've been in pairs like Henry said,'' he protested. ''And we've had the wind.''

I don't believe this. . . . ''From now on, until we

know what's going on, *no one* comes out to these fields.''

''But we have to keep on eye on the sheep.''

''Why?'' Vicki snapped, waving a hand toward the flock. ''Do they do something?''

''Besides eat and sleep? No, not really. But the reason there's so few commercial sheep operations in Canada is a problem with predators.'' Peter's lips drew back off his teeth and under his hair, his ears went back. ''We don't *have* problems with predators.''

''But you've gotta keep a pretty constant eye out,'' Rose continued, ''so someone's got to come out here.''

''Can't you move the sheep closer to the house?''

''We rotate the pastures,'' Peter explained. ''It doesn't quite work like that.''

''Bugger the pastures and bugger the sheep,'' Vicki said, her tone, in direct contrast to her words, reminiscent of a lecture on basic street safety to a kindergarten class. ''Your lives are more important. Either leave these sheep alone for a while or move them closer to the house.''

Rose and Peter exchanged worried glances.

''It's not just the sheep . . .'' Rose began.

''Then what?''

''Well, this is the border of our family's territory. It has to be marked.''

''What do you mean, marked?'' Vicki asked even though she had a pretty good idea.

Rose waved her hands, her palms were filthy. ''You know, marked. Scent marked.''

''I would have thought that had been done already.''

''Well, yeah, but you've got to keep doing it.''

Vicki sighed. ''So you're willing to risk your life in order to pee on a post?''

''It's not quite that simple.'' Rose sighed as well. ''But I guess not.''

''I guess we could talk to Uncle Stuart . . .'' Peter offered.

"You do that," Vicki told him agreeably. "But you do that back at the house. Now."

"But. . . ."

"No." Things had been a little strange for Vicki lately—her eyes, Henry, werewolves—but she was working now and, regardless of the circumstances, that put her back on firm ground. Two shots had been fired from those trees and somewhere in the woods would be the tiny bits of flotsam that even the most meticulous of criminals left behind, evidence that would lead her out of the woods and right down the bastard's throat.

The twins heard the change in her voice, saw the change in her manner, and responded. Cloud stood and shook, surrounding herself for a moment in a nimbus of fine white hairs. Peter heaved himself to his feet, his hand on Cloud's shoulder. He tucked his thumbs behind the waist band of his shorts, then paused. "Would you *mind?*" he asked, gesturing at her shoulder bag with his chin.

Vicki sighed, suddenly feeling old. The distance between thirty-one and seventeen stretched far wider than the distance between thirty-one and four hundred and fifty. "I assume your nose tells you it's still safe?"

"Cross my heart and bite my tail."

"Then give them here," she said, holding out her hand.

He grinned, stripped them off, and tossed them to her. Peter stretched, then Storm stretched, then he and Cloud bounded back toward the house.

Vicki watched until they leapt the closer of the two fences, stuffed Peter's shorts in her bag, and turned toward the woods. The underbrush appeared to reach up to meet the treetops reaching down, every leaf hanging still and sullen in the August heat. Who knew what was in there? She sure as hell didn't.

At the edge of the field she stopped, squared her shoulders, took a deep breath, and pushed forward into the wilderness. Somehow, she doubted this was going to be fun.

Barry Wu blinked a drop of sweat from his eye, squinted through his front sights, and brought the barrel of his .30-06 Springfield down a millimeter.

Normally, he preferred to shoot at good old-fashioned targets set at the greatest distance accuracy would allow but he'd just finished loading a number of low velocity rounds—the kind that reacted ballistically at one hundred yards the way a normal round would react at five—and he wanted to try them out. He'd been reloading his own cartridges since he was about fourteen, but lately he'd been getting into more exotic varieties and these were the first of this type he'd attempted.

A hundred yards away, the lead silhouette of the grizzly waited, scaled in the same five to one ratio as the rounds he planned to put into it.

The bullet slammed into the target with a satisfyingly solid sound and Barry felt a little of the tension drain from his neck and shoulders as the grizzly went down. He worked the bolt, expelling the spent cartridge and moving the next round into the chamber. Shooting had always calmed him. When it was good, and lately it always was, he and the rifle became part of a single unit, one the extension of the other. All the petty grievances of his life could be shot away with a simple pull of the trigger.

All right, not all, he conceded as the moose and the mountain sheep fell in quick succession. *I'm going to have to do something about Colin Heerkens.* The trust necessary for them to do their job was in definite danger. Rising anger caused him to wing the elk, but the white-tailed deer he hit just behind the shoulder.

We clear this up tonight.

He centered the last target and squeezed the trigger. *One way or another.*

A hundred yards away, the lead silhouette of the timber wolf slammed flat under the impact of the slug.

Vicki rubbed at a welt on her cheek and waved her other hand about in an ineffectual effort to discourage the swarms of mosquitoes that rose around her with every step. Fortunately, most of them appeared to be males. *Or dieting females,* she amended, trying not to inhale any significant number. Barely a hundred yards into the trees, the field and the sheep had disappeared and looking back the way she'd come, all she could see were more trees. It hadn't been as hard a slog as she'd feared it would be but neither was it a stroll through the park. Fortunately, the sunlight blazed through to the forest floor in sufficient strength to be useful. The world was tinted green, but it was visible.

"Somebody should tidy this place up," she muttered, unhooking her hair from a bit of dead branch. "Preferably with a flamethrower."

She kept to as straight a path as she could, picking out a tree or a bush along the assumed line of fire and then struggling toward it. Somewhere in these woods, she knew she'd find a fixed place where their marksman had a clear line of sight. It hadn't taken her long to realize that this place could only exist up off the forest floor. Which explained why the wer had found nothing; if they hunted like wolves, it was nose to the ground.

Trouble was, every tree she passed had so far been unclimbable. Trees large enough to bear an adult's weight stretched relatively smooth and straight up toward the sun, not branching until there was a chance of some return for the effort.

"So, unless he brought in a ladder . . ." Vicki sighed and scrubbed a drop of sweat off her chin with the shoulder of her T-shirt. She could see what might be higher ground a little to the right of where she thought she should be heading and decided to make for it. Stepping over a fallen branch, she tripped as the smaller branches, hidden under a rotting layer of last year's leaves, gave way under her foot.

"Parking lots." Shoving her glasses back up her nose, she stood and scowled around her at Mother Nature in the height of her summer beauty. "I'm all in favor of parking lots. A couple of layers of asphalt would do wonders for this place." Off to one side a cicada started to buzz. "Shut up," she told it, trudging on.

The higher ground turned out to be the end of a low ridge of rock on which a massive pine had managed to gain, and maintain, a roothold. Brushing aside years of accumulated needles, Vicki sat down just outside the perimeter of its skirts and contemplated her scratched and bitten legs.

This was all Henry's fault. She could have been at home, comfortably settled in front of her eighteen inch, three speed, oscillating fan, watching Saturday morning cartoons, and . . .

". . . and the wer would continue to die." She sighed and began building the fallen pine needles into little piles. This was what she'd chosen to do with her life—to try to make a difference in the sewer the world was becoming—no point in complaining just because it wasn't always an easy job. And she had to admit, it was a job that had gotten a hell of a lot more interesting since Henry had come into her life. The jury was still out on whether or not that was a good thing given that the last time they'd worked together she'd come closer to getting killed than she ever had in nine years on the Metro Police.

"And this time, I'm being eaten alive." She rubbed at a bite on the back of her leg with the rough front of her sneaker. "Maybe I'm going at this the wrong way. Maybe I should have started with the people. What the hell am I going to recognize out here?" Then her hand froze over a patch of needles and slowly moved back until the needles were in full sunlight again.

The scorch mark was so faint she had to hold her

head at just the right angle to see it. About two inches long and half an inch wide, it was a marginally darker line across the pale brown carpet of dead pine—the mark a spent cartridge might make against a tinder dry resting place.

Oh, all right, honesty forced her to admit, *it could've been caused by any number of other things—like acid rain or bunny piss.* But it sure looked like a cartridge scorch to her. *Of course, it could've come from a legitimate hunter out here to blow away whatever it is legitimate hunters blow away.*

There were plenty of bits of bare rock nearby where the gunman could have stood to retrieve his brass and plenty of places Vicki had cleared herself but she searched for tracks anyway. Not expecting to find any didn't lessen the frustration when she didn't.

Better to find where the shot came from. The ridge stood barely two and a half feet higher than the forest floor and the lines of sight hadn't improved. Vicki looked up. The pine was higher than most of the trees around it but its branches drooped, heavy with needles, right to the ground. Then on the north side, she found a way in to a dimly lit cavern, roofed in living needles, carpeted in dead ones. It was quiet in there, and almost cool, and the branches rose up the trunk as regular as a ladder; which was a good thing because Vicki could barely see.

This was it. This had to be it.

Had she seen the pine from the field? She couldn't remember, trees all looked alike to her.

She peered at a few tiny spurs snapped off close to the trunk, her nose almost resting on the bark. They could have been broken by someone scrabbling for a foothold. *Or they could have been broken by overweight squirrels. There's only one way to be sure.* Settling her glasses more firmly on her face, she swung up onto the first branch.

Climbing wasn't as easy as it looked from the ground; a myriad of tiny branches poked and prodded and generally impeded progress and the whole damn thing moved. Vicki hadn't actually been up a tree since about 1972 and she was beginning to remember why.

If her nose hadn't scraped by an inch from the sneaker print, she probably wouldn't have seen it. Tucked tight up against the trunk on a flattened glob of pine resin, was almost a full square inch of tread signature. Not enough for a conviction, not with every man, woman, and child in the country owning at least one pair of running shoes, but it was a start. The stuff was so soft that removing it from the tree would destroy the print so she made a couple of quick sketches—balanced precariously on one trembling leg—then placed her foot as close to it as possible and heaved herself up.

Her head broke free into direct sunlight. She blinked and swore and when her vision cleared, swore again. "Jesus H. Christ on crutches. . . ."

She'd come farther into the woods than she'd thought. About five hundred yards away, due north, was the spot where Ebon had been shot. A half turn and she could see the small pasture where Silver had been killed, a little closer but still an amazing distance away. If Barry Wu had pulled the trigger, he should have no trouble making the Olympic team *or* bringing home a gold. Vicki knew that some telescopic sights incorporated range finders but even they took both innate skill and years of practice to acquire the accuracy necessary. Throw in a *moving* target at five hundred yards. . . .

She'd once heard that according to all the laws of physics, a human being should not be able to hit a major league fastball. By those same laws of physics, the assassin had hit not one, but two, and hit them out of the ballpark besides.

A quick search turned up rubs in the bark where he'd braced his weapon on the tree.

"Unfortunately," she sighed, leaning her head back against a convenient branch, "discovering how and where brings me no closer to finding the answers to why and who." Closing her eyes for a moment, the sun hot against the lids, she wondered if she'd actually go through with it; if when she found the killer, she'd actually turn him over to the wer for execution. She didn't have an answer. She didn't have an alternative either.

It was time to head back to the house and make some phone calls, although she had a sick feeling that a drive into town and a good look at Constable Barry Wu's sneakers would be more productive.

Climbing down the tree took less time than climbing up but only because gravity took a hand and dropped her seven feet before she landed on a branch thick enough to hold her weight. Heart pounding, she made it the rest of the way to the ground in a slightly less unorthodox fashion.

Had her Swiss army knife contained a saw, she would have attempted to remove that final branch, the one that lifted the climber out of the tree and into the light. Unfortunately, it didn't and whittling off a pine branch two inches in diameter didn't appeal to her. In fact, except for attempting to keep them out of those fields, there wasn't a damn thing she could do to prevent the tree from being used as a vantage point to shoot the wer.

"Never a beaver around when you need one," she muttered, wishing she'd brought an ax. She had, however, uncovered two facts about the murderer. He had to be at least five foot ten, her height—any shorter and his shoulder wouldn't be level with the place where the rifle barrel had rested—and the odds were good that his hair was short and straight. She dragged a handful of needles and a small branch out of her short, straight hair. Had her hair been long or curly, she'd never had made it out of the tree alive.

"Excuse me?"

The shriek was completely involuntary and as she caught it before it passed her lips Vicki figured it didn't count. Her hand on her bag—it had made a useful weapon in the past—she whirled around to confront two puzzled looking middle-aged women, both wearing high-powered binoculars, one of them carrying a canvas bag about a meter long and twenty centimeters wide.

"We were just wondering," said the shorter, "what you were doing up that tree."

Vicki shrugged, waning adrenaline jerking her shoulders up and down. "Oh, just looking around." She waved a not quite nonchalant hand at the canvas bag. "You out here to do a little shooting?"

"In a manner of speaking. Although this is our camera tripod, not a rifle."

"It's illegal to shoot on conservation authority property," added the other woman. She glared at Vicki, obviously still unhappy at having found her up in a tree. "We would report *anyone* we found shooting out here, you can be certain of that."

"Hey." Vicki raised both hands to shoulder height. "I'm unarmed." As neither woman seemed to appreciate her sense of humor, she lowered them again. "You're birders, aren't you?" A recent newspaper nature column had mentioned that *birders* was now the preferred term; *bird-watcher* having gone out of vogue.

Apparently, the column had been correct.

Twenty minutes later, Vicki had learned more about nature photography than she wanted to know; learned that in spite of the high-power binoculars the two women had seen nothing strange on the Heerkens farm—*"We don't look at other people's property, we look at birds."*—and, in fact, didn't even know where the Heerkens farm was; learned that a .30 caliber rifle and scope would easily fit into a tripod bag, allowing it to be carried into the woods without arousing suspicion. Although neither woman had ever come across a hunter, they'd both found spent shell casings and so were always on the look out. With middle-class confidence that no one would ever want to hurt them, they laughed at Vicki's warnings to be careful.

There were two bird-watching clubs in London as well as a photography group run by the YMCA that often came out to the conservation area. Armed with names and phone numbers of people to contact—"Although the members of that *other* club are really nothing more than a group of dilettantes. You'd do much better to join us."—Vicki bade farewell to the birders and tromped off through the bush, willing to bet big money that not everyone with a pair of binoculars kept then trained exclusively on birds and that someone was shooting more than film.

"Henry Fitzroy?" Dave Graham peered over his partner's shoulder at the pile of papers on the desk. "Isn't that the guy that Vicki's seeing?"

"What if it is?" Celluci growled, pointedly turning the entire pile over.

"Nothing, nothing." Dave went around to his side of the desk and sat down. "Did, uh, Vicki ask you to check into his background?"

"No. She didn't."

Dave recognized the tone and knew he should drop it, but some temptations were more than mortal man could resist. "I thought you and Vicki had a relationship based on, what was it, 'trust and mutual respect'?"

Celluci's eyes narrowed and he drummed his fingers against the paper. "Yeah. So?"

"Well . . ." Dave took a long, slow drink of his coffee. "It seems to me that checking up on the other men in her life doesn't exactly fit into those parameters."

Slamming his chair back, Celluci stood. "It's none of your damned business."

"You're right. Sorry." David smiled blandly up at him.

"I'm just looking out for a friend. Okay? He's a writer, god knows what he's been into."

"Right."

Seemingly of their own volition, Celluci's fingers crumpled the uppermost paper into a tightly wadded ball. "She can see who she wants," he ground out through clenched teeth and stomped out of the office.

Dave snickered into his coffee. "Of course she can," he said to the air, "as long as she doesn't see them very often and they meet with your approval." He made plans to be as far out of range as possible when Vicki found out and the shit hit the fan.

By 10:27, Vicki was pretty sure she was lost. She'd already taken twice as long coming out of the woods as she'd spent going in. The trees all looked the same and under the thick summer canopy it was impossible to take any kind of a bearing on the sun. Two paths had petered out into nothing and a blue jay had spent three minutes dive-bombing her, screaming insults. Various rustlings in the underbrush seemed to indicate that the locals found the whole thing pretty funny.

She glared at a pale green moss growing all around a tree.

"Where the hell are the Boy Scouts when you need one?"

Six

Vicki saw no apparent thinning of the woods; one moment she was in them, the next she was stepping out into a field. It wasn't a field she recognized either. There were no sheep, no fences, and no indication of where she might be.

Settling her bag more firmly on her shoulder, she started toward the white frame house and cluster of outbuildings that the other end of the field rolled up against. Maybe she could get directions, or use their phone . . .

". . . or get run off for trespassing by a large dog and a farmer with a pitchfork." She was pretty sure they did that sort of thing in the country, that it was effectively legal, and that it didn't matter because she wasn't going back into those woods. She'd take on half a dozen farmers with pitchforks first.

As she approached, wading knee-deep through grass and goldenrod and thistles, she became convinced that no one had worked this farm for quite some time. The barn had a faded, unused look about it and she could actually smell the roses that climbed all over one wall of the white frame house.

The field ended in a large vegetable garden. Vicki recognized the cabbages, the tomato plants, and the raspberry bushes—nothing else seemed familiar. *Which isn't really surprising.* She picked her way around the perimeter. *My vegetables usually come with a picture of the jolly green.* . . . "Oh. Hello."

"Hello." The elderly man, who had appeared so

suddenly in her path, continued to stare, obviously waiting for her to elaborate further.

"I, uh, got lost in the woods."

His gaze started at her sneakers, ran up her scratched and bitten legs, past her walking shorts, paused for a moment on her Blue Jays' T-shirt, flicked over to her shoulder bag, and finally came to rest on her face. "Oh," he said, a small smile lifting the edges of his precise gray mustache.

The single word covered a lot of ground, and the conclusion it drew would've annoyed the hell out of Vicki if it hadn't been so accurate. She held out her hand. "Vicki Nelson."

"Carl Biehn."

His palm was dry and leathery, his grip firm. Over the years, Vicki had discovered she could tell a lot about a man based on how he shook hands with her—or if he'd shake hands at all. Some men still seemed absolutely confused about what to do when the offered hand belonged to a woman. Carl Biehn shook hands with an economy of movement that said he had nothing to prove. She liked him for it.

"You look like you could use some water, Ms. Nelson."

"I could use a lake," Vicki admitted, rubbing at the sweat collected under her chin.

His smile broadened. "Well, no lake, but I'll see what I can do." He led the way around the raspberry bushes and Vicki fell into step beside him. Her first view of the rest of the garden brought an involuntary exclamation of delight.

"Do you like it?" He sounded almost shy.

"It's . . ." She discarded a pile of adjectives as inadequate and finished simply. ". . . the most beautiful thing I've ever seen."

"Thank you." He beamed; first at her and then out over the flower beds where a fallen rainbow, shattered into a thousand brilliant pieces, perched against every possible shade of green. "The Lord has been good to me this summer."

Vicki tensed, but he made no other reference to God. *And thank God for that.* She had no idea if her admiration had broken through the elderly man's reserve or if he simply had none when it came to the garden. As they walked between the beds, he introduced the flowers they passed as though they were old friends—here adjusting a stake that held a blood red gladioli upright, there swiftly beheading a dying blossom.

". . . dusty orange beauties are dwarf hemerocallis, day lilies. If you make the effort to plant early, middle, and late varieties, they'll bloom beautifully from June on into September. They're not a fussy grower, not hard to work with, just give them a little phosphate and potash and they'll show their appreciation. Now these shasta daisies over here. . . ."

Having spent most of her life in apartments, Vicki understood next to nothing about gardens or the plants that grew in them but she could—and did—appreciate the amount of work that had gone into creating and maintaining such an oasis of color amid the summer-toasted fields. She also could appreciate the depth of emotion that Carl Biehn lavished on his creation. He wasn't soppy or twee about it but the garden was a living being to him; it showed subtly in his voice, his expressions, his actions. People who cared that much about something outside themselves were rare in Vicki's world and it reinforced her first favorable impression.

An old-fashioned hand pump stood on a cement platform, close by the back door. Carl led the way across the lawn toward it, finishing his enthusiastic monologue about the new heritage roses just as he reached for the handle.

"The cup appears to be missing again, Ms. Nelson. I hope you don't mind."

Vicki grinned. "I may just stick my entire head under if that's all right with you."

"Be my guest."

For all its apparent age, the pump worked smoothly, pulling up clear, cold water with only the slightest taste of iron. Vicki couldn't remember the last time she'd tasted anything as good and the sudden shock of it hitting the back of her head erased much of the morning's stickiness. If the pump had been a little higher off the ground, she'd have stuck her entire body under it.

Flicking her wet hair back off her face, she straightened and indicated the pump. "May I?" When Carl admitted that he wouldn't mind, they changed places. There was more pressure against the handle than Vicki had anticipated and she found herself having to lean into the mechanism. Gardening had obviously kept her elderly benefactor in good condition.

"It really is incredible," she murmured. "I've never seen anything like it."

"You should have seen it last week. Then it was really something." He stood, wiping his hands dry on his pants and gazing proudly out over the vast expanse of color. "Still, I have to admit, it doesn't look bad. Everything out there from A to Zee, from asters to zinnias."

Vicki stepped back as a bumblebee, leg pouches bulging with pollen, flew a slightly wobbly course just past the end of her nose. From this angle, she could look out over the flowers, to the vegetables, to the fields beyond. The contrast was incredible. "It looks like shredded wheat out there. How do you keep the garden watered? It must be almost a full-time job."

"Not at all." He rested one foot up on the cement platform and leaned a forearm across his thigh. "I use an underground irrigation system, developed by the Israelis. I merely turn on the tap and the system does all the work. Just to be on the safe side, however, I've run a water line out into the garden with a hundred feet of hose, in case a specific plant needs a little attention."

She waved a hand between the brown and the green. "I just can't get over the difference."

"Well, sometimes even the Lord needs a little help, his wonders to perform. Have you been saved, Ms. Nelson?"

The question came so unexpectedly, in such a rational tone, that it took Vicki a moment to realize what had been said and a moment beyond that to come up with what she hoped would be a definitive reply. "I'm an Anglican." She wasn't, really, but her mother was, sort of.

"Ah." He nodded, stepping back off the platform. "Church of England." For just a second, caught between the sun and the concrete, the damp sole of his shoe left a print—concentric half circles of tread last seen pressed into pine gum in the crotch of a tree.

Her expression carefully neutral over a sudden surge of adrenaline, Vicki put her own foot up on the platform and bent to tie her shoe. In the heat of the sun, the print dried quickly but it was a definite match.

Unfortunately, so was the print she left behind.

A quick look told her they were wearing the same brand of running shoe. A brand that seemed to cover the feet of half the civilized world.

Shit. Shit. Shit! Good news and bad news. Or bad news and good news, she wasn't quite sure. Evidence no longer pointed directly to the feet of Carl Biehn but her suspect list, based on the sneaker print at least, had just grown by millions. There'd be small differences of course—size, cracks in the rubber, wear patterns—but the possibilities of an easy match had just evaporated.

"Are you all right, Ms. Nelson? Perhaps you should sit down for a moment, out of the sun."

"I'm fine." He was watching her with some concern so she pulled up a smile. "Thank you, Mr. Biehn."

"Well, maybe we'd best see about getting you back

where you belong. If I could offer you a lift somewhere. . . ."

"And if you can't, I most certainly will."

Vicki turned. The man standing in the doorway was
in his early thirties, of average height, average looks,
and above average self-opinion. He leered genially
down at her, his pose no doubt intended to show off
his manly physique—which, she admitted, wasn't bad.
If you like the squash and health club types. . . .
Which she didn't.

Slipping on a pair of expensive sunglasses, he
stepped out into the sunlight, hair gleaming like bur-
nished gold.

I bet he highlights it. A quick glance showed he wore
blue leather deck shoes. Without socks. Vicki hated
the look of shoes without socks. Although odds were
good he owned a pair of running shoes, she somehow
doubted he'd be willing to ruin his manicure by climbing a tree. Which was a pity as he seemed to be exactly the type of person she'd love to feed to the wer.

Beside her, she heard Carl suppress a sigh.

"Ms. Nelson, may I introduce you to my nephew,
Mark Williams."

The younger man grinned broadly at his uncle.
"And here I thought your only hobbies were gardening and bird-watching and saving souls." Then he
turned the force of his smile on Vicki.

Some expensive dental work there, she thought,
picking at a bit of dried pine gum on her T-shirt and
trying not to scowl.

"Ms. Nelson got lost in the conservation area," Carl
explained tersely. "I was just about to drive her
home."

"Oh please, allow me." Mark's voice stopped just
short of caressing and more than a little past what
Vicki considered insulting. "If I know my uncle, once
he gets a lovely woman alone in a car all he'll do is
preach."

"Please, don't put yourself out." Her tone made it

more a command than a polite reply and Mark looked
momentarily nonplussed. "If you wouldn't mind . . ."
she continued, turning to Carl. Being preached at
would be infinitely preferable to being with Mark. He
reminded her of a pimp she'd once busted.

"Not at all." Carl was doing an admirable job of
keeping a straight face, but Vicki caught sight of the
twinkle in his eye and a suspicious trembling at the ends
of his mustache. He waved a hand toward the driveway
and indicated Vicki should precede him.

It wasn't hard to connect the car with the man. The
late model, black jeep with the gold trim, the plush
interior, the sunroof, and the rust along the bottom of
the doors was practically a simulacrum of Mark. The
ten-year-old, beige sedan with the recent wax job just
as obviously—although not as loudly—said Carl.

Vicki had her hand on the door handle when Mark
called, "Hey! I don't even know your first name."

She turned and the air temperature plummeted
around her smile. "I know," she told him, and got
into the car.

The very expensive stereo system surprised her a
little.

"I like to listen to gospel music while I drive," Carl
explained, when he saw her looking at enough lights
and buttons and switches to fill an airplane cockpit.
He stopped the car at the end of the driveway. "Where
to?"

Where to, indeed; she had no idea of the address or
even the name of the road. "The, uh, Heerkens sheep
farm. Are you familiar with it?"

"Yes."

The suppressed emotion in that single word pulled
Vicki's brows down. "Is there a problem?"

His knuckles were white around the steering wheel.
"Are you family?"

"No. Just the friend of a friend. He thought I needed
some time out of the city and brought me here for the
weekend." Mike Celluci wouldn't have believed the

lie for a moment—he'd often said Vicki was the worst liar he'd ever met—but some of the tension went out of Carl's shoulders and he turned the car out onto the dirt road and headed north.

"I just met them this weekend," she continued matter-of-factly. Experience had taught her that the direct approach worked best with no nonsense people like her host. "Do you know them well?"

Carl's mouth thinned to a tight white line but after a moment he said, "When I first moved here, ten, eleven years ago now, I tried to get to know them. Tried to be a good neighbor. They were not interested."

"Well, they are pretty insular."

"Insular!" His bark of laughter held no humor. "I tried to do my duty as a Christian. Did you know, Ms. Nelson that not one of those children have been baptized?"

Vicki shook her head but before she could say anything, he continued. "I tried to bring that family to God, and do you know what I got for my caring? I was told to get off their property and to stay off if I couldn't leave my God at home."

You're lucky you didn't get bit, Vicki thought. "I bet that made you pretty mad."

"God is not something I carry around like a pocketbook, Ms. Nelson," he told her dryly. "He is a part of everything I do. Yes, it made me angry . . ."

Angry enough to kill? she wondered.

". . . but my anger was a righteous anger, and I gave it to the glory of the Lord."

"And what did the Lord do with it?"

He half turned toward her and smiled. "He put it to work in His service."

Now that *could mean any number of things.* Vicki stared out the window. *How* do *you bring up the subject of werewolves?* "Your nephew mentioned that you're a birder. . . ."

"When I can spare time away from the garden."

"Ever go into the conservation area?"

"On occasion."

"I have a cousin who's a birder." She had nothing of the sort; it was a textbook interrogation lie. "He tells me you can see all sorts of fascinating things out in the woods. He says the unusual and bizarre lurk around every corner."

"Does he? His list must be interesting then."

"What's the most interesting species you've ever identified?"

Gray brows drew down. "I had an Arctic tern once. No idea how it got so far south. I prayed for its safe flight home and as I only saw it the once, I like to think my prayers were answered."

"An Arctic tern?"

"That," he told her without taking his eyes off the road, "was exactly the reaction of the others I told. I never lie, Ms. Nelson. And I never give anyone a chance to call me a liar twice."

She felt as though he'd just slapped her on the wrist. "Sorry." *Well, that got me exactly nowhere.*

"Looks like good hunting out here," she said casually, peering out the car window, watching trees and fields, and more trees and more fields go by. "Do you hunt?"

"No." The single syllable held such abhorrence, such strength of emotion, Vicki had to believe it. "Taking the lives of God's creatures is an abomination."

She squirmed around to face him, wondering how he'd rationalize his diet. "You don't eat meat?"

"Not since 1954."

"Oh." His point. "What about your nephew?"

"In my house he follows my rules. I don't try to run the rest of his life."

Nor do you approve of the rest of his life, Vicki realized. "Has he been staying with you long?"

"No." Then he added, "Mark is my late sister's son. My only living relative."

Which explains why you let the slimebag stay around at all. She sensed his disapproval, but whether it was directed at her or at Mark she couldn't say. "I've, uh, never hunted," she told him, attempting to get back into his good graces. Technically it was the truth. She'd never hunted anything that ran on four legs.

"Good for you. Do you pray?"

"Probably not as much as I should."

That startled him into a smile. "Probably not," he agreed and pulled over at the end of the long lane leading to the Heerkens farm. "If you'll excuse me, this is as far as I can take you."

"Excuse you? You've saved me a long hot walk, I'm in your debt." She slid out of the car and with one finger holding her glasses, leaned back in through the open window. "Thanks for the ride. And the water. And the chance to see your garden."

He nodded solemnly. "You're welcome. Can I convince you to join me at worship tomorrow, Ms. Nelson?"

"No, I don't think so."

"Very well." He seemed resigned. "Be careful, Ms. Nelson; if you endanger your soul you endanger your chance of eternal life."

Vicki could feel his sincerity, knew he wasn't just saying the words, so she nodded and said, "I'll be careful." and stepped back onto the shoulder. She waited where she was until he maneuvered the big car around in a tight three point turn then shifted the weight of her bag on her shoulder, waved, and started toward the lane.

Which was when she saw Storm emerge from the hedgerow about a hundred meters down the road. Tongue lolling, he trotted toward her, sunlight shimmering in the golden highlights of his fur.

Tires growled against gravel, the big sedan picked up speed, and headed right for the young wer.

Vicki tried to yell—to Storm, to Carl, she wasn't

sure—but all that came out of a mouth gone suddenly dry was a strangled croak.

Then, in a spray of dirt and small stones, it was over.

Carl Biehn, his car, and his God, disappeared down the road and Storm danced a welcome around her.

As her heart started beating again, Vicki settled her glasses back on her nose, her free hand absently rubbing the warm fur between Storm's ears. She could have sworn. . . . *I must've got just a little too much sun.*

Finding nothing to interest him in the highly overrated great outdoors, Mark Williams wandered back into the house and pulled a cold beer out of the fridge. "Thank God dear Uncle Carl has nothing against 'alcohol in moderation.' " He laughed and repeated, "Thank God." Hopefully, that blonde bitch was getting an earful of peace and love and the rest of that religious crap from the crazy old coot.

She hadn't been his type anyway. He liked his women smaller, more complacent, willing to be overwhelmed. The kind he could be sure wouldn't go screaming to the police over every little bending of the rules.

"What I like is the kind of woman that doesn't land me in the middle of goddamned nowhere." He took a long swallow of beer and looked out the kitchen window at the fields shimmering in the heat. "Shit." He sighed. "This is all Annette's fault."

If Annette hadn't been ready to blow the sweet little operation he'd been running out of Vancouver, he wouldn't have had to have her killed so quickly that he'd had to hire professional help, and sloppy professional help at that. He shuddered to think of how close he'd come to spending his most productive years behind bars. Fortunately, he'd been able to arrange it so that the hired help had ended up taking the fall. He'd barely been able to close down the business, realize most of the projected profits, and get out of the province before the hired help's family had arrived to demand their share.

"And thus I find myself in the ass-end of civilization." He finished the beer and yawned. It could've been worse; the nights, at least, offered rare sport. Grinning, he tossed the empty into the case. Last night's bit of fun had proven his skills were still as sharp as they'd ever been.

A second yawn threatened to dislocate his jaw. He'd been up until the wee small hours of the morning and been awakened obscenely early. Maybe he should head upstairs for a nap. "Don't want the fingers trembling at a critical moment. Besides," he grabbed another beer to take with him, "there's bugger all else to do until dark."

When an overgrown lilac hedge blocked the line of sight from the road, Vicki silently handed Peter his shorts.

"Thanks. What were you doing with old man Biehn?"

"I came out of the woods on his property." It certainly wasn't going to hurt anything if Peter believed she'd chosen her direction on purpose. "He gave me a ride back."

"Oh. Good thing Uncle Stuart didn't see him."

"Your uncle really ran him off?"

"Oh yeah, and if Aunt Nadine hadn't stopped him, he'd have probably attacked."

Vicki felt her brows go up and she turned her head to look at Peter directly. She gotten used to the disembodied voices of the people walking beside her but occasionally she just had to see expressions. "He'd have attacked over a difference in religion?"

"Is that what old man Biehn said?" Peter snorted. "Jennifer and Marie were six, maybe seven, and Aunt Nadine was pregnant with Daniel. Old man Biehn came over—he dropped by pretty often back then, try-

ing to save our souls, and it was driving us all nuts—
and he started talking about hell. I don't know what
he said 'cause I wasn't there, but he really scared the
girls and they started to howl.'' Peter's brows drew
down and his ears went back. ''You don't do that to
cubs. Anyway, Uncle Stuart showed up and that was
that. He's never come back.''

''He was pretty angry about it,'' Vicki offered.

''Not as angry as Uncle Stuart.''

''But you must see him occasionally. . . .''

Peter looked confused. ''Why?''

Vicki thought about that for a moment. *Why, indeed?* She hadn't seen the two young men who lived
in the back basement apartment of her building since
the day they'd moved in. If in almost three years she
hadn't run into them in the hallway, by the only
door. . . . *Well, the odds are good you can miss someone indefinitely out here in all this space.* ''Never
mind.''

He shrugged, the fine spray of red-gold hair on his
chest glinting in the sun. ''Okay.''

They'd come to the end of lane and Vicki leaned
gracefully against the huge tree that anchored it to the
lawn. Mopping her dripping brow, she opened her
mouth to ask where everyone was when Peter threw
back his head and ran his voice wordlessly up and
down a double octave.

''Rose wants to tell you something,'' he said by way
of explanation.

Rose wanted to tell her about Frederick Kleinbein.

''I think she's imagining things,'' Peter volunteered
after his sister finished talking. ''What do you think,
Ms. Nelson?''

''I think,'' Vicki told them, ''that I'd better go speak
to Mr. Kleinbein.'' She didn't add that she doubted
the tree's falling at that time and in such a way had
been entirely natural. Off the top of her head, she could
think of at least two ways it could be done without
leaving a scent for the wer to trace. Had Peter actually

left the car, she was pretty certain he'd have returned to find his twin had been shot the same way as Silver and Ebon. Which meant the assassin's pattern wasn't tied to that tree in the woods. Which opened up a whole new can of worms.

Thank God for Frederick Kleinbein. His arrival had no doubt saved Cloud's life and, simultaneously, removed him from the suspect list.

All things considered though, she thought she'd better have a talk with him anyway.

Rose shot a triumphant look at her brother. "He lives just back of the crossroads. I can tell you how to get there if you want to take Henry's car."

"Henry's car?"

"Yeah. It's about three and a half miles, maybe a bit more. It's easy enough for four legs but a bit of a hike for two."

Peter leaned forward, nostrils flared. "What's wrong?"

Nothing's wrong. But, just as I suspected, I'm piss useless out here. You see, I can't. See that is. And I can't drive. How the hell am I supposed to do anything and what the hell can I tell you. . . .

She jumped as Rose reached out and stroked her arm, callused fingers lightly running over sweaty skin. She realized the touch was for comfort, not pity, and stopped herself from jerking the arm away.

"I don't drive," she told them, her voice hard-edged to keep it from shaking. "I can't see well enough."

"Oh, is that all." Peter leaned back relieved. "No problem. We'll drive you. I'll just go get the keys." He flashed her a dazzling grin and loped off to the house.

Oh, is that all? Vicki watched Peter disappear into the kitchen then turned to look at Rose, who smiled, pleased that the problem had been solved. *Don't judge them by human standards.* The phrase was rapidly becoming a litany.

* * *

". . . anyway, Uncle Stuart says that if you want the wood, it's yours."

"Good, good. You tell your uncle, I get it when heat breaks." Frederick Kleinbein swiped at his dripping face with the palm of one beefy hand. "So, I have late raspberries that rot because I am too fat and lazy to pick; you interested?"

The twins turned to Vicki, who shrugged. "Just don't ask me to help. I'll stay here in the shade and talk to Mr. Kleinbein." And as Mr. Kleinbein very obviously wanted to talk to her. . . .

"So," he began a moment later, "you are visiting from the city. You know Heerkens for long?"

"Not long at all. I'm a friend of a friend. Do you know them well?"

"Not what you call well. No." He glanced over to where Rose and Peter were barely visible behind a thick row of raspberry canes. "They keep apart that family. Not unfriendly, distant."

"And people respect that?"

"Why not? Farm is paid for. Kids go to school." The finger he waggled in her direction looked like a half cooked sausage. "No law says got to be party animals."

Vicki hid a smile. Party animals—now that was a concept.

He leaned forward, his whole bearing proclaiming he had a secret.

Here it comes, Vicki thought.

"You stay with them so you must know."

She shook her head, fighting to keep her expression vaguely confused. "Know what?"

"The Heerkens . . ."

"Yes?"

". . . the whole family . . ."

She leaned forward herself.

". . . are . . ."

Their noses were practically touching.

". . . nudists."

Vicki blinked and sat back, momentarily speechless.

Frederick Kleinbein sat back as well and nodded sagely, his jowls bobbing an independent emphasis. "They must keep clothes on for you so far." Then his entire face curved upward in a beatific smile. "Too bad, eh?"

"How do you know this?" Vicki managed at last.

The sausage finger waggled again. "I see things. Little things. Careful people, the Heerkens, but sometimes there are glimpses of bodies. That's why the big dogs, to warn them to put on clothes when people come." He shrugged. "Everyone knows. Most peoples, they say bodies are bad and go out of way to avoid Heerkens but me, I say who cares what they do on own land." He waved a hand at the raspberry bushes. "Kids are happy. What else matters? Besides," this time the smile came accompanied by a decidedly lascivious waggling of impressive eyebrows, "they are very nice bodies."

Vicki had to agree. So the surrounding countryside thought the Heerkens were nudists, did it? She doubted they'd have been able to deliberately create a more perfect camouflage. What people believe defines what people see, and people looking for flesh were not likely to find fur.

And it's a hell of a lot easier to believe in a nudist than a werewolf.

Except that someone, she reminded herself, feeling the weight of the second silver bullet dragging at her bag, *isn't following the party line.*

Although his nephew's jeep was still in the driveway, Mark himself appeared to be nowhere around. Carl sat down at the kitchen table and leaned his head in his hands, thankful for the time alone. The boy was his only sister's only son, flesh of his flesh, blood of his blood, and the only family he had remaining. Family must be more important then personal opinion.

Was it a sin, he wondered, that he couldn't find it in his heart to care for Mark? That he didn't even like him very much?

Carl suspected he was being used as a refuge of some sort. Why else would this nephew he hadn't seen in years suddenly appear on his doorstep for an indefinite stay? The boy—the man—was a sinner, there was no doubt about that. But he was also family and that fact had to outweigh the other.

Perhaps the Lord had sent Mark here, at this time, to be saved. Carl sighed and rubbed at a coffee ring on the table with his thumb. He was an old man and the Lord had asked a great deal of him lately.

Should I ask Mark where he goes at night?

Do I have the strength to know?

Seven

"These are our south fields, this is the conservation area, Mr. Kleinbein lives here, and here's old man Biehn's place." Peter squinted down at his sketch, then dragged another three lines into the dirt. "These are the roads."

"The Old School Road's crooked," Rose pointed out, leaning over his shoulder.

"There's a rock in the way."

"So do it here . . ." She suited the action to the words, smoothing her palm over his road and drawing in a new one with her fingertip. ". . . and you avoid the rock."

Peter snorted. "Then it's at the wrong angle."

"Not really. It still goes from the corner down. . . ."

"Down the wrong way," her brother interrupted.

"Does not!"

"Does so!"

They both had lips and fingers stained with berry juices and Vicki marveled at how easily they could switch from adults to children and back again. She'd decided on the drive back from Mr. Kleinbein's—who had parted from her with a "wink, wink, nudge, nudge" adjuration to keep her eyes open—not to tell them about the local belief that they were nudists. She hadn't quite decided whether or nor she was going to mention it to their Uncle Stuart; mostly because she doubted he'd care.

"You've got to bring the crossroads up here!"

"Do not."

"Do so!"

"It doesn't matter," Vicki told them, stopping the argument cold. The wer, she'd realized while watching them draw the neighborhood on a bald patch of lawn, had very little sense of mapping. Although they probably knew every bush and every fence post on their own territory, the dimensions Peter had drawn were not the dimensions Vicki remembered. She frowned and pushed her glasses back up her nose. "As near as I can tell, here's the tree. And here's where I ended up coming out of the woods."

"But *why* didn't you just follow your back trail?" Rose asked, still confused on that point despite explanations.

Vicki sighed. The wer also had a little trouble dealing with the concept of *getting lost*.

Before they could reopen the subject of noses, a small black head shoved itself under Vicki's hand as Shadow crept forward, trying to get a better look at what was going on.

Peter grabbed him by the scruff of the neck and hauled him back. "Get out of there you, you'll mess it up."

"No, it's all right." Vicki stood, dusting off the seat of her shorts. The grass on the lawn was sparse and bare dusty patches were common. "I think I've seen as much as I can here." She should be inside making phone calls; this really wasn't helping.

Shadow squirmed in his cousin's grasp and, when Peter released him, turned into a very excited small boy. "Show Vicki your trick, Peter!"

Under his tan, Peter turned a little red. "I don't think she wants to see it, kiddo."

"Yes she does!" Daniel bounced over to Vicki. "You do, don't you?"

She didn't, but how could she say no in the face of such determined enthusiasm? "Sure I do."

He bounced back over to Peter. "See!"

Peter sighed and surrendered. "All right," he reached out and tugged at the lock of hair falling into Daniel's eyes. "Go and get it."

Barking shrilly, Shadow raced off to the front of the house.

"Is he talking when he does that?" Vicki wondered aloud.

"Not really." Rose's ears pricked forward toward the sound. "Fur-form noises are kind of emoting out loud."

"So Shadow's barking translates into 'Oh boy! Oh boy! Oh boy'?"

The twins looked at each other and laughed. "Close enough," Rose admitted.

Shadow raced back silently, but only, Vicki suspected, because the huge yellow frisbee he carried made barking impossible. He dropped it at Peter's feet—it looked more than a little chewed—and sat back, panting expectantly.

Peter skimmed out of his shorts and scooped up the plastic disk. "You ready?" he asked.

The entire back end of Shadow's body wagged.

Looking not unlike an ancient Greek discus thrower, Peter whipped the frisbee into the air. Shadow took off after it and a heartbeat later so did Storm. Muscles rippling under his russet coat, he raced past the smaller wer, drew his hindquarters under and flung himself into the air, jaws spread, ready to clamp his teeth down on the rim of the disk.

Only to have it snatched out of his grasp by a larger black wer who hit the ground running with both Storm and Shadow in hot pursuit.

Rose giggled, thrust her sundress into Vicki's hands and Cloud took off after them. They raced around the yard for a moment or two then, working as a team, Cloud and Storm cut the larger wer off and jumped it. Shadow, still barking whenever he managed to find a spare breath, threw himself on the mix of tumbling bodies.

A moment later, Nadine looked up out of the pile of multicolored fur, tossed the frisbee to one side and grinned at Vicki. "So, you about ready for lunch?"

"We found tracks, not five hundred yards from the house." The words were almost an unintelligible growl. The silence that followed them took only a few seconds to fill with answering anger.

Nadine crossed the kitchen and clutched at her mate's arm. "Whose?" she demanded. "Whose tracks?"

"We don't know."

"But the scent. . . ."

"Garlic. The trail reeks of nothing but garlic."

"How old?" Peter wanted to know.

"Twelve hours. Maybe a little more. Maybe a little less." Stuart's hair was up and he couldn't remain still, pacing back and forth with jerky steps.

If Ebon had been shot from that tree in the woods, as all evidence seemed to suggest he had, five hundred yards and twelve hours meant the assassin had come within range of the house sometime last night.

"Maybe you'd all better stay at a hotel, in town, until this is over," Vicki suggested, knowing even as the words left her mouth what the reaction was going to be.

"No!" Stuart snapped, turning on her. "This is our territory and we will defend it!"

"He's not after your territory," Vicki pointed out, her own voice rising. "He's after your lives! Take them out of his range, just for a time. It's the only sensible thing to do!"

"We will not run."

"But if he can get that close, you can't protect yourselves from him."

Stuart's eyes narrowed and his words were nearly lost in his snarl. "It will not happen again."

"How do you propose to stop it?" This was worse than arguing with Celluci.

"We will guard. . . ."

"You haven't *been* guarding!"

"He has not been on our territory before!"

Vicki took a deep breath. This was getting nowhere fast. "At least send the children away."

"NO!"

Stuart's response was explosive and Vicki turned to Nadine for help. Surely *she'd* understand the necessity of sending the children to safety.

"The children must stay within the safety of the pack." Nadine held a solemn looking Daniel very tightly, one hand stroking his hair. Daniel, in turn, held tight to his mother.

"This coward with a gun does not run this pack." Stuart yanked his chair out from the table and threw himself down on it. "And his actions will not rule this pack. We will live as we live." He jabbed his finger at Vicki. "You will find him!"

He wasn't angry at her, Vicki realized, but at himself, at his perceived failure to protect his family. Even so, the heat of his gaze forced her to look away. "I will find him," she said, trying not to resent the strength of his rage. *Let's just hope I find him in time.*

Lunch began as an assault; meat ripped and torn between gleaming teeth, an obvious surrogate for an enemy's throat. Fortunately for Vicki's piece of mind, things calmed down fairly quickly, the wer—especially the younger wer—being incapable of sustaining a mood for any length of time when distracted by the more immediate concerns of who forgot to take the butter out of the fridge and just where exactly was the salt.

The entire family ate in human form, more or less in human style.

"It makes it easier on the kids when they go back to school," Nadine explained, putting Daniel's fork into his hand and suggesting that he use it.

The cold mutton accompanying the salad was greasy and not particularly palatable, but Vicki was so relieved it was cooked that she ate it gladly.

''Ms. Nelson went to see Carl Biehn this morning,'' Peter announced suddenly.

''Carl Biehn?'' Donald glanced over at Stuart, whose ears had gone back again, then at Vicki. ''Why?''

''It's important I talk to the neighbors,'' Vicki explained, shooting a look of her own at the dominant male. ''I need to know what they might have seen.''

''He hasn't been around here for years,'' Nadine said emphatically. ''Not since Stuart ran him off for frightening the girls. Jennifer had nightmares about his *God* for months.''

Stuart snorted. ''God. He wouldn't know a real God if it bit him on the butt. Old fool's a grasseater.''

Vicki blinked. ''What?''

''Vegetarian,'' Rose translated.

''Did he tell you that?''

''Didn't have to.'' Stuart cracked a bone and sucked out the marrow. ''He smells like a grasseater.''

Donald tossed a heel of bread onto the table and dusted his hands off against his bare thighs. ''He stopped me in town once and pointed out the evils of giving life to animals only to kill them.''

''He did it to me once too but I pointed out that killing animals was easier than eating them alive.'' Peter tossed a radish up into the air, caught it between his teeth, and crunched down with the maximum possible noise.

''Like majorly gross, Peter!'' Jennifer made a disgusted face at her cousin, who only grinned and continued devouring his lunch.

''You don't think it's old man Biehn, do you, Vicki?'' Rose asked quietly, pitching her voice under the general noise level around the table.

Did she? Living so close, Carl Biehn had opportunity to both accidentally discover the wers' secret and access the tree the shots had come from. He was in good physical condition for a man his age and deeply held religious beliefs were historically a tried and true motive for murder. He had, however, expressed an abhorrence for killing that Vicki believed and, besides a sneaker tread he shared with all and sundry, no evidence linked him to the crimes. The fact that she'd liked him, as subjective as that was, had to be considered. Good cops develop a sensitivity to certain personality types that, no matter how carefully hidden, set off subconscious alarms. Carl Biehn seemed like a decent human being and they were rare.

On the other hand, the next likeliest suspect was a police officer and Vicki didn't want to believe that Barry Wu was responsible. She glanced down the table at Colin who, while larger than his uncle and father, was still a small, wiry man and probably wouldn't have made the force under the old size requirements. He looked like someone had a knife in his heart and was slowly twisting the blade. He hadn't said two words since he'd sat down.

Did she think it was old man Biehn? No. Nor did she want to think it was Colin's partner. Nor could she completely rule either of them out, not until the murderer was found. A great many people had access to the woods, however, and in spite of the statistics, the most obvious suspects didn't always turn out to be guilty.

She turned back to Rose, waiting predator patient for an answer.

"Until I get more information, I have to suspect everyone, Rose, even Mr. Kleinbein. This is too important not to."

Having cleared the table of anything remotely like food, the wer were rising and going their separate ways. Donald had already changed, padded out to the porch, and collapsed in a dark triangle of shade. Shadow, with permission from his mother, had taken a bone into a corner and, holding it between his front paws, was chewing it into submission.

Vicki stood as Colin did, but he turned and headed

out of the kitchen without acknowledging her in any way.

"Colin!" Even Vicki stiffened at the command in Stuart's voice and Colin stopped dead, shoulders hunched. "Vicki wants to talk to you."

Slowly, Colin turned, canines gleaming.

"Colin. . . ." The name was a growl, low and menacing.

The younger wer hesitated for a moment, then his shoulders dropped and a curt motion of his head indicated Vicki should follow him.

It was far from gracious, but it would have to do. She fell into step behind him as he started up the stairs.

"It's too hot to walk outside, so we'll talk in my room," he said without turning. "Then the kids won't interrupt."

Vicki wasn't so sure of that, given the wer sense of privacy but, if it made Colin more comfortable, they could talk on the roof for all she cared.

His room was one of three in the addition built on over the woodshed and the door next to his was the first closed door Vicki had seen in the house.

"Henry," Colin said by way of explanation as they passed. "He bolts it from the inside."

"It's not a bedroom. . . ."

"No. It's a storage closet. But it doesn't have a window, and if we shuffle stuff around there's room for a cot."

Vicki brushed her palm over the dark wood and wondered if Henry could sense her in the hallway. Wondered what it was like, lying there in the dark.

"I haven't seen the sun in over four hundred years."

She sighed and entered Colin's room. He threw himself down on the bed, fingers laced behind his head, watching her through narrowed eyes. Despite the outwardly relaxed position, every muscle in his body hummed with tension, ready for fight or flight. Vicki wasn't sure which, nor did she want to find out.

"I used to get the laundry to do mine, too," she

told him, nodding at the half dozen clean uniform shirts hanging on the closet door, still in their plastic bags. Pushing a pair of sweatpants off a wooden chair, she sat down. "I had better things to do with my time than iron.

"So," she leaned forward, elbows resting on her knees, "do you think your partner did it?" Colin's eyes narrowed further and his lips drew back but before he could move she added matter-of-factly, "Or do you want to help me prove he didn't?"

Slowly, his eyes never leaving her face, Colin sat up. Vicki accepted his puzzled scrutiny with her blandest expression and waited. The next line was his.

"You don't think Barry did it," he said at last.

"I didn't say that." She rested her chin on her folded hands. "But I don't *want* to believe he did it and you're the best person to prove he didn't. For Chrissakes, Colin, start thinking like a cop, not a . . . a sheepdog." He flinched. "Did he have the opportunity?"

For a moment she wasn't sure he was going to answer her, then he mirrored her position on the edge of the bed and sighed. "Yeah. We were working days both times it happened. He knows the farm and he knows the conservation area. We got off at eleven last night and he could have easily come out here after shift and made those tracks."

"Okay, that's one against, and we know he has the skill. . . ."

"He's going to the next Olympics, he's that good. But if he's casting silver bullets I couldn't find any evidence of it and, believe me, I looked."

"Does he have a motive?"

Colin shook his head. "How should I know? If he's doing it, maybe he's crazy."

"Is he?"

"Is he what?"

"Crazy? You spend eight hours a day with the man. If he's crazy, you should have noticed something." She rolled her eyes at his bewildered expression and used her voice like a club. ''Think, damn it! Use your training!''

Colin's ears went back and his breathing sped up but he held himself in check and Vicki could actually see him thinking about it. She was impressed by his control. If a stranger had used that tone on her, she'd have probably done something stupid.

After a moment, he frowned. ''I wouldn't swear to this in court,'' he said slowly, ''but I'd bet my life on his sanity.''

''You are betting your life on his sanity,'' Vicki pointed out dryly, ''every time you walk out of the station with him. Now we've settled that, why don't we concentrate on proving he *didn't* do it.''

''But. . . .''

''But what?'' Vicki snapped, getting a little tired of Colin's attitude. She recognized that he was in a terrible position, torn between his family and his partner, but that was no reason to shut off his brain. ''Just tell me about the man.''

''We, uh, we were at the Police College together.'' He ran his hands through his hair, the cropped cut accentuating the point of both chin and ears. ''I wouldn't even be a cop if it wasn't for Barry, and I guess he wouldn't be one if it wasn't for me. He was the only 'visible ethnic minority' cadet there and I was, well, what I am. We ended up together to survive. When we graduated, we managed to stay together—well, mostly, it's not like we're mated or anything. . . .''

Vicki wasn't surprised by Barry's philosophical reaction to his partner's actual race. In the ''us against them'' attitude that the job forced police officers to develop, finding out that one of ''us'' was a werewolf could be dealt with, at least on an individual basis. *Can I depend on my partner to back me up?* was the crucial question, not, *Does my partner bay at the moon?* And now that she thought about it, Vicki had known a number of cops who bayed at the moon.

''. . . and the night I got shot. . . .''

"Wait a minute, you what?"

Colin shrugged it off. "We surprised a couple of punks during a holdup. They came out shooting. I took a slug in the leg. It was nothing."

"Wrong. Very wrong." Vicki grinned. "Barry was there?"

"Course he was."

"He saw you bleed?"

"Yeah."

"You probably talked later about dying, about how you thought you were going to be killed?"

"Yeah, but. . . ."

"Why would Barry shoot at the wer with silver bullets—expensive rounds that he'd have to make himself, risking discovery—when he knows that good old lead will do the job?"

"To throw us off his trail?"

"Colin!" Vicki threw her hands up. "That would take a crazy person and you've already told me Barry is sane. Trust your instincts. At least when you've got enough facts to back them up."

Colin opened his mouth, closed it, and then shuddered as if a great weight had been lifted off of him. He leapt to his feet, threw back his head, and howled.

Vicki, who had pretty much forgotten that he was naked, found herself suddenly made very aware of it. The wer might react sexually to scent and therefore not react at all to humans, but humans had a visually based libido and Vicki's had just belted her in the crotch.

Oh, lord, why me? she thought as huge black paws came down on her shoulders and a large pink tongue swept vigorously across her face.

After Colin had galloped off to confront his pack leader—he needed Stuart's permission to finally speak to Barry about what had been going on—Vicki spent the early part of the afternoon on the phone, confirming that the game warden had, indeed, been up north since the beginning of August and had, in fact, been there on the two nights of the murders, his location supported by a bar full of witnesses. That done, and his name crossed off her list, she changed her clothes and had Rose and Peter drive her into London.

Storm spent the entire trip with his head out the window, mouth open, eyes slitted against the wind, ears flat against his skull.

The membership lists of both bird-watching clubs were relatively easy to get. She merely showed the presidents of each her identification and told them she'd been hired to find a distant relative of a very rich man.

"All I have to go on is that they once lived in the London area and enjoyed bird-watching. There's a great deal of money involved if I find them."

"But are you looking for a man or a woman?"

"I don't know," Vicki looked peeved. *"He's lost almost all his marbles and that's all he can remember. Oh, yes, he mumbled something about this relative being a marksman."*

Neither president rose to the bait. If the killer was one of the birders, he or she hadn't mentioned his or her interest in firearms to the executive of either club.

"You don't have a third cousin named Anthony Carmaletti, do you?" Vicki crossed her fingers as she asked. *If either of them did have a third cousin named Anthony Carmaletti it was going to blow her rich, dying relative story right out of the water.*

She received one definite no with a twenty minute lecture on genealogy, one "I'll ask my mother, can you get back to me tomorrow?" from an octogenarian, and both lists. *And Celluci says I'm a lousy liar. Ha.*

"Now what?" Rose asked as she got back into the car after the second stop.

"Now, I need the membership list of the photography club, but I doubt the YMCA will just hand it over, and I need the OPP list of registered firearms, which should be a little easier to get . . ." Cops tended to cooperate with their own. ". . . but right at the moment, I need to talk to Dr. Dixon."

First impressions said Dr. Dixon could not have been the killer. He was a frail old man who wouldn't have made it to the tree, let alone climbed it carrying a high-powered rifle and scope.

They had a short but pleasant visit. Dr. Dixon told Vicki embarrassing stories about Rose and Peter when they were children, which the twins paid no attention to as they were busy in the next room decimating his record collection.

"Opera," the doctor explained when Vicki wondered what was going on. "Every wer I've ever met is crazy about it."

"Every wer?" Vicki asked.

"Every wer *I've* met," he reiterated. "Stuart's old pack in Vermont prefers Italian, but they're close enough to civilization they can afford to be picky. Most of the rest, at least in Canada, particularly the pack just by Algonquin Park and the lot up by Mooseane, are glued to the CBC Sunday afternoons."

"How many packs are there?"

"Well, I just mentioned four, and there's at least two up in the Yukon, one in northern Manitoba. . . ." He frowned. "How the hell should I know? Enough for genetic diversity. Although at some point they seem to have inbred for opera. Can't get enough. I lend this lot records and," he raised his voice, "occasionally they bring them back."

"Next time, Dr. Dixon," Peter called. "We promise."

"Sure you will," he muttered. "If that damned pup's been chewing on them again I'll. . . ."

"Scratch him behind the ears and tell him he's adorable," Rose finished, coming into the room with a half dozen albums under her arm, "just like you always do."

While they were leaving, Vicki paused on the front step and watched Storm race across the lawn after a butterfly.

"What happens when you die?" she asked the doctor.

He snorted. "I rot. Why?"

"I mean, what happens to them? They won't stop needing a doctor just because you're gone."

"When the time is right, I'll tell the young doctor who took over my practice." He laughed suddenly. "She grew up not knowing if she wanted to be a vet or a GP. The wer should be right up her alley."

"Don't wait too long," Vicki warned.

"Don't stick that investigating nose of yours in where it doesn't belong," Dr. Dixon shot back. "I've known the Heerkens family for years, longer than you've been alive. I have no intention of dropping dead and leaving them to face the world alone."

"They *won't* be alone."

He grinned at her defensive tone, but his voice was soft as he said, "No, I don't suppose they will be."

Jennifer and Marie didn't bother coming in for dinner.

"They shared a rabbit about an hour ago," Nadine explained, smiling fondly, sadly, out the window at them. They were curled so tightly around each other that it was difficult to see where one fur-form ended and the other began.

Colin had long since left for work so only the seven of them sat down at the table. Daniel did his best to make up for the missing three.

After dinner, Vicki worked on her notes—impressions of Carl Biehn, Frederick Kleinbein, the birders, the doctor, the new set of tracks—and then she just sat, attempting to put the day and the day's discoveries in order. Order kept escaping her, she had a number of bits and pieces but nothing that definitely fit into the pattern. The opera in the background wasn't a lot of help and the weird harmonics added by her hosts could only be called distracting.

Actually, Vicki could think of a number of other

things to call them, but she went to the pond to watch Shadow hunt frogs instead. Under the circumstances, it seemed safer—not only for Shadow but for herself as well.

"Don't let him eat too many," Nadine called over the music as they left, "or he'll make himself sick."

"I'm not at all surprised," Vicki muttered, but she ended up letting him eat both frogs he caught. He'd worked so hard at it, bounding this way and that, barking hysterically, that she felt he deserved them.

Back at the house, dusk seemed to stretch for hours, the crickets and Pavarotti singing duets to the setting sun. Vicki's vision dimmed and the sound of the wind moving in the trees became the sound of death quietly approaching the house: the tap of two twigs, a rifle bolt drawn back. She knew she was allowing her imagination to overrule common sense even while she waited for the gunshot that would tell her it wasn't imagination at all. Finally, the darkness drove her to the kitchen table where the hanging bulb surrounded her with a hard edged circle of sight.

At last, Donald lifted his head and, nostrils flaring, announced, "Henry's up."

Vicki pulled her glasses off and rubbed at her eyes. It was about time. *You know it's been a strange day,* she mused, *when you're looking forward to the arrival of the bloodsucking undead.*

Eight

Usually, when he awoke in a place other than his carefully shielded sanctuary, there would be a moment of near panic while memory fought to reestablish itself. Tonight, he knew even before full consciousness returned, for the unmistakable scent of the wer saturated his tiny chamber.

He stretched and lay still for a moment, senses extended until they touched Vicki's life. The hunger rose to pulse in time with her heartbeat. He would feed tonight.

As Henry made his way downstairs, Mozart's *Don Giovanni* filled the old farmhouse and, he suspected, a good portion of the surrounding countryside. Stereo systems had been one piece of human culture the wer had embraced wholeheartedly. Henry winced as a descant Mozart could never have imagined soared up and over and around the recorded soprano.

Oh, well, I suppose it could be worse. He braced himself against Shadow's enthusiastic welcome. *It could be New Kids on the Block.*

With one hand fondling Shadow's ears, Henry paused on the kitchen's threshold, allowing his eyes to become accustomed to the light. He half expected to see Vicki seated at the table, but the room was empty save for Donald who sat, feet up, watching Jennifer and Marie work their way through a sink full of dishes. Seconds later, this simple domestic scene shattered as Shadow bounded forward and shoved a cold, wet nose against the back of Marie's bare legs. A plate hit the floor, bounced, and lay there forgotten as both twins chased their younger brother out of the house.

"Evening," Donald grunted as Henry bent to pick up the plate. "Don't suppose you know any opera singers?"

He'd known an opera dancer once, almost two hundred years ago, but that wasn't quite the same thing. "Sorry, no. Why?"

"Thought if you knew one, you could bring her out." Donald waved an arm in the air, the gesture encompassing *Don Giovanni*. "Be nice to hear this stuff live for a change."

Henry was about to point out that Toronto wasn't that long a drive and that the Royal Canadian Opera Company, while not Vienna, definitely had its moments when he had a sudden vision of wer at the theater and blanched. "Where is everyone?" he asked instead.

"Tag and Sky . . ."

Stuart and Nadine, Henry translated.

". . . are out hunting, in spite of protests from your Ms. Nelson. You saw the exit of the terrible trio. Colin is at work, and my other two are . . ."

The descant rose above the tenor solo, wrapping the notes almost sideways to each other.

". . . in the living room with their heads between the speakers. They got a couple of old recordings from the doctor today, obscure companies that aren't out yet on CD." He scratched at the mat of red hair on his chest and frowned. "Personally, I think the tenor is a little sharp."

"Why the doctor? Was someone hurt?"

"Everyone is fine." Vicki's voice came from behind him, from the door leading to the bathroom, and her tone added, *so far.* Henry turned as she continued. "I needed to talk to him to make sure he wasn't the killer."

"And are you sure."

"Quite. It's not him, it's not Colin's partner, and

it's not the game warden. Unfortunately, at least another thirty-seven people regularly go wandering through the woods with high-powered binoculars and it could be any one of them. Not to mention an unknown number of nature photographers whose names I don't have yet.''

Henry raised a brow and smiled. ''Sounds like you've had a productive day.''

Vicki snorted. ''I've had a day,'' she amended, shoving her glasses back up her nose. ''I'm not really any closer to finding out who *did* do it. And Stuart and Nadine have gone for a little nocturnal hike.'' Her opinion of that dripped off her voice.

''They're hunters, they. . . .''

''They can hunt at the local supermarket until this is over,'' she snapped. ''Like the rest of us.''

''They aren't like the rest of us,'' Henry reminded her. ''You can't judge them by. . . .''

''Leave it! I've had just about as much of that observation as I can take.'' She sighed at his expression and shook her head. ''I'm sorry. I'm just a little frustrated by illogical behavior. Can we go somewhere and talk?''

''Outside?''

She scowled. ''It's dark, I won't be able to see, and besides, outside is crawling with bugs. What about my room?''

''What about mine?'' While it wasn't large, his was the only room in the house with a door that could be bolted from the inside. If they began in his room, they wouldn't have to move later when it came time to feed. He felt her blood calling him and the plate he still held snapped between his hands. ''Oh, hell. Donald, I'm sorry.''

Donald only shrugged, a suspiciously knowing smile lurking around the edges of his mouth. ''Don't worry about it. We're kinda hard on dishes around here anyway.''

Giving thanks that his nature no longer allowed him

to blush—his fair Tudor coloring had been the curse of his short life—Henry dropped both halves of the plate in the garbage and turned once again to Vicki. For a change, he found her expression unreadable. "Shall we?" he asked, taking refuge in formality.

Scalloped glass light fixtures illuminated the stairs and the upper hall in the original section of the house but the wer, who could see almost as well in the dark, hadn't bothered extending them down the hall of the addition.

Vicki swore and stopped dead at the edge of the twilight. "Maybe my room is better after all. . . ."

Henry tucked her arm in his and pulled her gently forward. "It isn't far," he said soothingly.

"Don't patronize me," she snapped. "I'm going blind, not senile."

But her fingers tightened against the bend of his elbow and Henry could feel the tension in her step.

The bare forty watt bulb hanging from the center of Henry's closet—it was gross exaggeration to call it a room—threw enough light for Vicki to see Henry's face but the piled junk held shadows layered upon shadows. Dragging his pillow up behind her back, she leaned against the far wall and watched him bolt the door.

He could scent the beginning of her desire.

Slowly, he turned, hunger rising.

"So." She kicked off her sandals and scratched at a mosquito bite. *Nothing like taking care of one itch to distract you from another.* "Sit down and I'll tell you about my day."

He sat. There wasn't much else he could do.

". . . and that's the suspect list as it stands right now."

"You really believe it could be one of these bird-watchers?"

"Or the photographers. Hell, I'd rather it was Carl Biehn or his slimy nephew than some lone hiker we'll never track down."

"You don't think it was Mr. Biehn."

"Get real. He's a nice guy." She sighed. "Course, I have been wrong before and I haven't taken him off the list. Mind you, at this point, I've only got three people who I have taken off the list."

"I don't believe that." Henry picked up the bare leg stretched out on the cot beside him and began kneading her calf, digging his thumbs deep behind the muscle and then rolling it between his palms.

After a half-hearted attempt to drag it out of his grip, Vicki left her leg where it was. "Believe what?"

"That you've been wrong before."

"Yeah. Well. It happens . . ." She had to swallow before she could answer. ". . . occasionally."

Henry knew he could have her now, she'd made her point and would be willing. More than willing—the tiny room all but vibrated to the pounding of her heart. He wrapped iron control around his hunger.

"So." Slapping her lightly on the bottom of the foot, he laid her leg aside. "What did you want me to do?"

Her eyes snapped open and her brows drew down.

Henry waited, his expression one of polite interest.

For a heartbeat, Vicki teetered between anger and amusement. Amusement won and she grinned.

"You can stake out that tree I found. What wind there is—and there's bugger all air moving that I can tell—has changed again so that it's off the fields. If someone shows up with a .30 caliber rifle waiting for a target, grab him and it's case over."

"All right." He began to rise, but she swung her leg across his lap, barring his way.

"Hold it right there . . . and don't raise that eyebrow at me. We keep this up much longer and we'll end up ripping each other's clothes off in the kitchen and embarrassing ourselves. I don't want that to happen, this is one of my favorite T-shirts. Now that we've both exhibited control over our baser natures, what do you say we call it a draw and get on with things?"

"Fair enough." He held out his hand, intending to scoop her up into his arms in the best romantic tradition, but instead found himself yanked down hard against her mouth.

They didn't rip the T-shirt, but they did stretch it a little.

At the end, he took control and when his teeth broke through the skin of her wrist, she cried out, digging the fingers of her free hand hard into his shoulder. She kept moving as he drank and only stilled as he licked the wound clean, the coagulant in his saliva sealing the tiny puncture.

"That was . . . amazing," she sighed a moment later, her breath warm against the top of his head.

"Thank you." The salty smell of her skin filled nose and throat and lungs. "I was pretty amazed myself." He squirmed around until he could see her face. "Tell me, do you always make love with your glasses on?"

She grinned and pushed them higher with an unsteady finger. "Only the first time. After that, I can rely on memory. And for some things, I have a phenomenal memory." She moved, just to feel him move against her. "Are you always this cool?"

"Lower body temperature. Do you mind?"

"It's August and we're in a closet with no ventilation. What do you think?" Her fingernails traced intricate patterns along his spine. "You feel great. This feels great."

"Feels great," he echoed, "but I've got to go." He said it gently, as he sat up, one hand trailing along the slick length of her body. "The nights are short and if you want me to solve this case for you. . . ."

"For the wer," she corrected, yawning, too mellow to react to his smart-ass comment. "Sure, go ahead, eat and run." She snatched her foot back, away from his grab, and watched him dress. "When can we do this again?"

"Not for a while. The blood has to renew."

''You couldn't have taken more than a few mouthfuls; how long is a while?''

Tucking his shirt into his jeans, he leaned down and kissed her, sucking for a moment on her lower lip. ''We have lots of time.''

''Maybe you do,'' she muttered, ''but I'll be dead in sixty, seventy years tops and I don't want to waste any more of it.''

Police Constable Barry Wu glanced over at his partner and wished he knew what the hell was going on. Whatever had been bothering Colin for the last few weeks, getting under his skin and twisting, bothered him no longer—which was great, a depressed werewolf was not the most pleasant companion in a patrol car—but Colin still wouldn't say what the problem had been and Barry didn't like that. If Colin was in some kind of trouble, he should be the first to know. They were partners, for Chrissakes. ''So.'' He peered up and down Fellner Avenue as they crossed the intersection; it looked quiet. ''Everything's all right now?''

Colin sighed. ''Like I told you at the beginning of shift, we're working on it. I'll tell you what's happening the moment Stuart releases me.'' Stuart had proven damned elusive this afternoon, but Colin had every intention of tracking the pack leader down the moment he got off shift and laying Vicki's conclusions before him. Now that loyalties no longer pulled him in two directions, the sooner he could talk this whole thing over with Barry the better.

''But it's about me?'' Barry prodded.

''No, I told you, not anymore.''

''But it *was* about me?''

''Listen, can you just trust me until tomorrow night? I swear, I'll be able to tell you everything by then.''

''Tomorrow night?''

''Yeah.''

Barry maneuvered the car around the corner onto Ashland Avenue; on hot summer nights, gangs of kids often hung out around the Arena and the police liked to keep an eye on the place. "All right, sheep-fucker. I can wait."

Colin's lip curled. "You're lucky you're driving."

Barry grinned. "I wouldn't have said it if I hadn't been. . . ."

Henry stood for a moment, staring into the woods, one hand resting on the top rail of the cedar fence. In high summer, the woods seethed with life, with hunters and hunted, far too many for him to separate one from the other. He sensed no human lives near but couldn't be sure if that was due to their absence or to the masking of the smaller lives around them.

Had it been a mistake to feed? he wondered. Hunger would have increased his sensitivity to the presence of blood. *Mind you,* he admitted, smiling at the memory of Vicki moving beneath him, *in the end, I don't think I had much choice.*

In the past, when he stayed with the wer for longer than three days and it became imperative to feed, he'd drive into London for a couple of hours and hire a prostitute. He didn't mind paying occasionally—spread over time it was still cheaper than buying groceries. Upon a moment's reflection, he decided not to share that thought with Vicki.

The fence was barely a barrier, and a moment later he moved shadow silent through the trees, following the trail Vicki had laid that morning. A small creature crossed his path, then, catching the scent of so large a predator, froze, its heart beating like a trip-hammer. He heard it scurry away once he'd passed and wished it Godspeed; the odds were good it wouldn't survive the night. The wer had come this way, probably on the hunt, but not lately as the spoor had faded to hints and that only where the forest floor retained some dampness.

He ducked under a branch and plucked free a single golden-brown hair from the twig that had captured it.

Vicki hadn't done too well in the woods, the evidence of that was all around him—a faint signature of her blood marked much of the trail. Coming as she did from a world of steel and glass, he supposed this was hardly surprising. Tucking the hair safely in his pocket, he continued along her path, allowing his mind to wander with her memory while he walked.

He hadn't intended to come out tonight, but he hadn't been able to sleep so he took that as a sign. Settling back in the tree, drawing in deep breaths of the warm, pine-scented air, he brushed away a rivulet of sweat and squinted at the sky. The stars were a hundred thousand gleaming jewels and the waning moon basked in reflected glory. There would be light enough.

Below and behind him, some large creature blundered about. Perhaps a cow or sheep had wandered into the conservation area from one of the nearby farms. It didn't matter. Now that the wind had changed, his interest lay in the pale rectangles of field beyond the woods. They would come to check the sheep and he would be waiting.

With the barrel of his rifle braced against a convenient limb, he laid his cheek gently against the butt and flicked on the receiver of his night scope. He'd ordered the simplest infrared scope from a Bushnell catalog back in early summer, when he'd first known what he had to do. It had cost him more than he could really afford, but the money had been well spent. Nor did he begrudge the continuing outlay for lithium batteries, replaced before every mission. A man is only as good as his equipment—his old sergeant had made sure every man he commanded remembered that.

Under the cross hairs, the ghostly outline of trees began to show, punctuated here and there by the dim red heat signatures of small animals. Without bothering to turn on the emitter, he scanned both fields, registering nothing more than the sheep. The sheep were innocent. They had no control over the masters they had. Then he came back to the trees.

They hunted the conservation area on occasion. He knew it. Perhaps tonight *they* would hunt and he would. . . .

He frowned at a flash of red between two trees. Showing too dim for the size, he had no idea what it might be. Moving slowly, silently, he flicked on the emitter, playing the beam of infrared light over the area. Although the naked eye could see no difference, his scope brightened as if he'd turned on a high-powered red flashlight.

The creature he'd scanned should be. . . .

With an effort, Henry brought himself back to the woods. It was infinitely pleasanter replaying the earlier part of the night, but he knew he must be getting close to the pine. He lifted his head to scan the treetops . . .

. . . and snapped it back snarling as a beam of red light raked across his eyes.

"Holy shit!" Mark Williams raised his uncle's shotgun in trembling hands. He didn't know what that was. He didn't care. He'd had nightmares about things like that, the kind of nightmares that jerked you awake sweating, scrabbling for the light, desperately trying to push back the darkness.

It didn't look human. It didn't look safe.

He pulled the trigger.

The buckshot had spread enough that it did little real damage when it hit, tracing a pattern of holes down the outside of his right hip and thigh. The light had been an annoyance. This was an attack.

Henry had warned Vicki once that his kind held the beast much closer to the surface than mortals did. As blood began to slowly seep into his jeans, he let it loose.

A heartbeat later, a slug hit him in high in the left

shoulder and spun him around, lifting him off his feet. His skull cracked hard against the trunk of a tree and he dropped, barely conscious, to the ground.

Through the pain, through the throbbing of his life in his ears, he thought he heard voices, men's voices, one almost hysterical, the other low and intense. He knew it was important that he listen, that he learn, but he couldn't seem to focus. The pain he could deal with. He'd been shot before and knew that even now his body had begun to mend. He fought against the waves of gray, trying to hold onto self, but it was like trying to hold sand that kept seeping out of his grasp.

The voices were gone; where, he had no idea.

Then a hand reached down and turned him gently over. A voice he knew said quietly, "We've got to get him back to the house."

"I don't think he can walk. Go for Donald, he's too heavy for you to carry."

Stuart. He recognized Stuart. That gave him a place to start from. By the time Nadine returned with Donald, he'd managed to grab onto his scattered wits and force them into a semblance of reason. His head felt eggshell fragile, but if he held it carefully, very carefully, he could keep the world from twisting too far off center.

In spite of rough handling, Henry's head had almost cleared by the time the wer got him to the house. A number of gray patches continued to drift up from the swelling at the base of his skull but, essentially, he was back.

He could see Vicki waiting on the porch, peering anxiously into the darkness. She looked softer and more vulnerable than he'd ever seen her. As Stuart and Donald carried him into her reach, she stretched out a hand and lightly touched his cheek.

Her brows snapped down. "What the fuck happened to you?"

"Of course I followed you!" Mark Williams gulped a little more whiskey from the water glass in his hand.

"I get back a little early from a friendly poker game and see my aged uncle sneaking out of the house in the middle of the night carrying . . ." He waved a hand at the rifle now lying in pieces on the kitchen table. ". . . that, off to do God knows what. . . ."

"God knows," Carl interrupted quietly, working the oily rag along the barrel.

"Fine. God knows. But I don't. And," he slammed the now empty glass down on the table, "after what I just went through, I think I deserve an explanation."

Carl stared up at his nephew for a moment, then sighed. "Sit down."

"Okay. I'll sit." Mark threw himself into a kitchen chair. "You talk. What the hell were you planning on hunting out there and what was that thing that attacked me?"

Ever since the Lord had shown him what lived on the Heerkens farm and had let him know where his duty lay, Carl Biehn had been afraid he wouldn't be strong enough. He was an old man, older than he looked, and the Lord had given one old man a terrible burden to carry. Mark was not who he would have chosen to help him bear his cross, but the Lord worked in mysterious ways and apparently Mark had also been chosen. It made a certain sense he supposed, the boy was his only living relative, and by pulling that trigger tonight he'd proven he had the strength to enter the fray. Perhaps his own sins would be washed away in the blood of the ungodly he was to help destroy.

Carl made his decision and took the three rounds he'd prepared from his vest pocket, standing them on the table. They gleamed in the overhead light like tiny missiles.

"Holy shit! That's silver!"

"Yes."

Mark stroked one finger down the bullet head and laughed a bit hysterically. "You trying to tell me you're hunting werewolves?"

"Yes."

In the sudden silence the ticking of the kitchen clock sounded unnaturally loud.

The old boy's flipped. He's right out of his tiny little mind. Werewolves. He's crazy.

And then Carl started to talk. Of how he'd been out bird-watching in late spring and seen the first change by accident. How he'd seen the others by design. How he'd recognized a creature of the devil. Realized that this was why none of the cursed family ever entered God's house. Realized they were not God's creatures but Satan's, sent by the Great Deceiver to spread darkness on the earth. Gradually came to know what he must do.

They must be sent back to hell. And they must be sent back in the form that was not a mockery of God's image. It must be done in secret under the cover of the night lest the Lord of Lies try to stop him.

To his surprise, Mark found himself believing. It was the weirdest goddamned story he'd ever heard, but it had the undeniable ring of truth.

"Werewolves," he muttered, shaking his head.

"Creatures of the evil one," his uncle agreed.

"And you're killing them?" *And this is the guy who thinks eating a burger is a sin.*

"I am sending them back to their dark master. Demons cannot actually be killed."

"But you're sending them with silver bullets?"

"Silver is the Lord's metal as it paid for the life of His son."

"Jesus H. Christ."

"Do *not* blaspheme."

Mark looked down at the rifle, now cleaned and reassembled, then back up at his uncle. The man was a moral nut case, something that had to be remembered. A well armed moral nut case and one hell of a shot. "Yeah. Sorry. So, uh, what about that thing in the woods tonight?"

"I don't know." Carl laced his fingers together and sighed. "I shot him to protect you."

Sweat beaded Mark's forehead as he remembered and his heart began to race. For an instant, he thought he might lose control of his bladder again. He'd looked at Death tonight and he'd never forget the feel of icy fingers closing around his life, no matter how badly he might want to. That experience, primal and terrifying, made it easier to believe the rest. "Maybe," he offered, swallowing heavily, "it was Old Nick himself, come to check on his charges."

Carl nodded slowly. "Perhaps, but if so, I will leave him to the Lord."

Easy for you to say. Mark wiped damp hands on his jeans. *It wasn't going for your throat.* "What about the woman?"

"The woman?"

"Yeah, that Nelson babe who wandered by this morning."

"An innocent bystander, nothing more. You will leave her out of this."

But Mark remembered the bits of pine stuck to a Blue Jays T-shirt and wasn't so sure.

"A .30 caliber rifle at that range should've blown your fucking shoulder off." Vicki secured the end of the gauze and frowned down at her handiwork. "There's no way your collarbone should've been able to deflect that shot."

Henry smiled at the incredulous disbelief in Vicki's voice. The pain had fallen to tolerable levels and the damage had been much less than he'd feared. Theoretically, he should be able to regenerate a lost limb but he had no real desire to test the theory. A broken collarbone and a chunk of flesh blown off the top of his shoulder, he could live with. "My kind has stronger bones than yours," he told her, attempting to flex the arm. Vicki made a fist and looked ready to use it, so he stopped.

"Stronger?" She snorted. "Fucking titanium."

"Not quite. Titanium wouldn't have broken." He winced as Donald dug yet another piece of buckshot out of his thigh then turned back to Vicki. "Do you realize your language deteriorates when you're worried?"

"What the hell are you talking about?"

"You've done more swearing in the last hour than you have since we've met."

"Yeah?" She snapped the first aid kit shut with unnecessary force. "Well, I've had more to swear about, haven't I? I don't understand how this happened. You're supposed to be so great at night. What were you thinking about?"

He didn't see any reason to lie. "You. Us. What happened earlier."

Vicki's eyes narrowed. "Isn't that just like a man. Four hundred and fifty fucking years old and he's still thinking with his balls."

"That's the lot." Donald straightened and threw the tweezers into the bowl with the shot. "Few hours and you'll be good as new. Some of the shallower holes are healing already."

"You're pretty good at that," Henry noted, elevating his leg a little to get a better look.

Donald shrugged. "Used to get lots of practice twenty, thirty years ago. Folks were faster on the trigger back then and fur only deflects so much. Used to have a pattern much like that on my butt." Twisting around in a way no human spine could handle, he studied the body part in question. "Seems to be gone now." He picked up the bowl and headed for the door. "If you were one of us, I'd suggest you change a few times to clear out any possible infection. Or lick it. As it is. . . ." He shrugged and was gone.

"I wasn't even going to ask!" Henry protested as Vicki glared down at him.

"Good thing." Lick buckshot holes indeed! She couldn't hold the glare. It became a grin, then a worried frown as a new problem occurred to her. "Will you need to feed again?"

He shook his head, regretting it almost immediately. "Tomorrow maybe, not tonight."

"After the attack by the demon, you needed to feed right away."

"Trust me, I was in much worse shape after the attack by the demon."

Vicki rested her hand lightly on the flat expanse of Henry's stomach, just where the line of red-gold hair began below his navel. The motion was proprietary without being overtly sexual. *"Can* you feed tomorrow?"

He covered her hand with his good one. "We'll work something out."

She nodded, if not satisfied at least willing to wait. The desire she felt was embarrassing and she hoped like hell Henry's vampiric vibrations were responsible. Overactive hormones were the last thing she needed. "You know, I'm amazed you've managed to survive for four centuries; first the demon, now this, and in only five short months."

"You may not believe this, but until I met you I lived the staid, boring life of a romance writer."

Both her brows rose and her glasses slipped to the end of her nose.

"Oh, all right," he admitted, "the night life was a bit better, but these sorts of things never happened to me."

"Never?"

He grinned as he remembered, although the event had been far from funny at the time. A woman—all right, his preoccupation with a woman—had been responsible for that disaster too. "Well, hardly ever. . . ."

His right knee felt twice its normal size and barely held his weight. A lucky blow from the blacksmith's iron hammer had slammed into the side of the joint.

A man would never have walked again. Henry Fitzroy, vampire, had gotten up and run but the damage and the pain held him to a mortal's pace.

He could hear the dogs. They were close.

He should have sensed the trap. Heard or smelled or seen the men waiting in the dark corners of the room. But he'd been so anxious to feed, so anxious to lose himself in the arms of his little Mila, that he never suspected a thing. Never suspected that little Mila, of the sweet smile and soft thighs and hot blood, had confessed her sin to the priest and he had roused the village.

The presence of a vampire outweighed the sanctity of the confessional.

The dogs were gaining. Behind them came the torches and the stakes and the final death.

Had they not placed their faith so strongly in the cross, they would have had him. Only the blacksmith had presence of mind enough to swing as he broke through their circle and made for the door.

His leg twisted and white fire shot through his entire body. The sound of his own blood loud in his ears, he clutched desperately at a tree, fighting to stay upright. He couldn't go on. He couldn't stop.

It hurts. Oh, God, how it hurts.

The dogs were closer.

He couldn't die like this, not after barely a hundred years; hunted down like a beast in the night. His ribs pressed tight around his straining heart, as though they already felt the final pressure of the stake.

The dogs were almost on him. The night had narrowed to their baying and the pain.

He didn't see the cliff.

He missed the rocks at the water's edge by little more than the width of a prayer, then the world turned over and around and he almost drowned before he managed to claw his way back to the air. Unable to fight the current, he gave himself over to it. Fortunately, it was spring and the river ran deep—most of its teeth were safely submerged under three or four feet of water. Most. Not all.

Just before dawn, Henry dragged himself up onto the shore and wedged his battered body as deep as it would go into a narrow stone cleft. It was damp and cold, but the sun would not reach so far and, for the moment, he was safe.

It had never meant more.

"No, sir. Never any trouble from Mr. Fitzroy." Greg squared his shoulders and looked the police officer in the eye. "He's a good tenant."

"No wild parties?" Celluci asked. "Complaints from the neighbors?"

"No sir. Not at all. Mr. Fitzroy is a very quiet gentleman."

"He has no company at all?"

"Oh, he has company, sir." The old security guard's ears burned. "There's a young woman. . . ."

"Tall, short blonde hair, glasses? Early thirties?"

Greg winced a little at the tone. "Yes, sir."

"We know her. Go on."

"Well, there's a boy, late teens. He's kind of scruffy, tough like. Not the kind you'd expect Mr. Fitzroy to have over."

The boy's presence wasn't much of a surprise. It only added another piece to the puzzle, bringing it a step close to completion. "Is that all?"

"All the company, sir, but. . . ."

Celluci pounced on the hesitation. "But what?"

"Well, it's just you never see Mr. Fitzroy in the daytime sir. And when you ask him questions about his past. . . ."

Yes, I've a few questions myself about his past. In fact, Fitzroy had turned out to be more questions than answers. Celluci didn't like that in a man and he liked it even less now that he was beginning to see how he could fill in the blanks.

If Henry Fitzroy thought he could hide what he was, he was due for a nasty surprise.

The old man was asleep; Mark could hear him snoring through the wall that separated their bedrooms.

"The sleep of the just," he murmured, linking his hands behind his head and staring at a watermark on the ceiling. Although he'd agreed to help in his uncle's holy war—*And* that's *one elderly gentleman who's a few pickles short of a barrel.*—nothing had actually been said about what this entailed. Whether or not the werewolves were creatures of the devil was a moot point as far as he was concerned—more importantly, they were creatures apparently outside the law.

He was a businessman; there had to be a way he could make a profit out of that.

If he could capture one of them, he knew a number of people who would be more than willing to purchase such a curiosity. Unfortunately, that idea came with an obvious problem. The creature could just refuse to change—and they appeared to have complete control over the process—ruining any credibility he might have. And in sales, credibility was everything.

"All right, if I can't make a buck out of them live. . . ."

He smiled.

Were*wolves*.

Wolves.

Dead wolves meant pelts. Take the head as well and there'd be a dandy rug.

People were always willing to pay for the unique and the unusual.

Nine

"Has anybody seen Daniel this morning?"

Jennifer glanced up from the burr she was working out of her sister's fur. "He headed up the lane about an hour ago. Said he was going to wait for the mail."

"But it's Sunday." Nadine rolled her eyes. "Honestly, that child and the day of the week. Peter, could you go get him." Her tone fell between an order and a request.

Good sergeants used much the same tone, Vicki reflected; maybe the wer could integrate more easily than she'd expected.

Peter dragged his T-shirt over his head and tossed it at Rose. "You think you can find the car keys before I get back?"

"They're in here somewhere," she muttered, shuffling through yet another pile of papers. "I know they are, I can smell them."

"Don't worry about it," Vicki advised, rescuing a lopsided stack of *Ontario Farmers* from sliding to the floor. "If we don't find them by the time Peter gets back, we'll take Henry's car."

"We'll take the BMW?" Peter kicked his sneakers off. "You know where Henry's keys are?"

Vicki grinned. "Sure, he gave them to me in case we needed to move it."

"All right!" He dropped his shorts on Rose's head. "Don't look too hard," he instructed, then changed and barreled out the door, heading at full speed up the lane.

* * *

Mark had intended to just drive by the farm, to see if he could spot any of these alleged werewolves and get a good look at their pelts, but when he saw the shape sitting by the mailbox it seemed like a gift from God.

"And as I have been assured, God is on our side."

So he stopped.

It didn't look like a wolf, but neither did it look quite like a dog. About the size of a small German shepherd, it sat watching him, head cocked to one side, panting a little in the heat. Its pure black coat definitely appeared to have the characteristics of a wolf pelt, with the long silky hairs that women loved to run their hands through.

He stretched an arm out the open window of the car and snapped his fingers. "Here, uh, boy. Come-ere. . . ."

The creature stood, stretched, and yawned, its teeth showing very white against the black of its muzzle.

Why hadn't he brought a biscuit or a pork chop or something? "Come on." Pity it was black; a more exotic color would fetch a higher price.

And then he saw a flash of red coming up the lane. When it reached the mailbox, he realized that the black must only be about half grown. The red creature was huge with the most beautiful pelt Mark had ever seen. Long thick hair shaded from a deep russet to almost a red-gold in the sunlight. Every time it moved, new highlights flickered along the length of its body. Both muzzle and ears were sharply pointed and its eyes were delineated with darker fur, giving it an almost humanly expressive face.

He knew people who would pay big bucks to own a fur like that.

It studied him for a moment, head high, ignoring the attempts of the smaller one to knock it over. There was something in its gaze that made Mark feel intensely uncomfortable and any doubts he might have had about these creatures being more than they seemed vanished under that steady stare. Then it turned and both creatures headed back down the lane.

"Oh, yes," he murmured, watching them run. "I have found my fortune." Best of all, if anything went wrong this time, crazy Uncle Carl and his high caliber mission from God would take the rap.

First on the agenda, a drive into London to do a little research.

It didn't take long for Vicki to discover the attraction Henry's BMW held; low on the dashboard, discreetly out of sight from prying eyes and further camouflaged by the mat black finish—on everything including the buttons and the digital display—was a state of the art compact disk player. She was perfectly willing to admire the sound quality, she was even willing to listen to Peter enthuse about woofers and tweeters and internal stabilization somethings, but she was not willing to listen to opera all the way into London, especially not with the two wer singing along.

They compromised and sang along with Conway Twitty instead. As far as the wer were concerned, the Grand Ol' Opry ran a poor second to grand old opera, but it was better than no music at all. Vicki could tolerate country. At least she understood the language, and Rose had a hysterical gift for mimicking twang and heartache.

They cut through the east end of the city, down Highbury Avenue—Highway 126—heading for the 401. The moment they hit traffic, Rose reached over and turned the music off. To Vicki's surprise, Peter, reclining in the back with his head half out the window, made no protest.

"We don't see things quite the same way you do," Rose explained, very carefully changing lanes and passing an eighteen wheeler. "So we have to pay a lot more attention when we drive."

"Most of the world should pay more attention when

they drive," Vicki muttered. "Peter, stop kicking the back of my seat."

"Sorry." Peter rearranged his legs. "Vicki, I was wondering, how come you're going to see the OPP on a Sunday? Won't the place be closed down?"

Vicki snorted. "Closed down? Peter, the police don't ever close down, it's a twenty-four hour a day, seven day a week job. You should know that, your brother's a cop."

"Yeah, but he's city."

"The Ontario Provincial Police are police just like any others . . . except no one keeps messing with the color of their cars." Vicki liked the old black and whites and hadn't approved the Metro Toronto Police cars going bright yellow and then white. "In fact," she continued, "in a lot of places they're the only police. That said, on a hot Sunday afternoon in August, everyone with a good reason to be out of district headquarters should be and I might be able to get the information I need."

"I thought you were just going to go in and ask them for the names of everyone who has a .30 caliber rifle registered?" A Chevy cut in front of them and Rose dropped back a careful three car lengths, muttering, "Dickhead," under her breath.

"I am. But as they have no reason to tell me, a lot is going to depend on how I ask. And who."

Peter snorted. "You're going to try to intimidate some poor rookie, aren't you?"

Vicki pushed her glasses up her nose. "Of course not." It was actually more a combination of a subtle pulling of rank and an invoking of the "We're all in this together" attitude shared by cops all over the world. Granted, she wasn't a cop anymore, but that shouldn't affect the ultimate result.

The OPP District Headquarters overlooked the 401 on the south side of Exidor Road, the red brick building tucked in behind a Ramada Inn. Vicki had the twins wait by the car.

Had she still been a cop, it would've worked. Unfortunately, that she *used* to be a cop, wasn't good enough. Had she not then tried to "intimidate a poor rookie" it might still have worked, but the very intense young woman she spoke to knew Vicki had no right to the information, "working on a case" or not, and, her back up, refused to show it to her.

Things would have gone better with the sergeant if Vicki hadn't lost her temper.

By the time she left the building, most of the anger was self-directed. Her lips had thinned to a tight, white line and her nostrils flared with every breath. She'd handled the whole thing badly and she knew it.

I am not a cop. I cannot expect to be treated like one. The sooner I get that through my fat head, the better. It was a litany easy to forget back in Toronto where everyone knew her and she could still access many of her old privileges, but she'd just been given a nasty preview of what would happen when the people on the Metro force were no longer the men and women she'd served with. Her hands clenched and unclenched as though they were looking for a throat to wrap around.

She started for the car, standing in solitary splendor at the edge of the lot. With every step, she could feel the waves of heat rising up off the pavement, but they were nothing compared to the heat rising off her. *Where the hell are the twins?* She half hoped they'd done something stupid just so she could blow off some steam. With most of the distance to the car covered, she saw them heading across the parking lot from the Ramada Inn carrying bottles of water.

When they met, both wer took one look at her and dropped their eyes.

"It didn't work, did it?" Rose asked tentatively, peering up through her eyelashes. Under her hair, her ears were forward.

"No. It didn't."

"We just went for some water," Peter offered, his

posture identical to his sister's. He held out the second
of the plastic bottles he carried. "We, uh, brought you
one."

Vicki looked from the bottle to the twins and back
to the bottle. Finally she snorted and took it. "Thank
you." It was cold and it helped. "Oh, chill out. I'm
not going to bite you." Which was when she realized
that they thought she might.

Which was so absurd that she had to laugh.

Both sets of ears perked up and both twins looked
relieved. If they'd been in fur, they probably would
have bounced; as they weren't, they merely grinned
and drank their water.

Dominant/submissive behavior, Vicki thought drain-
ing her bottle. She worried about that a little. If all
the wer but the dominant couple were conditioned to
be submissive as a response to anger or aggression,
that could cause major problems out in the world.

As Rose went around the car to the driver's side,
two heavily muscled young men lounging around the
Ramada Inn pool began calling out lurid invitations.
Rose yawned, turned her back on them, and got into
the car.

And then again, Vicki reconsidered, *maybe there's
nothing to worry about.*

She tossed her empty bottle into the back seat with
Peter. "Let's go get lunch while I come up with another
brilliant idea."

Unlike a number of other places, London had managed to grow from a small town serving the surrounding farming community into a fair sized city without
losing its dignity. Vicki approved of what she saw as
they drove into the center of town. The city planners
had left plenty of parks, from acres of land to tiny
playgrounds tucked in odd corners. New development
had gone up around mature trees and where that hadn't
been possible new trees had been planted. Cicadas
sang accompaniment throughout most of the drive and

the whole city looked quiet and peaceful, basking in the heat.

Vicki, who liked a little more grit in her cities, strongly suspected that the place would bore her to tears in less than twenty-four hours. Although she emphatically denied sharing the commonly held Torontonian delusion that Toronto occupied the center of the universe, she couldn't imagine working, or living, anywhere else.

"The place is called Bob's Steak House," Peter explained as Rose pulled into a small, nearly empty parking lot. "It's actually up on Clarence Street, but if we leave the car there we have to parallel park."

"Which we're not exactly very good at," Rose added, cutting the engine with a sigh of relief.

Vicki would have been perfectly happy stopping for fast food—all she really demanded at this point was air conditioning—but the twins had argued for a restaurant "where the meat isn't so dead."

A short block east of the lot, Rose rocked to a halt in front of a little corner store and exclaimed, "Baseball stickers!"

Peter nodded. "Make him feel better."

"Is this a coded conversation," Vicki asked of no one in particular, "or can anyone join in?"

"Daniel collects baseball stickers," Rose translated. Her brow furrowed. "No one's quite sure why, but he does. If we bring a few packages back, it'll make up for him not being able to come with us."

"You two go ahead." Vicki rummaged in her bag for the car keys. "I've got this urge to go back and check the car doors."

"I locked mine," Peter told her, paused a moment, and added, "I think."

"Exactly," Vicki grunted. "And I don't want to have to tell Henry that we borrowed his BMW and lost half the pieces."

Rose waved a hand at the empty street. "But there's no one around."

"I have a naturally suspicious nature. Get the stickers. I'll meet you back here."

What's the point of new legislation on Sunday openings, Mark Williams wondered, heading back to the alley where he'd left his jeep, *if the places I need to go are still closed? A truly civilized country wouldn't try to cramp a man's style and . . . hello!*

He sidestepped quickly behind a huge old maple and with one hand resting lightly on the bark, leaned forward to take another look. It *was* Ms. "No First Name" Nelson. He thought he recognized the walk. Few women covered the ground with that kind of an aggressive stride. In fact. . . .

He frowned, watching her check the car doors, wondering why the body language seemed so familiar.

Drives a BMW, eh. Not too shabby.

As she turned away from the car, he ducked back, not wanting to be seen. A number of his most profitable enterprises had begun with him watching and keeping his mouth shut. When he felt enough time had passed, he took another look.

Jesus H. Christ. She's a cop.

For those who took the trouble to learn certain subtle signs, playing spot-the-cop became a game easy to win. Mark Williams had long ago taken the trouble to learn the signs. It never hurt to be prepared and this wasn't the first time that preparation had paid off.

What's she got to do with those werewolves though, that's the question. Maybe the aged uncle hasn't been as clever as he thought. If she's a friend of the family, and a cop. . . .

He came out from behind the tree as she disappeared up a side street at the other end of the parking lot. He couldn't tell if she was packing heat, but then, she could be packing a cannon in that oversized bag of hers and no one would be the wiser. Thinking furiously, he sauntered slowly across the street. If she could prove the aged uncle had been blowing away the neighbor's dogs, she didn't have to bring up the subject of werewolves at all. Uncle Carl would. And Uncle Carl would get locked away in a loonybin. And there would go his own chance to score big.

She was onto something. The pine needles on yesterday's T-shirt proved she'd found the tree and he'd be willing to bet that that little lost waif routine she'd pulled in the aged uncle's flower factory was just a ploy to get close.

He laid his hand against the sun-warmed metal of the BMW.

I'm not going to lose this chance.

She wouldn't appreciate it. She'd say he was interfering, that she could take care of herself, that he should stop being such a patronizing s.o.b.. Mike Celluci put down the electric razor and glared at his reflection in the bathroom mirror.

He'd made up his mind. He was going to London. And Vicki Nelson could just fold that into corners and sit on it.

He had no idea what this Henry Fitzroy had gotten her involved with nor did he really care. London, Ontario probably couldn't come up with something Vicki couldn't handle—as far as he knew, the city didn't have nuclear capabilities. Fitzroy himself, however, that was a different matter.

Yanking a clean golf shirt down over his head, Celluci reviewed all he had learned about this historical romance writer. *Historical romances, for God's sake. What kind of job is that for a man?* He paid his parking tickets on time, he hadn't fought the speeding ticket he'd received a year ago, and he had no criminal record of any kind. His books sold well, he banked at Canada Trust, he paid his taxes, and his charity of choice appeared to be the Red Cross. Not many people knew him and the night guard at his condo both respected and feared him.

All this was fine as far as it went, but a lot of the

paper records that modern man carried around with him from birth, were missing from Mr. Fitzroy's life. Not the important things, Celluci admitted, shoving his shirttails down behind the waistband of his pants, but enough of the little things that it set off warning bells. He couldn't dig any deeper, not without having his initial less than ethical investigations come to light, but he could lay his findings before Vicki. She used to be a cop. She'd know what the holes in Fitzroy's background meant.

Organized crime. The police didn't run into it often in Canada, but the pattern fit.

Celluci grinned. Vicki would demand an immediate explanation. He hoped he'd be there to hear Fitzroy try and talk his way out of it.

2:15. Family obligations would keep him in Scarborough until five at the earliest and even at that his sisters would squawk. He shuddered. Two hours of eating burned hamburgers, surrounded by a horde of shrieking nieces and nephews, listening to his brothers-in-law discussing the rising crime statistics and criticizing the police; what a way to spend a Sunday afternoon.

"Okay, so if the gun part of *Rod and Gun Club* refers to the rifle range and stuff," Peter, having convinced Rose that he should have a chance to drive, pulled carefully out of the parking lot, "what's the rod mean?"

"I haven't the faintest idea," Vicki admitted, smoothing the directions out on her knee. The napkin had a few grease stains on it, but the map was actually quite legible. "Maybe they teach fly-tying or something."

"Fly-tying?" Rose repeated.

"That'd take one real small lasso, there, pardner," Peter added, turning north.

Vicki spent the next few blocks explaining what she knew about tying bits of feathers to hooks. As explanations went, it was sketchy. Neither, when asked, did she have any idea why theoretically mature adults would want to stand thigh deep in an ice cold stream being eaten alive by insects so that they could, if lucky, eat something that didn't even look like food when cooked but rather stared up at them off the plate in its full fishy entirety. She was, however, willing to allow that it took all types.

Although Peter drove as meticulously as Rose, he was more easily distracted—any number of bright or moving things pulled his attention from the road.

So once again the wer are inside statistical norms, Vicki thought, squinting through the glare on the windshield, *and we see why teenage girls have fewer accidents than teenage boys.* "Red light, Peter."

"I see it."

It took Vicki a moment to realize they weren't slowing. "Peter. . . ."

His eyes were wide and his canines showed. His right leg pumped desperately at the floor. "The brakes, they aren't catching."

"Shit!"

And then they were in the intersection.

Vicki heard the squeal of tires. The world slowed. She turned, could see the truck, too close already to read the license plate, and knew they didn't have a hope in hell of not being hit. She screamed at Peter to hit the gas and the car lurched forward. The grille of the truck filled the window and then, with an almost delicate precision, it began to push through the rear passenger door. Bits of broken glass danced in the air, refracting the sunlight into a million sharp-edged rainbows.

The world returned to normal speed as the two vehicles spun together across the intersection, tortured metal and rubber shrieking, until the back of the BMW slammed into a light pole and the truck bounced free.

Vicki straightened. Covering her face to protect it had kept her glasses where they belonged. Thankfully, she pushed them up her nose, then reached over and turned off the ignition. For the first sudden instant of silence, her heart was the only sound she could hear, booming in her ears like an entire percussion section, then, from a distance, as though the volume were slowing being turned up, came voices, horns, and, farther away still, sirens. She ignored it all.

Peter had his head down on the steering wheel, pillowed on his folded arms. Vicki unsnapped her seat belt and gripped his shoulder lightly.

"Peter?"

The lower half of his face dripped blood but, as far as she could tell, it came from his nose.

"The brakes," he panted. "They—they didn't work."

"I know." She tightened her grip slightly. He was beginning to tremble and although he deserved it, although they all deserved it, this was not the time for hysterics. "Are you all right?"

He blinked, glanced down the length of his body, then back at her. "I think so."

"Good. Take off your seat belt and see if your door will open." Her tone was an echo of the one Nadine had used that morning and Peter responded to it without questions. Giving thanks for learned behaviors, Vicki pulled herself up on her knees and leaned over into the back to check on Rose.

The rear passenger side door had buckled, but essentially held. The inner covering and twisted pieces of the actual mechanisms it contained spread across three quarters of the seat which now tilted crazily up toward the roof. The rear window had blown out. The side window had blown in. Most of the glass had crumbled into a million tiny pieces, but here and there sizable shards had been driven into the upholstery.

A triangular blade about eight inches long trembled just above Rose's fetal curl, its point buried deep in the door lining. Glass glittered in her pale hair like ice in a snow field and her arms and legs were covered with a number of superficial cuts.

Vicki reached over and yanked the glass dagger free. A 1976 BMW didn't have plastic-coated safety glass.

"Rose?"

She slowly uncurled. "Is it over?"

"It's over."

"Am I alive?"

"You're alive." Although she wouldn't have been had she been sitting on the other side of the car.

"Peter. . . ."

"Is fine."

"I want to howl."

"Later," Vicki promised. "Right now, unlock your door so Peter can get it open."

While Peter helped his sister from the back, Vicki clambered over the gearshift and out the driver's door, dragging her bag behind her, and throwing it up on her shoulder the moment she was clear, its familiar weight a reassurance in the chaos. A small crowd had gathered and more cars were stopping. One of them, she was pleased to note, belonged to the London Police and other sirens could be heard coming closer.

With the twins comforting each other and essentially unharmed, Vicki made her way around the car to check on the driver of the truck. Blood ran down one side of his face from a cut over his left eye and the right side of his neck was marked by a angry red friction burn from the shoulder strap of his seat belt.

"Jesus Christ, lady," he moaned as she stopped beside him. "Just look at my truck." Although the massive bumper had absorbed most of the impact, the grille had been driven back into the radiator. "Man, I didn't even have fifty klicks on this things yet. My wife is going to have my ass." He reached down and lightly touched the one whole headlight. "Quartz-halogen. Seventy-nine bucks a pop."

"Is everyone all right here?"

Vicki knew what she'd see before she turned: she'd

used that exact tone too many times herself. The London police constable was an older man, gray hair, regulation mustache, regulation neutral expression. His younger partner was with the twins, and the two uniforms from the second car were taking charge of traffic and crowd control. She could hear Peter beginning to babble about the brake failure and decided to let him be for the moment. A little bit of hysteria would only help convince the police they were telling the truth. People who were too calm were often perceived as having something to hide.

"As far as I can tell," she said, "we're all fine."

His brows rose. "And you are?"

"Oh. Sorry. Vicki Nelson. I was a detective with the Metro Toronto Police until my eyes went." It didn't even hurt to say it anymore. Maybe she was in shock. "I was in the BMW." She dug out her ID and passed it over.

"You were driving?"

"No, Peter was."

"It's your car?"

"No, a friend's. He lent it to us for the day. When Peter tried to stop for the light, the brakes had gone. We couldn't stop." She waved a hand at the truck. "He didn't have a chance of missing us."

"Right out in front of me," the driver of the truck agreed, swiping at the blood on his cheek. "Not even fifty klicks on this baby. And the whole front end'll have to be repainted." He sighed deeply, his belly rising and falling. "The wife is going to have my ass."

"They were working earlier?"

"We stopped just down the road without any . . ." The world slid a little sideways. ". . . trouble."

"I think you'd better sit down." The constable's hand was around her elbow.

"I'm fine," Vicki protested.

He smiled slightly. "You've got a purple lump the size of a goose egg on your temple. Offhand, I'd say you're not quite fine."

She touched her temple lightly and brilliant white stars shot inward from her fingertips. All of a sudden, it hurt. A lot. Her whole body hurt. And she had no memory of how or when it had happened. "I'm getting too old for this shit," she muttered, letting the constable lead her to the side of the road.

"Tell me about it." He lowered her gently to the curb. "You just sit there for a minute. We'll have the ambulance people take a look at you."

Everything appeared to be about six inches beside where it should be. "I think," she said slowly. "That might not be a bad idea. The ownership, insurance, everything, is in the glove compartment."

He nodded and headed for the car. Vicki stopped keeping track of things for a while.

When the ambulance attendants suggested she go to the hospital, she didn't put up much of a fight, only pulled Dr. Dixon's phone number from the depths of her bag, asked that he be called immediately, and insisted on Rose and Peter coming with her. The police, who had soon recognized the family resemblance between the twins and one of their own people, overruled the protests of the attendants and helped all three of them into the back of the ambulance.

"We're not charging you with anything," the older constable told her, handing up the tow truck driver's card, "but we will be checking with the mechanics about those brakes. This is the garage he's taking the car to."

Vicki nodded carefully and stowed the card in her bag.

As the ambulance pulled away, the tow truck driver looked down at the wreck of the BMW and shook his head. "Good thing they weren't driving domestic."

"Storm. Storm!"

Storm gave Cloud one last frenzied lick and looked up at Dr. Dixon.

"Go into the kitchen and get me a glass of water,

please." Vicki made a motion to rise out of her chair, but the old man waved her back. "No, I want Storm to go. Run the water good and cold. If there's ice in the freezer, you'd better use it."

Nails clicking against the hardwood, Storm left the room. The sound continued down the hall and then stopped. Vicki assumed he'd changed. Cloud, her fur stuck up in damp spikes from Storm's tongue, shook herself briskly then lay her head down on her front paws and closed her eyes.

Dr. Dixon sighed. "She's getting too close," he said softly to Vicki, "and her twin's beginning to sense it."

Vicki frowned. "She's getting too close to what?"

"Her first heat. I imagine he'll be sent away as soon as this trouble's over. I only hope it isn't too late."

"Too late?" Vicki echoed, remembering Nadine had spoken of Cloud's first heat on Saturday morning.

"Usually it happens in late September, early October, that way if there's a pregnancy, the baby, or babies, will be born in early summer, ensuring a good food supply for the last few months of gestation and the first few months of life." He chuckled. "The wer aren't born with teeth, but they come up damn soon after. Of course, all this meant more when they lived solely by hunting, but the basic biology still rules. Thank God the baby's changes are tied to the mother's for the first couple of years."

Vicki dropped her hand on the old man's arm. The hospital had cleared her of any damage except a nasty bump but her head hurt and she knew she was missing something. "Dr. Dixon, what the hell are you talking about?"

"Huh?" He turned to look at her and shook his head. "I'm sorry, I'm old, I forgot you've only known the wer for a short time." His voice took on a lecturing tone, slow and precise. "Cloud is nearing sexual maturity. Her scent is changing. Storm is responding. Didn't you notice the way he was licking her?"

"I thought that was for comfort, to clean the cuts."

"It was, partially, but I didn't like the look of what it was turning into. That's why I sent him to the kitchen."

"But he's her brother," Vicki protested.

"Which is why the family will be sending him away. It's hard on twins. You simply can't keep them together during a first heat; he'd injure himself trying to get to her. When he's older, he'll be able to control his response but this first time, this first time for both of them. . . ." Dr. Dixon let his voice trail off and shook his head.

He remained silent as Peter came back into the room.

"I brought you some water, too," he said, handing Vicki the second glass he carried.

She thanked him. She needed a drink. Water would have to do. She watched carefully as Storm flopped down and rested his muzzle across Cloud's back, sighed deeply, and appeared to go instantly to sleep. It all looked perfectly innocent to her. She glanced at Dr. Dixon. He didn't look worried so apparently this was within the parameters of acceptable behavior.

The tableau shattered a moment later when a car door slammed outside and both wer leapt up and raced for the front of the house, barking excitedly.

"Their father," Dr. Dixon explained. "I called him as we were leaving the hospital. No sense worrying him before that and now he can take you back to the farm."

"Do they know it's going to happen?" Vicki asked. "That he's going to be sent away?"

Dr. Dixon looked momentarily puzzled. "Who? Oh. Cloud and Storm? Rose and Peter?" At her nod, he sighed. "They know intellectually that it's what happens, but for all they're wer, they're still teenagers and they don't believe it will happen to them." He shook his head. "Teenagers. You couldn't pay me enough to go through that again."

Vicki reached over and clinked her glass against his. "Amen," she said. "Amen."

Brows lowered, Mike Celluci worked his fingers around the steering wheel. He'd left his sister's later than he'd planned and felt lucky to get away at all. No one had warned him that their Aunt Maria would be at the "little family barbecue," probably because they knew he'd refuse to come.

"Well, surely you didn't expect Grandma to come on her own, Mike. I mean the woman is eighty-three years old."

If they'd mentioned Grandma was coming he'd have driven out to get her himself. A trip to Dufferin and St. Clair beat the hell out of an afternoon with Aunt Maria. Although he'd tried, it had been impossible to avoid her for the entire afternoon and eventually he'd had to endure the litany he'd heard from her at every meeting practically since puberty.

When are you getting married, Michele? You can't forget, you're the last of the Cellucis, Michele. I told your father, my brother, rest his soul, that a man needs many sons to carry on the name but he didn't listen. Daughters, he had three daughters. When are you getting married, Michele?

This afternoon he'd managed to keep his temper, but only barely. If his grandmother hadn't stepped in. . . .

"And the last thing I need now is a fucking traffic jam on the four-oh-goddamed-one." He had his light and siren in the glove compartment. The urge to slap it on the roof and go tearing up the paved shoulder, around the Sunday evening traffic, was intense.

He wanted to be in London before dark, but he wasn't going to make it. If traffic didn't open up, he doubted he'd be there before eleven. Time wasn't a problem, he had three days off, but he wanted to confront Vicki tonight.

He'd called Dave Graham, to let him know where

he was heading, and ended up slamming the receiver down when the other man started to laugh.

"Jealous," he growled, scowling up at the setting sun. It wasn't funny. Vicki had to be told what kind of person she'd gotten involved with. He'd do the same for any friend.

Suddenly, he grinned. Maybe he should introduce Vicki to Aunt Maria; the old lady'd never know what hit her.

"What are you so nervous about?"

Vicki jumped, whirled, and glared up at Henry. "Don't *do* that!"

"Do wha. . . . Sweet Jesu, Vicki, what happened?" He reached out to touch the purple and green lump on her temple but stopped when she flinched back.

"There was an accident."

"An accident?" He glanced around, nostrils flared. "Where is everyone?"

"Outside." Vicki took a deep breath and released it slowly. "We agreed I should be the one to tell you." Peter had wanted to, but Vicki had overruled him; he'd been through enough for one day.

Henry frowned. There were strange undercurrents in Vicki's voice he didn't understand. "Has someone else been shot?"

"No, not that." She glanced out the window. Although the sun had set, the sky was still a deep sapphire blue. "The wer have been staying out of those fields, patrolling around the house; it seems to be working for now. No, this involves something else."

"Something that involves . . ." He flicked his gaze over to the lump and she nodded. ". . . and me."

"In a manner of speaking. The brakes failed on the BMW today. We—Peter, Rose, and I—were broadsided by a truck. The car, well, the car was pretty badly damaged."

"And the three of you? You weren't badly hurt?"

"If we had been," Vicki snapped, "I'd have more to worry about than totaling your car." She winced. "Sorry. It's been a day."

Henry smiled. "Another one." He cupped her chin lightly with his right hand and looked up into her eyes. "No concussion?"

"No. Peter got a bloody nose and Rose has a few cuts from flying bits of glass. We were lucky." His hazel eyes appeared almost green in the lamplight. She could feel his hand on her skin through every nerve in her body, which was strange because as far as she could remember her chin had never been an erogenous zone before. She moved back and his hand dropped.

"You were *very* lucky," Henry agreed, pulling out a chair and settling into it. He wasn't sure if Vicki was responding to his hunger—his own injuries would heal faster if he fed—or if his hunger rose with her response, but for the moment he ignored both possibilities. "I don't understand about the brakes, though. I had a full service check done in the spring and they were fine. I've hardly driven the car since."

Vicki dropped into a chair beside him. "The garage was closed today, it being Sunday and all, so I'll talk to the mechanic tomorrow." She leaned her elbows on the table and peered into his face. "You're being very understanding about this. If someone trashed *my* BMW, I'd be furious."

"Four hundred and fifty years gives you a different perspective on possessions," he explained. "You learn not to grow too attached to *things.*"

"Or people?" Vicki asked quietly.

His smile twisted. "No, I've never managed to learn that. Although every now and then, I make the attempt."

Vicki couldn't imagine watching everyone she cared about grow old and die while she went on without them and she wondered where Henry found the strength. Which set her to wondering. . . .

"How are *you* tonight?" She plucked gently at the sling around his left arm.

"Bruised thigh, bruised head, shoulder's healing." It was frustrating more than painful. Especially with her blood so close.

"You've got that look on your face."

"What look?"

"Like you're listening to something."

To her heartbeat. To the sound of her blood as it pulsed just under the skin. "I'd better go."

She stood with him.

"No, Vicki."

Just in time she remembered not to raise her brows. "No, Vicki? Henry, you need to feed, I need to relax. I'm a grown woman and if I think I can spare you another few mouthfuls of my precious bodily fluids, you have no room for argument."

Henry opened his mouth, closed it again, and surrendered. Healing had used up whatever reserves he had and the hunger was too strong to fight. At least that's what he told himself as they climbed the stairs.

"How dare you! How fucking dare you!" Barry Wu couldn't remember ever being so furious. "You goddamned fucking son of a bitch, you actually believed I'd do something like that!"

Colin was trying desperately hard to keep his own temper, but he could feel himself responding to Barry's anger. He'd been pulled out of the car for special duty tonight, and this was the first chance they'd had to talk. "If you'd listen—I said I didn't believe you did it!"

Barry slammed his palm down on the hood of Colin's truck. "But you didn't believe I didn't! It took a fucking Toronto PI to convince you!"

"You've got to admit the evidence. . . ."

"I don't have to admit shit!" He stomped off half a dozen paces, whirled around, and stomped back.

"And another thing, where the fuck do you get off searching my place?"

"What? I was supposed to just sit on my ass and wait for the guy to strike again?"

"You could've fucking told me!"

"I *couldn't* fucking tell you!"

"Hey!"

Neither of them had heard the car pull up. They spun simultaneously, shoulder to shoulder, dropped into a defensive position, and went for their guns.

Which neither of them are wearing. Celluci lifted a sardonic eyebrow. *How lucky for all three of us.* "You two might want to find another place to have your disagreement. Police officers screaming profanities at each other in the station parking lot looks bad to civilians." If he remembered correctly, a sergeant had once said the same to him and Vicki.

Neither Barry nor Colin wasted a moment wondering how the stranger had known they were police officers even out of uniform. They were young. They hadn't been on the force very long. They weren't stupid.

"No, sir!" they replied in unison, almost but not quite coming to attention.

Celluci hid a smile. "I'm looking for someone. A woman. Her name is Vicki Nelson. She's a private investigator from Toronto. She's working for some people who own a sheep farm north of the city. I figure by now she'll have contacted the police, for information if nothing else. Can you help?"

Colin stepped toward the car, trying to paste a neutral expression over concern. "Excuse me, sir, but why are you looking for her? Is she in trouble?"

Jackpot first try. She's probably had this poor kid breaking into police files for her. "I'm a friend. I have information about the man she's traveling with."

"About Henry?" The concern broke through. Information about Henry could mean trouble.

Barry frowned at the tone but moved forward, ready if Colin needed him.

"You *know* him?"

"Uh, yeah, I do." Barry looked a little surprised at the change in Colin's voice and more surprised when he continued with, "I'm Colin Heerkens. Henry and Vicki are out at my family's farm," and then proceeded to give detailed directions. There was an undercurrent of amusement about Colin's whole attitude that made Barry very nervous.

As the car pulled away, Colin gave a shout of laughter and slapped Barry on the back. "Come on," he yanked open the truck door and climbed in, "you're not going to want to miss this!"

"Miss what?"

"What happens when he gets to the farm."

"What happens?"

Colin rolled his eyes. "Christ, Barry, I know your nose isn't worth much but I don't believe you didn't smell that. That guy was so jealous he was practically green." He leaned over and opened the passenger door. "You know, if you'd learn to read nonverbal clues you'd be a better cop."

"Yeah?" Barry swung up into the truck. "And if I'd wanted to be in the canine corps, I'd have joined it." He settled back against the seat cushions and buckled in. "I still want to know what happens when he gets to the farm."

"Beats me." Colin shot him a grin as he pulled out onto the street. "But it oughta be interesting."

"You think this is pretty funny, don't you?"

"We think most of you humans are pretty funny. Laugh a minute."

"Sheep-fucker."

"Yellow peril."

"You know, Colin, your uncle's probably not going to be too thrilled by you sending this guy out to the farm." Barry drummed his fingers against the dash and shot a look at his partner. "I mean, you lot aren't big on company just generally and right now. . . ."

Colin frowned. "You know, you're right. I guess I was reacting to his scent and the situation. Uncle Stuart's going to have my throat." He sucked in a deep breath through his teeth. "I guess I just didn't think."

"It's your least endearing trait." And one that would keep him from promotion; keep him on the street, in uniform. Barry doubted that Colin would ever rise any higher than constable and sometimes he wondered how the wer would manage when he moved on.

"Barry, I did *want* to tell you."

"I know. Forget it." And he knew that Colin could, the wer lived very much in the here-and-now. It would take a little longer for him.

Ten

This is ridiculous. It's 11:30. Vicki's likely asleep. Celluci sat in his car and stared at the dark bulk of the farmhouse. *Or at least in bed.* He decided not to take that thought any further. *The lights are on in the kitchen. Someone's up. I could at least make sure this is the right. . . .* "Jesus!"

The white head staring in the driver's side window belonged to the biggest dog he'd ever seen. It looked to be part shepherd, part malamute, and, if he didn't know better, he'd swear, part wolf. It didn't look angry, just curious and its eyes. . . . Unable to decide if the eyes were as strange as he thought or if the glass was distorting them somehow, he cracked open the window enough for the head, but not the shoulders, and kept his finger on the switch in case the beast should lunge.

Not so much as a whisker crossed the edge of the window, but the wet black nose twitched once, twice as the cool air inside the car flowed out into the night.

The eyes were strange; it wasn't just the glass. Celluci wasn't quite sure what the difference was but he'd never seen a dog of any kind with eyes that looked so human.

Suddenly, the big dog whirled and ran barking for the house, its pale form flickering like a negative image against the night.

Realizing his choice had just been made for him, Celluci shut off the engine. He'd been announced. He might as well go in.

* * *
''Vicki. Come on, Vicki. Wake up.''

Vicki tried to ignore both the voice and the hand gently shaking her shoulder but, in spite of her best efforts, her body betrayed her and began losing its hold on sleep. Finally she surrendered, muttered an obscenity, and groped for her glasses. Cool fingers gripped her wrist, guiding her search. She didn't bother opening her eyes until she actually had the glasses in place—not much point when she wouldn't be able to see anything anyway.

In the dim spill of light from the hallway, she could just barely make out the darker outline of a man. It had to be Henry, not only was he the only adult male in the house who habitually wore clothes, but the temperature of his touch was a dead giveaway.

''Henry, I'm flattered but I'm exhausted. Get lost.''

She could hear the smile in his reply. ''Next time I'll be able to do more of the work. But that wasn't why I woke you. We've got company and I think you'd better get up.''

''What time is it?''

''11:33.''

Vicki really disliked digital watches, only race horses and defense attorneys needed to time life to the second. ''I just got to sleep. Can't it wait until morning?''

''I don't think so.''

''All right.'' She sighed and swung her legs out from under the sheet. ''Who is it?''

''Detective-Sergeant Michael Celluci.''

''Say what!''

''Detec . . .''

''I heard you the first time. Close the door and turn on the light.''

He did as she requested, shielding his eyes against the sudden glare.

The clothes she'd worn this afternoon would have to

do, Celluci had certainly seen her look worse. "Are you sure?"

"Very. Cloud checked out the car when it first pulled up. She said she could smell a gun, so I took a quick look. It's Michael Celluci. Keeping in mind how we met, I'm not likely to forget him."

Vicki had very little memory of how Henry and Celluci had met, but considering that she was tired and bleeding and about to become a demonic sacrifice at the time, that was hardly surprising. "What the hell is *he* doing here?"

"I don't know." Henry leaned back against the wall and waited while she pulled a T-shirt over her head before he continued. "But I thought you might like to be there when we found out."

"Be there?" She stuffed her feet into sandals and stood, running both hands through her hair rather than search for a brush. "You couldn't pay me enough to miss this explanation and if something isn't very wrong that I *have* to know about immediately—and I'll be damned if I can think of what that might be—I'll have a few words to say in return."

Because Henry had every intention of living for another four hundred and fifty years, he kept his initial response to that clamped firmly behind his teeth.

"Detective-Sergeant Michael Celluci, ma'am. Is Vicki Nelson here?"

"Yes, she's here. Henry's gone to wake her."

"That isn't necessary." Henry must've seen him approaching the house and recognized him. *He's got eyes like an owl if that's the case. I couldn't see my hand a foot in front of my face out there, cloud cover's got everything blocked off.* "It's late. Now I know this is the right place, I can return tomorrow."

"Nonsense." The woman stepped back out of the way and motioned him into the kitchen. "You've driven all the way from Toronto, you might as well wait. She'll be right down."

If they'd gone to get her up, he didn't really have a choice. The only thing worse than having Vicki dragged out of bed, would be having her dragged out of bed and not staying around to explain why. Slipping his shield and his ID back into his pocket, he followed a gesture into a chair, keeping a wary eye on the huge white dog who watched him from across the room. *This is ridiculous. One more night isn't going to make a difference. And she's not going to be happy about being woken up.*

A red dog came out and sat beside the white. It looked less than happy to see him. It also looked larger although, considering the size of the first, Celluci found that difficult to believe. He shifted a little in his chair. "What, uh, kind of dogs are they?"

"They're descended from an obscure European hunting breed. You've probably never heard of it."

"Something like wolfhounds?"

"Something like, yes." She pulled out a chair and sat down, pinning him under a curiously intent gaze. "My name is Nadine Heerkens-Wells, my husband and I run this farm. Vicki is working for us at the moment. Is there something I should know, Detective?"

"No, ma'am. This doesn't concern you." In fact, Celluci was having a little trouble dealing with a friendship between the man he perceived Henry Fitzroy to be and this woman. Although physically she was quite striking, with her widow's peak and sharp, almost exotic features, the quality of her surroundings said poor white trash. Her wrinkled sleeveless dress looked as if it had just been picked up off the floor and thrown on. *And there's enough stuff scattered around to dress a half a dozen people, provided they're not too fussy about the condition of their clothes.* None of the furniture could be less than ten years old, clumps of hair had piled up in every corner, and the whole kitchen had a kind of shabby ambience that indicated money was scarce.

Of course, all their spare cash could be going into dog food.

He heard footsteps on the stairs and stood, turning to face the door leading into the hall.

"All right, Celluci, what's wrong?" Vicki stopped barely a handspan from his chest and glared up into his face. "Someone had better be dying. . . ." Her tone added, *or someone's going to be.*

"What the hell happened to your head?"

"My what? Oh that. I was in a car accident this afternoon. I guess I hit the dash." The fingers on her right hand patted the air over the purple and green swelling. "The hospital says it's just a bump. Looks bad but no real damage." Her eyes narrowed, glasses sliding down her nose with the motion. "Your turn."

Henry, standing just inside the kitchen, hid a smile. Vicki obviously thought Celluci was entitled to hear about the accident; while she was telling him, the challenge dropped from her voice and posture. The moment she finished, it was back.

Celluci drew in a deep breath and let it out slowly. "Can we talk somewhere privately?"

"Privately?"

He glanced over her shoulder at Henry. "Yeah. Privately. As in I'd like to speak with you alone."

Vicki frowned. She'd seen that look before. Politely translated, it meant he was ready to make an arrest. Why he should be aiming it at Henry. . . . "We'll go out to your car."

"I thought you couldn't see in the dark?"

"I know what you look like." She grabbed his arm just above the elbow and propelled him toward the kitchen door, throwing an "I won't be long" to the room in general as they left.

The moment they were clear of the house, Peter stretched and said, "I wonder why she didn't want to use the living room?"

Henry grinned. "Where you could've heard every word they said?"

"Well. . . ."

"Vicki has a pretty good idea of how well the wer can hear." He walked to the window and stared across the dark lawn at Celluci's car. "And she *knows* how well I can."

"Well?"

He tapped his fingers against the steering wheel. Where to start? "It's about your friend, Mr. Fitzroy."

Vicki snorted. "No kidding."

"I did some checking into his background . . ."

"You *what?*"

He ignored the interruption and continued. ". . . and there're a number of discrepancies I think you should know about."

"And I suppose you had a good *reason* for abusing police privilege?" The tension in her jaw pulled at her temple, sharpening the pain and spreading it out over her skull, but Vicki didn't dare unclench her teeth. If Celluci had discovered Henry's secret, she had to know about it and couldn't risk it getting lost in a screaming fight. *Later.*

Celluci could hear the suppressed anger in her voice, could see the tightening of her lips in the pale oval of her face. He had no idea why she was hanging onto her temper but he knew it wouldn't last so he'd better use the time he had.

"Your *reason,* Celluci."

"You think what happened last spring wasn't reason enough?"

"Not if you just started searching now, no, I don't."

"What makes you think I just started searching now?"

He could see the lighter slash of her smile. It didn't look friendly.

"You drive all the way from Toronto, you barge into a strange house at 11:30 at night, you have me roused from sleep and dragged from bed, and I'm supposed to believe this is information you've had for months? Cop a plea, Celluci, the evidence is against you.''

"Look," he turned to face her, "your friend isn't what you think he is."

"What do I think he is?" This didn't sound good.

"Oh, I don't know." Celluci drove both hands up through his hair. "Hell, yes I do. You think he's some sort of exotic literary figure, who can wine you and dine you and offer you moonlit nights of romance . . ."

Vicki felt her jaw drop.

". . . but he's got holes in his background you could drive a truck through. Everything points to only one answer; he's got to be deeply involved in organized crime."

"Organized crime?" Her voice came out flat, no inflection.

"It's the only solution that fits all the facts."

She sputtered. She just couldn't help it. She just couldn't hold it in any longer.

Celluci leaned toward her, trying to read her expression. When she got over the initial shock, she'd want to hear what he'd found.

Vicki managed to repeat *organized crime* one more time before she lost it.

He watched her laugh and wondered if he should smack her. He could always use hysteria as an excuse.

Finally, she managed to get hold of herself.

"Are you ready to listen?" he asked through gritted teeth.

Vicki shook her head, reached up and brushed the long curl of hair back off his forehead—she didn't have to see it to know it was there. "Leaving aside your reasons for the moment, you couldn't be more wrong. Trust me, Mike. Henry Fitzroy is not involved in organized crime. At any level, of any kind."

"You're sleeping with him, aren't you?"

So much for his reasons. *You are mine* resonated over, under, and through that question. Unfortunately, she couldn't deal with his archaic perceptions right now; this was too potentially dangerous for Henry. "What does that have to do with this?"

"You wouldn't be willing to believe. . . ."

"Bullshit! I'm perfectly willing to believe that you're a chauvinistic, possessive bastard and I sleep with you." So much for good intentions.

He hadn't intended to be so loud, but his voice practically echoed in the confines of the car. "Vicki, I'm telling you, beyond a certain point, Henry Fitzroy has no. . . . What the hell was that?"

"Was what?" Vicki peered out the windows but couldn't see past the night. She shoved her glasses up her nose. It didn't help.

"Something ran past out there. It might have been one of those big dogs. It looked like it might be hurt."

"Shit!" She was out of the car and racing toward the house before the final explosive "t" had passed her lips. The darkness was absolute save for the faint square of light that was the kitchen window. *It's a big building. How can I miss it?* Then she remembered Henry warning her the first night about the curve in the path. Too late. She stumbled and fell, burying her hands in the loose dirt of the garden.

"Come on." Celluci heaved her to her feet and kept a tight hold on her arm. "If it's that important, I'll be your eyes."

They pounded through the kitchen door together, just in time to see a massive russet shape crash to the floor, the fur on its chest a darker, more deadly shade of red.

"Too big to be Storm," Vicki panted, fighting free of Celluci's grip. "Has to be. . . ."

And then there wasn't any question as outlines blurred and blood began pumping from an ugly gash across the right side of Donald's ribs.

Vicki and Nadine hit the floor beside the wounded wer at roughly the same time. Nadine, who had grabbed a first aid kit from over the kitchen sink, was expertly pinching the torn edges of flesh together and wrapping them in place.

"We do most of our own doctoring," she said, in response to Vicki's silent question.

All things considered, it made sense. The presence of Dr. Dixon didn't carry much weight against an entire history with no physicians. "Doesn't look like a gunshot wound." Together they got the gauze around Donald's neck. "Looks like he got hit with a chunk of flying rock."

Nadine snorted. "Comforting."

"I thought," Vicki grunted, holding Donald's weight while Nadine continued to wind the gauze, "that you'd all agreed to stay out of those fields."

"It isn't that easy to overcome a territorial imperative."

"It isn't that easy to overcome a .30 caliber slug either."

"What the hell are you two *talking* about?" Celluci took a step forward. "What the *hell* is going on around here?"

"Later, Mike. I think he's going to need a hospital."

"I think you're right. Cloud!"

To Celluci's astonishment, the big white dog galloped out of the room. "What's it going to do? Call 911?"

"Yes," Vicki snapped, pushing at her glasses with the back of a bloody hand.

Henry started across the kitchen. Someone was going to have to take care of Michael Celluci and, as much as he might wish otherwise, it looked like it was going to have to be him. *No need for concern, Detective, it's just werewolves.* Coercion would be safer than explanation; get him outside and twist his mind until he no longer knew exactly what he'd seen.

Unfortunately, by the time Henry had covered the four meters to Celluci, the situation had changed again.

Stuart, who had seen a stranger's car parked at the

end of the lane, had grabbed a pair of shorts from the barn and changed before coming to the house. A voice and a pair of hands could often make a difference in an unplanned confrontation, but now he wished he'd stayed with tooth and claw. A member of his pack was down and the blood scent drew his lips back from his teeth.

"What's going on?" he growled.

"Donald got hit. Vicki thinks it was a ricochet. There's an ambulance coming." Nadine shot the words out without looking up.

"He changed?"

"As he went out."

Stuart turned to face the stranger, hackles rising, ears tight against his head. "And this one saw?"

"Yeah, *this one* saw." Celluci's jaw jutted out at a dangerous angle. "And I want some explanations of *what* I saw and I want them now."

"Don't push, Detective." Henry could see that Stuart was close to the edge and was facing Celluci's aggression the way he'd face a challenge from a dominant male of his own kind.

"Stay out of this, Fitzroy!" His fingers curled into fists, Celluci locked eyes with the man in the doorway. He'd taken as much abuse as he was going to. Dogs *did not* change into men. "I want answers *now.*"

The growl was a warning and something deep in Celluci's hindbrain recognized it as such. He didn't listen. "Well? I'm waiting!" He didn't have to wait long. His tottering world view fell and shattered as thumbs were shoved behind shorts, shorts hit the floor, and a great black beast that seemed mostly teeth leapt suddenly for his throat. Then something pushed him back and Henry and the beast were on the floor.

Henry had thrown his good shoulder under the charge and managed to force Stuart's fur-form down. With only one arm, however, he couldn't keep him there without injuring him. *At least his anger's been redirected. . . .*

Celluci knew a man couldn't possibly move as fast as Henry Fitzroy was moving. The beast lunged and Fitzroy was somewhere else. Instantly. Or as near as made no difference. Again. And again. And again. With barely a heartbeat between. And through it all came the deep-throated growl of an enraged animal, building to a savage crescendo with each attack.

A deadly little dance, Henry realized as teeth snapped closed on the air beside his hip. Even with one bad arm he knew he could force the wer to submit—he was stronger and faster, but then what? Defeat the dominant male and rule the pack. *No thank you,* he thought as they scrabbled through another movement. But he could feel himself responding to the scents and the sounds and the anger and wondered how much longer he'd be able to maintain control. *There has to be a way to break through. . . .*

Suddenly, it was no longer his problem.

With Donald still on the floor, the red wer attacking had to be Storm. Henry backed quickly out of the way while the two rolled snarling and snapping then sprang apart, circled, and charged together again.

Enough! Celluci dropped to one knee and pulled his gun from his ankle holster. He wasn't thinking exactly clearly, he had no real idea of what he was going to shoot—*This is someone's kitchen for Chrissakes!*—but he felt more in control with the weight of the weapon in his hand.

Then Storm yelped and threw himself down on his back, all four feet in the air and the edge of one ear split. Long white teeth closed around his throat.

Celluci raised the gun.

A high-pitched, piercing howl cut through the chaos and everyone froze, looking like they'd been playing a demented game of statues. Then, in near unison, they turned. Shadow sat just inside the hall door, muzzle raised and throat working as his howl undulated mournfully up and down the scale. It lasted just over a minute, bouncing off the walls, reverberating through bone and blood, impossible to ignore, and then trailing off into a series of hiccuping yelps.

Nadine responded first, leaving Donald with Vicki and racing across the room to gather Shadow up into her arms. He pushed closer and tried to bury his head under her breasts. She lifted his head and gazed anxiously down into his eyes. "What is it, baby? What's wrong?"

Given encouragement to speak, and therefore to change, Daniel peered over his mother's shoulder and wailed. "That man's going to shoot my papa!"

All heads now turned to follow Daniel's pointing finger—all except Storm who had been pinned by one of his uncle's huge paws and was now having his bitten ear vigorously licked.

Vicki sat back on her knees, one hand resting lightly on the thick pad of gauze wrapped around Donald's chest, monitoring the rise and fall of his labored breathing with her fingertips. She rolled her eyes and sighed. "Oh for Chrissake, Celluci, put the penis substitute away."

A shout of laughter from outside the screen door was the immediate and unexpected response. Everyone turned yet again as Colin and Barry came into the kitchen, Colin saying, "I told you we'd miss all the good stuff if we stopped for gas."

"I'm sure I saw this once in an old Marx Brothers' movie," Vicki muttered to no one in particular. She raised her voice. "People, what are the odds we could pull ourselves together before the ambulance arrives?"

Colin glanced around the kitchen, nostrils flaring as they caught the varied scents, smile vanishing as he saw the body on the floor. "Dad!" He threw himself to his knees, pushing Vicki away. "What happened to my father?"

"Ricochet. Our marksman missed."

"Is he . . ?"

"At least one busted rib and some torn up muscle. I don't know about internal injuries."

"Why is he just lying here? We've got to get him to a hospital!" He put his hands under his father's shoulders.

Vicki lifted them away. "Calm down, there's an ambulance coming."

"If you're being shot at in human form now, we'll *have* to report it," Barry put in, touching Colin lightly on the back.

"He wasn't," Vicki told him, getting to her feet. "He changed when he hit the house. You must be Barry Wu."

"Yes, ma'am."

"I want to talk to you."

"Yes, ma'am. Later. Uh, if he changed in the house, then. . . ." His gaze flickered to Celluci and back.

Vicki sighed. "Yes, he saw." She turned to Celluci, wiping her bloody fingers on her shorts. "Please put the gun away, Mike."

Breathing heavily, he looked down at the gun as if he'd never seen it before.

"Put it away, Mike."

He looked up at her and his brows drew down into a deep vee. "This is crazy," he said.

"There's a perfectly simple explanation," she told him, moving closer. She'd jump him if she had to. With luck, he'd hesitate before shooting her and she'd be able to disarm him.

"Okay." He tossed the curl of hair back off his forehead. "Let's hear it."

Vicki glanced back at Nadine who shrugged.

"Go ahead," she said. "If you think he can handle it."

Vicki thought they didn't have much choice, at least not until they got that gun back where it belonged.

"Your simple explanation?" Celluci prodded.

Squaring her shoulders, she met his eyes and said, as matter-of-factly as she was able, "Werewolves."

"Werewolves," he repeated blankly, then he bent and slipped the .38 into its holster, twitching the leg

of his jeans back into place before he straightened. He
looked down at Shadow, rubbing himself up against
his father's fur, at Storm and Cloud who were doing
much the same, and then over at Henry.

"You, too?" he asked.

Henry shook his head. "No."

Celluci nodded. "Good." He drew in a deep breath
and then he started to swear. In Italian. He kept it up
for almost three minutes and managed to dredge up
words and phrases he hadn't used since childhood.
Most of them, he screamed at Vicki who waited patiently for him to run down.

Henry, who spoke fluent if slightly archaic Italian,
noted, moderately impressed, that he only repeated
himself in order to add adjectives to the profanity.

His vocabulary ran out just as the lights of the ambulance turned in at the top of the lane.

The moment they showed, Nadine took charge.
"Cloud! Get Shadow back upstairs and make sure he
and the twins stay there. Storm stay in fur-form; your
ear is still bleeding. Tag, get some clothes on."

Tag? Vicki repeated silently as Stuart scooped up a
pair of sweatpants. *Stuart's fur-form name is Tag?*

"Colin," Nadine continued, closing the hall door
behind Cloud and Shadow, "you follow them into town
in case he needs blood. Vicki, could you go in the
ambulance? If he wakes up. . . ."

"No problem."

She'd told the others and asked Vicki—Henry noted
the distinction with some amusement.

As the paramedics carried Donald out on the
stretcher, Celluci grabbed Vicki's arm and pulled her
to one side.

"I'm going to follow you in. We have to talk."

"I'll be looking forward to it."

"Good." He drew his lips back off his teeth in a
parody of a smile. No one in the room, vampire or
wer, could have done it better.

Eleven

"Because the hospital has to report gunshot wounds, you should know that."

Colin glanced over at Barry and the two Ontario Provincial Police constables standing talking by the nurses' station. "You said it was a ricochet."

Vicki rolled her eyes. "Colin. . . ."

"Okay, sorry. It's just, well, what am I going to tell them?"

"You aren't going to tell them anything." She smothered a yawn with her fist. "I am. Trust me. I've been at this longer than you have, I know the things a police department wants to hear and the way they want to hear them."

"Vicki." Celluci leaned forward and tapped her on the shoulder. "I hate to burst your bubble, but you are quite possibly the worst liar I know."

She turned to face him, pushing her glasses up her nose. "Lie to the police? I wouldn't think of it. Every word out of my mouth is going to be the truth."

"So there's been someone taking potshots out of those woods for a while now?"

"Well, I'm not sure three shots counts as *potshots*, Constable."

"Still should've been reported, ma'am. If someone's firing a hunting rifle out in the conservation area we'd like to know about it."

"The family figured it was just because Arthur Fortrin was out of town," Colin put in.

Given a little direction, Colin was remarkably good at half-truths. *But then, he'd have to be,* Vicki realized. *All things considered.*

The OPP constable looked dubious. "I don't think the absence of one game warden's going to make much difference. And *you* should've known better." He snapped his occurrence book shut. "Tell your family next time they hear a shot, to call us immediately. Maybe we can spot the guy's car."

"I'll tell them. . . ." Colin shrugged.

"Yeah, I know, but will they listen." The constable sighed and glanced over at Vicki. He didn't think much of a Toronto private detective messing around in his neck of the woods, although her police background did lend credibility. His warning to be careful died in his throat when he caught her eye. She looked like a person who could take care of herself—and anything else that crossed her path. "So," he turned back to Colin, "this have anything to do with your Aunt Sylvia leaving?"

Colin snorted. "Well, she did say it was the last straw."

"Didn't she head up to the Yukon?"

"Yeah, her brother, my Uncle Robert, has a place just outside Whitehorse. She said it was getting too crowded around here."

"Your Uncle Jason just took off too, didn't he?"

"Yeah, Father accused Aunt Sylvia of starting an exodus and threatened to lock Peter, Rose, and I in the house until things calmed down."

"Well, frankly I was surprised he stayed around as long as he did. Man needs a place of his own." The OPP constable poked Colin in the ribs with his pen. "When'll you be moving out?"

"When I feel suicidal enough to live on my own cooking."

Both men laughed and the conversation turned to a general discussion of food.

Vicki realized that the wer were perhaps not as iso-

lated as she'd originally thought. Colin leaving the
farm and taking a job had brought them to the attention of the police if nothing else. Fortunately, the police tended to take care of their own. As for the
shooting; she knew there wasn't much the OPP could
do. She could only hope that a few extra patrols up
and around the area would give her time to find this
psycho before anyone else got killed. The wer would
just have to recognize their higher visibility and be
more careful when they changed for a while. It seemed
a small price to pay.

". . . anyway, Donald's fine. The hospital released
him into Dr. Dixon's care—that's one persuasive old
man—and he'll probably be able to come home tomorrow. Apparently because he was shot in one form
and then changed there's no danger of infection. Colin's on his way back, but I thought I should call and
fill you in. Oh, and Nadine, I'll be spending the night
in town."

"Explanations?"

"Uh-huh."

"Do you trust him with this?"

"I trust Mike Celluci with my life."

"Good. Because you're trusting him with ours."

Vicki half turned so she could see Celluci leaning
on the hospital wall across from the phones. He looked
tired but impassive, with all professional barriers
raised. "It'll be okay. Can I speak to Henry?"

"Hang on." Nadine held the receiver out to the
vampire. "You were right," she told him as he took
it.

He didn't appear particularly gratified by this information. If Celluci's face was impassive, Henry's was
stone. "Vicki?"

"Hi. I thought I should tell you, I'm staying in town
tonight. I need a little time alone."

"Alone?"

"Well, away."

"I can't say as I'm surprised. You and Mr. Celluci have a great deal to discuss."

"Tell me about it. Do me a favor?"

"Anything." Before she could speak, he reconsidered and added. "Almost anything."

"Stay around the house tonight."

"Why?"

"Because it's 3:40 in the morning and sunrise is around 6:00."

"Vicki, I have been avoiding the dawn for a long time. Don't patronize me."

Okay. Maybe she deserved that. "Look, Henry, it's late, you've only got one good arm—at best one and a half—I've had a very rough day, and it isn't over yet. Please, give me one less person to worry about over the next few hours. We know this guy is coming right up to the house and we don't know for sure just where exactly Donald was shot."

"You didn't ask him?"

"I didn't get the chance. Look," she sagged against the wall, "let's just assume that the farm is under a state of siege and act accordingly. Okay?"

"You're asking me to do this for your peace of mind?"

She drew in a deep breath and let it out slowly. She had no right to ask him such a thing for such a reason. "Yes."

"All right. I'll sit quietly in the kitchen and work on an outline for my next book."

"Thank you. And keep the wer in the house. Even if you have to nail the doors shut." She slid a finger and thumb up under the edge of her glasses and rubbed the bridge of her nose. "I mean, how many times do I have to tell them to stay out of those fields?"

"An enemy they can't see or smell isn't very real to them."

She snorted. "Well, death is. I'll see you tomorrow night."

"Count on it. Vicki? Is he likely to be difficult?"

She shot another glance at Celluci, who was attempting to cover a massive yawn. "He excels at being difficult, but I can usually make him see reason if I thump him hard enough."

After she hung up, she rested her head for a few seconds on the cool plastic top of the phone. She couldn't remember the last time she'd wanted to sleep this badly.

"Come on." Celluci pulled her arm through his and steered her out into the parking lot where the heat hit them like a moist and semi-solid wall. "I know a cheap, clean motel out by the airport where they don't care what time you show up as long as you pay cash."

"How the hell did you find a place like that?" The yawn threatened to split her head in two and the pain came down on her bruised temple with hobnailed boots. "Never mind. I don't want to know." She slid into the car and let her head fall back against the seat. "I know you're dying to begin the interrogation—why don't I just start at the beginning and tell it in my own words?" If she had a nickel for every time she'd said that to a witness, she'd be a rich woman.

Eyes closed, she started with Rose and Peter in Henry's condo. She finished, with Donald being shot, as they pulled in at the motel. The only thing she left out was Henry's actual nature. That wasn't her story to tell.

To her surprise, Celluci's only response was, "Wait in the car. I'll go get us a room."

As she had no intention of moving farther or more often than she had to, she ignored his tone and waited. Fortunately, the keys he returned with were to a room on the ground floor. At this point, she doubted her ability to climb stairs.

"Why so quiet?" she asked at last, easing herself gently down on one of the double beds. "I was expecting another fine set of Italian hysterics at the very least."

"I'm thinking." He sat on the other bed, unbuckled

his holster, and laid it carefully on the bedside table. "A concept I know you're unfamiliar with."

Except he didn't know *what* he was thinking. There were a number of things Vicki wasn't telling him and exhaustion had distanced the events of the night so they felt as though they'd happened to someone else. He couldn't believe he'd actually pulled his gun. It was easier to believe in werewolves.

"Werewolves," he muttered. "What next?"

"Sleep?" Vicki suggested hopefully, her voice slurred.

"Does this have anything to do with what happened last spring?"

"Sleeping?" Something about that didn't make sense but she couldn't quite get her brain around it.

"Never mind." He pulled her glasses off her face and set them down beside his gun, then quickly undressed her. She let him. She hated sleeping in her clothes and didn't have the energy to get rid of them herself.

"Good night, Vicki."

"Night, Mike. Don't worry." She fought with her mouth to get the last words out. "It'll all make sense in the morning."

He leaned over and pulled the sheet up around her shoulders. "Somehow, I doubt it," he told her softly, although he suspected she could no longer hear him.

Henry stood and stared up at the night, trying to decide how he felt. Jealousy was an emotion his kind learned to deal with early on or they didn't survive long. *You are mine!* sounded very dramatic, especially when accompanied by a swirling cape and ominous music, but real life just didn't work that way.

The trouble, therefore, had to be Celluci. "The man throws his life out like a challenge," Henry muttered. He wasn't at all surprised Stuart had attacked the detective—dominant males usually came to blows. His continuing presence probably hadn't helped. Although he had a special status within the family, while he was around Stuart remained on edge, instincts demanding that one of them submit. It was the alpha male's responsibility to protect the pack and his frustration at having to call in outside help had no doubt destabilized Stuart further.

Given Celluci's attitude and Stuart's state of mind, a fight had been inevitable. Storm's intervention, on the other hand, had been a complete surprise to everyone involved, including Storm. Cloud must be getting very close for her twin to be behaving so irrationally.

Which brought them back around, more or less, to Vicki.

Henry grinned. If Celluci was a wer, he'd piss a circle around her, telling the world, *This is mine!* And then Vicki would get up and walk out of it.

"I'm not jealous of him," he told the night, aware as he spoke that it was almost a lie.

"Can we love?" The process had begun although the final change had not yet been made.

Christina turned to him, dark eyes veiled behind the ebony fan of her lashes. "Do you doubt it?" she asked, and came into his arms.

He had loved half a dozen times in the centuries since and each time it had shone like a beacon in the long darkness of his life.

Was it happening again? He wasn't sure. He only knew he wanted to tell Mike Celluci, "The day is yours, but the night is *mine.*"

Celluci would be as unlikely to agree to such a division as Vicki would.

"You cannot resent what they do in the daylight hours." Christina laid his head upon her breast and lightly stroked his hair. "For if you do, it will fester in your heart and twist your nature and you will be-

*come one of those creatures of darkness they are right
to fear. Fear is what kills us.''*

Perhaps, when the wer were safe, he would ask her,
''Will you give me your nights?''
Perhaps.

He wanted to touch her, hold her . . . no . . . he
wanted to catch her up and throw her down and reestablish his claim on her. The intensity of his desire
frightened him, stopped him. Confused, he sat on the
edge of his bed, watching her sleep, listening to the soft
sound of her breathing play a counterpoint to the
helicopter roar of cheap air-conditioning.

They'd never had an exclusive relationship. They'd
both had other lovers. *She'd* had other lovers.

Mike Celluci forced his hands to relax against his
bare thighs and took a deep breath of the chilled air.
Nothing had changed between him and Vicki since
Henry Fitzroy came on the scene.

Suddenly, he couldn't stop thinking about the first
eight months after she'd left the force. They'd had one
last bitter fight and then no contact at all as the days
dragged into weeks and the world had become more
and more impossible to deal with. Until she was gone,
he hadn't realized how important a part of his life she'd
been. And it wasn't the sex he'd missed. He'd missed
conversations and arguments—even considering that
most of their conversations became arguments—and
just having someone around who'd get the joke. He'd
lost his best friend and had barely learned to live with
the loss when fate had thrown them together again.

No one should have to go through that twice.

But Fitzroy wasn't taking her anywhere.

Was he?

''Look, if you think that after last night I'm going
meekly back to Toronto, think again. I'm driving you
back to the farm. Get in the car.''

Vicki sighed and surrendered. She recognized Celluci's *"There's more going on here than meets the eye and I'm going to get to the bottom of it regardless of how you feel"* tone, and it was just too hot to keep arguing. Besides, if he didn't drive her, someone would have to come out from the farm to get her and that didn't seem entirely fair.

And he already knew about the wer, so what harm would it do with Henry safely locked away?

"So," he started the engine and flipped the air-conditioning on full, "what are the odds your furry friend is going to go for my throat again?"

"Depends. What are the odds you're going to act like a jackass?"

He frowned. "Did I?"

Vicki shook her head. *Just when you think he has no redeeming characteristics.* . . . "Well," she said aloud, "you did challenge Stuart's authority in his own house."

"I was a little upset, werewolves are a new concept for me. I wasn't myself."

"You were definitely yourself," Vicki corrected with a smile. "But I think that under normal circumstances Stuart will be able to deal with that."

They stopped for breakfast at a hotel down the road and Vicki allowed Celluci to pump her about the case while they ate, giving the waitress only one bad moment when Vicki exclaimed, ". . . and to blow the top of his head off from that distance was one hell of a shot!" just as she put the plates down. If Celluci noticed she talked around Henry's involvement, he didn't mention it. She couldn't decide if he was being tactful or deep.

"You do realize," Celluci said, mashing the last of his hash browns into the leftover yoke on his plate, "that there're two of them out there? One with a shotgun and one with a rifle?"

She shook her head, setting down her empty coffee mug with just a little too much force. "I don't think so; this has all the earmarks of being a one-person setup. I know, I know,'' she raised her hand and cut off his protest, ''Henry got shot at twice.'' Henry's injuries had been considerably downplayed over the course of the conversation. ''But one man can operate two guns and up until now there's been no evidence of a second player.''

Celluci snorted. ''There's been bugger all evidence, period.''

''But the tracks, the tree, the type of shot, all point to a single obsessed personality. I think he,'' she spread her hands as Celluci's brows went up, ''or she, just kept the shotgun handy in case anyone got too close.''

''Like your *writer* friend.'' His tone made it perfectly clear what he thought about both Henry *and* Henry wandering around in the woods playing the great detective.

''Henry Fitzroy can take care of himself.''

''Oh, obviously.'' He stood and tossed a twenty down on the table. ''That's why he got shot. Twice. Still, I'm amazed you let an amateur wander around out there at night, considering the danger.''

''I didn't know about the shotgun,'' she protested as they left the coffee shop, then wished she could recall the words the moment they left her mouth. ''Henry's a grown man,'' she muttered getting into the car. ''I didn't *let* him do anything.''

''That's a surprise.''

''I'm not going to discuss him with you.''

''Did I say I wanted to?'' He pulled out of the parking lot and headed north. ''You've gotten yourself involved with a pack of werewolves, Vicki. For the moment, that makes organized crime seem just a little tame.''

''Henry is *not* involved in organized crime.''

''All right. Fine. It makes whatever he is involved with seem just a little tame.''

Vicki pushed her glasses up her nose and slouched

down in the seat. *That's all you know,* she thought. She recognized the set of Celluci's jaw and knew that although he might be temporarily distracted by the wer, he wasn't going to let his suspicions about Henry drop. *Fine. Henry can deal with it. In four hundred odd years, this can't be the first time.* While she had no intention of getting caught in the cross fire, she would be perfectly willing to bash their heads together if it became necessary.

"Look," she said just before they reached Highbury Avenue, "if you're going to hang around, you might as well make yourself useful."

He scowled suspiciously. "Doing what?"

"Turn right. You're going to pay a visit to the OPP for me."

She had to give him credit for brains, he understood the reason for the visit immediately.

"You haven't got the firearms registration list, have you? Why the hell not?"

"Well . . ." Vicki flicked the air-conditioner vents back and forth a time or two. "The OPP and I had a little misunderstanding." She hated admitting even that much, knowing that Celluci would blow it all out of proportion.

"I'll bet," he grunted and, to her surprise, let it drop.

Twenty minutes later when he came out of the station, he made up for his silence.

"A little misunderstanding?" He slammed the car door and twisted around to glare at her. "Vicki, you may have destroyed any chance of provincial cooperation with local police forces for now and for always. What the hell did you say?"

She told him.

He shook his head. "I'm amazed the Duty Sergeant let you leave the building alive."

"I take it then that you didn't get the list."

"Dead on, Sherlock, but I did get an earful concerning proper police procedure."

"Damn it! I need that list."

"Should've thought of that before you made the crack about his mother." Celluci stopped the car at the parking lot exit. "Which way?"

"Left." Vicki waited until he'd maneuvered the car around the turn and into traffic before she added. "I want you to pick up a membership list from the Y."

"Have you alienated them, too?"

She supposed it was a legitimate question, all things considered. "No, but I have no right to ask them for the list and they have no reason to hand it over. You, however, are a cop." She poked him in the biceps. "Nice people, like those at the Y, are used to trusting the police. If *you* ask them for their firstborn child, they'll hand the little nipper over."

"You want me to lie for you?"

Vicki smiled at him, showing her teeth. "You're always bragging about how good you are at it."

The nice people at the YMCA proved fully as cooperative as Vicki had suggested and Celluci threw the membership list of the photography club on her lap as he climbed into the car.

"Anything else," he grumbled, starting the engine.

"You're the one who decided to stick around," Vicki pointed out, scanning the membership for names she recognized. No one looked familiar, so she folded it carefully and put it in her purse. "That's it for this morning. Let's head out to the farm, I'm desperate for a change of clothes." Although she'd had a lovely long shower behind the locked door of the motel bathroom, she was still wearing yesterday's shorts and shirt and they were both a bit the worse for wear.

"I was wondering what that smell was."

"Piss off, Celluci. You sure you can find your way out of the city?"

He could. Although he had to start from the police station to do it.

They drove in silence for a while, Vicki half dozing

as she stared out the window at the passing fields and trees and trees and fields and. . . .

Suddenly she straightened. "I think you missed the turn."

"What are you talking about?"

"I don't remember seeing that ruined schoolhouse before."

"Just because you didn't see it. . . ."

"Look, I've been out this way three times now. Twice," she used the word to cut off his next comment, "in the daylight when I could see. I think you missed the turn."

"You might be right," he conceded, searching the surrounding farmland for landmarks. "Should we turn around now or cut east at the next opportunity?"

"Well, county roads are usually laid out on a simple grid pattern. As long as we head south at the first opportunity we should be fine."

"The next east it is, then."

Vicki slid down in the seat and braced her knees against the dashboard. They both knew it would make more sense to turn around now and look for the correct crossroad, but Vicki was comfortable and relaxed for the first time in days and didn't think a few extra moments would make a difference. She understood Mike Celluci. He had come to represent the natural in the face of the supernatural, and that meant she could let her guard down in a way she couldn't with either Henry or the wer. If they turned and went back, the interlude would only be over that much earlier.

She didn't dare guess what Celluci's reasons were for driving on.

The side road they turned onto petered out in a farmyard after six kilometers. The farmer, not bothering to hide his amusement, gave them directions while his dog marked a rear tire. They'd driven past the south turnoff, thinking it was only a lane.

"This thing has more potholes than Spadina Avenue," Vicki grunted, blocking the ceiling's attempt to smack her in the head. "Do you think maybe you could slow down?"

"Just watch for the red barn."

The red barn had either fallen or faded; it certainly wasn't where the farmer had said. They finally turned east on the second crossroad, which after two kilometers swung around a gentle, banked curve and headed due south.

"We're going to end up back in London at this rate."

Celluci sighed. "Hasn't anyone out here ever heard of street signs? There's a building up ahead. Let's see if we can get some coherent directions this time."

They'd turned into the driveway before Vicki recognized the white farm house.

"Lost again, Ms. Nelson?" Carl Biehn approached the passenger side of the car, brushing dirt off his hands.

Vicki smiled up at him. "Not this time, Mr. Biehn." She hooked a thumb back over her shoulder. *"He* was driving."

Carl bent so he could see into the car and nodded at Celluci who nodded back and said, "We seem to have taken a wrong turn."

"Easy to do in the country," the older man told him, straightening.

Vicki thought he looked tired. His eyes were ringed in purple shadows and the lines running past the corners of his mouth had deepened. "Trouble in the garden?" she asked, and wondered why he started.

"No. No trouble." He rubbed at a bit of mud dried to the edge of his thumb, his hands washing around and around themselves.

"Well, well, well. Lost again, Ms. Nelson?" The words were identical, but the tone sat just this side of insult. "I think you'll have to face the fact that some people aren't cut out for country life."

Vicki considered returning a smile as false as the one Mark Williams offered her but decided not to bother. She didn't like him; she didn't care if he knew it.

He pushed past his uncle and leaned into the car, resting one hand on the bottom edge of the open window. "I see this morning you've managed to lead someone else astray." His left hand stretched across Vicki into the car. "Mark Williams."

"Celluci. Michael Celluci."

They shook briefly. Vicki found herself tempted to take a bite out of the tanned arm as it withdrew. She restrained herself; time spent with the wer had obviously influenced her thinking. *Besides, odds are I'd catch something disgusting.*

"What happened to your head?" He sounded concerned.

"I had an accident." And it was none of his business.

"You weren't badly hurt?" Carl looked down over his nephew's shoulder, brow furrowed.

"Just a bump," Vicki assured him. He nodded, satisfied, and she shot Mark a look that warned against further questions.

"We're trying to get to the Heerkens farm." Celluci wore his neutral expression—not friendly, not unfriendly, just there. Vicki had one like it. She didn't bother to put it on.

"No problem. Three or four kilometers down this road and the first left. Their lane's about two K in." He laughed companionably. His breath spilled into the car, smelling like mint. "And about two K long once you get there."

"Nothing wrong with privacy," Celluci said mildly.

"Nothing at all," the other man agreed. He stood and spread his hands, the gold hair on his forearms glinting in the sun. "I'm all for it myself."

I bet you are, Vicki thought. *And wouldn't I just love a look at the dirty little secrets your privacy hides. Probably good for five to ten just for starters. . . .*

"Ms. Nelson?" Carl had stopped rubbing at the dirt

but he still appeared disturbed. "Will you be staying with the Heerkens long?"

"I hope not."

"That sounds almost like a prayer."

She sighed. "Maybe it is." She was staying until she nailed the bastard with the rifle and if prayer would help then she had nothing against it. Pushing her glasses up her nose, she turned to wave as Celluci did a three point turn in the driveway and headed back to the road.

Carl raised a strained hand in a reserved salute but Mark, who knew full well he hadn't been included in the farewell gesture, responded with a flamboyant movement of his arm.

"Well?"

"Well, what?" He half turned toward her, brows up. "You aren't actually asking my opinion, are you?"

"Celluci."

He pursed his lips and turned back to face the road. "The older man's upset by something, probably the younger—pity you can't choose your relatives. Given what you told me over breakfast and what I observed just now, my brilliant powers of deduction conclude you like Mr. Biehn, who I admit seems to be a decent sort, but you don't like Mr. Williams."

Vicki snorted. "Don't tell me you do?"

"He didn't seem so bad. Hey! Don't assault the driver."

"Then don't bullshit me."

Celluci grinned. "What? You want your opinion confirmed? That's gotta be a first."

Vicki waited. She knew he wouldn't miss an opportunity to tell her what he thought.

"I think," he continued right on cue, "that Mark Williams would sell his own mother if he figured he could make a profit from the deal. I guarantee he's up to something else; his kind always are."

Vicki shoved at her glasses even though they were

sitting firmly at the top of her nose. It'd be a cold day in hell before Mark Williams had the discipline to become the kind of marksman who was picking off the wer.

Carl Biehn turned away the moment the car left the drive. He'd always been able to find peace in the garden but this morning it had eluded him. He kept hearing, over and over, the cry of the creature he had wounded in the night. It was not one of God's creatures so its pain should have no power to move him but he couldn't block the cry from his mind or his heart.

The Lord tested him, to see if his resolve was strong. Evil must not be pitied, it must be cast out.

"Two cops." Mark Williams pursed his lips thoughtfully. "She seems to have brought in reinforcements." It was too bad yesterday's accident hadn't removed the problem but, as he always said, nothing ventured, nothing gained. Even if Ms. Nelson's friend was here to investigate the crash, he'd been very careful to leave nothing on the car that would incriminate him.

On the other hand, with the two of them rummaging about, he'd better get a move on or between the police and his trigger-happy uncle, there'd be nothing left of his lovely little plan.

"Are you going to fight with my father again?"

"Not unless he fights with me."

Daniel turned and looked up at Stuart, who had risen as Vicki and Celluci came in and was now standing behind his chair growling low in his throat. "Daddy?"

Stuart ignored him. The two men locked eyes.

"Daddy? Can I bite him for you?"

Stuart started and glanced down at his son. "Can you what?"

"Can I bite him for you?" Daniel bared small white teeth.

"Daniel, you don't just go around biting people. You've been taught better than that."

The youngest wer narrowed his eyes. "You were going to," he pointed out.

"That's different."

"Why?"

"You'll understand when you're older."

"Understand what?"

"Well. . . ." He shot a helpless look at Celluci who spread his hands, equally at a loss for an answer. "It's a . . . man thing."

Daniel snorted. "I never get to bite anybody," he complained, kicked the screen door open, and stomped out into the yard.

Although laughter might be the spark in the tinder, Vicki couldn't help herself. She collapsed back onto the sagging couch, holding her sides and gasping for breath. "A man thing," she managed to wheeze finally, and started up harder than ever.

The two men looked down at her and then at each other, expressions identical.

"Stuart Heerkens-Wells."

"Michael Celluci."

"Is she with you?"

"Never saw her before in my life."

When Vicki came downstairs from changing her clothes, only Nadine was in the kitchen.

"Where is everyone?" she asked, shoving her glasses up her nose and setting her bag on the floor.

"Well, my daughters are out in the barn chasing rats, my son is hopefully wearing himself out chasing that frisbee. . . ."

Vicki peered out the kitchen window and saw, to her surprise, Celluci throwing the frisbee for Shadow. "What's *he* still doing here?"

"I think he's waiting for you."

Vicki sighed. "You know, when we turned in the lane, I thanked him for his help and told him to get lost. I wonder what made me think he'd listen?"

"He's a man. I think you're expecting too much of him. Anyway, Rose and Peter are getting dressed to take you back into town and Tag's gone to check the flock."

Which reminded Vicki of something she'd meant to ask. "Tag? He doesn't look much like a Tag."

"Maybe not now," Nadine agreed, "but he was the youngest and the smallest in a set of triplets and I guess it suited him then."

"The smallest?"

Nadine grinned. "Yes, well, he grew."

Just then Celluci came into the kitchen leaving Shadow out on the lawn, tongue lolling, frisbee safe under both front paws. "Good, you're ready. Let's get going, it's almost noon. I hear Henry Fitzroy's still in bed." He kept himself from sneering but only just.

"He had a busy night."

"Didn't we all."

Then it hit her. "Going where?"

"Back into town. You need to check with the mechanic—unless you don't care if Peter's charged with operating an unsafe vehicle—someone somewhere has to know who has the skill to make those shots so I suggest we go where the boys are, and Donald has to be picked up and brought home."

"Yeah? So?" She folded her arms across her chest. "What does any of that have to do with you?"

"I've decided to stick around." He inclined his head toward Nadine. "No extra charge."

Vicki bit off the *Fuck you!* before she actually vocalized it. It almost choked her, but her pride, measured against the lives of the wer, meant nothing. On the other hand, in spite of what he thought, Mike Celluci did not have a direct line to truth and he had no right to butt in.

"What's up?" Peter followed his sister into the

kitchen and looked from Vicki to Celluci, nostrils
flared. There were some strange scents in the air.

"Vicki's just deciding who's going to be driving into
town," Nadine told him.

"Rose," Peter said promptly. "I'm still traumatized
from yesterday."

Rose rolled her eyes. "You want to sit with your
head out the window."

He grinned. "That, too."

"I'm driving because we're taking my car."

The twins turned as one to look at Vicki.

*I should tell him to go home and this time make it
stick, even if I have to break a few bones. I don't need
his high-handed help.*

Reading her indecision, Peter moved a step closer,
and lowered his voice. "Uh, Vicki, about *him* being
around, I don't think Henry's going to approve."

Her eyes narrowed to slits. What the hell did Henry
have to do with this? She grabbed her purse up off the
floor and headed for the door. "What are you standing
around for?" she snapped as she passed Celluci. "I
thought you were driving."

Celluci glanced speculatively at Peter, then followed.

"What was all that about?" Peter wondered as the
twins hurried to catch up. "Why did Aunt Nadine start
laughing?"

"You really don't know?"

"No. I really don't."

Rose sighed and shook her head. "Peter, you are
such a dork sometimes."

"Am not."

"Are too."

They'd have continued the argument all the way into
London if Vicki hadn't threatened to muzzle them
both.

Twelve

"There's your problem."

Vicki peered down into the engine of Henry's BMW. Nothing looked obviously wrong. "Where's the problem?"

"There." The mechanic pointed with the screwdriver he held. "Brakeline, up by the master cylinder."

"There's something wrong with the brakeline?"

"Yeah. Holed."

"What do you mean, holed?"

The mechanic sighed. His expression said *"Women!"* as clearly as if he'd spoken the word aloud. "Holed. Like, not solid."

"Someone put a hole in it?" It took a moment for the implications of that to sink in. Had the stakes just gone up? Had the killer become aware of her involvement and decided to do something about it? She frowned; that didn't fit the established pattern. Suddenly the air in the garage, already redolent with iron and oil and gasoline, grew thicker and harder to breathe.

"Didn't say someone did it. See here?" He lifted the black rubber hose on the end of his screwdriver. "Rubbed against that piece of metal. Rubbed just right between the ribs and broke through." Shrugging, he let the hose drop. "Happens. Brakes work for a while but lose fluid. Lose enough fluid and. . . ." A greasy finger cut a line across his throat.

"Yes, I know." Vicki straightened. "I was there. So you'll be telling the police. . . ?"

"Accident. Tough luck. Nobody's fault." He shrugged again and turned to shake his head at the destroyed side of the car. "Hard to believe everyone walked away. Lucky."

Very lucky, Vicki realized. Death had missed her by less than a couple of feet and if Rose had been riding on the passenger side, she wouldn't have survived. Holding her glasses on her nose, Vicki bent over the brakeline again; something didn't look right.

"Why the hell would anyone build a car so that the brakeline rubbed?"

She could hear the shrug in the mechanic's voice. "Could be 'cause it's an old car. Built in '76, things go wrong. Could've been a mistake on the line. No two cars are exactly alike."

All right, it made sense, bad luck and nothing more had put her and Rose and Peter in the car when that little mistake had paid off. *Jesus, if you can't count on a BMW. . . .*

Except. . . . There were two spots bracketing the tear where the yellow markings on the hose showed brighter, places where accumulated dirt could have rubbed off on someone's fingers as they gave that little mistake a helping hand. Careful not to touch the rubber, Vicki pressed her finger against the protruding bit of metal that had done the actual damage. While not exactly sharp, it held a definite edge.

"Suppose you wanted to hole someone's brakeline and yet made it look like an accident," she gestured down into the engine, "how long would it take you to duplicate that?"

The mechanic looked speculative. "Not long."

They'd been in the restaurant for an hour and a half. Plenty of time.

Intrigued by the idea, he reached down into the car. "I'd grab it here . . ."

"Don't touch it!"

He jerked back as though stung. ''You don't think. . . .''

''I don't think I want to take any chances. I want you to call the police. I have the number of the officer at the scene if you don't.''

''No. I got it.''

''Good. Tell him you've found suspicions of tampering and, if nothing else, they should take prints.'' She had her own small kit, not exactly high tech but certainly up to lifting prints off greasy hoses. If, however, police technology could be brought to bear, so much the better.

''Why don't you call?''

''Because you're the expert.''

He scowled at her for a moment then sighed and said, ''Okay, lady. You win. I'll call.''

''Now,'' she suggested.

''Okay. Now. You don't touch nothing while I'm gone.''

''Fine. And you don't touch anything until the ident man has come and gone.''

The scowl returned. He went two steps, stopped, and looked back. ''Someone tried to kill you, eh?''

''Maybe.'' Or Peter. Or Rose.

He shook his head, his expression hovering between respect and disgust. ''Bet it isn't the first time.'' He continued to the office without waiting for a reply.

Vicki rubbed her right thumb against the faint scars on her left wrist, saw again the inhuman smile, and heard the demon say, *''So you are to be the sacrifice.''* A trickle of sweat that had nothing to do with the heat ran down between her breasts and behind it, she could feel her heart begin to race. Death had been so close that a shadow of it remained long after the substance had been defeated. With practiced skill, she pushed the memory away and buried it deep.

The world outside the memory seemed strange for a moment then she shook her head and forced herself back to the present. Out by the car, Rose was telling

Celluci some kind of story that involved a great deal
of arm waving, Peter hovering protectively at her side.
When Celluci laughed at something Rose said, Vicki
saw Peter's shoulders stiffen.

"Peter! Could you come here, please?"

Reluctantly, he came.

She nodded toward the car. "What are the odds that
you could pick up someone's scent off a rubber brakeline?"

Peter glanced down into the engine and wrinkled his
nose. "Slim to none. The smell of the brake fluid is
kind of strong. Why?"

Vicki saw no point in lying, the wer already knew
they were under the threat of death. "I think someone
engineered yesterday's accident."

"Wow. Henry's going to be pissed."

"Henry?"

"Well, they totaled his car."

"And almost killed us," Vicki reminded him.

"Oh. Yeah."

The office door opened and the mechanic walked
back into the garage. He didn't look thrilled. "Okay.
I called. He says someone'll come around. Later." He
glared at the car and then up at Vicki. "He says he
wants to talk to you. Don't leave town."

"I wouldn't dream of it. Thanks, you've been a big
help."

He returned her smile with a snort and pointedly
bent to work on a late model, blue Saab that had seen
better days.

Vicki recognized a dismissal when she saw it. As
there was nothing more she could do here, she even
decided to pay attention to it. "Come on, Peter."

Frowning thoughtfully, Peter followed her out of the
garage.

"What?" she asked as they crossed the parking lot
to Celluci's car.

"It's probably nothing, but while you were talking
to Mr. Sunshine I had a sniff around the edges of the

hood. I mean, if someone messed with the brakes they had to get the hood open first.'' He took a deep breath. ''Anyway, for just a second there, I thought I caught a scent I recognized. Then I lost it. Sorry.''

''Would you know it again?''

''I think so.''

''Okay, if you do come across it, tell me immediately. This guy is dangerous.''

''Hey,'' he protested. ''I know. It's my dad that got shot.''

Vicki wondered if she should tell him that the person who'd shot his father and the person who'd tampered with Henry's car weren't likely to be the same man—the actions were far too different—and in her book this new threat, with no pattern to make it predictable, was a lot more dangerous. She decided against it. What good would it do?

Celluci watched until Peter and Rose had gone inside then he backed out of Dr. Dixon's driveway and headed downtown. ''It's hard not to like them, isn't it?''

''What's not to like?''

''This from the woman who once said that teenagers should be against the law?''

''Well, they're not exactly your typical teenagers, are they?''

Celluci glanced sideways at her. ''All right, what's bothering you? You've been in a mood since we left the garage.''

Vicki shoved her glasses up her nose and sighed. ''I was just thinking . . .''

''That's a first.''

She ignored him. ''. . . that if someone's taking the trouble to try to kill me, I must know something I'm not aware of knowing. The killer thinks I'm getting too close.''

''Or you weren't the target, Rose and Peter were. You were just there.''

"No, there's already a system set up to kill the wer, why change it? It's still working. I have a feeling this was aimed at me."

"A hunch?"

"Call it what you like, but if you call it woman's intuition, I'll rip your face off."

As he had no intention of saying anything so blatantly suicidal, he ignored the threat. "So let's go over what you do know."

"Shouldn't take that long." Knees braced against the dash, Vicki ticked the points off on her fingers. "I know Barry Wu didn't do it. I know Dr. Dixon didn't do it. I know Arthur Fortrin didn't do it. *Anyone* else might have, up to and including a chance acquaintance either of those three might have bragged to in a bar. Once Barry tells me who around London is capable of that kind of shot, well, I'll make some comparisons with those lists of the people who use the conservation area regularly. Hopefully we can decode these directions to his apartment before he leaves for work."

Celluci plucked the sheet of paper off her lap, scanned it, and tossed it back. He had complete faith in his ability to find his way around in spite of the morning's scenic tour of the countryside. "And if Barry doesn't know?"

"Someone knows. I'll find them." She smoothed the map out on her leg. "Oh, and it isn't Frederick Kleinbein either."

"Who?"

"Technically, I guess you could call him their nearest neighbor. He informed me that the Heerkens have a deep, dark secret." She grinned. "They're nudists, you know."

"Nudists?"

"So he tells me. Apparently, the locals prefer to believe in nudists over werewolves."

He shot her a sour look. "Hardly surprising. I am, however, surprised it hasn't brought flocks of young men out armed with telephoto lenses."

"I got the impression the 'dogs' took care of that problem."

Celluci who had been on the receiving end of one of those "dogs" in action could see how it might discourage a casual voyeur.

Vicki interpreted his grunt as agreement and went on. "The only other people I've really talked to are Carl Biehn and Mark Williams."

It took him a moment to place the names. "The two guys this morning?"

"That's right."

"So maybe it's them."

"Not likely." She snorted. "Can you see someone like Williams taking the time and trouble to become a marksman? Uh uh. The way I read him, it's instant gratification or he's not interested."

"And the older man? The uncle?"

Vicki sighed. "He's a vegetarian."

"He's not eating the wer, Vicki, he's just killing them."

"And he's a deeply religious man."

"So are a lot of nut cakes. It's not mutually exclusive."

"And he gardens."

"*And* you like him."

She sighed again, flicking the air-conditioning vent open and closed. "Yeah. And I like him. He seems like such a basically decent person."

"Another feeling?"

"Piss off, Celluci." Between the bright sunlight, yesterday's injury, and the lack of sleep, she was developing one mother of a headache. "Having a slimebag for a nephew is hardly grounds to accuse someone of multiple murders. I am, however, going to ask Barry to check out Mr. Williams for priors, just in case. If *you* want to be helpful, and the wind is in the right direction, you can spend tonight watching the tree."

"Thank you very much. Just what I always wanted to do, spend the night out in the woods being eaten alive by mosquitoes.'' *While you and Henry are comfy cozy inside? Not fucking likely.* He glanced over at her and then back at the road. "Who says he'll go back to it?''

"It's part of his pattern when the wind's off the field.''

"Then why don't you cut it down?''

"I've thought about it.''

"While you're thinking about that, here's another one. If you know he keeps going back to that tree, why haven't *you* staked it out?''

"How? *You* know I can't see a damned thing after dark. Besides, Henry went out. . . .''

"You sent a civilian!''

"He volunteered!'' Vicki snapped, ignoring the fact that she herself was now a civilian.

"And did he volunteer to get shot?''

"Henry's a grown man. He knew the risks.''

"A grown man. Right. And that's another thing, according to his driver's license, Fitzroy is only twenty-four years old.'' He took his eyes off the road long enough to glare at her. "You're almost eight years older than he is, or doesn't that . . . What's so funny?''

Although the vibrations were doing nasty things to the inside of her head, Vicki couldn't stop laughing. *Eight whole years. Good God.* Finally, the frigid silence on the other side of the car got through and she managed to get ahold of herself. *Eight whole years.* . . . She took her glasses off and wiped her eyes on the shoulder of her shirt. "Mike, you have no idea of how little that matters.''

"Obviously not,'' Celluci grunted through gritted teeth.

"Hey! Are we in hot pursuit or something? You just accelerated through a yellow light.'' Vicki took one look at the set of his jaw and decided the time had come to change the subject. "What could I possibly know that's worth killing to protect?''

It wasn't the most graceful of conversational transitions but Celluci grabbed at it. He suddenly did *not* want to know what she'd been laughing at. At a full twelve years older than Henry fucking Fitzroy, he didn't think his ego was up to it. "If I were you, I'd have Carl Biehn and his nephew pulled in for questioning."

"On what grounds?"

"Someone thinks you're getting too close and they're the only *someones* you've talked to who haven't been cleared."

"Well, you're not me." Vicki scratched at a mosquito bite on the back of her calf. "And in case you've missed the point, not only is this not a police case but we can't get the police involved."

"They're already involved, or have you forgotten last night's reported gunshot wound?"

"Queen Street. Turn here. Barry's apartment building is number 321." Pushing her glasses up her nose, she added. "The police only think they're involved. They haven't a clue about what's really going on."

"And you don't think they'll find out?" he asked while swinging wide around the corner to avoid a small boy on a bicycle.

Vicki spread her hands. "How are they going to find out? You going to tell them?"

"They'll investigate."

"Sure they will. The OPP'll swing around by the conservation area a little more frequently for a couple of weeks and then something more important than an accidental shooting'll come up for them to allot man-hours to."

"But it wasn't an accident," Celluci pointed out, making an effort and keeping his temper.

"*They* don't know that." Vicki forced herself to relax. Clenched teeth just made her temple throb and had no effect on the thickhead sitting next to her. "Nor are they going to find out."

"Well, they're going to have to get involved when you find out who's doing the killing. Or," he continued sarcastically, "had you planned on arranging an accident that would take care of everything?"

"There." She pointed. "Three twenty-one. Sign says visitor's parking is in the rear."

The silence around the words spoke volumes.

"Jesus Christ, Vicki. You *aren't* going to bring this to trial, are you?"

She studied the toes of her sneakers.

"Answer me, damn it!" He slammed on the brakes and, almost before the car had stopped, grabbed her shoulder, twisting her around to face him.

"Trial?" She jerked her shoulder free. God, he was so dense sometimes. "And what happens to the wer at a trial?"

"The law . . ."

"They don't want the law, Celluci, they want justice and if the killer goes to trial they won't get it. You know as well as I do that the victim goes on trial with the accused. What kind of a chance would the wer have? If you're not white, or you're poor, or, God forbid, you're a woman, the system sees you as less than human. The wer *aren't* human! How do you think the system is going to see them? And what kind of a life would they have after it was finished with them?"

He couldn't believe what he was hearing. "Are you trying to convince me or are you trying to convince yourself?"

"Shut up, Celluci!" He was deliberately not understanding. *His own neat little world view gets screwed and he can't adapt. That's not my fault.*

His voice rose in volume to match hers. "I'm not going to stand around and watch you throw away everything you've believed in for so long."

"Then leave!"

"You're willing to be judge and jury—who's to be the executioner? Or are you going to do *that,* too?"

They stared at each other for moment then Vicki closed her eyes. The pounding of her heart became rifle fire and on the inside of her lids she saw Donald, bleeding, then one by one the rest of the pack, sprawled where the bullets dropped them, their fur splattered with blood, and only she was left to mourn. She drew in a long shuddering breath, and then another, and then she opened her eyes.

"I don't know," she said quietly. "I'll do what I have to."

"And if that includes murder?"

"Leave it, Mike. Please. I said I didn't know."

He forced both hands up through his hair, closing his lips around all but one of the things he wanted to say. He even managed to keep his voice sounding reasonably calm. "You used to know."

"Life used to be a lot simpler. Besides," she unhooked the seat belt, gave a shaky and totally unconvincing laugh, and opened the car door. "I haven't even caught the son-of-a-bitch yet. Let's worry about this shit when it hits the fan."

Celluci followed her into Barry Wu's building, concern and anger in about equal proportions grinding together inside his head. *Life used to be a lot simpler.* He sure couldn't argue with that.

"Most of all, you need a good set of knives."

"I have the knives."

"Pah. New knives. Factory edges are crap."

"I'll have them sharpened this afternoon."

"Pah." The elderly man pulled a torn envelope out of the mess of papers on the kitchen table and scribbled an address on the back of it. "Go here," he commanded as he passed it to his visitor, "last place in town that might do a decent job."

Mark Williams folded the paper in half and tucked it in his wallet. A few questions asked around the fur trade had gotten him the old man's name. A fifty had bought him a couple of hours of instruction. Considering what the pelts were going to net him, he considered it money well spent.

"Okay. Listen up. We go over this one more time

and if you go slow you shouldn't have any trouble. Your first cut is along the length of the belly—almost a seam there anyway—then . . ."

"The problem is, there isn't anyone else. In fact, I'm not positive I could make those shots myself. Not at night." Barry stuck his head out of the bedroom where he was getting dressed for work. "I haven't done much scope work."

"What about one of the special weapons and tactics people?"

His eyebrows drew down. "You mean a cop?"

Celluci sighed. In his opinion, young men always looked petulant when they tried to scowl. "You trying to tell me London's never had a bad cop?"

"Well . . . no . . . but it's not like we're Toronto or anything." He disappeared back into the bedroom and emerged a moment later, uniform shirt hanging open and carrying his boots. "I guess I could ask around," he offered, perching on the edge of the one remaining empty chair. The apartment was a little short of furniture although both the television and stereo system were first rate. "But frankly, I don't think any of those guys could do it either." He took a deep breath. "I know it sounds like bragging but even considering my lack of scope work, none of them are in my league."

Vicki picked Barry's police college graduation picture up from its place of honor on top of the television. Only one of the earnestly smiling faces in the photograph belonged to a visible minority; Barry Wu. *Plus five women and a werewolf. What a great mix.* All the women were white. Technically, so was the werewolf. *And the police wonder why community relations are falling apart.* Actually, she had to admit, the police knew why community relations were falling apart, they just couldn't come up with the quick fix solution everybody wanted in the face of such a long-term problem. Unfortunately, "it'll take time" wasn't much of an answer when time was running out.

"I'm surprised the S.W.A.T. boys haven't scooped you up." She carefully set the picture back down. It was still strange thinking of herself and *the police* as separate units.

He smiled a little self-consciously. "I've been warned the moment I come back with Olympic gold, I'm theirs." The smile faded as he bent to lace his boots. "I guess I'd better check them out, hadn't I?"

"Well, if you can find out what their best marksmen were doing on the nights of the murders, it would help."

"Yeah." He sighed. "Pity we didn't have some big hostage crisis those nights that'd clear them."

"Pity," Vicki agreed, and hid a totally inappropriate smile. The boy—young man—had been completely serious.

"I just can't believe that someone'd be shooting at Colin's family. I mean," he sat up and began buttoning his shirt, fingers trembling with indignation, "they're probably the nicest people I know."

"It doesn't bother you that these people turn into animals?" Celluci asked.

Barry stiffened. "They don't turn into animals," he snapped. "Just because they have a fur-form doesn't make them animals. And anyway, most of the animals I've met lately have been on two legs! And besides, Colin's a great cop. Once he picks up a suspect's scent the perp's had it. You couldn't ask for a better guy to back you up in a tight situation, and what's more, the wer practically invented the concept of the team-player."

"I only wondered if it bothered you," Celluci told him mildly.

"No." Savagely shoving his shirttails into his pants, Barry turned faintly red. "Not anymore. I mean, once you get to know a guy, you can't hate him just because he's a werewolf."

Words of wisdom for our time, Vicki thought. "Back to the shooting . . ."

"Yeah, I think I know someone who might be able to help. Bertie Reid. She's a real buff, you know, one of those people who can quote facts and figures at you from the last fifty years. If there's someone in the area capable of making those shots, she'll know it. Or she'll be able to find it out."

"Does she shoot?"

"Occasionally small arms but not the high caliber stuff anymore. She must be over seventy."

"Do you know her address?"

"No, I don't, and her phone number is unlisted—I heard her mention it one day at the range—but she's not hard to find. She drops by the Grove Road Sportsman's Club most afternoons, sits up in the clubroom, has a few cups of tea and criticizes everyone's shooting." He glanced up from the piece of paper he was writing the directions on. "She told me I kept my forward arm too tense." Flexing the arm in question, he added, "She was right."

"Why don't you practice at the police range?" Celluci asked.

Barry looked a little sheepish as he handed over the address of the club. "I do occasionally. But I always end up with an audience and, well, the targets there all look like people. I don't like that."

"I never cared for it much myself," Vicki told him, dropping the folded piece of paper in her purse. It might be realistic, certainly anything a cop would have to shoot would be people-shaped, but the yearly weapons qualifying always left her feeling slightly ashamed of her skill.

They accompanied Barry down to the parking lot, watched him shrug into a leather jacket—"I'd rather sweat than leave my elbows on the pavement."—and a helmet with a day-glow orange strip down the back, carefully pack his cap under the seat of his motorcycle, and roar away.

Vicki sighed, carefully leaning back on the hot metal

of Celluci's car. "Please tell me I was never that gung ho."

"You weren't," Celluci snorted. "You were worse." He opened the car door and eased himself down onto the vinyl seat. There hadn't been any shade to park in, not that he would have seen it given the conversation they'd been involved in when they arrived. Swearing under his breath as his elbow brushed the heated seatback, he unlocked Vicki's door and was busying himself with the air conditioning when she got in.

The echoes of their fight hung in the car. Neither of them spoke, afraid it might begin again.

Celluci had no desire to do a monologue on the dangers of making moral judgments and he knew that as far as Vicki was concerned the topic was closed. *But if she thinks I'm leaving before this is over, she can think again.* He didn't have to be back at work until Thursday and after that, if he had to, he'd use sick time. It was more than Henry Fitzroy now, Vicki needed saving from herself.

For the moment, they'd maintain the truce.

"It's almost 2:30 and I'm starved. How about stopping for something to eat?"

Vicki glanced up from Barry's scribbled directions and gratefully acknowledged the peace offering. "Only if we eat in the car on the way."

"Fine." He pulled out onto the street. "Only if it's not chicken. In this heat the car'll suck up the smell of the Colonel and I'll never be free of it."

They stopped at the first fast food place they came to. Sitting in the car, eating french fries and waiting for Vicki to get out of the washroom, Celluci's attention kept wandering to a black and gold jeep parked across the street. He knew he'd seen it before but not where, only that the memory carried vaguely unpleasant connotations.

The driver had parked in front of an ancient shoe repair shop. A faded sign in the half of the window Celluci could see proclaimed, *You don't look neat if your shoes are beat.* He puzzled over the fragment of memory until the answer walked out of the shop.

"Mark Williams. No wonder I had a bad feeling about it." Williams had the kind of attitude Celluci hated. He'd take out-and-out obnoxiousness over superficial charm any day. He grinned around a mouthful of burger. *Which certainly explains my relationship with Vicki.*

Whistling cheerfully, Williams came around to the driver's side of the jeep, opened the door, and tossed a bulky brown paper package onto the passenger seat before climbing in himself.

Had he been in his own jurisdiction, Celluci might have gone over for a chat, just on principle; let the man know he was being watched, try to find out what was in the package. He strongly believed in staying on top of the kind of potential situations Mark Williams represented. As it was, he sat and watched him drive away.

With the jeep gone, a second sign became visible in the shoe shop window.

Knives sharpened.

"Bertie Reid?" The middle-aged man sitting behind the desk frowned. "I don't think she's come in yet but . . ." The phone rang and he rolled his eyes as he answered. "Grove Road Sportsman's Club. That's correct, tomorrow night in the pistol range. No, ma'am, there'll be no shooting while the function is going on. Thank you. Hope to see you there. Damn phones," he continued as he hung up. "Alexander Graham Bell should've been given a pair of cement overshoes and dropped off the continental shelf. Now then, where were we?"

"Bertie Reid," Vicki prompted.

"Right." He glanced up at the wall clock. "It's only just turned three, Bertie's not likely to be here for another hour. If you don't mind my askin', what's a couple of Toronto PI's want with Bertie anyway?"

More than a little amused by his assumption that her ID covered Celluci as well, Vicki gave him her best professional smile, designed to install confidence in the general public. "We're looking for some information on competition shooting and Barry Wu told us that Ms. Reid was our best bet."

"You know Barry?"

"We make it our business to work closely with the police." Celluci had no problem with being perceived as Vicki's partner. Better that than flashing his badge all over London—behavior guaranteed to be unpopular with his superiors in Toronto.

"And so do we." His voice grew defensive. "Gun club members take responsibility for their weapons. Every piece of equipment that comes into this place is registered with both the OPP and local police and we keep no ammunition on the premises. It's the assholes who think a gun is a high-powered pecker extension— begging your pardon—who start blasting away in restaurants and school yards or who accidentally blow away Uncle Ralph while showing off their new .30 caliber toy, not our people."

"Not that it's better to be shot on purpose than by accident," Vicki pointed out acerbically. Still, she acknowledged his point. If the entire concept of firearms couldn't be stuffed back into Pandora's box, better the glamour be removed and they become just another tool or hobby. Personally, however, she'd prefer worldwide gun control legislation so tight that everyone from manufacturers to consumers would give up rather than face the paperwork, and the punishment for the use of a gun while committing a crime would fit the crime . . . and they could use the bastard's own weapon then bury it with the body. She'd developed this philosophy when she saw what a twelve gauge shotgun at close range could do to the body of a seven-year-old boy.

"Do you mind if we wait for Ms. Reid to arrive?" Celluci asked, before the man at the desk could decide if Vicki's words had been agreement or attack. He fig-

ured he'd already gone through his allotment of im-
passioned diatribes for the day.

Frowning slightly, the man shrugged. "I guess it
won't hurt if Barry sent you. He's the club's pride and
joy, you know; nobody around here comes close to
being in his league. He'll be going to the next Olympics and, if there's any justice in the world, coming
back with gold. Damn!" As he reached for the phone,
he motioned toward the stairs. "Clubroom's on the
second floor, you can wait for Bertie up there."

The clubroom had been furnished with a number of
brown or gold institutional sofas and chairs, a couple
of good sized tables, and a trophy case. A small
kitchen in one corner held a large coffee urn, a few
jars of instant coffee, an electric kettle and four tea-
pots in varying sizes. The room's only inhabitant at
3:00 on a Monday afternoon was a small gray cat
curled up on a copy of the *Shooter's Bible* who looked
up as Vicki and Celluci came in then pointedly ignored them.

From behind the large windows in the north wall
came the sound of rifle fire.

Celluci glanced outside then picked up a pair of binoculars from one of the tables and pointed them down-
range at the targets. "Unless they're cleverly trying to
throw us off the trail," he said a moment later passing
them to Vicki, "neither of these two are the marksman
we're looking for."

Vicki set the binoculars back on the table without
bothering to use them. "Look, Celluci, there's no reason for both of us to be stuck here until four. Why
don't you swing around by Dr. Dixon's, take the twins
and their father home, and then come back and pick
me up."

"While you do what?"

"Ask a few questions around the club then talk to
Bertie. Nothing you'd need to baby-sit me during."

"Are you trying to get rid of me?" he asked, leaning back against the cinder block wall.

"I'm trying to be considerate." She watched him fold his arms and stifled a sigh. "Look, I know how much you hate waiting for things and I doubt there's enough going on around here to keep both of us busy for an hour."

As much as he disliked admitting it, she had a point. "We could talk," he suggested warily.

Vicki shook her head. Another *talk* with Michael Celluci was the last thing she needed right now. "When it's over, we'll talk."

He reached out and pushed her glasses up her nose. "I'll hold you to that." It sounded more like a threat than a promise. "Call the farm when you want me to start back. No point in me arriving in the middle of things."

"Thanks, Mike."

"No problem."

"Now why did I do that?" she wondered once she had the clubroom to herself. "I know exactly what he's going to do." The chairs were more comfortable than they looked and she sank gratefully into the gold velour. "He only agreed to go so he could pump the wer about Henry without me around to interfere." Did she *want* him to find out about Henry?

"He's already been searching into Henry's background," she told the cat. "Better he finds out under controlled conditions than by accident."

It was a perfectly plausible reason and Vicki decided to believe it. She only hoped Henry would.

Thirteen

"I'm sorry, you just missed him. He's gone back to bed."

"Gone back to bed?" Celluci glanced down at his watch. "It's ten to four in the afternoon. Is he sick?"

Nadine shook her head. "Not exactly, but his allergies were acting up, so he took some medicine and went upstairs to lie down." She placed the folded sheet carefully in the laundry basket, reminding herself to inform Henry of his allergies when darkness finally awakened him.

"I'd hoped for a chance to talk to him."

"He said he'd be up around dusk. The pollen count doesn't seem to be as high after dark." As she spoke, she reached out to take the next piece of clean laundry from the line and overbalanced. Instantly, Celluci's strong grip on her elbow steadied her. *Almost a pity he isn't a wer,* she thought, simultaneously thanking him and shaking off his hand. *And it's a very good thing Stuart is out in the barn.* "If you stay for supper," she continued, "you can talk to Henry later."

Allergies. Henry Fitzroy did not look like the type of man to be laid low by allergies. As much as Celluci wanted to believe that a writer, and a romance writer yet, was an ineffectual weakling living in a fantasy world, he couldn't deny the feeling of strength he got from the man. He was still more than half convinced the writing covered connections to organized crime. After all, how long could it take to write a book?

There'd be plenty of time left over to get involved in a great many unsavory things.

Unfortunately, he couldn't wait around indefinitely.

"Thank you for the invitation, but . . ."

"Detective?"

He turned toward the summons.

"It's Ms. Nelson. On the phone for you."

"If you'll excuse me?"

Nadine nodded, barely visible under the folds of a slightly ragged fitted sheet. Nocturnal changes were hard on the linens.

Wondering what had gone wrong, Celluci went into the house and followed the redheaded teenager into a small office just off the kitchen. The office was obviously the remains of a larger room, left over when indoor plumbing and a bathroom had been put into the farmhouse.

"Thank you, uh . . ." He'd met the younger set of twins not fifteen minutes before, when they'd appeared to help Peter and Rose get Donald upstairs and into bed, but he had no idea which one this was.

"Jennifer." She giggled and tossed her mane of russet hair back off her face. "I'm the prettier one."

"Pardon me." Celluci smiled down at her. "I'll remember that for next time."

She giggled again and fled.

Still smiling, he picked up the old black receiver—probably the original phone from when the line had been put in thirty years before. "Celluci."

Vicki, who'd learned her phone manners in the same school, had no problem with the lack of pleasantries. She seldom used them herself. "I just found out that Bertie Reid won't be in until five at the earliest."

"You going to wait?"

"I don't see as I have an option."

"Shall I come in?"

"No point, really. Stay around the farm so I can reach you and try to keep the we . . . Heerkens from going out to those south fields."

"Should be safe enough in the daytime."

"I don't care. No one else gets shot if I have to leash the lot of them."

She hung up without asking about Henry. Celluci found that a little surprising, as though she'd known he wouldn't be around. Of course, she could just be showing more tact than usual, but he doubted it.

Mulling over possibilities, he returned to the yard and Nadine. "It looks like I'll be staying around for a while, the woman Vicki needs to speak with is going to be late."

"No problem." Which wasn't the exact truth, but in Nadine's opinion, Stuart needed to work on tolerating non-wer dominants. This Toronto detective would be good practice for the next time Stuart had to go into the co-op; the last time had almost been a disaster. It was getting hard enough to keep their existence a secret without Stuart wanting to challenge every alpha male he met. And while she recognized her mate's difficulty in accepting outsiders as protectors of the pack, it was done and he was just going to have to learn to live with it. *Or we all die without it. Like Silver.* She passed Celluci a handful of clothespins. "Put these in that basket, please."

Frowning a little at her sudden sadness, Celluci complied, wondering if he should say something. And if so, what?

"Mom?" The perfect picture of six-year-old dejection, Daniel dragged himself around the corner of the house and collapsed against the step. "I wanna go to the pond, but there's no one to take me. Daddy's got his head stuck in a tractor and he says Peter and Rose gotta fix that fence up by the road and Uncle Donald's sick and Colin's gone to work and Jennifer and Marie are taking care of Uncle Donald . . ." He let his voice trail off and sighed deeply. "I was wondering. . . ?"

"Not right now, sweetie." She reached down and stroked his hair back out of his eyes. "Maybe later."

Daniel's ebony brows drew down. "But I wanna go now. I'm hot."

"I can take him." Celluci spread his hands as Nadine turned to look at him. "I don't have anything else to do." Which was true as far as it went. It had also occurred to him that children, of any species, often knew more than adults suspected. If Fitzroy was an old family friend then Daniel might be able to fill in some of those irritating blanks.

"Can you swim?" Nadine asked at last.

"Like a fish."

"Please, Mom."

She weighed her child's comfort against her child's safety with this virtual stranger. In all fairness, last night couldn't be weighed against him. Males were not accountable for their actions when their blood was up.

"Mommy!"

And the challenge had, essentially, given him a position of sorts within the pack. "All right."

Daniel threw his arms around her legs with what came very close to a bark of joy, and bounded away, throwing an excited, "Come on!" back over his shoulder at Celluci, who followed at a more sedate pace.

"Hey!"

He turned, barely managing to snag the towel before it hit him in the face.

Nadine grinned, tongue protruding just a little from between very white teeth. "You'll probably need that. And don't let him eat any frogs. He'll spoil his dinner."

"I dunno. He's been coming for my whole life."

Translation; three or four years. "Does he come very often?"

"Sure. Lots of times."

"Do you like him?"

Daniel turned around and walked backward down the path, peering up at Celluci through a wild shock of dusty black hair. "Course I do. Henry brings me stuff."

"Like what?"

"Action figures. You know, like superheros and stuff." He frowned. "They chew up awful easy though." A bare heel slammed into a hummock of grass and, arms windmilling, he sat down. He growled at the offending obstacle then, having warned it against further attempts to trip him, accepted Celluci's offered hand.

"Are you okay?"

"Sure." He ran a little bit ahead then came back, just to prove he was all right. "I've fallen farther than that."

Celluci slapped at a mosquito. "Is the pond far?" He pulled the squashed insect out of the hair of his arm and wiped the mess on his jeans.

"Nope." Three jumps proved that an overhanging branch was still too high and he moved on.

"Is it part of the farm?"

"Uh-huh. Grandpa had it dugged a gizillion years ago. When Mommy was little," he added, just in case Celluci had no idea how long a gizillion years was.

"Does Henry take you swimming?"

"Nah. I'm not allowed to swim at night 'less everybody's there."

"Isn't Henry ever here in the daytime?"

Daniel sighed and stared up at Celluci like he was some kind of idiot. "Course he is. It's daytime now."

"But he's asleep."

"Yeah." A butterfly distracted him and he bounded off after it until it flew high up into one of the poplars bordering the path and stayed there.

"Why doesn't he ever take you swimming in the daytime."

"Cause he's asleep."

"Just when you want to go swimming?"

Daniel wrinkled his nose and looked up from the bug he was investigating. "No."

The security guard at Fitzroy's building had already told Celluci that Henry Fitzroy seemed to live his life at night. Working nights and sleeping days wasn't that unusual but added to all the other bits and pieces—or to the lack of bits and pieces—it certainly didn't help allay suspicion. "Does Henry ever bring anyone with him?"

"Course. Brought Vicki."

"Anyone else?"

"Nope."

"Do you know what Henry does when he's at home?"

Daniel knew he wasn't supposed to tell that Henry was a vampire, just as he wasn't to tell about his family being werewolves. It was one of the earliest lessons he'd been taught. But the policeman knew about the fur-forms and he was a friend of Vicki's and she knew about Henry. So maybe he did, too. Daniel decided to play it safe. "I'm not supposed to tell."

That sounded promising. "Not supposed to tell what?"

Daniel scowled. This grown-up was real dull, all he wanted to do was talk and that meant no fur-form. Vicki had been lots more fun; she'd thrown sticks for him to chase. "You mad at Henry 'cause he's with your mate?"

"She's not my mate," Celluci snapped, before he considered the wisdom of answering the question at all.

"You smell like she is." His brow furrowed. "She doesn't though."

He had to ask. "And what does she smell like?"

"Herself."

This is not the type of conversation to have with a six-year-old, Celluci reminded himself as the path opened out into a small meadow, the pond shimmering blue-green in a hollow at the far end.

"Oh, boy! Ducks!" Daniel tore out of his shorts and raced across the field, barking shrilly, tail thrashing from side to side. The half dozen ducks waited until he was almost at the pond before taking wing. He plunged in after them, splashing and barking until they were out of sight behind the trees then sat down in the shallows, had a quick drink, and looked back, panting, to see if his companion had witnessed his routing of the enemy.

Celluci laughed and scooped up the discarded shorts. "Well done!" he called. He'd felt a superstitious prickling up his spine when the boy had first changed, but it hadn't been able to maintain itself against the rest of the scene. Crossing the meadow, he decided to leave Henry for the rest of the afternoon and just enjoy himself.

"Is it deep?" he asked, arriving at the pond.

" 'Bout as deep as you near the middle," Daniel told him after a moment's study.

Over six feet was pretty deep for such a little guy. "Can you swim."

Daniel licked a drip of water off his nose. "Course I can," he declared indignantly. "I can dog paddle."

"Think we'll get this done by supper time?" Rose asked, scrubbing a dribble of sweat off her forehead.

"I didn't think Uncle Stuart gave us an option," Peter panted, leaning on the mallet. "He's sure been growly lately."

"In case you'd forgotten, the family's under attack. He has a good reason."

"Sure, but that doesn't mean he has to growl at me."

Rose only shrugged and started stomping the earth tightly around the base of the metal fence post. She hated the amount of clothing she had to wear for this— shoes, jeans, shirt—but fences couldn't be fixed in a sundress, especially not when every section seemed determined to support at least one raspberry bush.

"I mean," Peter clipped an eight-inch length of wire off the bale and began reattaching the lower part of the fence to the post, "everything you do, he snaps at you."

Everything you *do, you mean.* Rose sighed and kept her mouth shut. She'd been feeling so strange herself lately, she certainly wasn't going to criticize her twin.

He squinted up at the sun, burning yellow-white in the late afternoon sky, and fought the urge to pant. "What a day to be working outside. I don't believe how hot it is."

"At least you can work without a shirt on."

"So could you."

"Not right next to the road."

"Why not?" He grinned. "There's never any traffic along here and besides, they're so little no one'll be able to see them anyway."

"Peter!"

"Peter!" he echoed, as she took a swing at him. "Okay, if you don't like that idea, why don't you trot back to the house and get us some water."

Rose snorted. "Right. While you lean on the fence and watch the world go by."

"No." He bent and picked up the brush shears. "While I clear the crap from around the next post."

She looked from the post to her brother, then turned and started walking back to the house. "You better have that done . . ." she warned, over her shoulder.

"Or what?"

"Or . . . Or I'll bite your tail off!" She laughed as Peter cowered at their favorite childhood threat, and then she broke into a run, feeling his gaze on her back until she left the field and started down the lane.

Peter yanked at the waistband of his jeans. They were too tight, too constrictive, too hot. He wanted . . . Actually, he didn't know what he wanted anymore.

"This has been one hell of a summer," he muttered, moving along the fence. He missed his Aunt Sylvia and his Uncle Jason. With the two older wer gone, it seemed like he and Rose had no choice but to become adults in their place.

He suddenly wanted to howl but worked off some of his frustrations in hacking at the brush instead. Maybe he should get a life outside the pack, like Colin had. He tossed that idea almost the instant he had it. Colin didn't have a twin and Peter couldn't imagine living without Rose beside him. They almost hadn't made it through grade eleven when class schedules kept them apart for most of the day. The guidance counselor had no idea how close she'd come to being bitten when she refused to change things. She'd said it was time they broke free of an unhealthy emotional dependency. Peter beheaded a few daisies, working the shears like two-handed scissors. *That's all she knew. Maybe if humans developed a little emotional dependency the world wouldn't be so fucked up.*

The sound of an approaching car brought him over to the fence where he could get a look at the driver. The black and gold jeep slowed as it drew even with him, stopped a few feet down the road, then backed up spraying gravel. It was the same jeep that had been parked at the end of the lane Sunday morning when he'd gone to the mailbox to fetch Shadow. Hackles rising, he put down the shears and jumped the fence. Time to find out why this guy was hanging around.

Mark Williams couldn't believe his luck. Not only was there a solitary werewolf right up by the road where he could get to it, but it was one of the red-heads. One of the young redheads. And in his experience, teenage anythings could be easily manipulated into impulsive, reckless behavior.

Even in jeans and running shoes, the creature had a certain wolflike grace, and as Mark watched it jump the fence and start toward the car he became convinced that this was the other version of the animal he'd seen by the mailbox yesterday. The set of its head, the expression of wary curiosity, was, given the variation in form, identical.

He rolled down the window, having already determined how to take advantage of this chance meeting. He'd always believed he did his best work off the cuff.

"You one of the Heerkens?"

"Yeah. What of it?"

"You may have noticed me around a bit lately."

"Yeah."

Mark recognized the stance. The creature wanted to be a hero. *Well, keep your pants on, you'll get your chance.* "I've, uh, had my eye on your little problem."

"What problem's that?"

He pointed his finger and said, "Bang. Hear you lost two members of your family this month. I have, uh . . ." The sudden noise startled him, especially when he realized what it was. The creature was growling, the sound beginning deep in its throat and emerging clearly as threat. Mark pulled his arm into the car and kept one finger on the window control. No point taking unnecessary chances. "I have information that might help you catch the person responsible. Are you interested?"

Russet brows drew down. "Why tell me?"

Mark smiled, being careful not to show his teeth. "Do you see anyone else to tell? I thought you might want to do something about it."

The growling faded and stopped. "But . . ."

"Never mind." Mark shrugged. *Careful now, it's almost hooked.* . . . "If you'd rather sit safely at home while other people save your family. . . ." He started to raise the window.

"No! Wait! Tell me."

Got him. "My uncle, Carl Biehn . . ."

"The grasseater?"

The disgust in the interruption couldn't be missed. Mark hid a grin. He'd been about to say his uncle had seen something through his binoculars while bird-watching but hurriedly rewrote the script to take advantage of the prejudice of a predator for a vegetarian. Even if it did throw his uncle to the wolves. So to speak. "Yeah. The grasseater. He's the one. But no one'll believe you if you just *tell* them, so meet me in his old barn tonight after dark and I'll give you the proof."

"*I* don't believe you."

"Suit yourself. But just in case you decide your family's worth a bit of your time, I'll be in the barn at sunset. I suppose you can tell your . . . people anyway." He sighed deeply, shaking his head. "But you *know* that without proof they won't believe you—A grasseater? Ha!—not any more than you believe me and if you don't come, you'll have missed your only chance. Not something I'd like to have on my conscience."

Mark raised the window and drove away before the creature had a chance to sort out the convolutions of that last sentence and ask more questions. A number of things could go wrong with the plan, but he was pretty sure he'd read the beast correctly and the risk fell within acceptable limits.

He glanced in the rearview mirror to see the creature still standing by the side of the road. Pretty soon it would convince itself that, regardless of the stranger's motives, it couldn't hurt to check out the proof. In the way of the young, it wouldn't bother telling anyone else, not until it was sure.

"Come on, save the world. Be a hero. Impress the girls." Mark patted the bundle of leg-hold traps on the seat beside him. "Make me rich."

Rose got back to the fence with the jug of water just as the dust trail behind the car began to settle. She'd seen Peter talking to someone but hadn't been able to either see or smell who it was.

"Hey!" she called. "You standing in the road for a reason?"

Peter started.

"Peter? What's wrong?"

"Nothing." He shook himself and came back over the fence. "Nothing's wrong."

Rose frowned. *That* was a blatant lie. About to call him on it, she remembered the advice Aunt Nadine had given her when she'd mentioned Peter's recent moodiness. *"Let him have a little space, Rose. It's hard for boys around this age."* They'd never had secrets from each other before, but perhaps Aunt Nadine was right.

"Here." She held out the jug. "Maybe this will make you feel better."

"Maybe." But he doubted it. Then their fingers touched and he felt the light caress sizzle up his arm and resonate though his entire body. The world went away as he drank in her scent, musky and warm and so very, very close. He swayed. He felt the jug pulled from his lax grip and then the freezing cold splash of water over his head and torso.

Rose tried not to laugh. He looked furious but that she could deal with. "I thought you were going to faint," she offered, backing up a step.

"If we could change," Peter growled, tossing his head and spraying water from his hair, "I'd chase you into the next county and when I caught you I'd . . ."

"You'd what?" she taunted, dancing out of his reach, suddenly conscious of a strange sense of power. If only she weren't wearing so many clothes.

"I'd . . ." A rivulet of water worked its way past the waistband of his jeans. "I'd . . . Damn it, Rose, that's cold! I'd bite your tail off, that's what I'd do!"

She laughed then, it was impossible not to, and the moment passed.

"Come on." She picked up the mallet and headed toward the fence. "Let's get this done before Uncle Stuart bites both our tails off."

Peter grabbed the bale of wire and followed. "But

I'm all wet," he muttered, rubbing at the moisture beading the hair on his chest.

"Quit complaining. Mere moments ago, you were too hot."

She lifted the mallet over her head and the smell of her sweat washed down over him. Peter felt his ears begin to burn and all at once, he came to a decision. He would go to Carl Biehn's barn tonight.

He toyed with the idea of telling his Uncle Stuart and then discarded it. One of two things would happen, either he'd dismiss the information about the grasseater out of hand and want to know what this human was up to, or he'd believe the information and want to receive the proof himself. Either way, he, Peter, would be out of the action. *That* wasn't going to happen.

He'd tell Uncle Stuart when he had the proof. Present it to him as a fait accompli. That would show the older wer he was someone to be reckoned with. Not a child any longer. Peter's head filled with visions of challenging the alpha male and winning. Of running the pack. Of winning the right to mate.

His nostrils flared. If he came back with the information that saved the family, it couldn't help but impress Rose.

"You the young woman who's waiting to see me?"

Vicki came awake with a start and glanced down at her watch. It was 6:10. "Damn!" she muttered, shoving her glasses back up her nose. Her mouth tasted like the inside of a sewer.

"Here, maybe this'll help."

Vicki stared down at the cup of tea that had suddenly appeared in her hand and thought, *Why not?*

A moment later she had her answer.

Because I hate tea. Why did I do that?

She very carefully set the cup down and forced her scattered wits to regroup. *This is the clubroom at the*

Grove Road Sportman's Club. So this little old lady in blue jeans must be . . .

"Bertie Reid?"

"In the flesh. Such as remains of it." The older woman smiled, showing a mouthful of teeth too regular to be real. "And you must be Vicki Nelson, Private Investigator." The smile broadened, the face around it compressing into an even tighter network of fine lines. "I hear you need my help."

"Yeah." Vicki stretched, apologized, and watched as Bertie settled carefully into one of the gold velour chairs, teacup balanced precisely on one knee. "Barry Wu tells me that if anyone in this city can help, it's you."

She looked pleased. "He said that? What a sweetie. Nice boy, Barry, bound to be in the medals at the next Olympics."

"So everyone says."

"No, everyone says he'll take the gold. I don't. I don't want to jinx the boy before he gets there, neither do I want him to feel badly if he comes home with the silver. Second best in the entire world is nothing to feel badly about and all those armchair athletes who sneer at second deserve a good swift kick in the butt." She took a deep breath and a long draught of tea. "Now then, what did you want to know?"

"Is there anyone around London, not just at this club, who can shoot with anything approaching Barry Wu's accuracy?"

"No. Was there anything else?"

Vicki blinked. "No?" she repeated.

"Not that I know of. Oh, there're a couple of kids who might be decent if they practiced and one or two old-timers who occasionally show a flash of what they once had but people with Barry's ability and the discipline necessary to develop it are rare." She grinned and saluted with the cup. "That's why they only give out one gold."

"Shit!"

The old woman studied Vicki's face for a moment, then put down the teacup and settled back in the chair, crossing one denim clad leg over the other, the lime green laces in her hightops the brightest spot of color in the room. "How much do you know about competition shooting?"

"Not much," Vicki admitted.

"Then tell me why you're asking that question, and I'll tell you if you're asking the right one."

Vicki took off her glasses and scrubbed at her face with her hands. It didn't make things any clearer. In fact, she realized as the movement pulled at the bruise on her temple, it was a pretty stupid thing to do. She shoved her glasses back on and scrambled in her bag for the bottle of pills they'd given her at the hospital. *There was a time I could make love to a vampire, walk away from major car accident, rush a client to the hospital, stay up until dawn, and spend the day arguing ethics with Celluci, no problem. I must be getting old.* She took the pill dry. The only alternative was another mouthful of tea and she didn't think she was up to that.

"Cracked my head," she explained as she tossed the small plastic bottle back in her bag.

"In the line of duty?" Bertie asked, looking intrigued.

"Sort of." Vicki sighed. Somehow in the last couple of minutes, she'd come to the conclusion that Bertie was right. Without knowing more about competition shooting, she *couldn't* know if she was asking the right questions. Her voice low to prevent the only other occupant of the clubroom from overhearing, she presented an edited version of the events that had brought her to London.

Bertie whistled softly at the description of the shots that killed "two of the family dogs," then she said, "Let me be sure I've got this straight, five hundred yards on a moving target at night from twenty feet up in a pine tree?"

"As much as five, maybe as little as three."

"As little as three?" Bertie snorted. "And both dogs were killed with a single, identical head shot? Come on." Setting the teacup aside, she heaved herself out of the chair, pale blue eyes gleaming behind the split glass of her bifocals.

"Where are we going?"

"My place. One shot like that might have been a fluke, luck, nothing more. But two, two means a trained talent and you don't acquire skill like that overnight. Like I said before, there's damned few people in the world who can do that kind of shooting and this marksman of yours didn't spring full grown from the head of Zeus. I think I can help you find him, but we've got to go to my place to do it. That's where all my reference material is. This lot wouldn't know a book if it bit them on the butt." She waved a hand around the clubroom. The fortyish man sitting at one of the tables stroking the cat looked startled and waved back. "Gun magazines, that's all they ever read. I keep telling them they need a library. Probably leave them mine when I die and it'll spend ten or twenty years sitting around getting outdated then they'll throw it out. Did you drive?"

"No . . ."

"No? I thought every PI owned a sexy red convertible. Never mind. We'll take my car. I live pretty close." A sudden flurry of shots caught her attention and she strode over to the window. "Ha! I told him not to buy a Winchester if he wants to compete this fall. He'll be months getting used to that offset scope. Fool should've listened. Robert!"

The man at the table looked even more startled at being directly addressed. "Yes?"

"If Gary comes up tell him I said, I told you so."

"Uh, sure, Bertie."

"His wife's down in the pistol range," Bertie confided to Vicki as they headed out the door. "They come by most evenings after work. He hates guns but he loves her so they compromised; she only shoots targets, he doesn't watch.''

Bertie's car was a huge old Country Squire station wagon, white, with wood-colored panels. The eight cylinders roared as they headed out onto the highway and then settled down into a steady seventy-five kilometers an hour purr.

Vicki tried not to fidget at the speed—or lack of it—but the passing time gnawed at her. Hopefully Donald's wound would remind the wer of why they had to stay close to the house after dark, but she wasn't counting on it: As long as the wer insisted on their right to move around their land, every sunset, every extra day she spent solving this case, put another one of them in danger. If she couldn't convince them to stay safe, and so far she'd had remarkably little luck at that, she had to find this guy as fast as possible.

A car surged past, horn honking.

''I wanted to get a bumper sticker that read, 'Honk at me and I'll shoot your tires out' but a friend talked me out of it.'' Bertie sighed. ''Waste of diminishing natural resources driving that speed.'' She dropped another five kilometers as she spoke, just to prove her point.

Vicki sighed as well, but her reasons were a little different.

Fourteen

Bertie Reid lived in a small bungalow about a ten-minute drive from the range.

Ten minutes had anyone else been driving, Vicki sighed silently as she got out of the car and followed the older woman into the house. "May I use your phone, I'd better call—*Oh, hell, what do I call Celluci?*—my driver and let him know where I am."

"Phone's right there." She pointed into the living room. "I'll just go put the kettle on for tea. Unless you'd rather have coffee."

"I would actually."

"It's only instant."

"That's fine. Thank you." Vicki was not a coffee snob and anything was better than tea.

The phone, a white touch-tone, sat on of a pile of newspapers beside an overstuffed floral armchair with a matching footstool. A pole lamp with three adjustable lights rose up behind the chair and the remote for the television lay on one wide arm, partially buried under an open *TV Guide*.

Obviously the command center. Vicki punched in the Heerkens number and looked around the living room while she waited for someone at the farm to answer. The room bulged with books, on shelves, on the floor, on the other pieces of furniture, classics, romances—she spotted two by Elizabeth Fitzroy, Henry's pseudonym—mysteries, nonfiction. Vicki had seen bookstores with a less eclectic collection.

"Hello?"

"Rose? It's Vicki Nelson. Is Mike Celluci still there?"

"Uh-huh, Aunt Nadine invited him to dinner. I'll get him."

Dinner. Vicki shook her head. That should prove interesting, a little alpha male posturing over the hot dogs. She heard voices in the background, then someone lifted the receiver.

"Great timing, we just sat down. You ready to be picked up?"

"No, not yet. Ms. Reid arrived late. I'm at her place now and likely to be for some time. She doesn't know who the marksman is, but she thinks we can find out."

"How?"

"Anyone as good as this guy is has to have left some kind of a record and if someone made a record of it, she says she has a copy. But," she glanced around the living room, nothing appeared to be shelved in any particular order, "it may take a while to find it."

"Do you want me to come in?"

"No." The less time she spent with him, the less likely he'd restage the afternoon's fight and she just didn't want to deal with that right now. Letting Celluci tie her in knots wouldn't help anyone. Her job was to find the killer and stop him, not argue the ethics of the case. "I'd rather you stayed there and kept an eye on things."

"What about Henry?"

What about Henry? She wondered how his absence had been explained. Celluci swore he always knew when she lied so she chose her words carefully. "He hasn't any training."

"Christ, Vicki, these are werewolves; *I* haven't any training." In her mind's eye she saw him tossing the curl of hair back off his forehead. "And that wasn't what I meant."

"Listen, Mike, I told you what I think of your organized crime theory and I haven't got time to pander to your bruised male ego right now. You and Henry work it out.'' The best defense is a good offense—she didn't know where she'd first heard it but it made sense. ''I'll call you when I get done.'' She could hear him speaking as she hung up. He didn't sound happy. *Odds are he'll repeat it later so I haven't missed anything.*

The early evening sunlight stretched long golden fingers into the living room. Almost two and a half hours remained until dark. Vicki found herself wishing she could push that pulsing golden ball down below the horizon, releasing Henry from the hold of day. Henry understood, unlike Mike Celluci who was trying to apply rules to a game no one was playing.

And wasn't I just thinking it was nice to have Celluci around, lending an aura of normality to all this? When did my life get so complicated?

''Cream and sugar?'' Bertie called from the kitchen.

Vicki shook her head, trying to clear the cobwebs. ''Just cream,'' she said, moving toward the voice. Nothing to do but keep going and hope it all untangled itself in the end.

The second bedroom had been turned into a library, with bookshelves on three of the four walls and filing cabinets on the fourth. A huge paper-piled desk took up much of the central floor space. The desk caught Vicki's eye.

''It's called a partnership desk,'' Bertie told her, caressing a gleaming edge of dark brown wood with a fingertip. ''It's really two desks in a single piece of furniture.'' She lifted a pile of newspapers off one of the chairs and motioned for Vicki to sit down. ''Ruth and I bought it almost twenty-five years ago now. If you don't count the cars or the house, it's the most expensive thing we ever bought.''

''Ruth?'' Vicki asked, leveling a space on the desk blotter for her coffee.

The older woman picked up a framed photograph off one of the bookshelves, smiled down at it for an instant, then passed it over. ''Ruth was my partner.

We were together for thirty-two years. She died three years ago. Heart attack.'' Her smile held more grief than humor. ''There hasn't seemed to be much point in housecleaning without her around. You'll have to excuse the mess.''

Vicki returned the picture. ''It's hard to lose someone close,'' she said softly, thinking that Nadine's eyes had held the same stricken look when she'd spoken of her twin. ''And I'd be the last person to criticize housecleaning. As long as you can find things when you need them.''

''Yes, well . . .'' Bertie set the photograph of Ruth carefully back on the shelf and waved a hand at the rows and rows of titles; *History of Marksmanship, Rifle Shooting as a Sport, Position Rifle Shooting, The Complete Book of Target Shooting.* ''Where do we start?''

Reaching into her purse, Vicki drew out the lists of those who used the conservation area with any frequency—both sets of birders, the nature photography club—and laid it on the desk. ''I thought we'd start at the top and compare these names with first the Canadian Olympic teams, then regional award winners, then down to local winners.''

Bertie bent over and scanned the lists. ''Be easier though if you knew who had registered weapons in this group. Doesn't the OPP have . . . ?''

''Yes.''

The older woman looked a little startled at the tone and the muscles moved around her mouth, but Vicki's expression helped her to hold back her curiosity. After a moment she asked, ''Just the Canadian teams?''

''To start with, yes.'' Vicki took a long swallow of coffee and wondered if she should apologize. After all, it had been her own damned fault she didn't have that registration list. ''If they turn up empty, we'll start on other countries. If you have . . .''

''I have every Olympic shooting team for the last forty years as well as the American nationals, most of the regionals, and local competitions from Pennsylvania, Michigan, and New York.''

The Canadian teams were in seven fat red binders. Even ignoring all the statistics, the photocopies of newspaper articles, and the final results, the daunting number of names to wade through started Vicki's head throbbing again.

If this were a television show, I'd have found a bit of shirt caught in that tree that could have belonged to only one man, there'd have been a car chase, a fight, time out to go to the bathroom, and everything wrapped up in a nice, neat tidy package in less than an hour. She laid the first list of birders beside the first binder and pushed her glasses up her nose. *Welcome to the real world.*

A half a dozen times during dinner, Peter changed his mind about telling the rest of the family what he knew. A half a dozen times, he changed it back. They deserved to know. But if *he* could present them with the proof. . . . Back and forth. Forth and back.

A part of him just wanted to dump the whole thing on the older wer and let them take care of it but Rose's knee bumping randomly against his under the table kept knocking that thought out of his head. He hardly tasted a mouthful of his food because every time he inhaled, the only thing he could smell was his twin and the only thing he could think of was proving himself to her.

''Peter! The bread?''

''Sorry, Aunt Nadine.'' He couldn't remember her asking for the bread but her tone made it obvious she had. As he passed the plate of heavy black bread up the table he realized that whatever else he decided, he couldn't tell his aunt. To say *I think I might know who killed your twin* without having the proof so she could act would just be worrying at the wound. Besides, she thought he was still a cub and treated him not much different than Daniel. He had to prove to her that he

was a man. He hadn't noticed before, but Aunt Nadine
smelled very much like Rose.

He couldn't tell his father. His father was wounded.
He couldn't even talk it over with his father because
his father didn't do anything without talking it over
with Uncle Stuart first.

Uncle Stuart. Peter tore at a piece of meat as Uncle
Stuart accepted the saltshaker from Rose. *He didn't
have to touch her. Thinks he's so . . . so shit hot.
Thinks he knows everything. Well, I know something
he doesn't.*

"Whacha angry about, Peter?"

Peter glared at his young cousin. "I'm not angry."

Daniel shrugged. "Smell angry. You going to jump
on Daddy again?"

"I said I'm *not* angry."

"Peter." Stuart leaned around Daniel, brows down
and teeth bared.

Peter fought the urge to toss his head back, exposing
his throat. His ears were tight against the sides of his
skull, the torn edge throbbing in time with his pulse.
"I didn't do anything!" he growled, shoving away
from the table and stomping out of the kitchen. *You
just wait,* he thought as he stripped and changed. *I'll
show you.*

Rose made as if to follow but Nadine reached out
and pushed her back into her chair. "No," she said.

Stuart sighed and scratched at a scar over his eyebrow, the result of his first challenge fight as an adult
male. This had to happen when there was a stranger
with the family. He looked over at Celluci who was
calmly wiping ketchup off his elbow—Daniel had been
overly enthusiastic with the squeeze bottle again—and
then at Nadine. Arrangements to separate Rose and
Peter would have to be made this evening. They
couldn't put it off any longer.

Storm skulked around the barn, looking for rats to
take out his bad temper on. He didn't find any. That

didn't help his mood. He chased a flock of starlings into the air but he didn't manage to sink his teeth into any of them. Flopping down in the shade beside Celluci's car, he worried at a bit of matted fur on his shoulder.

Life sucks, he decided.

It would be almost two hours until dark. Hours until he could prove himself. Hours until he could take that human's throat in his teeth and shake the truth out of him. He imagined the reactions of his family, of Rose, when he walked in and declared, *I know who the killer is.* Or better yet, when he walked in and threw the body down on the floor.

Then faintly, over the smell of steel and gas and oil, he caught a whiff of a familiar scent. He rose. On the passenger side of Celluci's car, up along the edge of the window was an area that smelled very clearly of the man in the black and gold jeep.

He frowned and licked his nose.

Then he remembered.

The scent he'd caught at the garage, the trace clinging to the hood release of Henry's wrecked car, was, except for intensity, identical to the scent here and now.

This changed things. Tonight's meeting could only be a trap. Storm scratched at the ground and whined a little in his excitement. This was great. This alone would convince everyone to take him seriously.

"Peter?"

He pricked up his ears. That was his uncle's voice, over by the house, not calling him, talking about him. Storm inched forward, until he could see around the front of the car but not be seen. Fortunately for eavesdropping, he was downwind.

His uncle and Detective Celluci were sitting on the back porch.

"He's all right," Stuart continued. "He's just, well, a teenager."

Celluci snorted. "I understand. Teenagers."

The two men shook their heads.

Storm growled softly. So they could dismiss him with one word could they? Say *teenager* like it was some kind of disease. Like it explained everything. Like he was still a child. His hackles rose and his lips curled back, exposing the full gleaming length of his fangs. He'd show them.

Tonight.

". . . course, up until the early 60s, most shooters thought that no one would ever shoot a score above 1150 in an international style competition but then in 1962, a fellow named Gary Anderson shot 1157 in free-rifle. Well, there were some jaws hitting the floor that day and most folks believed he'd never be beat." Bertie shook her head at the things most folks believed. "They were wrong, of course. That 1150 was just what they call a psychological factor and once Gary broke it, well, it got shot all to shit. So to speak. I'll just make another pot of tea. You sure you don't want more coffee?"

"No, thanks." Since she'd left the force, Vicki's caffeine tolerance had dropped and she could feel the effect of the three cups she'd already had. Her nerves were stretched so tightly, she could almost hear them ring every time she moved. Leaving Bertie in the kitchen, she hurried to the living room and the phone.

The evening had passed unnoticed while she'd been comparing lists of names. The sun, a disk so huge and red and clearly defined against the sky that it looked fake, trembled on the edge of the horizon. Vicki checked her watch. 8:33. Thirty-five minutes to sunset. Thirty-five minutes to Henry.

He said his arm would be healed by tonight so maybe he and Celluci could stake out that tree together and she could get Peter to drive in and pick her up. She snickered at the vision that idea presented as she sat down in the armchair and flicked on one of the lights. She'd definitely had too much coffee.

The surnames of eleven Olympic shooters had matched with members in the local clubs. Time for the next step.

"Hello, Mrs. Scott? My name is Terri Hanover, I'm a writer, and I'm doing an article on Olympic contestants. I was wondering if you were related to a Brian Scott who was a member of the Canadian rifle team at the '76 Olympics in Montreal? No? But you went to Montreal. . . . That's very interesting but, unfortunately, I really need to talk to the contestants themselves." Vicki stifled a sigh. "Sorry to bother you. Good night."

One down. Ten to go. Lies to get at truth.

Hi, there. My name is Vicki Nelson and I'm a private investigator. Have you or any members of your family been shooting werewolves?

She pushed her glasses up her nose and punched in the next number without any real hope of success.

For Henry the moment of sunset came like the moment between life and death. Or perhaps, death and life. One instant he wasn't. The next, awareness began to lift the shroud of day from his senses. He lay still, listening to his heartbeat, his breathing, the rustle of the sheet against the hairs on his chest as his lungs filled and emptied. He felt the weave of the fabric beneath him, the mattress beneath that, the bed beneath both. The scent of wer wiped out even the scent of self but, all things considered, that didn't surprise him. Redefined for another night, he opened his eyes and sat up, extending his senses beyond his sanctuary.

Vicki wasn't in the house. Mike Celluci was.

Wonderful. Why hadn't she gotten rid of him? And for that matter, where *was* she?

He flexed his arm and peered down at the patch of new skin along the top of his shoulder. Although still a little tender, the flesh dimpled where the new muscle fiber had yet to add bulk, the wound had essentially healed. The day had given him back his strength and the hunger had faded to a whisper he could easily ignore.

As he dressed, he considered Detective-Sergeant Celluci. The wer had obviously accepted him, for Henry could feel no fear or anger in his sensing of the mortal. While he still thought that burning the memory of the wer and the witnessed change out of Celluci's mind was the safest plan, he couldn't make a decision without knowing how things had progressed over the course of the day. He wished he knew what suspicions the man harbored about him, what he'd said to Vicki last night, and what Vicki had said in return.

"Only one way to find out." He threw open the door and stepped out into the hall. Mike Celluci was in the kitchen. He'd join him there.

Just before the sun slid below the horizon, Storm leapt the fence behind the barn and using the fence bottom as cover, moved away from the house. If his uncle saw him, he'd call him back. If Rose saw him, she'd demand an explanation of where he thought he was going without her. Both would mean disaster so he used every trick he'd learned in stalking prey to stay hidden.

It didn't matter how long it took, the human would wait for him. He was sure of that. His ears flattened and his eyes gleamed. The human would get more than he bargained for.

"No luck?"

"No." Vicki rubbed her eyes and sighed. "And I've about had it for tonight. I don't think I can face those lists again without at least twelve hours sleep."

"No reason why you should," Bertie told her, clearing away the sandwich plates. "And it's not like it's an emergency or anything. Surely those people can keep their dogs tied up for a few days."

"It's not that simple."

"Why not?"

"Because it never is." A facetious explanation, but she didn't have a better one. Even if she'd been able to discuss it, Vicki doubted she could do justice to the territorial imperatives of the wer—not when it involved such incredibly stupid actions as presenting oneself as a target. She checked her watch and dug another two pain killers out of her purse, swallowing them dry. At eleven, Colin would be off shift. In an hour or so she'd head over to the police department and catch a ride back to the farm with him. In the meantime. . . .

"If you can put up with me for a little while longer, I think I'd better get started on the non-Canadian teams."

Bertie looked dubious. "I don't mind. If you think you're up to it. . . ."

"I have to be." Vicki dragged herself up out of the depths of the armchair, which seemed to be dragging back. "The people I talked to tonight will probably mention the call." She raised her voice so she could hear herself over the percussion group that had set up inside her skull. "I have to move quickly before our marksman spooks and goes to ground." She gave her head a quick shake, trying to settle things back where they belonged. The percussion group added a brass section, her knees buckled, and she clutched desperately at the nearest bookcase for support, knocking three books off the shelf and onto the floor.

With the bookcase still supporting most of her weight, she bent to pick them up and froze.

"Are you all right?" Bertie's worried question seemed to come from very far away.

"Yeah. Fine." She straightened slowly, holding the third book which had fallen faceup at her feet. *MacBeth.*

This morning Carl Biehn had been wringing his hands, trying to scrub off a bit of dirt. Like Lady MacBeth, she thought, hefting the book, and wondered what had happened to make the old man so anxious. But Lady MacBeth's scrubbing had been motivated by guilt not anxiety. What was Carl Biehn feeling guilty about?

Something his slimy nephew had done? Possibly, but Vicki doubted it. She'd bet on Carl Biehn being the type of man who took full responsibility for his actions and expected everyone else to do the same. If he felt guilty, he'd done something.

Vicki still couldn't believe he was a murderer. And she knew that her belief had nothing to do with it.

Most murders are committed by someone the victim knows.

Strongly held religious beliefs had justified arbitrary bloodbaths throughout history.

It wouldn't hurt to check him out. Just to make sure.

He hadn't been on any of the Canadian teams but Biehn was a European name and although he didn't have an accent, that didn't mean much.

"Are you *sure* you're all right?" Bertie asked as Vicki turned to face her. "You're looking, well, kind of peculiar."

Vicki placed the copy of *MacBeth* back on the shelf. "I need to look at the European shooting teams. Germans, Dutch . . ."

"I think you'd be better off sitting down with a cold compress. Can't it wait until tomorrow?"

There was no reason why it couldn't.

"No." Vicki stopped herself before she shook her head, the vision of the old man's hands washing themselves over and over caught in her mind. "I don't think it can."

Storm tested the wind as he crouched at the edge of the woods, watching the old Biehn barn. The man from the black and gold jeep was alone in the building. The grasseater remained in the house.

The most direct route was straight across the field but even with the masking darkness, Storm had no intention of being that exposed. Not far to the south an old fence bottom ran from the woods to the road, passing only twenty meters from the barn on its way, the scraggly line of trees and bushes breaking the night into irregular patterns. Secure in the knowledge that even another wer would have difficulty spotting him, Storm moved quickly along its corridor of shifting shadows.

Although he longed to give chase, he ignored the panicked flight of a flushed cottontail. Tonight he hunted larger game.

Neither the East nor West Germans had ever had a Carl Biehn on their shooting teams. Vicki sighed as she flipped through the binder looking for the lists from the Netherlands. When she closed her eyes, all she could see were little black marks on sheets of white.

The way people move around these days, Biehn could come from anywhere. Maybe I should do this alphabetically. Alphabetically . . . She stared blankly down at the page, not seeing it, and her heart began to beat unnaturally loud.

Rows of flowers stretched before her and a man's voice said, *"Everything from A to Zee."*

Zee. Canadians pronounced the last letter of the alphabet as Zed. Americans said Zee.

She reached for the binder that held the information on the U. S. Olympic teams, already certain of what she'd find.

Henry stood in the shadows of the lower hall and listened to Celluci patiently explain to Daniel that it was now too dark to play catch with the frisbee. He hadn't thought the mortal the type who cared for children but then, he hadn't thought much about this mortal at all. Obviously, he would have to rectify that.

The man was close to Vicki, a good friend, a colleague, a lover. If only through Vicki, they would continue to come into contact. Their relationship must therefore be defined, for the safety of them both.

Like most of his kind, Henry preferred to keep his

dealings with the mortal world to a minimum and those dealings under his control. Mike Celluci was not the sort of man he would normally associate with. He was too . . .

Henry frowned. Too honest? Too strong? Was this where a prince had fallen then, avoiding the honest and the strong for the weak and the rogue? In his life, he had commanded the loyalty of men like this one. He was not now less than he had been. He stepped out into the light.

Mike Celluci didn't hear Henry's approach, but he felt something at his back and turned. For a moment, he didn't recognize the man who stood just inside the kitchen door. Power and presence acquired over centuries hit him with almost physical force and when the hazel eyes met his and he saw they considered him worthy, he had to fight the totally irrational urge to drop to one knee.

What the hell is going on here? He shook his head to clear it, recognized Henry Fitzroy, and to cover his confusion, snarled, "I want to talk to you."

The phone rang, freezing them where they stood.

A moment later Nadine came into the kitchen, glanced from one to the other and sighed. "It's Vicki. She sounds a little strange. She wants to talk to . . ."

Celluci didn't wait to hear a name, but even as he stomped into the office and snatched up the receiver, he had to acknowledge that Henry Fitzroy had allowed him to take the call; that without Fitzroy's implicit permission, he wouldn't have been able to move. *If that man's nothing but a romance writer, I'm a . . .* He couldn't think of a sufficiently strong comparison. "What?"

"Where's Henry?"

"Why?" He knew better than to take his anger out on Vicki. He did it anyway. "Want to make kissy-face over the phone?"

"Fuck off, Celluci." Exhaustion colored the words.

"Carl Biehn was a member of the American shooting team in the 1960 summer Olympics in Rome."

Anger no longer had a place in the conversation, so he ignored it. "You've found your marksman, then."

"Looks that way." She didn't sound happy about it.

"Vicki, this information has to go to the police."

"Just put Henry on. I don't even know why I'm talking to you."

"If you don't report this, I will."

"No. You won't."

He'd been about to say that their friendship, that the wer, couldn't come before the law but the cold finality in her voice stopped him. For a moment, he felt afraid. Then he just felt tired. "Look, Vicki, I'll come and get you. We won't do anything until we talk."

A sudden burst of noise from the kitchen drowned out her reply and, tucking the phone under one arm, he moved to the door to close it. Then he stopped. And he listened.

And he knew.

Good cops don't ever laugh at intuition, too often a life hangs in the balance.

"The situation's changed." He cut Vicki off, not hearing what she said. "You'll have to make it back here on your own. Peter's missing."

Storm crept across the open twenty meters from the fence bottom to the barn crouched so low the fur on his stomach brushed the ground. When he reached the stone foundation of the barn wall, he froze.

The boards were old and warped and most had a line of light running between them. He changed—to get his muzzle out of the way, not because one form had better vision than the other—and placed one eye up against a crack.

A kerosene lantern burned on one end of a long table, illuminating the profile of the man from the jeep as he stood, back to the door, fiddling with something

Peter couldn't see. A shotgun leaned against the table edge, in easy reach.

Under the man-scent, the smell of the lantern, and the lingering odor of the animals the barn had once held there was a strong scent of oiled steel, more than the gun alone could possibly account for. Peter frowned, changed, and padded silently around to the big front doors. One stood slightly ajar, wide enough for him to slip through in either form but angled so that he couldn't charge straight into the barn and attack the man at the table. His lips curled his teeth and his throat vibrated with an unvoiced growl. The human underestimated him; a wer that didn't want to be heard, wasn't. He could get in, turn, and attack before the human could reach the gun, let alone aim and fire it.

He moved forward. The scent of oiled steel grew stronger. The dirt floor shifted under his front paw and he froze. Then he saw the traps. Three of them, set in the opening angle of the door, in hollows dug out of the floor then covered with something too light to set them off or hinder their movement when the jaws snapped shut. He couldn't be sure, but it smelled like the moss stuff Aunt Nadine put in the garden.

He could jump them easily, but the floor beyond had been disturbed as well and he couldn't tell for certain where safe footing began. Nor could he change and spring the traps without becoming a target for the shotgun.

Nose to the walls, he circled the building. Every possible entry had the same scent.

Every possible entry but one.

High on the east wall, almost hidden behind the branches of a young horse-chestnut tree was a small square opening used, back when the barn had held cattle, for passing hay bales into the loft. As a rule, the wer didn't climb trees, but that didn't mean they couldn't and callused fingers and toes found grips that mere human hands and feet might not have been able to use.

Moving carefully along a dangerously narrow limb, Peter checked out the hole, found no traps, and slipped silently through, congratulating himself on outwitting his enemy.

The old loft smelled only of stale hay and dust. Crouched low, Peter padded along a huge square cut beam until he could see down into the barn. He was almost directly over the table which contained, besides the lantern, a brown paper package, a notebook, and a heavy canvas apron.

The man from the jeep checked his watch and stood, head cocked, listening.

The whole setup was a trap and a trap set specifically for fur-form.

There could no longer be any question about it, this was the man who was killing his family. A man who knew them well enough to judge correctly what form he'd wear tonight.

Peter grinned and his eyes gleamed in the lantern light. He'd never felt so alive. His entire body thrummed. He had no intention of disappointing the human; he wanted fur-form, he'd get it. Tooth and claw would take him down. Moving to the edge of the beam, he changed and launched himself snarling through the air, landing with all four feet on the back of the human below.

Together, they crashed to the ground.

For one brief instant, Mark Williams had been pleased to see the shape that dropped out of the loft. He'd called the creature's reactions correctly right down the line. Except he hadn't thought about the loft or realized exactly what he'd be facing.

More terrified than he'd ever been in his life, he fought like a man possessed. He'd once seen a German shepherd kill a gopher by grabbing the back of its neck and crushing the spine. That wasn't going to happen to him. He felt claws tear through his thin shirt and into his skin, hot breath on his ear, and managed to twist around and shove one forearm between the beast's open jaws while his other hand groped frantically around on the floor for the fallen gun.

Storm tossed back his head, releasing the arm, and dove forward for the suddenly exposed throat.

Mark saw death approaching. Then he saw it pause. *Shit, man. I can't just rip out some guy's throat! What am I doing?* Abruptly, the blood lust was gone.

With his legs up under the belly of the beast, Mark heaved.

Completely disoriented, Storm hit the ground with a heavy thud and scrambled to regain his feet. The floor moved under his left rear paw. Steel jaws closed.

The snap, the yelp of pain and fear combined, brought Mark slowly to his knees. He smiled as he saw the russet wolf struggling against the trap, twisting and snarling in a panicked effort to get free. His smile broadened as the struggles grew weaker and creature finally lay panting on the floor.

No! Please, no! He couldn't change. Not while his foot remained held in the trap. *It hurts. Oh, God, it hurts.* He could smell his own blood, his own terror. *I can't breathe! It hurts.*

Dimly, Storm knew the trap was the lesser danger. That the human approaching, teeth showing, was far, far more deadly. He whined and his front paws scrabbled against the ground but he couldn't seem to rise. His head suddenly become too heavy to lift.

"Got you now, you son of a bitch." The poison had been guaranteed. Mark was pleased to see he'd got his money's worth. Wincing, he reached over his shoulder and his hand came away red. Staying carefully out of range, just in case, he spat on the floor by the creature's face. "I hope it hurts like hell."

Maybe . . . if I howl . . . they'll hear me. . . .

Then the convulsions started and it was too late.

Fifteen

". . . I don't know! He's been acting so strangely lately!"

Stuart and Nadine exchanged glances over Rose's head. Nadine opened her mouth to speak but her mate's expression caused her to close it again. Now was not the time for explanations.

"Rose." Celluci came out of the office and walked quickly across the kitchen, until he could gaze directly into the girl's face. "This is important. Besides the family, Vicki, Mr. Fitzroy, and myself, who did Peter talk with today?"

He knows something, Henry thought. *I should never have let him take that call.*

Rose frowned. "Well, he talked to the mechanic at the garage, Dr. Dixon, Dr. Levin—the one who took over from Dr. Dixon, she was at his house for a while—um, Mrs. Von Thorne, next door to Dr. Dixon, and somebody driving by up on the road, but I didn't see who."

"Did you see the car?"

"Yeah. It was black, mostly, with gold trim and fake gold spokes on the wheels." Her nose wrinkled. "A real poser's car." Then her expression changed again as she read Celluci's reaction. "That's the one you were waiting for, wasn't it? Wasn't it?" She stepped toward him, teeth bared. "Where's Peter? What's happened to my brother?"

"I think," Stuart said flatly, coming around from

behind his niece, "you'd better tell us what you know."

Only Henry had some idea of the conflict Celluci was going through and he had no sympathy for it. The question of law versus justice could have only one answer. He watched the muscles on Celluci's back tense and heard his heartbeat quicken.

Everything in Celluci's training said he leave them with an ambiguous answer and take care of this himself. If werewolves expected to be treated like the rest of society, within the law, then they couldn't act outside the law. And if the only way he could do his duty was to fight his way out of this house. . . . his hands curled into fists.

A low growl began to build in Stuart's throat.

And Rose's.

And Nadine's.

Henry stepped forward. He'd had enough.

Then Daniel began to whimper. He threw himself on his mother's legs and buried his face in her skirt. "Peter's gonna get killed!" The fabric did little to muffle the howl of a six-year-old child who only understood one small part of what was going on.

Celluci looked down at Daniel, who seemed to have an uncanny knack for bringing the focus back to the important matters, then over at Rose. "Can't you let me take care of this?" he asked softly.

She shook her head, panic beginning to build. "You don't understand."

"You *can't* understand," Nadine added, clutching at Daniel so tightly he squirmed in her grasp.

Celluci saw the pain in the older woman's eyes, pain that cut and twisted and would continue far longer than anyone should be forced to endure. His decision might possibly keep that pain from Rose.

"Carl Biehn was an Olympic marksman. His nephew, Mark Williams, drives a black and gold jeep."

Rose's eyes widened. "If he was talking to Peter this

afternoon . . ." She whirled, her sundress hit the floor, and Cloud streaked out of the kitchen and into the night.

"Rose, no!" Unencumbered by the need to change, Henry raced after her before Stuart, still caught in challenge with Celluci, began to react.

Jesus Christ! Nobody moves that fast! Celluci grabbed Stuart's arm as Henry disappeared into the night. "Wait!" he barked. "I need you to show me the way to Carl Biehn's farm."

"Let me go, human!"

"Damn it, Stuart, the man's got guns. He's taken Henry out once already! Charging in will only get everyone shot. We can get there before them in my car."

"Don't count on it." Stuart laughed but the sound held no humor. "And this is our hunt. You have no right to be there."

"Take him, Stuart!" Nadine's tone left no room for her mate to argue. "Think of after."

The male wer snarled but after an instant he yanked his arm free of Celluci's hold and started for the door. "Come on, then."

After? Celluci wondered as the two of them charged across the lawn. *Mary, Mother of God, they want me there to explain the body. . . .*

"What is taking him so long!" Vicki shoved at her glasses and turned away from the living room window. With the sun down she could see nothing past her reflection on the glass but that didn't stop her from pacing the length of the room and back then peering out into the darkness again.

"He has to come all the way from Adelaide and Dundas," Bertie pointed out. "It's going to take him a few minutes."

"I *know* that!" She sighed and took a deep breath. "I'm sorry. I had no right to snap at you. It's just that . . . well, if it wasn't for my damned eyes, I'd be driving myself. I'd be halfway there by now!"

Bertie pursed her lips and looked thoughtful. "You don't trust your partner to deal with it?"

"Celluci's not a partner, he's a friend. I don't have a partner. Exactly." And although Henry could be counted on to keep Celluci from doing anything stupid, who would save Peter, or watch the wer, or grab the murdering bastard—Vicki always saw him with Mark Williams' face, convinced that he had been the reason for the deaths even if he hadn't pulled the trigger—and . . . and then what? "I *have* to be there! How can I *know* it's justice if I'm not there?"

Realizing that some questions weren't meant to be answered, Bertie wisely kept silent. Questions of her own would have to wait.

"Damn it, I told him it was an emergency!" Vicki whirled back to the window and squinted into the night. "Where is he?" With an hour left in the shift, and Colin already back in the station, it hadn't been hard for Vicki to convince the duty sergeant to release him for a family emergency. "Why the . . . There!" Headlights turned up the driveway.

Vicki snatched up her bag and ran for the door, shouting back over her shoulder, "Don't talk about this to anyone. I'll be in touch."

Outside, and effectively blind, she aimed for the headlights and narrowly missed being run down by one of London's old blue and white police cars. She grabbed for the rear door as it screeched to a stop and threw herself into the back seat.

Barry slammed the car into reverse and laid rubber back down the length of the driveway while Colin twisted around and snarled, "What the hell is going on?"

Vicki pushed her glasses back into place and clutched at the seat as the car took a corner on two wheels.

"Carl Biehn was an Olympic marksman by way of Korea and the marines."

"That grasseater?"

"He may be," Vicki snapped, "but his nephew . . ."

"Was charged with fraud in '86, possession of stolen goods in '88, and accessory to murder nine months ago," Barry broke in. "No convictions. Got off on a technicality all three times. I ran him this afternoon."

"And the emergency," Colin growled, teeth bared. "Peter's missing."

Grasses and weeds whipped at his legs; trees flickered past in the periphery of his sight, unreal shadow images barely seen before they were gone; the barrier of a fence became no barrier at all as he vaulted the wire net and landed still running. Henry had always known that the wer were capable of incredible bursts of speed but he never knew how fast until that night. Making no effort to elude him, Cloud merely raced toward her twin, not far ahead but far enough that he feared he could never catch her.

With her moonlight-silvered shape remaining so horribly just out of reach, Henry would have traded his immortal life for the ability to shapechange given to his kind by tradition. All else being equal, four legs were faster and more sure than two.

All else, therefore, could not be equal.

He hadn't run like this in many years, and he threw all he was into the effort to close the gap. This was a race he had to win, for if one couldn't be saved, the other had to be.

Spraying dirt and gravel in a great fan-shaped tail, Celluci fought the car through the turn at the end of the lane without losing speed. The suspension bottomed out as they drove into and out of a massive pothole and the oil pan shrieked a protest as it dragged across a protruding rock. The constant machine gun staccato of stones thrown up against the undercarriage of the car made conversation impossible.

Stuart kept up a continuous deep-throated growl.

Over it all, Celluci kept hearing the voice of memory.

"You're willing to be judge and jury—who's to be the executioner? Or are you going to do that, too?"

He very much feared he was about to get his answer and he prayed Vicki would arrive too late to be a part of it.

By the time Cloud reached the open door of the barn, Henry ran right at her tail. Another step, maybe two and he could stop her, just barely in time.

Then Cloud caught the scent of her twin and, snarling, sprang forward.

As her feet left the packed dirt, Henry saw with horror where she'd land. Saw the false floor. Saw the steel jaws beneath. With all he had left, he threw himself at her in a desperate flying tackle.

He knew as he grabbed her that it wasn't going to be quite enough so he twisted and shielded the struggling wer with his body as they hit the floor and rolled.

Two traps sprang shut, one closing impotently on a few silver-white hairs, the other cheated entirely of a prize.

From the floor, Henry took in a kaleidoscope of images—the russet body lying motionless on the table, the mortal standing over it, covered neck to knees with a canvas apron, the slender knife gleaming dully in the lamplight—and by the time he rose to a crouch, one arm still holding the panting Cloud, he knew. Anger, red and hot, surged through him.

Then Cloud squirmed free and attacked.

For the second time that night Mark Williams looked death in the face; only this time, he knew it wouldn't pause. He screamed and fell back against the table, felt hot breath against his throat and the kiss of one ivory fang then suddenly, nothing. Self preservation took over and without stopping to think, he grabbed for the shotgun.

Henry fought with Cloud, fought with his own blood

lust. *She's a seventeen-year-old girl, barely more than a child. She must not be allowed to kill.* The wer no longer lived apart from humans and their values. What point victory now if she spent the rest of her life with that kind of a stain on her soul? Over and over, as she tried to tear herself out of his grip, he said the only words he knew would get through to her.

"He's still alive, Cloud. Storm is still alive."

Finally she stilled, whimpered once, then turned toward the table, muzzle raised to catch her brother's scent. A second whimper turned to a howl.

With her attention now fixed on Storm rather than death, Henry stood. "Stay where you are," he commanded and Cloud dropped to the floor, trembling with the need to get to her twin but unable to disobey. As he lifted his head, he came face-to-face with both barrels of the shotgun.

"So, he's still alive, is he?" Both the gun and the laugh were shaky. "I couldn't feel a heartbeat. You sure?"

Henry could hear the slow and labored beating of Storm's heart, could feel the blood struggling to keep moving through passages constricted by poison. He allowed his own blood lust to rise. "I know life," he said, stepping forward. "And I know death."

"Yeah?" Mark wet his lips. "And I know Bo Jackson. Hold it right there."

Henry smiled. "No." Vampire. Prince of Darkness. Child of the Night. It all showed in Henry's smile.

The table against his back made retreat impossible; Mark had no choice but to stand fast. Sweat beaded on his forehead and dribbled down the side of his nose. This was the demon he'd shot in the forest. Man-shaped but nothing manlike in its expression. "I—I don't know what you are," he stammered, forcing his trembling fingers to maintain their grip on the gun, "but I know you can be hurt."

One more step would move the barrel of the weapon

around enough so that Cloud would be out of the line of fire. *One more step*, Henry told himself fueling the hunger with rage, *and this* thing *is mine*. He raised his foot.

The barn door slammed back, crashing against the wall and breaking the tableau.

"Drop it!" Celluci commanded from the doorway.

Stuart snarled a counterpoint beside him, the effort of will it took to hold his attack while Cloud remained in danger sending tremors rippling across the muscles of his back. Her howl had yanked him from the car before it had quite stopped and pulled him unthinking into the barn in human form where the clothes he wore confined his shape.

The shotgun barrel dipped then rose again. "I don't think so."

"What the hell is going on out here?" Carl Biehn demanded, rifle covering the two men standing in the open doorway. He'd heard the car race down the driveway; heard it stop, spraying gravel; heard the howl and known that Satan's creatures were involved. It had taken him only a moment to snatch up his rifle and he'd arrived at the barn just behind the men from the car. He still didn't know what was going on, but his nephew needed his help, that much was obvious. "Put the safety on and toss your revolver to the ground." He gestured with the rifle. "Over there, away from everyone."

Teeth gritted, Celluci did as he was told. He couldn't see as he had an option. The snap of steel jaws closing as the gun hit the floor startled everyone about equally.

"Traps," Stuart said, pointing. "There and there." The dirt floor just beyond his bare foot had been disturbed. "And here."

Mark smiled. "Pity you don't take longer strides."

"Now move over there," Carl commanded, "by the others so I can get a . . ." As they picked their way between the traps and into the lamplight, he recognized Stuart and his eyes narrowed. All day he had prayed for an answer to his doubts and now the Lord delivered the leader of the ungodly into his hands. Then he saw Cloud, still crouched behind Henry, ignoring everything but the body on the table.

Then he saw Storm.

He lowered the rifle from his shoulder to his hip, holding it balanced by the pistol grip, finger still resting on the trigger. Keeping the muzzle carefully pointed toward the group of intruders now clustered together at one side of the barn, he moved to stand beside the table. "What," he repeated, "is going on here? How did this creature die?"

"He's not dead!" Rose threw herself into Stuart's arms. "He's not dead, Uncle Stuart! He's not."

"I know, Rose. And we'll save him." He stroked her hair, glaring at the younger human who stared at her as though he'd never seen skin before. She needed comfort but, if they were to save themselves and Storm, too, better she have the use of tooth and claw. Silently he cursed the clothing that held him to human form. "Change now," he told her. "Watch. Be ready."

"Stop that!" The rifle swung from Stuart to Cloud and back again. "You will do no more devil's tricks!"

Cloud whined but Stuart buried his hand in the thick fur behind her head and said quietly, "Wait."

Carl swallowed hard. The pain in the creature's eyes as it, no, she, gazed up at him added itself to the cry of the creature he had wounded and the weight of doubt settled heavier around his heart. The work of the Lord should not bring pain. He turned and gazed down at Storm with horrified fascination. "I asked you a question, nephew."

Mark put a little more distance between himself and Henry before he answered—coincidentally moving himself closer to the door, just in case—fighting the silent command that called him to *look at me*. "I assume," he said with a forced grin, "that as we've been assured my guest isn't dead you want to know,

how did you put it, 'What the hell is going on here?'
It's simple, really. I decided to combine your policy
of holy extermination with a profit-making plan of my
own.''

''You do *not* find profit in doing the Lord's work!''
Suddenly unsure of so many other things, this belief,
at least, Carl held to firmly.

''Bullshit! You reap your rewards in heaven, I want
mine . . . Hold it right there!'' He gestured with the
shotgun and Henry froze. ''I don't know what you are,
but I'm pretty damned sure both barrels at this range
will blow you to hell and gone and I'd be more than
willing to prove it.'' White showed all around his eyes
and he was breathing heavily, sweat burning in the
scratches on his back.

Celluci glanced at Henry's profile and wondered
what the other man could see that had him so terrified.
He wondered, but he really didn't want to know. In
his opinion their best chance lay with Carl Biehn, who
looked confused and somehow, in spite of his unques-
tionable ability with the rifle, fragile and old. ''This
has gone too far,'' he said calmly, making his voice
the voice of reason, laying it over the tension like a
balm. ''Whatever you thought when you started this,
things have changed. It's up to you to end it.''

''Shut up!'' Mark snapped. ''We don't need your
two cents worth.''

Carl lifted his hand from where it lay almost in
benediction on Storm's head and took a firmer grip on
the rifle. ''And what do you plan to do now?'' he
asked pointedly, desperation tinting his voice, the
question echoing prayers that had remained unan-
swered.

''You said yourself the devil's creatures must die.
That one,'' Mark nodded at Storm, ''has been taken
care of. This one,'' Cloud whined again and pressed
close to Stuart's legs, ''I could use as well. Pity we
can't get the big one to change before he dies.''

Stuart snarled and tensed to spring.

"No!" Henry's command snapped Stuart back on his heels, furious and impotent. With both weapons pointing at them from different angles, an attack, whether it succeeded or not, would be fatal to at least one of their company. There had to be another way and they had to find it quickly for although Storm's heart still fought to survive, Henry could hear how much it had weakened, how tenuously it clung to life.

"You keep your goddamned mouth shut," Mark suggested. His hands were sweating around the shotgun but even with his uncle covering their "guests" he dared not wipe his palms. He was well aware that the moment the shooting started and it no longer had anything to lose that creature would charge. This had to be carefully choreographed so that he and his pelts came out in one piece. And if he couldn't bring Uncle Carl around . . . *Poor old man, he wasn't entirely sane, you know.* "All right, the lot of you, turn around and line up facing that wall."

"Why, Mark?"

"So that I can cover them and you can send them back to hell where they belong." With a sudden flash of inspiration, he added, "God's will be done."

Carl's head came up. "God's will be done." It was not for him to question the will of God.

"Mr. Biehn." Celluci wet his lips. Time to lay all the cards on the table. "I'm a Detective-Sergeant with the Metropolitan Toronto Police Department. My badge is in the front left-hand pocket of my pants."

"You're with the police?" The rifle barrel dipped toward the floor.

"He's consorting with Satan's creatures!" Mark snapped. The cop would die by a rifle bullet. *Poor Uncle Carl* . . .

The rifle barrel came up. "The police are not immune to the temptations of the devil." He peered at Celluci. "Have you been saved?"

"Mr. Biehn, I'm a practicing Catholic, and I will recite for you the 'Lord's Prayer,' the 'Apostles'

Creed,' and three 'Hail Marys,' if you like." Celluci's
voice grew gentle, the voice of a man who could be
trusted. "I understand why you've been shooting these
people. I really do. But hasn't it occurred to you that
God has plans you're not aware of and maybe, just
maybe, you're wrong?" As they were still alive, it had
obviously occurred to him; Celluci attempted to make
the most of it. "Why don't you put down that gun,
and we'll talk, you and I, see if we can't find a way
out of this mess." And then, up out of the depths of
childhood when his tiny, black-clad grandmother had
made him learn a Bible verse every Sunday, he added,
" 'For there is nothing covered that shall not be re-
vealed; neither hid, that shall not be known.' "

"St. Luke, chapter twelve, verse two." Carl shuddered and Mark saw that he was losing him.

"Even the devil quotes scripture, Uncle."

"And if he is not the devil, what then?" A muscle
jumped in the old man's cheek. "Would you murder
an officer of the law?"

"Man's law, Uncle, not God's law!"

"Answer my question!"

"Yes, answer him, Mark. Would you commit murder? Break a commandment?" Now, Celluci used his
voice like a chisel, hoping to expose the rotten core.
"Thou shalt not kill. What about that?"

Mark had escaped death twice already this night.
From the moment he'd recognized the creature that
had attacked him in the woods, he'd known that escaping death a third time would take more than luck.
In order for him to live, everyone in the barn would
have to die. And he was *going* to live. This goddamned
bastard of a fucking cop was manipulating the one
thing he needed to pull his ass out of the fire and still
be able to make a profit. The old man as a live stooge
was preferable to the old man as a dead excuse.

"Uncle Carl . . ." Stress the relationship. Remind
him of where the blood ties lay, of family loyalty.

"These are not God's creatures. You said so yourself."

Carl looked down at Cloud and shuddered. "They are *not* God's creatures." Then he raised his tormented eyes to Celluci's face. "But what of him?"

"Condemned by his own actions. Willingly consorting with Satan's minions."

"But if he is a police officer, the law . . ."

"Don't worry, Uncle Carl." Mark didn't bother to hide the sudden rush of relief. If the old man was concerned about repercussions, then he'd already decided to take action. It was in the bag. "I can make the whole thing look like an accident. Just be careful when you kill the white wolf—dog, whatever—that you don't ruin the pelt."

Just a little too late, he realized he'd said the wrong thing.

The old man shuddered and then straightened, as though he were shouldering a terrible weight. "So much I'm unsure of, but this I know; whatever happens tonight will be for the grace of God. You will not profit from it." He swung the rifle around until it pointed at Mark. "Put down the gun and get over there with them."

Mark opened his mouth and closed it, but no sound came out.

"What are you going to do?" Celluci asked, voice and expression carefully neutral.

"I don't know. But *he* isn't going to be a part of it."

"You can't do this to me." Mark found his tongue. "I'm family. Your own flesh and blood."

"Put down the gun and go over there with them." Carl knew now where he'd made his mistake, where he'd left the path the Lord had shown him. The burden was his to bear alone, he should never have shared it.

"No." Mark shot a horrified glance at Henry, whose expression invited him to come as close as he liked. "I can't . . . I won't . . . you can't make me."

Carl gestured with the rifle. "I can."

Mark saw the death he'd been holding off approaching as Henry's smile broadened. "NO!" He swung the shotgun around at the one who drove him to it.

Carl Biehn saw the muzzle come around and prepared to die. He couldn't, not even to save himself, shoot his only sister's only son. *Into your hands, I commend my spir . . .*

Cloud reacted without thinking and flung herself through the air. Her front paws hit the middle of the old man's chest and the shot sprayed harmlessly over the east wall as the two of them hit the ground together.

Then Henry moved.

One moment, almost ten feet between them. The next, Henry ripped the shotgun out of Mark's grasp and threw it with such force it broke through the wall of the barn. His fingers closed around the mortal's throat and tightened, blood welling around his fingertips where his nails pierced the skin.

"No!" Celluci charged forward. "You can't!"

"I'm not going to," Henry said quietly. And he backed his burden up; one step, two. The trap snapped closed and Henry released his grip.

The arm that stopped Celluci was an impassable barrier. He couldn't move it. He couldn't get around it.

It took a moment for the pain to penetrate through the terror. With both hands at his throat, Mark pulled his eyes from Henry's face and looked down. Soft leather deck shoes had done little to protect against the steel bite; his blood welled up thick and red. He cried out, a hoarse, strangled sound, and dropped to his knees, pushing at the hinge with nerveless fingers. Then the convulsions started. Three minutes later, he was dead.

Henry dropped his arm.

Mike Celluci looked from the body to Henry and said, through a mouth dry with fear. "You aren't human, are you?"

"Not exactly, no." The two men stared at each other.

"Are you going to kill me, too?" Celluci asked at last.

Henry shook his head and smiled. It wasn't the smile Mark Williams took with him into death. It was the smile of a man who had survived for four hundred and fifty years by knowing when he could turn his back. He did so now, joining Cloud and Stuart beside Storm's body.

Now what? Celluci wondered. *Do I just go away and forget all this happened? Do I deal with the body? What?* Technically, he'd just been a witness to a murder. "Hang on, if Storm's still alive, maybe . . ."

"You've seen enough death to recognize it, Detective."

Fitzroy was right. He *had* seen enough death to know he saw it sprawled at his feet on the dirt floor; not even the flickering lamplight could hide it. "But why so quickly?"

"He," Stuart snarled, "was only human." The last word sounded like a curse.

"Jesus H. Christ, what happened?"

Celluci whirled around, hands curling into fists, even though—or perhaps because—he recognized the voice. "What the hell are you doing here? You're stone blind in the dark!"

Vicki ignored him.

Colin pushed past her, into the barn, desperate to get to his brother.

Barry moved to follow. One step, two, and the floor shifted under his foot. He felt the impact of steel teeth slamming into a leather police boot all the way up his leg. "Colin!"

Colin stopped and half turned back toward his partner, caught in the beam of the flashlight Vicki had pulled from her purse, his face twisted with the need to be in two places at once.

Vicki couldn't make him choose. "Go," she commanded. "I'll take care of Barry."

He went.

Dropping carefully to one knee, Vicki trained the light on Barry's foot. The muscles of his leg trembled where they rested against her shoulder. Tucking the flashlight securely under her chin, she studied the construction of the steel jaws. "Can you tell if it's gone through the boot?"

She heard him swallow. "I don't know."

"Okay. I don't think it has, but I'll have to get it off to be sure." Her fingers had barely touched the metal before Celluci slapped them aside.

"Poisoned," he said before she could protest, and slipped a rusty iron bar in at the hinge. "Hold his leg steady."

Both sole and reinforced toe had taken a beating but had held. Barry sagged against Vicki's arm, relief finally allowing a reaction. *I could have died,* he thought and swallowed hard. The heat had little to do with the sweat that plastered his shirt to his back. *I could have died.* His foot hurt. It didn't seem to matter. *I could have died.* He took a deep breath. *But I didn't.*

"Are you all right?" Vicki asked, playing the circular definition of her vision over his face.

He nodded, straightened, and took a step. Then another slightly less shaky one back to her side. "Yeah. I'm okay."

Vicki smiled at him and swept the flashlight beam over the interior of the barn. There was a body on the floor. Carl Biehn sat on a barrel of some kind looking stunned. Everyone else—Colin, Cloud, Henry, Stuart—was with Storm."

"Is Storm . . ?"

"He's alive," Celluci told her. "Apparently Williams caught him in another one of those traps. Which are buried all over this place so walk only where I tell you."

"Williams?"

"Is dead." Celluci jerked his head in the direction of Carl Biehn and said to Barry, "Get over there. Watch him."

Barry nodded, thankful for some direction, and limped across the barn.

All the long way here in the back of the police car, Vicki had thought only about arriving in time to make a difference. Now she was here, it was over, and the flashlight showed her only broken scenes suspended in darkness. "Mike, what happened?"

For a second, he weighed the alternatives, then he quickly laid out the facts, attempting to keep them uncolored by emotions he himself wasn't certain of. He watched her face carefully when he told her what Henry had done but she let nothing show he could use.

"And Peter? I mean, Storm?" she asked when he finished.

"I don't know."

Sixteen

Vicki launched herself toward the blur of light, the dim figures moving through it taking on solid form as she came closer. If Storm died, she didn't think she'd be able to forgive herself. If only she hadn't been so stupidly wrong about Carl Biehn, so sure he couldn't be the killer. She felt Celluci take her arm and allowed herself to be guided the last few feet, flashlight hanging forgotten in her hand.

Cloud had her front paws up on the table and was desperately licking her brother's face, her tongue alternately smoothing and spiking the fur on his muzzle. Stuart's arms were around Storm's shoulders, supporting his weight. Colin stroked trembling fingers down the russet back, whimpering low in his throat.

Henry . . . Vicki squinted at Henry, bent over one of Storm's back legs. As she watched, he straightened and spat.

"The poison's spread through his system. I'd kill him if I tried to take it all."

Colin began to make a noise, low in his throat, not quite a howl, not quite a moan.

"Get him to Dr. Dixon." Cloud ignored her. The rest turned to stare.

"We can't move him, Vicki," Henry told her softly. "He's trembling on the edge right now. It would be so easy to tip him over."

"If only we could get him to change," Stuart rested his cheek on the top of Storm's head, the anger in his voice only emphasizing the pain in his expression.

Vicki remembered what the doctor had said about the change somehow neutralizing infection. She supposed poison could be considered a type of infection. "He can't change because he isn't conscious?"

Stuart nodded, tears marking the russet fur with a darker pattern.

"Then what about forcing an unconscious change?"

"You don't know anything about us, human."

"I know as much as I need to." Vicki's heart began to pound as she gathered up everything Dr. Dixon had told her, added it to her own observations, and knew she had something that might work. "If he won't change on his own, maybe he'll change for Rose. Twins are linked. Dr. Dixon said it, Nadine said it, hell, you can see it. And Rose and Peter are . . ." She couldn't think of a way to phrase it, not with Rose—Cloud—right there. *Oh, hell, no way around it.* "As Rose goes into heat, she's pulling Peter with her. Their reactions are linked more now than they ever have been. If Rose, not Cloud, would, uh, well, maybe it would pull Storm over into Peter."

Stuart raised his head. "Do you realize what might happen? How strong a bond this is with our kind?"

Vicki sighed. "Look, even if it works, he's too sick to do anything and besides . . ." She reached out and stroked one finger down the limp length of Storm's front leg. *Incest or death, what a choice.* ". . . isn't it better than the alternative?"

"Yes. Oh, yes." Rose didn't wait for Stuart to reply. She threw herself down beside her twin, gathering him as close as she could, rubbing her face over his.

Stuart released Storm and straightened, one hand resting lightly on his nephew's shoulder. "Call him," he said, his voice resigned, his expression watchful. He would not allow this to go any further than it had to. "Bring him back to us, Rose." *But try not to lose yourself.* The last thing they needed now was Rose going into heat without Nadine around to protect her. Breeding reaction had destroyed packs in the past.

"Peter?"

The fine hair along her spine rising, Vicki could feel the power in a name. *This is who you are*, it said. *Come back to us.*

"Peter, oh, please. Please, Peter don't leave me!"

For agonizing moments it looked as though nothing was happening. Rose continued to call, the grief, the pain, the longing, the love enough to raise the dead. Surely it must have some effect on one not yet gone.

"He moved," Henry said suddenly. "I saw his nostrils twitch."

"He's got the scent," Stuart said, and he and Colin both shifted uncomfortably.

Then it happened. Slowly enough this time that Vicki always after swore she'd seen the exact moment of change.

Peter tossed his head and moaned, his skin gray and clammy, left foot horribly cut by the steel jaws of the trap.

Rose pressed kisses on his lips, his throat, his eyes, until her uncle moved her bodily off the table and shook her, hard. She burst into tears and buried her face on Peter's chest, both hands tightly wrapped around one of his.

"His heartbeat is stronger." Henry listened to it struggling, forcing the sluggish blood to flow. "His life has a better hold. I think it's safe to move him now."

"In a minute." Vicki took a deep breath. It felt like the first in some time and even the dusty, kerosene scented air of the barn smelled sweet. *Jesus Christ, how the hell are we going to explain this to the police?* "Here's what we're going to do. . . ."

"Excuse me."

She started and for a moment didn't recognize the old man who crept forward into the lamplight, Barry Wu trailing behind like an anxious shadow.

Carl Biehn reached out a trembling hand and lightly brushed the silver spray of Rose's hair. She rubbed her nose on the back of her wrist and looked up, eyes narrowing when she saw who it was.

"I know it won't be enough," he said, speaking only to her, the words rough-edged with pain, "but I realize now I was wrong. In spite of all I'd done to you and yours, even in the midst of your grief, you saved my life at the risk of your own. *That* is the way of the Lord." He had to pause to clear his throat. "I wanted to thank you, and say I'm sorry even though I know I have no right to your forgiveness."

He turned away then, and Vicki met his eyes.

They were red rimmed with weeping but surprisingly clear. Although pain had become a part of them, no doubt lingered. This was a man who had made his peace with himself. Vicki heard the voice of memory say, *"He's a decent human being and they're rare."* She nodded, once. He echoed it and moved past, bowed but somehow still possessing a quiet dignity.

"Okay people, we're going to keep this as uncomplicated as possible." She blinked rapidly to clear her eyes and shoved at her glasses. "This is what happened. The police already know someone has been taking potshots at the Heerkens dogs—and the Heerkens—and that I'm looking into it. Obviously Peter found something out . . ."

"He spoke with Mark Williams this afternoon," Celluci told her, wondering how far he was going to let this vaguely surreal explanation go on.

"Great. Suspicious, he headed over here. Meanwhile, I found out the same information, called, discovered that Peter was missing, pulled Colin off shift, and started out here. Meanwhile, you," she pointed at Celluci, "and you," the finger moved to Stuart, "raced to the rescue. We stick to the truth as far as we can. Now then, Henry, you weren't here."

Henry nodded. Staying clear of police investigations had always been one of his tenets of survival.

"Colin, you and Barry, get Peter into the back of your car. Rose, stay with him. Don't let him change again. And Rose, you weren't here either. The boys picked you up on their way back into town as you were running along the road, trying to get here, furious that Stuart and Celluci wouldn't take you with them. Got that?''

Rose sniffed again and nodded, letting go of her twin only long enough to pull on the T-shirt Stuart stripped off and gave her. It fell to mid-thigh and would do as clothing until they reached the doctor's where the entire family kept something to wear.

Gently Colin lifted his brother and, with Peter's head lolling in the hollow of his throat, made for the door, Rose close at his side, her hands chasing each other up and down her twin's body.

"Wait by the car," Vicki called, sending Barry after them. "There're a few more things you'll have to know."

"Like what you're planning to do about the corpse," Celluci snapped, running both hands up through his hair, his patience nearly at an end. "I don't know if you've taken a good look at it, but someone obviously helped it achieve its current condition, which is going to be just a little hard to explain. Or were you just going to bury it in the woods and conveniently forget about it? And what about Mr. Biehn? Where does he fit into this fairy tale you're wea . . ?''

The gunshot, even strangely muffled as it was, jerked Celluci around. Stuart growled and fought to get himself free of the confining sweatpants. Even Henry whirled to face the sound, and from outside the barn came questioning exclamations and running footsteps.

Vicki only closed her eyes and tried not to listen, tried to think of flowers spread across an August morning like a fallen rainbow.

"He went into the corner, put the rifle muzzle in his mouth and pulled the trigger with his toe."

She felt Celluci's hands on her shoulders and opened her eyes.

"You knew he was going to do that, didn't you?"

She shrugged as well as she was able considering his grip. "I suspected."

"No, you knew!" He started to shake her. "Why the hell didn't you stop him?"

She brought her arms up between his and broke his hold. They stood glaring at each other for a moment and when she thought he'd actually hear her, she said, "He couldn't live with what he'd done, Mike. Who was I to say he had to?" Sliding her glasses up her nose, she looked past him and drew a long shuddering breath. "We're not done yet. Is there a can of kerosene around for that lamp?"

"Here, by the table." Stuart bent to lift the five gallon can.

"No, don't touch it."

Celluci knew at that moment what she was going to do and knew this was his last chance to stop her, to bring this entire night back under the cover of the law. He strongly suspected that if he tried, both Henry and Stuart would align themselves firmly on her side. Trouble was, if it came to choosing sides. . . .

Vicki dug a pair of leather driving gloves out of the bottom of her purse and as though she was reading his mind asked him, as she pulled them on. "Did you want to add something, Celluci?"

Slowly, realizing he had no choice at all, he shook his head, forgetting that she couldn't see him. He'd decided where he stood back at the farmhouse when he'd passed on the information she'd given him. She knew that as well as he did. *Maybe better.*

Gloves in place, Vicki bent and carefully picked up the can. It felt nearly full. She unscrewed the cap, and paused. She needed both hands on the can but would be unable to see without her flashlight the moment she left the immediate area of the lamp. "God damn it all to . . ."

Celluci found himself looking at Henry, whose expression so clearly said, *It's up to you,* that it took a moment before he realized it hadn't been said out loud.

Up to me. Right. As if I had a choice. But he walked forward and picked up the flashlight anyway.

Vicki squinted up into his face, but the light was too bad to make out nuances. *Not that Celluci tends to do nuances.* It was enough he was there; it helped. *Let's get on with it.*

She walked along the beam of light toward Mark Williams body, pouring the kerosene carefully on the packed earth floor as she went, thankful that her grip on the can hid the trembling of her fingers. The law had meant everything to her once. "As far as anyone will be able to piece together, there was a fight, probably because Carl Biehn walked in on whatever it was his nephew was doing to Peter. During the fight, Mark Williams stepped in one of his own grisly little bits of ironmongery. Out of grief, or guilt, or God knows what, Carl Biehn shot himself. Unfortunately, at some point during the fight, the can of kerosene got knocked over."

The light slid across the body. It was evident that Mark Williams had died in great pain, the mark of Henry's fingers still apparent on his neck. Vicki couldn't find it in her to be sorry. The only thing she'd felt for Mark Williams in life had been contempt and his death hadn't changed that. *As soon feel sorry for squashing a cockroach,* she thought, setting the can down beside the corpse and tipping it over.

"What about Carl Biehn?"

"Leave him alone. Let him lie where he chose." She walked back along the light to the table and picked up the lantern. The dancing flame made patterns against the darkness that continued to dance in her vision after she looked away. "Also unfortunately, at some time during the fight, the lantern shattered."

The force with which the lantern hit the floor eloquently expressed the emotions that lurked behind her matter-of-fact tones.

The kerosene in the shattered reservoir caught first, and then the path Vicki had poured.

"Take a good look, Mike, Stuart. This what you saw when you arrived." She took a deep breath and peeled off the gloves, shoving them down into the depths of her bag. "Plus Peter's body, lying naked on the table. The two of you rushed in, grabbed Peter, and got out. The flames were then too high for you to go back. Now, I suggest *we* get out of here, as this barn is ancient, tinder dry, and likely to go up in very little time."

With a hungry woosh, Mark Williams' clothes caught, the burning kerosene outlining his body in flame.

She paused at the door, her hand dropping from Celluci's guiding arm, and looked back. A splash of orange had to be fire climbing the surface of the north wall. They couldn't stop it now, even if they wanted to. She wondered for an instant just who *they* were, then squared her shoulders and went out to talk to Colin and Barry by their car.

"When we arrived," she told them, "Celluci and Stuart had Peter lying out on the grass. The barn was burning. Forget everything else. You put Peter in the car, called in the fire, and headed back to town, picking Rose up on the way."

"But what about . . ." Barry didn't sound happy.

Vicki stood quietly, waiting. She couldn't see his face but she had a good idea of what must be going through his mind.

She heard him sigh. "There isn't any other way, is there? Not without exposing the wer and . . ." She heard Henry in his pause, heard him decide not to voice his suspicions. ". . . other things."

"No, there isn't any other way. And don't let anyone get a good look at your boot."

She watched their taillights pull away, saw them speed down the highway, then turned and walked back to the three men—the vampire, the werewolf, and the cop—outlined in the flickering flames from the burning building. There would be ash and not much more remaining when the fire burned out.

As though his turn had now come to read her mind, Celluci said dryly, "If they sift the ashes, any competent forensic team could poke a thousand holes in your story."

"Why should they investigate? With you and me and two of the local city police on the scene, I think they'll be happy to take our word for it."

He had to admit she was likely right. Three cops and an ex-cop with nothing to gain from lying—and covering for a family of werewolves would not likely occur to anyone—they'd wrap it up and write it off and get on to something they could solve.

"Still, there are a lot of loose ends," Stuart said thoughtfully.

Vicki snorted. "Police prefer loose ends. Wrap it up too neatly and they'll think you're handing them a package." The night was sultry, without a breath of wind, and the barn was now burning brightly, but Vicki hugged her arms close. They'd won, she should feel happy, relieved, something. All she felt was empty.

"Hey." Henry wished he could see her eyes. All he could see were the flames reflected on her glasses. "You all right?"

"Yeah. I'm fine. Why wouldn't I be?"

He reached out and slid her glasses up her nose. "No reason."

She grinned, a little shakily. "You'd better get going. I don't know how long it'll take the fire trucks and the OPP to get out here."

"Will you be back to the farmhouse?"

"As soon as the police are finished with me."

He shot a look at Celluci but managed to hold back the comment.

Vicki sighed. "Go," she told him.

He went.

Celluci took his place.

Vicki sighed again. "Look, if you're about to treat

me to another lecture on ethics or morals, I'm not in the mood.''

''Actually, I was wondering if a grass fire was part of your plan? Maybe as a diversion? We're starting to get some sparks and the field behind the barn is awfully dry.''

Flames were racing across the roof now, the entire structure wrapped in red and gold.

The last thing she wanted to do was more damage. ''There's a water hookup in the garden with plenty of hose. Just wet the field down.''

''Well, how the hell was I supposed to know?''

''You could have looked! Jesus H. Christ, do I have to do everything?''

''No, thanks. You've done quite enough!'' He wanted to recall the words the moment he said them but to his surprise, Vicki started to laugh. It didn't sound like hysteria, it just sounded like laughter. ''What?''

It was a moment before she could speak and even then, the threat of another outbreak seemed imminent. ''I was just thinking that it's all over but the shouting.''

''Yeah? So?''

''So?'' She waved one hand helplessly in the air as she went off again. ''So, now it's over.''

''You will come back and see us again? When you need to get out of the city?''

''I will.'' Vicki grinned. ''But right at the moment, the peace and quiet of the city seems pretty inviting.''

Nadine snorted. ''I don't know how you stand it. Bad smells and too many strangers on your territory. . . .'' Although she still bore the mark of her twin's loss, in the last twenty-four hours the wound had visibly healed. Whether it was due to the deaths of Mark Williams and Carl Biehn or the saving of Peter's life, Vicki wasn't sure. Neither did she want to know.

Rose had also changed, with less of the child she'd been and more of the woman she was becoming showing in her face. Nadine kept her close, snarling when any of the males approached.

Vicki moved toward the door where Henry stood waiting for her, tension stretching between him and Stuart in almost a visible line.

"In the barn, before you arrived," Henry'd explained earlier, *"I gave him an order he had no choice but to obey."*

"You vampired him?"

"If you like. We're both pretending it didn't happen, but it'll take him some time to forget that it did."

Shadow, his black fur marked with dust, crawled out from under the wood stove, his jaws straining around a huge soup bone. He trotted to the door and dropped it at Vicki's feet.

"It's my best bone," Daniel told her solemnly. "I want you to have it so you don't forget me."

"Thank you, Daniel." The bone disappeared into the depths of Vicki's bag. She reached out and picked a bit of fluff from the top of his head. "I think that I can pretty much guarantee that I'll never, ever forget you."

Daniel squirmed, then Shadow threw himself at her knees, barking excitedly.

Oh, what the hell, Vicki thought, crouched down and did what she'd done to Storm way back in the beginning, digging her fingers deep into the thick, soft fur of his ruff and giving him a good scratch.

It was hard to say which of them enjoyed it more.

Celluci leaned against the car and tossed the keys from hand to hand. It was an hour and a half after sunset and he wanted to get going; after the last two days, plain, old, big city crime would be a welcome relief.

He still wasn't certain why he'd offered Vicki and Henry a ride back to Toronto. No, that wasn't entirely true. He knew why he'd offered Vicki a lift, he just wasn't sure why he'd included Henry in the package. Granted, the man's BMW would be another week in the shop, at least, but that wasn't really much of a reason.

"What the hell is taking them so long?" he muttered.

As if in answer, the back door opened and Shadow bounded out, tail beating the air. Vicki and Henry followed, accompanied by all the rest of the family except Peter, who had remained at Dr. Dixon's.

Vicki had been right about the police investigation. The whole thing was just so weird and the witnesses so credible that the OPP had jumped to pretty much exactly the conclusions Vicki had outlined and were willing to write off the rest. Mark Williams' police record hadn't hurt either, especially when a report of his latest business venture had come in from Vancouver.

Celluci braced himself as Shadow leapt up on his chest, licked his face twice, then raced off to run noisy circles around the group approaching across the lawn. Werewolves. He'd never be able to look at anyone quite the same way again. If werewolves existed, who knew what other mythical creatures might turn up.

Vicki seemed to have taken the whole thing in stride, but then, he'd always known she was a remarkable woman. An obnoxious, arrogant, opinionated woman much of the time, but still, remarkable. On the other hand, he thought as he closed his fist around the keys, Vicki had known Henry since Easter so maybe none of this was new to her. Who knew what the two of them had been involved with?

During the gratitude and the good-byes, Stuart approached, hand held out. "Thank you for your help."

The tone wasn't exactly gracious, but Celluci understood about pride. He smiled, careful to keep his teeth covered, and took the offered hand. "You're welcome."

The grip started firmly enough but soon progressed so that the veins in both forearms were standing out against the muscle and Celluci, in spite of being nearly ten inches taller and proportionally heavier, began to worry about his knuckles popping.

Nadine, having caught scent of the competition, nudged Vicki and they both turned to watch.

"Do they keep this up until one of them breaks a hand?" Vicki wondered dryly, squinting at the joined silhouette straining in the fan of light from the car.

"Hard to tell with males," Nadine told her in much the same tone. "Their bodies seem to be able to go on for hours once their brains have shut off."

Vicki nodded. "I've noticed that."

If the sudden release came with any visible signals passing between the two men, Vicki didn't see them. One moment they were locked in stylized hand-to-hand combat, the next they were clapping each other on the shoulders like the best of friends. She figured that the correct internal pressure had finally been reached, tripping a switch and allowing life to go on—but she wasn't going to ask because she really didn't want to know.

While Stuart demanded to know what his mate was laughing at, Celluci found himself unexpectedly pre-occupied by a logistics problem; who was going to sit beside him in the front seat on the way home. It seemed a childish thing to worry about but although the seat should by rights go to Vicki—she was the taller and entitled to the greater leg room—he didn't want Henry Fitzroy sitting behind him in the dark for the three hour drive.

Vicki took the decision away from him. Running her fingers along the car until she found the rear door handle, she opened it, tossed her bag in and climbed in after it, carefully removing Shadow—who'd been trying to get a few more licks in—before she closed the door. She'd known Mike Celluci for eight years and she had a pretty good idea of what was going through his head concerning this. If he thought she was going to run interference between him and Henry, he could think again.

Henry kept his face expressionless as he slid into the front seat and buckled his seat belt.

Shadow chased the car to the end of the lane then sat by the mailbox barking until they were out of sight.

By the time they reached the 401, Celluci couldn't stand the silence a moment longer. "Well," he cleared his throat, "are all your cases that *interesting?*"

Vicki grinned. She knew he'd break first. "Not all of them," she said, "but then I have a pretty exclusive clientele."

"That's one word for it," Celluci grunted. "What's going to happen with Rose and Peter, did they say?"

"As soon as Peter's better, Stuart's sending him to stay with his family in Vermont. Rose is pretty broken up about it."

"At least he's alive to send away."

"True enough."

"Rose is probably going to spend the next week howling in her room while the three adult males make themselves scarce."

"Three males? You mean her father . . ."

"Apparently it's a pretty strong biological imperative."

"Yeah, but . . ."

"Don't get your shorts in a knot, Celluci, Nadine'll make sure nothing happens."

"Only the alpha female gets to breed," Henry said matter-of-factly.

"Yeah? Great." Celluci drummed his fingers on the steering wheel and shot a sideways glance at the other man. "I'm still not sure where you fit in."

Henry raised a red-gold brow. "Well, in this particular instance, I acted as intermediary. Usually though, I'm just a friend." And then, because he couldn't resist, he added, "Sometimes I help Vicki out with the night work."

"Yeah. I bet you do." The engine roared as Celluci gunned the car past a transport. "And you probably had more to do with that . . . that . . . thing, we ran into last spring than either of you are telling me."

"Perhaps."

"Perhaps nothing." Celluci ran one hand up through his hair. "Look, Vicki, you can get involved with as many ghoulies and ghosties and things that go bump in the night," he shot another look at Henry, "as you want. But from now on keep me out of it."

"No one invited you into it," Henry pointed out quietly before Vicki could respond.

"You should be damned glad I showed up!"

"Should we?"

"Yeah, you should."

"Perhaps you'd care to elaborate on that, Detective-Sergeant."

"Perhaps I would."

Vicki sighed, settled back, and closed her eyes. It was going to be a long ride home.